ACTUAL
INNOCENCE

ACTUAL INNOCENCE

Barry Siegel

BALLANTINE BOOKS   NEW YORK

A Ballantine Book
Published by The Ballantine Publishing Group

Copyright © 1999 by Barry Siegel

www.randomhouse.com/BB/

This is a work of fiction. Names, characters, places, and
incidents are the products of the author's imagination or are used fictitiously.
Any resemblance to actual events, locales, or persons, living or dead,
is entirely coincidental.

LIBRARY OF CONGRESS CATALOGING-IN-PUBLICATION DATA
Siegel, Barry.
Actual innocence / Barry Siegel. — 1st ed.
p.   cm.
ISBN 0-345-41309-1 (hc : alk. paper)
I. Title.
PS3569.I368A64   1999
813'.54—dc21   99-31266
                                                          CIP

Text design by Holly Johnson

Manufactured in the United States of America

First Edition: October 1999

10 9 8 7 6 5 4 3 2 1

To the memory of my mother,
and her enduring love of family

ACTUAL
INNOCENCE

—————— O N E ——————

The phone rang yet again. Greg Monarch reached for it, but his hand stopped short. His head ached so badly, he could barely see across his desk. He'd been reading case files since dawn, preparing for three trials at once. Now he longed only for a dim silence. Closing his eyes, he imagined himself back in Pecho Rancho State Park, where he'd spent the weekend. Eight thousand acres of lost Central California coastland. Hidden coves, wooded stream canyons, golden poppy fields . . .

At least the phone had stopped ringing.

Greg rose from his chair and walked to the window. Through the pane, he studied the creek winding past La Graciosa's central plaza. It was dusk, the sky a pale pink glow. Shoppers and families were gathering on the town plaza, local farmers were spreading their apples and avocados on the backs of pickup trucks, children were tossing bread crumbs to ducks at the creek's edge. Greg turned back to his desk. His head still hurt, but he could see now.

He almost wished he couldn't. There, on the desk's edge, sat the embossed, gold-lettered card. The invitation to the Chumash County Criminal Bar Association's annual awards dinner. And, beside it, the announcement of this year's Lawyer of the Year: Greg Monarch.

The Sullivan murder trial, the Plaskow business, the Danny McCloud case—Monarch had cultivated a singular reputation on the Central Coast. He'd won his share of acquittals, he'd shown his instinct for doing what was needed, but he'd not lunged for the spotlight. No showboating on TV, no tell-all books, no unctuous self-promotion. "His efforts have well served the legal community and the public at large," went the citation to be presented at tonight's dinner. "Greg Monarch has provided a standard of excellence for all others in his profession."

What would he say when it came time for his acceptance speech? Greg glanced at a legal pad where, during breaks from his trial preparation, he'd been trying to scribble out some comments. *We all play a critical role, a necessary role. . . . Without a zealous adversary for the defense, the system breaks down. . . . What's at stake is the integrity of the law as an institution. . . . What's at stake is the state's interest in a just society. . . .*

It was there Greg had lost his thread. He picked up a pen, started anew.

What's at stake is the mask of propriety. The defense attorney provides the mask. The defense attorney's unfettered advocacy of his client validates what the state does. . . . Without the defense attorney, the state would look mighty bad indeed. . . .

Greg stopped, put down his pen. That wouldn't do. No. He'd have to wing it. He'd ad-lib from the podium.

Greg was reaching for his coat when he heard a knock at the door in his anteroom. He ignored it. His office was closed; he was already late. The knock came again, three hard raps, insistently. Greg turned toward the door. Four, five, six.

"Monarch?" The man calling from the street was offering more a greeting than a question. The voice sounded patrician, and familiar. "Monarch, I know you're there. Let me in."

Greg wished he could ignore this summons. It wasn't every day, though, that Judge Daniel Solman came knocking at a lawyer's door. Solman, the chief federal district judge for the Central California region, could be found more often at a public podium, speaking before hundreds, if not thousands. That was so even back at Chumash State, where he and Greg had been passing friends and classmates, sharing the occasional teacher and lecture hall. Student government had been Solman's province in those days, and his stepping-stone. It was a shame really that he'd gotten himself appointed a federal judge seven years ago, for that development, however lustrous, had derailed a promising political career. The United States District Court did not offer Solman enough opportunities to orate.

No, he couldn't ignore Judge Solman. Greg reached for the doorknob.

"Evening, Judge," he said. "I was just heading out."

"Won't keep you long," Solman began, stepping inside without invitation.

Greg studied his guest. The sweeping breadth of the forehead, the mane of curly gray hair, the cast of the mouth, and the expression in his lively eyes all portrayed an uncommon flair—hardly the sensibility of a judge. Without his robes, Daniel Solman suggested a thriving entrepreneur more than a man of the law. He favored Italian crepe wools, cashmere blazers, hand-sewn calfskin moccasins. Greg wondered where he bought his clothes.

"In town for the weekend, and on my way to the county bar dinner," the judge was saying now. "Saw your light still on, so thought I'd stop by. Just an impulse. Had a notion you might be interested in what's crossed my desk."

"Did you?"

"Yes. . . . Quite a curious habeas corpus petition. Pro se, handwritten, pauper, rather hapless. Right up your alley, in other words. Another poor, vulnerable lass, fighting institutional power."

Greg took a step back from Solman. Despite his flip manner, the judge didn't appear all that relaxed. It was so unusual for him to show up like this. "Wouldn't say that's exactly my alley," Greg said. "Why come to me?"

"She needs a lawyer if she's going to proceed." Solman peered at Greg with curiosity. "And . . . well, Monarch, she's sort of asked for you."

Greg showed only mild interest. So many prisoners sent him urgent pleas these days. Urgent pleas and densely packed boxes of documents. "Sort of? What do you mean?"

"She attached a note to her petition, requesting that a copy be sent to Greg Monarch."

"But her petition has already been written and filed. She doesn't need me."

"This petition won't get her through the door."

"Why do you think anything will?"

Solman's eyes roamed about Greg's small unadorned office. "Well now, that's just the question. Probably not. Probably she has no chance at all. Still, the way she puts things, the way she writes . . . Hard to explain. You'll see if you take a look. No federal judge would act on this as it is, but—"

"What's she in for?"

The question stopped Solman for a moment. "Murder one," he offered finally, sounding uneasy with the notion. "Slashed an old man's throat, it seems, out by a riverbank in the El Nido Valley. One moonlit night five years ago. She's been losing appeals ever since."

As well she should, Greg reasoned. Why should throat slashers win their appeals? Why should murderers walk free? "Sorry, Judge, I've had my fill of death-row cases." He paused. "I've had my fill of defending killers."

Solman looked now as if he regretted this unplanned visit. "I understand," he said with sudden conviction. "Don't blame you." He stepped toward the door. "It was just something I thought you should see. As I say, I stopped by on impulse. Maybe because of the time issue . . . I'll be off now."

"Time issue?" Greg asked. "What do you mean?"

Solman slowly turned back to him. "She's only six months from the executioner. They've set the date. This is her last appeal."

Greg, without thinking, glanced at his watch. Habeas petitions were a particular quagmire. Unwinding the past with virtually no chance of getting anywhere. Courts weren't even interested anymore whether your client was innocent, just as long as the judges and prosecutors dotted all their *i*'s. Not more than a hundred out of ten thousand federal habeas petitions even won review each year, and of those, maybe four or five prevailed. A miserable waste of time.

"Sorry, Judge," Greg said. "Still not interested. My plate's pretty full. Our dedicated prosecutor here in Chumash County keeps throwing new criminal cases at me. I take it he's anxious to keep me gainfully employed. That leaves little time for a no-chance dance down a dead-end road. Give it to some eager young kid just out of law school."

Solman nodded his agreement but seemed lost in thought. He stood at the door, hand on the knob, not moving. Greg had never known Solman to cerebrate like this.

"Tell you what," the judge finally suggested. "I'm going to send this woman's petition over to your office by messenger. We'll slip it through your mail slot, despite your full plate. Read it with your nightcap this evening. Send it back tomorrow morning if you're not interested."

"That's just what I'll do," Greg promised.

HE WALKED DOWN THE brick path that followed the creek as it wound through La Graciosa. The evening air cleared Greg's head. From time to time, he paused to smell the jacaranda and watch the creek roll by. When others passed, he called out the casual greetings common in a small town. *Hey there . . . Been a while . . . Well, how you doing?* Two assistant prosecutors, knowing where he was headed, stopped to congratulate him and urge him to enjoy his night in the spotlight. "I intend to do just that," he informed them with a grin. "Just like every night."

The way she puts it, the way she writes. What an odd thing for Solman to say. *Hard to explain.* Greg, striding quickly now, shook off the judge's words.

The Apple Canyon Inn, that's where they were having this dinner. At the foot of Carmel Street, where the creek sank into an underground tunnel and began its ten-mile journey to the sea. Just five blocks away. Greg straightened his tie and ran a hand through short sandy hair. In this stretch, he had the creek path largely to himself. Through the rear windows of bars and cafés that backed onto the creek, he could see familiar faces leaning into the evening's first Graciosa Brew. Laughter and the lilting sound of a piano drifted through the perennial haze that gripped La Graciosa most evenings. Greg smelled camphor at the creek's edge, kelp from the sea ten miles distant. La Graciosa hadn't changed yet, he thought with satisfaction. The coastal mountain range still held back the world. So did the fog. For the time being, this town remained a lost outpost. Ranching, farming, fishing, that was it. That, and just enough transgression to keep a criminal defense attorney occupied.

He stood finally before the Apple Canyon Inn. Unsure whether to reflect a town forged in the Spanish-mission era, or one ripened in frontier ranching days, the inn had chosen a compromise: adobe and tile mixed freely with split timber. Yellow light poured from a bank of paned windows. Inside, scattered about the lobby, Greg could see dozens of lawyers lifting glasses to their lips. If nothing else, the criminal bar of Chumash County knew how to bend an elbow.

"Well, if it isn't Greg Monarch himself." A large damp hand gripped Greg's shoulder, a red meaty face loomed near his ear. Against his will, Greg inhaled Jerry Belson's whiskey breath. Jerry Belson, the ex-cop turned shoddy criminal defense lawyer. Greg had savaged him in the Sullivan trial. Why would Belson be so solicitous now? Was that what the Lawyer of the Year Award got you?

"Just a little winded," Greg muttered, hoping to avoid a conversation. "Long walk. Need to sit down. See you inside."

Breaking free of Belson's grip, Greg pushed through the inn's front door. More hands reached for him, more faces loomed. He grinned gamely, nodding and waving at those he knew. Arms propelled him forward. *Glad to see you, Greg. . . . Way to go, Greg. . . . Congratulations . . . Terrific . . .* At least now he was among close, valued colleagues. Tim Ruthman, Ron Carson, Jenny Blair, Art Parrish, all the usual gang. They were his compadres, lawyers renowned for their defense of everyone from white-collar swindlers to odd fellows waving knives under the downtown bridge. Ruthman was Greg's favorite. A big bear of a man with a bushy mustache and a constantly amused expression, Tim took his job seriously, but not himself.

"You sure you don't want to go fishing tonight instead?" Ruthman whispered in Greg's ear.

"You're reading my mind," Greg said. "My boat's bobbing on the lake, waiting for us."

"Looks like they're waiting for you here, too."

"If only you guys hadn't voted for me."

"If only you hadn't won all those cases."

Greg hesitated, weighing a response. Before he could speak, he felt a hand on his shoulder, pulling him away from Ruthman.

"This way, Greg. We need you up on the dais soon. Running a bit late."

Jonathan Clamber, president of the criminal bar association, twitched as he spoke. Rapid eye blinks, jaw clenches, that's how he got whenever timetables weren't being met. Clamber had Greg by the elbow. Together they weaved through the crowd.

"There'll be a few kickoff speeches," Clamber was saying. "Usual stuff. Membership drive, booster numbers, telegram from the governor. Still waiting on the president, not sure whether that son of a bitch will deliver on time. Then we do a couple toasts, a couple small change awards. After that, I do the presentation speech for the Lawyer of the Year Award. When I finish, you stand up."

Clamber peered at Greg, who appeared to be searching the room for something. "You listening to me, Monarch? You look distracted."

Greg offered what he hoped resembled an obliging smile. "Nice to see you too, Jonathan. Sorry I was late. A bit overwhelmed by work, that's all. Three cases that act as if they mean to end up inside a courtroom."

Clamber regarded Greg now with open irritation. He'd never been part of Greg Monarch's fan club. Hadn't even voted for him. Greg's courtroom style at times was a bit too audacious for Clamber's meticulous taste. "You could work on your attitude, Monarch. Should be grateful about this award. Lucky you're getting it."

"Yes, quite lucky. Much obliged."

"You don't look terribly appreciative, Monarch."

"Appearances can be deceiving."

Clamber's hands flexed. "If I had my way, you'd be pleading before the state bar ethics crowd, not accepting awards."

"Take comfort, Jonathan. Someday you may very well have your way."

They both knew Greg had won the bar association's annual award by a rather narrow margin. After they tallied the executive board's vote, two of the more straitlaced members clucked loudly in dismay, and one particularly crotchety septuagenarian stomped out in protest.

"Monarch, piece of advice." Clamber placed a tight wiry hand on Greg's shoulder. "Keep your acceptance speech short."

GREG TRIED HIS BEST to appear appreciative as he sat on the dais. He was a tall, rangy man with angular features, dark watchful eyes, and the long graceful fingers of a pianist. He raised those fingers to his brow now. Bright lights blazed in his face, so before him the crowd of five hundred appeared mainly as shadows. Only occasionally did a decipherable face swim into view. Yet clearly he was among friends and admirers, despite Clamber's venom. Out of their mouths came lavish praise for him.

For him, and for themselves as well. Speaker after speaker hailed their profession without qualm or censure. Everything merited an anecdote, everything drew enthusiastic huzzahs. Greg scanned the crowd, peering into a dark sea of murmuring voices. He saw Judge Solman near the front, nodding amiably at him. Halfway back, his once-close companion, the federal prosecutor Kimberly Rosen, offered a faint wink. In the rear, standing against the wall among the local journalists, the *News-Times* reporter Jimmy O'Brien waved a wide chunky hand. Greg lifted his eyes to the dinner hall's windows, which gave onto a side street just off the corner of Carmel. Nearly a full moon tonight, he realized. The lake would be shimmering.

Then it was time for the guest of honor to speak. Greg moved slowly toward the microphone, still composing his comments. He gripped the lectern with two hands and drew a breath. "We toil in a noble cause," he began. "You honor me too much." The rest he managed by rote, drawing from dozens of speeches he'd delivered over the years. *The pursuit of justice cannot be reduced to storytelling. . . . A trial is a search for truth. . . . We need to recommit ourselves to the faith that the state must prove, with honest evidence, its case against the accused. . . . The defense attorney who walks into the courtroom honestly defending the guilty also defends the innocent. He preserves the system. He makes the powerful state always prove its case against the powerless. . . .*

Enthusiastic applause interrupted Greg twice. When he finished, hands clasped his shoulders, voices murmured praise in his ear. Greg backed away from those surrounding him even as he offered his thanks. *Yes . . . Certainly . . . How kind of you . . . Much appreciated . . .* Spotting an exit at the rear of the podium, he inched toward it. *Could use some fresh air for a moment . . . Been working all day . . . Need to clear my head . . .* In a lull, finding himself alone, he turned to the door. Tim Ruthman, watching from the corner, knowing what he was up to, waved him on with a broad grin. Before many others noticed, Greg was gone.

Outside, the creek beckoned. Greg stood on the path above its bank, listening to the sound of water slapping against earthen barriers. He turned finally and began the short trek to his creekside cottage. Reaching La Graciosa's plaza, he decided instead to stop at his office. There he paced through the suite of rooms, unsure what he was seeking. He paused at the window. Slowly he sank onto the upholstered reading chair beside his desk. Only then did he spot the long manila envelope lying on the ground below the mail slot, just inside his office door. He studied it for a moment, puzzled, before recalling Judge Solman's peculiar visit. There it was: the habeas petition.

Greg rose, reached for the envelope, settled at his desk. So thin, he thought, holding the bundle in his hand. Not at all like a lawyer's legal brief, especially when a life was at stake. So devoid of a lawyer's voluminous oratory, a lawyer's ceaseless cascade of arguments and citations. Instead, no doubt, just as the judge promised: a simple hapless plea.

Greg pulled the document from the envelope. Only nine pages in all. Handwritten, but not sloppy. Straight lines, perfect circles, elegant curls. This woman had printed her words as if inscribing invitations to a birthday party. For all that, the substance of her message looked drearily commonplace. Four previous appeals denied, the last by the state supreme court. Each rejection issued after ventilation of the usual claims: newly discovered evidence, prosecutorial misconduct, ineffective defense counsel. Judges must yawn, seeing this type of stuff day in and day out.

Yet Judge Solman hadn't yawned; Solman had come knocking at his door. Greg leafed again through the nine pages, trying to gauge what the judge had seen. Was it the handwriting itself, the sense of a real person making this plea rather than a lawyer? Or was it the aura of something feminine in the curl of the letters? Something female and urgent and full of yearning? Or had Solman just never before read a forlorn plea from a guilty soul sitting on death row?

Greg flipped back to the document's front page. He scanned past the legal phrases, searching for this woman's name. He squinted, running a finger from line to line. Then he froze.

Sarah Marion Trant, Petitioner, vs. Mr. Bryce Chalmers, Superintendent, Respondent.

Sarah Marion Trant. Sarah Trant.

Greg closed his eyes.

Sarah Trant.

Did Judge Solman do this purposefully? Did Solman know? How

could he? Sarah had come along well after law school, many months after his shared classrooms with the judge.

Greg sat in the dark, fighting off memories. Sarah on the night they met, Sarah on the night they parted. Both times, her bright hazel eyes so urgent and hungry, so full of hope. *What a fight that was, Greg, what a scene. . . . I fear that irrevocable things have happened. . . . What should we do? . . . I don't want to feel such pain, I don't want to be confused. . . . I'll say goodbye to you for now. . . . Maybe we can face each other in the future on sturdier ground. . . . Oh, Greg, don't marry anyone, all right? . . . There is no one better than you. . . .*

An asylum, that's where he'd always imagined Sarah might end up. Instead, she'd landed in state prison. Slash an old man's throat on a dark riverbank? Yes, he had to admit . . . he'd seen that possibility in her. She could do that.

Again he leafed through the habeas petition. There was nothing there, nothing to suggest anything but yet another murderer who desired escape from the consequences of her actions. Yet another killer who wanted him to win for her. Why was Sarah turning to him after all these years? Reaching the end of the document, Greg stopped. There, stuck on the back page, he noticed Sarah's personal plea, scrawled on a small yellow card. *Please send copy of this to Greg Monarch in La Graciosa.* That's all it said.

Greg stared at the words, then rose and began to pace again. Through a narrow winding mountain pass—that's where El Nido lay, that's how you got there. A remote oak-thick river valley, some sixty miles southeast of La Graciosa, well across the county line. With his dad, Greg had hiked and fished there often in his youth. Less frequently, but always with rekindled memories, he'd returned in recent years. Didn't he even know a lawyer out there?

Greg studied the bare walls of his office. He tried to sit down but couldn't keep still. Three cases he had, all coming to trial. Unless they could be postponed. He reached for his phone. "Goddamn it, Judge," he snapped into Solman's answering machine. "What are you doing to me?"

——————————— T W O ———————————

The Chumash Dunes were wondrous. Those great white mounds, reaching south along the coast from Pirate's Beach, rose like an apparition in the misty drizzle. Greg, kicking a sturdy broad-shouldered roan into a gallop, felt the cold dank wind in his face as he threaded through a grove of willow and poplar, then opened onto the beach and flew across the hard sand at the surf's edge. Before him Sarah led the way, her long dark hair wild in the breeze. *There's something about you,* she murmured when they stopped to rest. *Something that I can't understand completely. The way you move, the way you won't give up, the way I know you'd fight for your beliefs.* Her cool smooth palm moved gently across his face. *You are one of a kind, Greg. . . . I know you understand about wonder. . . . I trust you. . . . I love you so much. . . .*

Greg awoke with a start, smelling gas fumes, or perhaps leaking oil. For a moment he thought of returning to his dream, but found he could not. One side of his head throbbed; something sticky clung to his face.

He stirred, pulled himself into a sitting position. In his car, that's where he was. On the side of a road, peering into a lush forest. The windshield cracked, shards of glass on the seat beside him. Greg recalled leaving La Graciosa early on the Saturday morning after the awards dinner. The drive toward El Nido; a treacherous mountain pass; a low rising sun in his eyes; a jolting collision. Nothing more. Greg slowly climbed out of his car. Now he grasped what had happened. Half awake, distracted, blinded by the sun, he'd cracked into a thick tree trunk fallen across his path. His car sat twisted on the road's shoulder. Greg's hand rose to his face, tracing the sticky substance on his forehead. Blood. No wonder his head hurt.

Greg looked about. He was standing on a wooded ridge in the high foothills of the El Nido Valley. Some hundred feet below him, in an oak-thick mountain gorge, a clear pebbly trout stream coursed through a tumble of rust-colored boulders. At one bend, he spotted a solitary fly fisherman, knee deep in the water, casting upstream into the current. At the next bend, he watched a woman swimming lazily across the river. A woman who now was rising, naked and willowy and distracted, from the deep blue-green pool where she'd been bathing. Rivulets of water, sparkling in the morning sun, ran down her back. She reached up and unpinned her hair, which fell, a tousled tawny mane, to her shoulders. Then, like a deer sensing a foreign presence in the wind, she looked up and spotted Greg. For a moment she stood still. Slowly, her eyes still on him, she reached for her clothes. Pulling a pale green dress over her damp body, she ran a hand through her hair. Turning, she began to climb out of the creek bed.

Greg turned too, and crossed the road. There a long steep slope rose to a yet higher plateau. He drew a breath, fighting off a wave of dizzy nausea. Then he scrambled up the slope, using tree roots as footholds. At the crest, facing to the southeast, he lifted his eyes to the vast El Nido Valley. It rolled before him to the horizon, ten miles long and three miles wide. Magnificent dense live oak forests backed up to towering seven-thousand-foot mountains ribbed with gray sandstone; pale morning sunlight played through deep foliage-thick ravines; dark green orchards climbed foothill slopes abundant with orange trees, avocado bushes, and grapevines. In the mid-distance rose the century-old tile roofs of El Nido Village, the valley's solitary town. No more than seven thousand dwelled there, perhaps another thirty thousand in the surrounding countryside. Coming from a misty coastal region, Greg marveled at this barricaded valley's startling clarity. In all his visits here, he'd never seen fog.

He pivoted away from the vista. He'd have to hike his way out, that much seemed certain. The descent down the slope, grasping tree branches, proved more treacherous but half as long as the trip up. Stepping past his battered car, he began walking up the mountain road. Around a bend, it turned from pavement to dirt. A hundred yards farther, it narrowed into a path. Then came a shed, and beyond it a splintered wooden gate, blocking his way. On the gate sat a board bearing hand-lettered words: "Do Not Trespass— Private Property."

Greg climbed over the gate, trying to ignore his aching head. He was now moving across what looked to be a vast empty campus of some sort. He circled structures, peered into windows. A central brick building, two wooden lodge houses, a half dozen cottages, a kitchen and mess hall, a football field, sports equipment, boxes and supplies. No people, though. No sign of life, only its residue.

Greg stopped before one of the lodge houses. Through a window he saw folding chairs, a long table, a dais, a white board. He stepped closer. Smudges discolored the board where someone had dragged a rag, wiping out whatever had been written. Greg squinted; through the blur, he thought he saw a trace of words, but the lines and curls had no shape, no meaning he could discern. He turned and walked on. A pair of boots lying on the porch before a cottage caught his eye. They were knee-high rubbers, black with blue trim, meant for back-country travel in deep snow. Men wore such boots in the far north, from Minnesota to Maine, not in Central California. Yet here they were. Greg looked through the cottage's window. In the small corner room, a single bed, a thin mattress, no sheets. In the main room, hanging on a hook, three pairs of white overalls. Also a fireplace, laid with fresh wood.

Greg meandered, listening for noises, hearing none. The utter silence felt like a presence, something alive, something watching. Nothing moved, though. No breeze here. No birds either. The sky was empty. Ancient oaks, ringing the campus, stood still in fields crowded with vines and mosses. Greg felt a sudden desire to get out of this place.

He turned, hiked toward the far end of the complex. Past another wooden gate and No Trespassing sign, he found himself in a wooded field. He followed a small dry wash to a ledge of sandrock and leaned against it. A piece of the sandrock broke off in his hand. It reeked strangely of rotten eggs. Greg looked down at his feet. He was standing on a dark tarlike material. Asphaltum, he judged, asphaltum that had seeped from a canyon wall. He kicked over the thick rotting trunk of a fallen oak tree. In the furrow it had created sat a pool of pale green liquid. He bent to study this peculiar fluid.

"Get up." The words sounded like a command, not a suggestion.

Lifting his head, Greg stared into the barrel of a rifle. Behind it stood a stout man with a ragged reddish-brown beard. The shirttails from his brown flannel shirt hung over a pair of denim overalls. He spat at Greg's feet.

"Get up, turn around, back out. You're trespassing."

Greg looked back and forth between the rifle and the dark tarry ground. "Trespassing on what?" he asked.

PAST THE ABANDONED CAMP, the mountain path broadened again. Heeding the rifleman's brusque command, Greg followed that road as it descended through two miles of sharp switchbacks. Around a final turn, the forest suddenly opened into a rolling meadow bordered by a low wooden fence. Studying the horizon, Greg realized he was standing at the edge of a vast ranch that reached across much of the valley floor. On a rise to the south stood a two-story structure made of stone and timber. It looked to Greg more like a hunting lodge than a home.

Twenty minutes later, he knocked at its front door. Dusty sweat glistened on the neck of the Latino who opened the door. He appeared to be fresh from the fields, but didn't hold himself like a ranch hand. He wore a straw hat, and had piercing brown eyes, and gnawed on a toothpick.

"May I see the master of the house?" Greg asked, offering his business card.

"There is no master," the man replied without glancing at the card. "We've got a mistress." He studied Greg's bloodied forehead for a moment, then ushered him into a cavernous room filled with furniture made of walnut and leather. "I'm Alex Ramirez," he said. "I'm the ranch foreman. You wait here."

Left alone, Greg glanced about the room. It had to be at least fifty feet long, he estimated, and thirty wide. The high beamed ceilings were made of polished oak logs. On one wall hung a large oil painting, the obvious portrait of a patriarch: Fierce, deep-socketed, ice-blue eyes stared out from under thick eyebrows, as if examining and judging those standing before him. A floor-to-ceiling brick fire-place occupied much of a second wall, a huge picture window a third. Through it Greg could see half of the El Nido Valley.

Edward Sanborn, it suddenly occurred to Greg. The oil portrait was of Edward P. Sanborn, the legendary founder of El Nido. How dim he'd been not to make the connection.

"Welcome to El Nido, Mr. Monarch. I'm Diana Sanborn."

Greg turned from the window. She appeared to be about seventy, a robust seventy. Her long loose gray hair spilled to her shoulders from under a dirty white cowboy hat; her scuffed black cowboy boots poked out from a long flowing lavender skirt. Her smile warmed the room. Her voice sounded like champagne.

"I've already been welcomed," Greg said.

Diana Sanborn's eyes danced with anticipation. She had high cheekbones and a generous mouth. "Tell me," she said. "Tell me who has welcomed you."

"He didn't introduce himself. Just waved a rifle, ordered me to stop trespassing, pointed me toward your ranch. An abandoned camp of some sort, down the road a couple of miles. That's where I left my car."

Greg's answer was not, it appeared, what Diana Sanborn had expected, or wanted. She no longer looked the least amused. "Left your car, Mr. Monarch?"

"I had an automobile accident. I didn't notice a tree trunk across the road."

Stepping closer to Greg, Diana Sanborn now could see the gash at the side of his forehead. "My goodness, Mr. Monarch, you're injured."

"Just a cut. It's stopped bleeding already. I'm okay."

"Alex," the old lady called. "Alex, bring us washcloths and hot water." Then to Greg she said, "Lose your way, Mr. Monarch?"

Without knowing exactly why, Greg felt uneasy. "No," he replied. "Just got blinded by the rising sun in my eyes."

Diana Sanborn's eyebrows arched. "Just what were you doing out on the edge of my property?"

Greg hesitated. For all her warmth, this grand woman couldn't mask the hint of interrogation in her voice. "Taking a drive, Mrs. Sanborn. Clearing my head."

"A drive to clear your head? That sounds marvelous, Mr. Monarch. So far from home, though."

"I had a lot to clear."

Sanborn's rich laughter filled the room. "Okay, I give up. Why don't you simply tell me what brings you to El Nido?"

"Must I?"

Sanborn's smile revealed a row of gleaming white teeth. "Strangers do not usually come here, Mr. Monarch."

THEY SETTLED ON THE veranda before a sloping lawn densely treed with live oak and sycamore. Beyond, Sanborn Ranch reached toward the foothills. Alex brought hot washcloths; a thin dark Latina brought iced tea and biscuits. "I'll talk first," Diana volunteered.

She'd grown up on this ranch, her mother and father distant figures to her, world travelers whom she hardly knew. She was raised by servants and her widowed grandfather. Yes, her grandfather was Edward Sanborn, the valley's honored patron. She'd married twice and divorced twice. With no male family members surviving, she ran the ranch herself now, helped by a foreman and small crew. She rode through her pastures, inspecting the stock, making notes for the boys. She counted how many deer she spotted. She watched to see whether the turkeys were here or gone. She looked to see if she had any quail.

"Just a real country life, Mr. Monarch. A real country life I wish dearly to preserve."

"You think it's threatened?"

Sanborn studied him. "No, I don't. But we remain always vigilant. Wouldn't you agree that is wise?"

Greg's forehead still throbbed. He had no interest in parrying with this lady. "Mrs. Sanborn, I'll be direct. Whatever your concerns about preserving your valley, I can assure you I'm not here to aggravate them. As you know from my card, I'm a lawyer from La Graciosa. I drove out here to see someone at the state prison. Just passing through, don't even intend to spend the night. That is, if I can get a little help here. You think I possibly could make a couple of calls? And maybe get a ride down to the village?"

At those words, Diana Sanborn turned toward the horizon and fell silent. When she next spoke, her voice had gone dry.

"Someone at the prison, Mr. Monarch?"

Beads of sweat dripped down Greg's face. He suddenly felt hot and cold at once. The room tilted before him. "Yes," he said. "Sarah Trant."

Squinting through his pain, Greg could only vaguely see Sanborn now as she jumped to her feet. "Bless your heart, Mr. Monarch," he could hear her saying as he drifted away. "You just rest yourself. We'll get you help right away. Don't you worry, we'll get you all straightened out."

GREG AWOKE TO FIND a narrow, pinched face hanging above him. Light from a window glinted off small gimlet eyes. The man was short and wiry, and smelled vaguely of aftershave lotion. On his hip he packed a holstered revolver. It took Greg a moment to realize he wore a uniform.

"Sheriff Roy Rimmer," the face offered by way of introduction. "Sheriff of El Nido County."

Greg slowly pushed himself into a sitting position. They were still on the veranda where he'd settled with Diana Sanborn, but the mistress of the house was nowhere to be seen. Greg glanced up at the sky. Late morning, he guessed. He'd been out at least an hour.

"Greg Monarch," he said. "Citizen of Chumash County."

"You're being too modest, Mr. Monarch. Such a celebrated lawyer, the toast of the Central Coast. They even gave you an award last night, didn't they? Right there in La Graciosa. We've made a couple of calls. You have quite a reputation."

Greg studied the sheriff. Rimmer suggested to him a man who always sat on the edge of his chair, if he sat at all.

"Don't believe everything you hear," Greg advised.

"It would be hard to do that, Mr. Monarch. After all, so much of what we hear sounds downright inconceivable."

Greg at last found his head clear and pain free. The nap had done some good. "I understand what you mean, Sheriff. Things I hear also sound downright inconceivable."

"Hear about what, Monarch?"

Greg pushed himself to his feet. A raspy edge had seeped into Rimmer's voice. El Nido no longer was feeling so insulated. "What happened to the 'mister,' Sheriff? I was getting used to it."

Rimmer took a step closer. The sheriff's head was level with Greg's chest. "Cracked your car up pretty bad down the road," Rimmer said. "Must have been quite a party over there in La Graciosa. Maybe you drank a bit too much. Maybe you inhaled something. Who knows about those Chumash County defense lawyers. It's a little late now, but maybe a blood test will tell us a story."

"Then again," Greg said, "maybe a few photographs of the accident scene will reveal a negligent county that leaves fallen tree trunks lying across public roads. Good idea, Sheriff. Let's do a real thorough investigation."

Rimmer's eyes grew more fixed. "Ms. Sanborn says you've come here to see Sarah Trant over at the prison."

"That's right."

"That may be a problem. She's in solitary confinement. Don't believe you can just arrive over there. At least not with first-degree murderers. You've got to arrange visits. Write the warden, set it up."

"In solitary? What for?"

"Wouldn't know. But that Trant woman, she's trouble. Always has been. Making a ruckus, I'm sure."

That was probably true, Greg thought. Sarah certainly was trouble. He bent over and put his mouth next to Rimmer's left ear. "County sheriffs have squat to do with state prisons," he said. "So get out of my face. I mean to get over to the prison one way or another. I mean to see Sarah Trant today."

Rimmer jerked his head back. "Sorry, Monarch. Don't think that's possible."

"Tell you what," Greg offered, walking to a phone he'd spotted in an alcove off the veranda. "Let's call the federal judge who sent me Trant's habeas petition. Let's tell Judge Solman that the sheriff of El Nido County says I can't see a state murder convict about a federal matter."

Greg picked up the phone, started punching numbers. "What's all this based on? Just why is it I can't see her? Want to make sure I get it right for the judge."

Rimmer reached Greg's side in two steps and took the phone from his hand. "Okay, Monarch," he said. "We'll let you have your little visit."

MORE THAN ANYTHING ELSE, geography protected El Nido. Cradled by mountain ranges on all sides, the valley offered no approach other than through a narrow pass. The access road from La Graciosa first curved past El Nido Lake at the basin's high northwest end, then descended through the La Luna foothills in a southeasterly slant toward the center of the valley floor. There rose the village, eight blocks of shops and cafés running along Main Street. To the south of this hub, a pergola led into sixty-acre Sanborn Park. To the north, stately old ranch houses filled the wooded slope that fronted the La Lunas. A walk from those residential foothills through the village, then into the park, and down to its southern border at El Nido Creek required no more than twenty minutes.

Even to the east, farther into the valley, where distances might be described in miles rather than blocks, a bike would do as well as a car. Just past the village, all signs of commerce gave way to lush citrus groves, interrupted only by a few isolated homes. Diana Sanborn's white timber lodge sat out there, on a bluff some two miles beyond the hamlet. On the far backside of her ranch, the valley narrowed into increasingly rugged terrain as it ascended to the foothills and the abandoned camp Greg had traversed. On the village side, El Nido Creek formed the ranch's southwest boundary as it flowed toward town. Throw an inner tube in there, Greg thought, and you could float all the way through Sanborn Park.

He didn't have an inner tube, though. Instead he had Sheriff Rimmer's patrol car, with Rimmer behind the wheel. They were winding their way west from Sanborn Ranch, through groves abundant with oranges and avocados and peaches. In an instant they were entering El Nido Village and moving slowly down Main Street. The place, Greg noted with appreciation, had hardly changed at all. As it had for one hundred years, a tile-roofed Spanish arcade spanned the long block across from Sanborn Park, sheltering a familiar mix of art galleries and dress shops, bookstores and folk-music cafés. There was the homemade ice cream stand he'd loved as a boy, and the dimly lit

Gaucho Tavern he'd wondered about. There was the toy store, and the tea shop, and the well-stocked newsstand. At the end of the block, the tile and adobe U.S. Post Office tower remained El Nido's tallest structure, reaching sixty-five feet into the air.

Just past that tower, Sheriff Rimmer turned left, then right onto Old Brook Road, which closely followed El Nido Creek as both rolled to the west. Greg studied the rippling water, preparing himself. Three miles down this bygone wagon trail, Sarah Trant resided in the state penitentiary.

Greg thought the La Luna Women's Correctional Center a site more suitable for respite than punishment. It sat on 160 acres of wooded tableland at the mouth of the valley, barely within the county's boundary. Dappled sunshine graced the front of the low whitewashed adobe buildings; El Nido Creek meandered along the prison's southern border; century-old sycamores shaded rolling green lawns. Only a barbed-wire fence and four security booths at each corner of the property marred the effect.

Rimmer drove Greg past the sentries. At a double wall of iron gates just inside the prison's entry hall, the sheriff reluctantly handed him off to a dour-looking prison guard, who led him to a small office. Thirty minutes of paperwork followed under the eyes of a clerk who pointed silently at where he wanted signatures. Then a second guard led Greg to a bare, fluorescent-lit holding area. "Wait here," he instructed as he turned on his heel.

They called his name a full hour later. He rose and headed toward the double gates. The first wall slid open, then slammed shut behind him as he stepped inside. He stood in what amounted to a large barred cell as a guard, hidden from view, took his time hitting the button that activated the second gate. When it opened finally, Greg walked into the heart of the prison. A female guard escorted him down a hallway to a compact interview room. There, hanging from the ceiling, a bare bright bulb lit pale green walls. Using his handkerchief, Greg reached up and unscrewed the bulb. The weak yellow hallway light seeping through a small window was enough. He wanted shadows for his reunion with Sarah Trant.

What would she look like these twenty years later? He couldn't say. He knew only that she'd still be searching for something.

"Counsel for the defense, I presume? My savior?"

Standing in the doorway, backlit by the hallway's dim illumination, Sarah for a moment appeared to Greg much as she had two decades before. The loose thick auburn hair fell across her shoulders. The intense hazel eyes sparkled with amused challenge. A thin white cotton shift clung to a still-slender body. Sarah watched him, hands on hips. He'd phoned ahead so that she'd be prepared.

"Not your savior, Sarah," Greg said. "Never was much good at that."

"You'll get no argument from me there."

He waved her to a chair. The guard retreated, closing the interview-room door. Greg studied the woman before him. Closer up, Sarah did not appear quite as she had when he'd last seen her. The years showed under her eyes, and at the corners of her mouth. A flicker of exuberance still played across her face, but so too did something else. Greg's heart sank. Sarah looked as if a part of her were missing.

They'd met the summer after he'd finished law school, she a graduate writing program. Both of them at loose ends, he not yet committed to being a lawyer, she not prepared for what it took to write. Living in rented single rooms on the rough edge of Clam Beach, their two cramped units part of a peeling wood-frame complex that stared out at a wind-whipped sea. Neither of them knew where they were headed, or what to do with themselves, so they spent their days at the water's edge, their evenings in bed with bottles of wine. She electrified him back then—she and her abandon and her unreasonable appetites. They were forever devising schemes, plunging into projects, scouring the Central Coast, meeting strange characters, gawking at the phantasmagoria. There were nights they never slept, nights they roamed the vast lost Chumash Dunes, nights they talked endlessly and made love and swam naked under a black starlit sky. Sarah so hungry, lying in the sand, her legs wrapped around him, crying and moaning, beating on his chest, holding him tightly inside her. . . . It didn't matter that she was constantly, even then, longing after something ineffable. For a time, it all seemed possible, it all seemed within their reach.

Her decline came slowly, over many months, as her writing stalled and Greg turned to his budding law practice. She still radiated delight and humor in most situations, but also an uncomfortable, growing urgency. Hers was a vibrant desolation, full of game resolve, and it moved Greg in ways he couldn't explain. When she started turning to him for solutions—seeking in him an energy she could appropriate—he tried his best. He yearned to see her once more striding cockily through her world. In time, though, he realized neither he nor anyone could provide what she sought. When Sarah also came to understand this much, her tremulous search turned frantic.

She began moving repeatedly, lurching from one apartment to another along the Central California coast, furiously arranging rooms for writing that never seemed to satisfy. *Just try to show me that I can provide you with things,* she begged Greg. *With information, with visions. Let me feel courageous sometimes. Let me have a hand in things. You've got to understand that I'm strong. . . . I'm just full of stories, I'm a whole big panorama, and I want to feel that way. . . . Sometimes I feel overshadowed by you. . . .*

Near the end, after he'd opened his own small law office in La Graciosa, he'd come home at night to find her waiting in his rented house. She'd stare impatiently at him, as if she were expecting something, as if she meant to siphon out his insides. She'd pull him onto her smooth flat belly, shake him, try to draw blows from him. She'd gobble Libriums, hunch over her typewriter, struggle to write the stories she felt so full of. She'd jump into her battered green Mustang, gun the engine, roar aimlessly north up Highway 101.

One day late in their third summer, with Greg in the passenger seat, she didn't stop driving until they were in Canada. It was as if she couldn't stop, was afraid to stop. Hour after hour they hurtled up the coast, pausing only for gas and sandwiches. I have friends up there, Sarah told Greg. Friends on an island off Vancouver. We'll go visit, it'll be such a surprise, these guys will love to see us. Greg nodded his agreement, as uncertain as he was excited by her wild, unstoppable quest.

When they finally arrived on that island off Vancouver, though, their hosts didn't appear particularly enchanted. They were a gray-haired couple, busy with their garden and pickling. How Sarah knew them, Greg never did learn. After an oddly strained hour in the living room, the lady of the house tactfully handed her visitors a bottle of homemade blueberry wine and sent them on their way. Greg and

Sarah ended up at a dark, drafty motel on a side street half a mile from the shore.

It was there, with nowhere else to ricochet, that Sarah finally unraveled. Greg sometimes thought she consciously chose to let go that night. More often, though, he imagined her charging full speed toward a precipice, unable to brake, plunging helplessly over the edge. Whatever its provenance, the descent didn't take long. Greg went out for ice and hamburgers. When he returned, she was crouched in a corner of their room, glowering at the motel manager's fat, lazy brown cat. Glowering, and clutching a twelve-inch carving knife she'd found in their kitchenette's back drawer.

"He's trying to kill me," Sarah hissed, waving her knife at the cat. "I have to get him first."

In the gloom it took Greg a moment to see she was stark naked. Her jeans and blouse lay crumpled by her side; she sat cross-legged, her long dark hair falling across full, milk-white breasts. He moved toward her, reaching for the knife. Realizing his intent, she leapt up and dived for the cat, swinging the blade in a broad sweeping arc. The cat hissed and jumped away. Sarah followed, wielding the knife like a dagger. From corner to corner they pounced, cat screeching, Sarah thrusting, until Greg finally tackled his winsome hazel-eyed girl and pinned her to the ground. That he felt aroused in this moment, lying atop Sarah's naked heaving body, he never told anyone. To the counselors and doctors who eventually appeared, that evening and in the following weeks, he confined himself to the facts as best he knew them.

"Oh, Greg," Sarah sighed on the morning they finally took her to a private psychiatric clinic. "I can't figure it out, Greg. I can't figure out how to get back."

At first he came by regularly, but as time passed his visits dwindled, then ceased. Eventually she moved to a sort of halfway house, then out on her own. For a while, living by herself, she wrote him letters.

At three this morning, I drove around Berkeley, winding up at the House of Pancakes for coffee and fresh fruit. The only fresh fruit was a banana, but I ordered it anyway. The waitress brought it to me sliced up, with a little pitcher of half-and-half. It was nice. I ate it slowly, reading through my brown phone book that I take everywhere. I longed for you. And before the banana and phone book, before all this, I longed for you. On my birthday I cried myself to sleep longing for your body to hold. You probably don't believe me. And even if you do, it doesn't matter. Your willpower is stronger than mine. And knowing you, I knew that it would be this way. You won't allow yourself to be confused. I am such a fool. . . .

After the letters stopped, he still occasionally found a postcard from her in his mailbox, usually reporting on one environmental cause or another she was promoting at the time. Once she sent him a newspaper clipping about her monthlong sojourn in the high branches of a thousand-year-old redwood that a lumber company wanted to cut down. Surrounded by an Earth First! crowd, she gradually receded into her own story. Years passed. The postcards tapered off. He lost track of her.

"Been a while," Greg said. "Hasn't it, Sarah?"

She offered a nervous little laugh. "That's not much of an opener, Greg."

"I was trying to start slowly."

"Expected something more interesting from you. Something like, 'Still waving knives around, Sarah?' That would be an icebreaker."

Greg watched how she held herself. Legs crossed and jaw pitched forward, resting now on her closed fist. As if she were willing herself to remain cogent. "Still Sarah, I see. Still Sarah after all these years."

"And what about you? Still Greg?"

He didn't know how to answer that one. He'd wanted her to need him those long years ago. He'd savored her need, he'd grown strong on her need. Yet she'd drained him, too. Drained him, and nearly unhinged him. He learned from her the dangers of misreading voracious hunger as allure. He learned from her the need to keep hold of himself. He'd learned from her the need to fend off certain types of unbridled emotional tumult.

"Sarah, you should know something. A federal judge sent me your habeas petition because you requested that I get a copy. He didn't realize we once knew each other. He just thought I'd be interested. I am, Sarah. As always. That's not changed. But I can't help. . . . I can't get involved. We're way past all that. I came here only because you asked for me. I'm not staying. I'll get your petition to the right lawyer."

Sarah looked at him through lowered eyelashes. "Don't even want to hear my story? Don't even want to hear how I ended up in this place?"

Greg glanced around the room. The skeptical smile, the longing in her eyes . . . He'd been seduced back then as much by her uncertainty as by her sensuousness. "Well, yes . . . ," he said. "Sure I do."

"Where do we start?"

Greg took a deep breath. "Why don't we start with whether you're still waving knives around."

For a moment, Sarah didn't appear to register what he'd said. Then she did, and it was as if the ground had collapsed under her. Her eyes slid swiftly from allure to anxiety to something dark and muddled. She wrapped her arms around her body. The sudden transformation startled Greg, even though he'd seen it often before. In an instant, Sarah became the girl he'd glimpsed at the end of their time together.

"Maybe so," Sarah whispered. "Maybe I am still waving knives."

She began to talk, her voice halting and faint, as if coming from somewhere far away. Her story started not in El Nido but in the woods of Northern California. She'd found her place there, she wanted Greg to know. She'd found meaning, reasons, a way to live. She'd fought for clean rivers, old-growth redwood forests, riparian watersheds, spotted owls. She'd joined groups that shared her concerns, she'd met comrades equally full of passion. With them she'd challenged corporations, educated homeowners, marched, picketed, traveled the state. Then, finally, a half-dozen years ago, she'd set off on her own and arrived in El Nido. For a time, she thought she'd fit in here. Then it all unraveled.

"Brewster Tomaz," she said. "That's who they say I killed."

"Who was he?"

"A sour prune, that's who he was. A crazy, mean-faced old geologist. Always glaring and hollering at us. Once he drove his pickup straight at us as we stood by the creek. Another time—"

"Who's 'us'?" Greg asked. "You and who else?"

The question seemed to sadden Sarah. "I wasn't alone," she said softly. "At least not at the start."

"Let's go back to the start."

She closed her eyes, then opened them. "It began when Modo-Corp came to El Nido. Big company out of San Francisco. Bought a gorgeous chunk of wilderness up in the foothills, announced plans to build a world-class health spa. Lot of folks in the valley sided with them, especially after they hired Brewster Tomaz to promote their cause. But not everyone. Not me. There were demonstrations. Confrontations down at the river, lots of pushing and shoving. One time . . ."

Sarah stopped and turned away.

"One time what, Sarah?"

"I don't want to say."

"Tell me."

"I . . . I think . . . One time I pushed Brewster and he fell backward into the water."

"What day was that, Sarah?"

Sarah frowned, nibbled at her lip. "It was the night of the murder. But I ran off right after that. Brewster was alive then. I didn't cut his throat."

"Yet you've been found guilty of doing just that."

"And sentenced to death . . . Six months to go."

As often with her, he felt baffled. What had happened? Was she really a killer? He couldn't ask. No defense attorney wants to hear a confession that will later handcuff him in court. A *defense attorney shouldn't hear what he doesn't need to know.* "Not just a verdict," Greg managed to say. "Four appellate rejections."

She studied her hands. "I think I've been framed."

"You think?"

Sarah looked up at him now, her eyes glistening with dismay. "I'm confused, Greg. I didn't kill Brewster. But I imagined it. I imagined slashing his throat."

Greg rose from his chair. He'd walked this road before. "Okay Sarah, okay" was all he could think to say.

"Won't you help me?"

"Someone will help you."

"No, Greg. No. You."

Greg had reached the interview room door. He yanked it open. "Not me," he said.

OUTSIDE THE PRISON, GREG stood blinking in the afternoon sunlight. A steady breeze pushed warm air against his face, reminding him of how dry and hot the valley could be. He began walking down a long gravel pathway, toward the sentry booth and the barbed-wire gate. Although his head no longer hurt, he found he had to step carefully to keep his balance. When he reached the prison's gate, he glanced about.

"I suspect you need a ride, Mr. Monarch."

Peering into the glare, Greg recognized Diana Sanborn. She stood leaning against a white rusted Dodge pickup that had its best years well behind it. She had a booted foot propped on the side fender, an arm stretched toward the roof. Her cowboy hat hung around her neck.

"What I need is a way out of El Nido," he said. "Just want to get my car fixed and drive away."

Diana patted her pickup as if it were a horse. "I'm so sorry, Mr. Monarch, I'm afraid that's not possible. We're having your car towed up here right now. But it's Saturday. We have no auto shops in El Nido, no parts. Also no taxi service."

"No rentals?"

"I'm afraid not."

"Then I'll call a friend. Someone from Chumash County."

"If you wish," Diana said. She hesitated. "I apologize about the sheriff. I thought it best to summon him because of your injury, and the automobile accident."

"Yet another warm El Nido welcoming party. Your valley teems with hospitality."

"You two left the ranch so suddenly, I didn't know you were departing. Otherwise I would have said goodbye."

"That's why you were waiting for me here? To say goodbye?"

"No, that's not why." Diana pushed herself off the pickup and stepped toward Greg. He saw something in her expression now that he couldn't read. "Please accept my hospitality," she said. "Please stay the weekend in El Nido."

Greg tried to take a step, but staggered instead. Diana, a yard from him, reached out to lend support. Leaning against her, he felt oddly comforted.

"Besides," Diana Sanborn said. "You are in no condition to travel."

——————— T H R E E ———————

Standing before the oil portrait of his hostess's forebear, Greg tried to imagine how El Nido must have looked to Edward P. Sanborn when he first rode into this valley near the turn of the century. The perpetual play of sunlight, the towering mountains, the warm dry air—he would have seen that, and more. Rather than the dusty truck farms and immaculate ranch houses and pockets of weathered cottages that now decorated the valley, the country beyond the small hamlet would have offered a vast solitude, acre after acre unbroken by human habitation. Grizzlies and mountain lions, but no people at all.

Greg's eyes moved slowly down Edward Sanborn's portrait to a small bronze plaque discreetly positioned under its thick walnut frame. He began to read. *It is difficult for newcomers to the valley to realize what Mr. Sanborn's generosity has meant, because they cannot visualize what existed before his day.* Below those words was verse:

> *There came to the El Nido Valley*
> *The peaceful El Nido*
> *A decade or so ago*
> *A man rich in goods and gold*
> *And rich in the love of the beautiful . . .*

It was late Saturday afternoon. Greg had been in El Nido less than a day, but felt himself already affected. The world beyond the valley had started to slip away. Greg recalled feeling that same sensation as a boy whenever he came here. He and his father, alone in a rowboat on El Nido Lake. They could talk in ways they never did back at home, sharing thoughts normally hidden, forgetting boundaries, achieving a fragile connection. Greg welcomed the chance to revisit that time, that place. He had no intention of representing Sarah Trant, yet he'd protested only momentarily before accepting Diana's invitation to stay the weekend.

From the living-room wall where Edward Sanborn's portrait hung, Greg walked to a small side room, just off Diana's veranda. She'd offered him this alcove for his personal use during his brief stay. Sunlight poured through a picture window giving onto a view of the El Nido Valley. In one corner there was a desk and phone, in another a lamp and reading chair. *Your private place to think, or work, or whatever it is you do,* Diana had explained, her voice a bright trill that left Greg struggling yet again to read her. Something about his presence in El Nido clearly unnerved this woman, yet she appeared curiously driven to keep him in the valley. She'd even summoned her personal physician to tend to his head wound.

Greg sat down at the desk, then turned again to the foot-high pile of news articles that he'd found an hour before in a bottom drawer while casually exploring his temporary domain. Whether Diana had purposefully placed them there, or simply forgotten where she'd stored them, he could not say. All he knew was that the small weekly newspaper's accounts of how Sarah Trant came to be on death row made for interesting reading.

Once more, Greg leafed through them. He'd assembled what had been a haphazard pile into chronological order. Viewed that way, he could see that the story began—as Sarah said—not with the cranky old geologist Brewster Tomaz's murder, but months before, with the arrival of ModoCorp. With the arrival, to be exact, of Charles Whit, identified as founder and managing director of ModoCorp. Sarah had mentioned the company, but not the man. And she hadn't mentioned that the "gorgeous chunk of wilderness" they bought was a long-closed thirty-six-acre religious complex called Camp Mahrah. Greg studied the newspaper map that located this camp. Here's where he must have cracked up his car. Here's where the rifleman welcomed him to El Nido.

Greg kept reading. Fronted by a public relations team, Whit had showered El Nido with soaring but vague talk about a world-class health spa at Camp Mahrah. There'd been town hall meetings, slide shows, and what looked to be Whit's calculated insinuation into the community. Whit had bought a home in the rustic El Nido neighborhood called Woodland, originally developed by Edward Sanborn. He'd paid calls to bankers, small-business merchants, local civic leaders, the Lions Club. He'd made the circuit of various Sunday church services. He'd bought the grand champion hog at El Nido County's livestock auction. He'd contributed to the Little League, the Firemen's Association, the El Nido High School's "Project Graduation." He'd donated $500 toward a scholarship for the newly crowned Miss El Nido.

Most important, he'd hired Brewster Tomaz.

Greg had to admit that was an astute move. Tomaz, the articles made clear, was a well-known El Nido native, born and raised in the valley, amusing and cantankerous at once, and much appreciated for both traits. He'd lived alone almost his entire seventy-three years, yet nearly everyone considered his solitary nature a mark of hardy individualism rather than misanthropy. They particularly respected Tomaz for his unmatched knowledge of the region. He knew the valley's terrain as well as anyone. With Tomaz on board, ModoCorp had gained both respectability and instant roots in the community. Support for the health spa at Camp Mahrah gradually mounted.

Yet why would a man like Tomaz sign on with an outfit such as ModoCorp? Greg studied the geologist's photos, as if his face might offer an answer. He saw only an old man's withered scowl. Sarah was right; Tomaz did indeed resemble a prune. A bloated prune, with a broad sunburned forehead and a perpetual five-day beard. Colorful and eccentric and amusing, yes, but to Greg there also was a look of menace about him. In almost every photo, the crusty old coot's thin lips curled in a manner that suggested genuine contempt; one color snapshot revealed cold pale blue eyes aimed with distaste at a subject beyond the camera's range.

Big plans for El Nido. That's what Sarah had said. *Confrontations at the river, pushing and shoving.* In the later articles, Greg saw what she meant. ModoCorp, having won provisional approval to clear their land, ostensibly for fire-control purposes, had suddenly rolled in a bulldozer with no advance notice and cut a new road through state forestland. Then they'd fenced off the segment of a public hiking and equestrian trail that crossed a corner of Camp Mahrah. Finally, they'd started digging diversion channels where El Nido Creek bordered their property high in the foothills. It had been a dry year in El Nido, so even Brewster Tomaz's involvement couldn't keep a few eyebrows from rising over this threat to a central source of valley water. Only after Charles Whit made clear they intended merely to construct an auxiliary water supply, again for firefighting purposes, did the valley's anxiety wane. Not Sarah's, though.

Here, Greg saw, was where she really started waving her banner. Speeches at local Grange meetings, petitions for restraining orders, demonstrations at the entrance of Camp Mahrah, confrontations at the El Nido Creek diversion site—Sarah was always present, and usually alone. A majority of citizens were behind ModoCorp by then. Despite some trepidation, even El Nido's city fathers, pushed by merchants hungry for growing tourist dollars, had voted to support the planned health spa. Sarah's strident objections were offending just about the entire community.

Greg read on. There'd been several face-to-face encounters between Sarah and Brewster Tomaz. Once the two had even ended up in a shoving match in front of ModoCorp's bulldozer, and Sarah had evidently gotten the best of him. Greg cringed as he studied the photo of Tomaz sprawled in El Nido Creek that day; it looked too much like foreshadowing. ModoCorp had finally gone to the local magistrate's court seeking an injunction against her physical intrusions. There was no way around the matter: It appeared that Sarah by then was just about stalking the quaint old geologist.

Flipping through the clips, Greg reached the murder itself.

It happened just past dusk on a chilly December evening, not near Camp Mahrah, but rather, at the stretch of El Nido Creek that formed the southern boundary of Sanborn Park. There'd been a concert that night in the park, one of a monthly series offered free by the amateur El Nido Band. A commotion at the river was heard. Then Brewster Tomaz's body was found, floating facedown in the rippling water. Accidental drowning, it might have seemed at first. Until they turned the body over and saw the geologist's slashed throat.

From the accounts before Greg, it did not appear authorities took more than a few hours to arrest Sarah Trant. No wonder: Who else was known to be hounding the victim, who else was known to have pushed him into the river, who else in all the valley would slash a man's neck ear to ear? In her statements to police, Sarah readily admitted that she'd been down at the river, that she'd confronted and argued there with Brewster Tomaz, that she'd once again pushed Tomaz into the water. That was all, though. She'd run off after that, she insisted, and had never looked back.

Perhaps the jury might have believed her, perhaps not. It was hard to say, because before those twelve citizens could commence deliberating, a final surprise witness had stepped forward for the prosecution. A witness who claimed to have rushed to the dying geologist's side. A witness who claimed that she heard Brewster Tomaz, with his last breath, whisper: "Sarah did this, Sarah had a knife."

Greg once more studied the accompanying photo of the witness. She'd been five years younger then, the face a bit thinner, the hair not quite as gray. Looking at her high cheekbones and wide dark amused eyes, he could easily imagine her as a young woman driving men to distraction as she walked the streets of El Nido. Now she was unnerving him. . . . Just how, he wondered, did Diana Sanborn come to be the star prosecution witness who sealed Sarah Trant's fate?

"AN INTERESTING READ?"

Greg looked up to see Alex Ramirez staring at him from the doorway. The ranch foreman apparently had the run of Diana's house.

"A puzzling read," Greg said.

"Yes, I suspect it is for you."

"Not for you?"

Alex shrugged. "I'm a little closer to it."

"What do you mean?"

Alex showed nothing in his expression. "I just mean I'm from here, I'm from El Nido. Fourth generation. My family has worked this land—other people's land—for more than a century. I understand this valley as an outsider could not."

"You must understand the valley to grasp the meaning of this murder case?"

"It wouldn't hurt. It was a fight over development of the valley that led to this killing, and there have been many such fights before. Each has its own story . . . but there are patterns."

On impulse Greg said, "Tell me about this place. I want to know."

"It wouldn't be of interest to you."

"Yes it would."

"You think so?" Alex was studying him with curiosity.

"Yes."

Alex pulled up a chair, sat down. He'd needed little persuading. He spoke warmly now, plainly savoring the memories, and the chance to recount them.

The Chumash were El Nido's original inhabitants, he began. They lived in peace, eating grain and berries, acorns and fish. Didn't own the land, though. The missions held title, then the Mexican government, which began handing out parcels to political favorites. Rancho El Nido, almost eighteen thousand acres in all, went to Federico Alvera in 1837. Title changed hands a half-dozen times over the next quarter century. Speculators made quick profits, then moved on. For a time it looked as if El Nido would fall to progress. Entrepreneurs built health spas around the region's natural hot springs. Wildcutters sank oil wells in ravines where petroleum seeped from crevices. Eastern settlers fueled a frantic land rush, doubling property values within weeks, then doubling them again.

Alex's eyes gleamed with pleasure at the thought of what followed. "That boom in 1887 lasted just months. The health spas had to shut their doors for lack of business, and the prospectors withdrew for lack of oil. No one much minded in the valley. By the turn of the century, El Nido had returned to being what it is now."

"Which is . . . ?" Greg asked.

Alex looked at Greg as if he should know. "A forgotten valley," he said.

"When did Edward Sanborn show up?"

"Just about then. Around 1901, I'd say. Came from Michigan. Made a fortune there manufacturing ball bearings or something. He favored progress also, but of his own sort. Looked at what was just another dusty western village and hired an architect. They built that arcade on Main Street."

"Spanish-mission style," Greg said.

"That's right."

"The post office tower and the El Nido Valley Inn had the same architect?"

"Right again," Alex said.

"Then there's Sanborn Park," Greg said. "Sixty acres of woodland right in the middle of the village. Edward Sanborn's gift to the valley. My father called it 'the soul of El Nido.' "

Alex appeared to appreciate that description. "If Sanborn had let them," he said, "they would have renamed the whole town after him. When he died, he willed millions of dollars to all sorts of groups across the valley. Folks staged a county-wide celebration over that. Called it 'Sanborn Day.' "

"That's where the plaque came from? The one below his portrait?"

"Yes."

They both fell silent. Greg tried to sort out his thoughts.

"So Alex," he asked after a while. "What does all this history have to do with Brewster Tomaz's murder? You also have insights about that?"

"No . . . just questions."

"Such as?"

"Why you're here."

Greg felt a growing interest in this ranch foreman. "Certainly," he said, "your boss has explained."

"Explain more. What draws you to Sarah Trant's case?"

"I'm not drawn to it," Greg said. "I'll be leaving on Monday."

At that, Alex appeared confused. "You're not drawn to it?"

"Why should I be?"

Alex looked over his shoulder, then rose and reached to close the door to the room. He stepped toward Greg. "No reason, really . . ." He stopped, frowning. "You've seen the autopsy report, I assume? And the autopsy photos?"

Greg shook his head. "What's the point? A habeas petition is about procedural errors and constitutional violations. You don't reinvestigate murders in federal court. You don't redo the trial."

Alex backed toward the door. "I see. Of course. That's what I thought. No point. No point at all."

NO POINT AT ALL. Greg had heard those words before, connected to another case. A notorious case. Sitting alone at dusk in Diana Sanborn's guest office, the memory filled his mind. Not just to defend a mentally unstable killer, but to keep him from being arrested, to let him walk the streets of La Graciosa undetected—Greg had to agree with his critics, such was not a commonplace legal maneuver.

The phone call had come unexpectedly, at home one Sunday morning. Almost five years before. Within minutes, he'd found himself standing in a gas station parking lot, listening to a gawky man in gray work clothes confess to an unsolved homicide. "I did it," Jason Pine reported shyly. "Killed that store clerk last night. Thought she was my ex-girlfriend. No point at all."

Greg never could figure out just why he didn't walk away right then. From news accounts, he knew about the shooting of Mary Ann Michaels, single mother of two little kids, up at the 7-Eleven on Crocker Highway. Itinerants on drugs usually committed that type of crime; only they would try to steal the few bucks not kept in a safe at a convenience store. Jason Pine didn't look like a druggie, though. With his unnerving smile and stiffly held arms and sideburns cut above his ears, Pine looked to Greg like a mental case. A mental case who had not yet managed to wipe out his ex-girlfriend.

By then, though, Pine also looked like his client. At least it seemed that way to Greg. He'd agreed to meet this man, he'd listened to his story. Greg felt ethically and legally bound to keep his client's confession confidential. Only if Pine directly threatened to kill someone could Greg inform authorities. Pine hadn't gone that far. He talked only of what he'd done to a store clerk, not what he might do to an ex-girlfriend.

Greg let him come to his office the next day. There Pine told his story at even greater length. He was thirty-three. He'd been under psychological treatment since he was fifteen. He'd stopped taking his Prozac and lithium after watching a TV counselor say drugs do bad things to you. He'd also stopped going to his therapist. He'd grown so lonely. That's why he tried to visit his former girlfriend. She ran him off. He drank beer all night, then started driving around, looking for her. Drove around until he came to that 7-Eleven. The clerk there was making a pot of coffee, just as his ex-girlfriend used to do. He pulled the trigger five times. He was horrified at what he'd done. He understood all too well he was ill. Sitting in bars, he watched everyone having a good time. He fantasized about being part of that. He knew he was different. He knew he was alone.

Greg scrawled on a yellow pad as Pine spoke. They would put him in prison, Greg knew. Pine was flat out crazy, but they'd put him behind bars forever if he talked. Better to get him committed to a hospital, get him examined. That would take him off the streets but still protect his rights. As long as the state asked for the exam, whatever Pine said to a doctor in the hospital was usable only on the issue of sanity, not guilt or innocence.

Goddamn Dennis Taylor. If only the Chumash County district attorney had agreed from the start to this plan, they wouldn't all have twisted in the wind for so long. Taylor wouldn't buy Greg's ploy, though. He had his own job, which was to build the best possible prosecutable case. He knew just how to do that, too—exploit Greg's desire to get his client off the streets. It became a high-stakes chess game. For two months, he and the DA two-stepped down their fine frightening line, Greg insisting he'd reveal his client's identity only for a hospital commitment, the DA insisting he'd take him only under arrest, each waiting for the other to blink.

"Monarch, forget it," Taylor snapped one day. "I'm not going to just pick up this guy and commit him based on your hearsay. I don't know who the guy is, even. Don't have a probable cause to hold him. If we got to trial, what's my case? Don't have one. You're a great lawyer, Greg, but how the hell you know this guy is crazy?"

Taylor rolled a pencil across his desk then, and looked out the window. "I believe there's a public-safety exception to the confidentiality privilege," he said. "If there's a threat to public safety, you can violate confidentiality. You can share this."

"Bull," Greg snorted. "Where'd you pull that out of?"

In the end, they'd called the hot line at the California state bar's board of professional responsibility. They'd laid out the deal to an ethics counselor, talking together on the speakerphone. Then they'd asked, Who's right? Is there a public-safety exception?

No doubt about it, the state expert declared. The defense attorney is right. There's no exception. Mr. Monarch can't betray his client.

GREG LEAFED THROUGH THE El Nido directory, then picked up the phone and punched in the residential number of Reginald Dodge. By newspaper accounts, Dodge had served as Sarah Trant's defense counsel at her state murder trial. On this early Saturday evening, Greg couldn't imagine El Nido citizens being anywhere but home. In this case, at least, his intuition proved right. Dodge answered on the second ring.

"Dodge here," he said.

Greg tried to imagine this man on the other end of the phone line. A criminal defense attorney in a place such as El Nido must spend most of his time doing—what? Car radio thefts, dope smokers in Sanborn Park, the occasional domestic squabble, that's what filled the police blotter reprinted in the valley's weekly newspaper. A murder trial must have been an extraordinary experience for him. In fact, it likely had been his first and only.

"Mr. Dodge, my name is Greg Monarch. I'm a lawyer from La Graciosa, here in El Nido for the weekend—"

Dodge interrupted. "Yes, Mr. Monarch, so I've heard. This is a small town. Your arrival has been noted."

"Then you know I'm here because of Sarah Trant's habeas petition?"

In the silence that followed, Greg thought he could hear the clink of ice cubes in a glass.

"Yessir," Dodge finally replied. "That I know." His voice sounded overly hearty.

"I'm wondering if I might browse a bit through your case files. Just to get up to speed. Especially interested in the autopsy report and photos on Brewster Tomaz."

Again a silence, and the clink of ice cubes. "Well, now," Dodge began. He was having trouble forming his words. "That would be difficult. Five years ago, that trial was. Those files got stored away long ago. Not sure where, tell the truth. That would take a while, track all that down. You'd be long gone by then."

"Maybe not," Greg said. "I like the air here."

Dodge erupted in a spasm of coughing. When he stopped he made the gulping noise of a man hungry for oxygen. "Watch out for her, Monarch, watch out for that woman. Sarah Trant told me six different stories. Never knew what she'd be saying day to day."

"The autopsy report," Greg said. "Surely that's public record. It would be much easier getting it from you than from the DA."

"Don't have it. That's the honest truth. Gave it to the pathologist who was going to testify for the defense, so he could prepare his expert testimony. Never got it back."

"What do you mean 'going to testify'?"

A bitter laugh came from somewhere deep in Dodge's throat. "Well, he did testify. But it's a matter of debate whether it was for the defense."

"Who called him as a witness?"

It sounded as if Dodge were draining his glass. "The defense called him, Mr. Monarch. I called him."

DR. GRANT MONTROSE ALSO answered his own phone when Greg punched in his number. "Yes, yes, this is Dr. Montrose," he snapped. "Who is this?"

The pathologist sounded like a busy man, or at least a harried one. He had a vague accent that Greg couldn't place.

"Greg Monarch here. I'm a lawyer from La Graciosa, here in El Nido for a day trying to help Sarah Trant with an appeal."

"What can I do for you, Mr. Monarch?" Montrose didn't sound any more surprised by his call than did Dodge.

"I need a copy of the autopsy report on Brewster Tomaz. Sarah's trial attorney tells me he sent his copy to you. Since for the time being at least I'm Sarah's lawyer, I'd like to get it back."

Montrose cleared his throat. Greg imagined someone rotund, with a pompous air and a monocle. Maybe a rug on his head.

"Well, Mr. Monarch," the pathologist said, "I don't know if I can give that to you. There are certain rules we have to follow. There's something called discovery, isn't there? If I just send you the autopsy report, we'd be going way outside that process."

Greg labored to keep his tone reasonable. "Dr. Montrose, I commend your concern about the discovery process. But the autopsy report and photographs would have come into the case even before the trial. They're part of the public record now. Sarah's lawyer had them, Sarah's lawyer gave them to you so you could prepare your testimony. They're actually part of Sarah's property, if you think about it. You just never got around to returning them."

A long pause. "Well, I don't know," Montrose said finally. "I don't think I can do this without getting the district attorney's approval. Why don't you just ask the DA for a copy?"

Greg stared out Diana's window toward the El Nido Valley. Dusk had turned to a pitch-black hue. He could no longer see where he was. Of course, he could call the DA. But why was this pathologist being so resistant?

"Dr. Montrose, wouldn't it be easier if you just pulled it from your files and sent me a copy?"

"Well, I don't know. We have to watch how we do these things. Anyway, I purge my files. Like everyone does. I may have thrown it away."

"Dr. Montrose, Sarah Trant needs the report and photos. What gives here? Why are you withholding them?"

Montrose's tone shifted now. Pomposity gave way to a certain high-pitched alarm. "Was she granted a new trial? Is that why you want this stuff?"

"No, not yet. But she's aiming for one." Greg could hear footsteps, as if Montrose were pacing about his phone. He continued. "Doctor, you were retained by Sarah Trant. You were given these documents by Sarah's lawyer."

"No!" Montrose cried. "No, I was not hired by Sarah Trant. I was hired by the state."

"Well now, you may have been paid by the state, Doctor, but you were paid to assist Sarah Trant."

"No, Mr. Monarch. I was paid by the state to analyze evidence fairly."

Greg tried to speak gently. Montrose, for all his bluster, sounded scared. "Why are you doing this, Doctor?"

Montrose lacked the polish to carry off what he was attempting.

He couldn't contain himself any longer: "Because I've been directed by the DA's office not to release either the autopsy report or photos to you, that's why. I've been directed. I've been ordered."

"Who in the DA's office?" Greg asked.

"The district attorney himself. James Mashburn."

Greg stiffened in his chair. He'd lost track of affairs here in this remote valley. He'd thought Karl Jackson was still the DA. But that couldn't be, come to think of it. Jackson was a state judge now. *James Mashburn.* Greg had once known a lawyer by that name. A lawyer who'd left La Graciosa years ago for the inland valleys. For El Nido, in fact. Yes. It must be him.

Looking about in the darkened room, Greg now realized that Alex Ramirez was standing in the doorway, listening to his half of the conversation. Slowly, he placed the receiver back on the phone without bothering with farewells.

"Tell me, Alex," he said. "Just how big is this?"

F O U R

Peering through the big picture window in his office, El Nido County District Attorney James Mashburn watched three laughing seven-year-old girls splash in the public fountain that fronted Sanborn Park. The fountain was an abstract free-form structure, but to Mashburn it looked like a woman bent over with one hand cupped, as if she were playing craps. He'd always wanted to hang big fake dice from her fingers.

"Mashburn, may I ask if you're listening to me?"

Slowly, the DA turned from the window. Sheriff Roy Rimmer's narrow, insistent face hadn't gone away. There it was still, floating in the air on the far side of the room. Mashburn had inherited that face when he first took office. By then Rimmer had been the El Nido County sheriff for a decade, and knew way too much about the valley to be ignored. The truth was, Mashburn needed Rimmer. Especially when he began, the DA had lacked a natural bent for the harsher aspects of prosecuting. He'd also lacked the grasp of El Nido that only a native possessed. Rimmer was his hammer. Also, his eyes and ears.

"Are you there, Jim?" Rimmer asked again. "Are you with me?"

Mashburn ran a hand through his salt-and-pepper beard. He was a sturdy man, pushing fifty now, with a high forehead, a perpetual frown, and dark wary eyes. "I'm here, Roy. Whether I'm with you is another matter."

"Okay, then. I'll settle for that right now. What I'm saying is, this Monarch fellow is out of control. Christ sake, look at these goddamn letters he's sending to the judge. Jesus. We have to respond, Jim. We have to do something to head this off."

As Rimmer talked, the DA thumbed again through Greg's correspondence. *This Monarch fellow.* To the sheriff, he was a stranger. Not to Mashburn, though. What he most recalled about Monarch was the way he drummed his fingers on the bar counter as they worked a pitcher of beer.

They'd never been friends. Not even colleagues, really. But for one summer they'd held a similar hand of cards. It must have been a dozen years ago. Mashburn still thought of those days with appreciation. He'd been on the other side then, working as a criminal defense attorney. His client, and Monarch's, were both targets of a Chumash County grand jury probe. The prosecutor thought one or the other might be the killer in a tangled drug deal gone wrong. The prosecutor had no real evidence, just a desire to charge someone. So he tried playing Monarch against Mashburn, dangling immunity, threatening death row, inviting either to deliver a client willing to sing. Usually, someone caved in such a situation, lunging after their self-interests. But not this time. One evening, Monarch hauled Mashburn to a funky old tavern called JB's Red Rooster, poured a vat of Graciosa Brew into him, and proposed they trust each other. For once, he urged, let's stand together.

What do you have in mind? Mashburn asked.

Monarch didn't answer at first. He tapped his fingers on the bar in that manner he had, humming along to the tune being pounded out by the piano player. Only after the music stopped did he turn back to Mashburn. A joint defense agreement, he said then. We negotiate a joint defense agreement.

It had been a clever suggestion, Mashburn had to admit. Each of them, in that way, could legitimately inform the other what the DA had been asking their client, and what their client had told the DA. Joint defense agreements invariably made it more difficult for authorities to flip a target. They countered the government's standard divide-and-conquer strategy in criminal cases.

"Helps level the playing field" was how Greg put it at JB's that night. "All those case agents and detectives and prosecutors get to share information. Why don't we?"

Stonewalling, of course, was another way to put it. Circling the wagons. A conspiracy backing up the original conspiracy that triggered the initial investigation. A way for wrongdoers to learn whether their version of events was fitting with other witnesses'. As DA in El Nido County, Mashburn had been forced to deal with such ploys more than once. Goddamn frustrating as hell, that's how he saw them now.

Not back then, though. Back then, the Chumash County DA had no recourse but to let both their clients go. The two defense lawyers toasted their success with a hike at dusk into the Chumash Dunes. Not long after, Mashburn moved inland to El Nido and started on the path that led to the DA's office. He hadn't seen or heard from Monarch in more than a decade.

Mashburn turned his attention back to Greg's letters. He knew less than he should about this whole Sarah Trant situation. Brewster Tomaz had been murdered well before he took office. It had been his predecessor Karl Jackson's prosecution, and Sheriff Rimmer's investigation. Just as well, really. He didn't want his thumbprints on this one. The whole case gave off a bad odor. The stink was there even though Sarah Trant's guilt seemed perfectly obvious. Take the matter of footprints along the riverbank, for just one example. The police in their official reports described only those of Brewster Tomaz and Sarah Trant, but the forensic technician's account—which Mashburn found in the investigative file—also included mention of a third set. Boot prints, to be precise. The left boot had distinctive half-soled nail marks, rows of tacks pounded in diagonally across the half-sole. Those prints held obvious importance. Yet the defense attorney Reggie Dodge had never introduced them at trial. Mashburn suspected Dodge had never been told about them. Mashburn wondered what else Dodge hadn't been told.

With irritation, the DA tossed Monarch's letters back on a desk already filled with a jumble of documents. He could see the cause for Sheriff Rimmer's concern. Greg Monarch still knew how to play his hand. He'd gone home after his first weekend in El Nido but hadn't backed off. From Chumash County he'd fired off letters and phone calls for a good week. He wasn't representing Sarah Trant, he explained to those few willing to ask. He was just poking around, helping out for the moment.

His first letter had gone to Dr. Grant Montrose, the pathologist who'd testified for the defense at Sarah Trant's trial. *The purpose of this letter is to confirm our telephone conversation last Saturday. I called to ask if you would give me a copy of the autopsy report and photos on Brewster Tomaz. You refused. "I wasn't hired by Sarah Trant, I was hired by the state," you told me. You also told me that you'd been "ordered" by the El Nido County DA's office not to provide anything. If you feel that the above inaccurately reflects our conversation, please so inform me in writing within seventy-two hours. If I don't hear from you, I'll assume that you agree with everything set forth in this letter.*

It was, Mashburn knew, the last line, under Greg Monarch's signature, that most bothered Rimmer:

cc: The Honorable Daniel Solman

Monarch had copied this letter to the federal judge.

And not just that letter; he'd copied everything he'd written. Including letters he'd sent to Mashburn.

Dear DA James Mashburn . . . I am writing to confirm certain instructions that your office has given to Dr. Montrose. The doctor has refused to provide me the autopsy report and photos on Brewster Tomaz. He has told me he can't do so without your express approval. He has also told me that you instructed him not to provide me those documents. I trust you agree with this account. If you disagree . . .

Again, there at the bottom, was *cc: The Honorable Daniel Solman.*

Mashburn's mouth started to curve into an appreciative smile. Then he caught himself, and quickly shook all expression off his face. He was a professional, after all. A prosecutor. His job, like it or not, was to represent the state and fight this habeas petition. His job was to protect the conviction his colleagues had won. You have to take a stand to be a prosecutor, or else you never get anything done. You can't be a prosecutor if you shrink from making the calls or fighting the battles. And once you're fighting, you simply can't entertain the possibility of being wrong. You have to act certain, even if you aren't. Goddamn hardass certain.

"Okay, Roy," Mashburn said. "So if it were up to you, which it isn't, how would you respond?"

Rimmer paced across the room, his hands clasped behind his back. "We deny everything, first off. We simply must, Jim. We deny his accounts of our conversations."

Mashburn nodded, and turned back to his picture window. The

little girls were still splashing in the fountain. "I see. Yes, of course. That makes perfect sense, Rimmer. Except for one thing. Monarch is absolutely right. He hasn't managed to get anything from us. We've stonewalled him quite nicely. How do we explain that?"

Rimmer flushed with exasperation. "We never said we wouldn't provide him documents, Jim. We told him we'd be happy to hand over anything, provided he had a subpoena."

Mashburn kept his eyes on the window. "Of course, you know Greg Monarch can't issue subpoenas, or, in this situation, get anyone else to issue them."

Rimmer walked to Mashburn's side. "Oh really?" he said. "I didn't realize that. I'm not a lawyer, after all."

Mashburn turned on him. "Let's cut the bullshit, Rimmer. For whatever reasons, you guys obviously rigged this one from start to finish, even though it looks like you damn well had the right target. You should have played it straight, you would have won anyway, but you didn't. Now I have to clean up your mess. That I'll do, because that's my goddamn job. I can't just blow this off. I'm not going to put a murderer back on the streets. But I don't like this game."

Rimmer offered a faint smile. "I knew I could count on you, Jim."

Mashburn picked up the letter he'd drafted in response to Greg Monarch's foray. Greg had kept it formal in his correspondence, not acknowledging any connection, so he'd done the same.

Dear Mr. Monarch: I am by copy of this note advising Judge Solman that the information contained in your letter is utterly false. I have never directed Dr. Montrose to withhold documents from you. I question why you are copying the judge on correspondence of this nature. . . .

"This ought to do it," the DA said.

As Rimmer scanned the page, his smile widened into a look of unbounded delight. "Very nice, Jim," he said. "Yes, this ought to do it."

AT DUSK, AS THE valley sky turned slowly from gold to pink, the bell atop the U.S. Post Office tower began to toll, signaling the start of the weekly El Nido Band concert. Parents watching their children splash in Sanborn Park's public fountain turned to listen. So did teenagers racing mountain bikes down the park's dirt pathways, and folks riding horses along its equestrian trail. Soon, families bearing beach chairs and coolers were strolling toward the open lawn that surrounded Sanborn Park's redwood bandstand. Under a spreading oak, two stout ladies from the Heritage Club sold homemade popcorn and lemonade.

It was the Sunday evening of Greg's second weekend in El Nido. His last evening, he told himself. He'd won postponements in his three most pressing cases, and farmed out other matters to Tim Ruthman, but the calls summoning him home kept coming. He couldn't stay away from La Graciosa for long. He'd stirred things up as much as he could here. He'd rattled a few cages, he'd alerted Judge Solman to the hint of funny business. Tomorrow he'd hand Sarah off to a local lawyer or the county public defender.

For the moment, though, he stood to one side of the concert bandstand, watching and remembering. There'd been past evenings like this one. He and his father, on a blanket, humming along to the unabashedly corny tunes. They'd felt a little odd, like spies intruding on a closed world. They'd also rolled their eyes in those moments when the town came close to reminding them of a stage set straight out of *The Music Man*. Yet they'd always been warmly welcomed by El Nido's natives, and that felt authentic. It was easy, Greg found now, to spot those longtime residents of El Nido amid the valley's more recent arrivals. They entered the park not with their families but in separate groups—men, women, children. From newspaper photos, Greg recognized El Nido's mayor, eighty-two-year-old Sam Rabe. He was leaning against one side of the bandstand, scratching his bristly white beard and spitting tobacco juice into the high grass. His wife Tammy Rabe loomed a few steps behind him. Greg could hear her booming out instructions on where to sit—"You over there, now don't argue, you to that corner"—as her two-inch silver crescent-moon earrings clanked and her five coral-and-turquoise rings glittered. Not one citizen passing her way objected to his assignment; at 205 pounds—much of those stuffed this evening into a pair of improbably tight Levi's—the mayor's wife did not brook much dispute.

Diana Sanborn had invited Greg to attend this concert. He'd dropped by Sanborn Ranch that morning, hoping for a final visit with the mistress of the house. He'd found her at the breakfast table, picking at a bowl of fresh blueberries. She'd seemed softer there in the morning light, less overpowering. She'd walked him around the ranch, explaining how she monitored the moods of her livestock. Pointing out the protected rise where she often watched the sun set, she talked of the peculiar pink light that filled El Nido's skies at dusk. "We will be doing our best imitation of *The Music Man* tonight in the park," she'd said finally, as if she'd overheard Greg and his father. "Come see for yourself." Now, returned to the public stage, wearing her trademark granny dress with boots and a cowboy hat, Diana stood in the center of the park crying *bless your heart* to half the population of El Nido. Greg watched her for a while, then glanced at the tall slender woman standing beside her. She was, Greg saw, already studying him.

She held his gaze. Her emerald dress matched her eyes. They were intriguing eyes, enormous and full of feeling. She had an oval face framed by a tangle of light brown hair, and the type of mouth that looked as if it were always on the edge of an arriving smile. She could be thirty, Greg thought, maybe thirty-five.

Diana waved him over. "Mr. Monarch, someone for you to meet," she sang out. "Jasmine Gest, Greg Monarch. Jas is quite our glamorous star. Writes articles and columns for the *El Nido News*. Also writes short stories and poems, which one day will surely be published. She even finds time to volunteer at El Nido's historical museum. She does it all. While Greg, alas"—here Diana whooped loudly—"is limited to being a lawyer."

Jas smiled faintly at Diana's words. She looked down, then up at Greg. "We've met already," she said.

It took Greg a moment to understand. Then he realized: Here was the woman he'd seen bathing at the river on his first morning in El Nido. She appeared as coolly composed now as she had then.

"You were an inspiring introduction to El Nido," he said.

Jas rolled her eyes. "You have me at a disadvantage. You know more about me than I know of you."

Bless your heart, bless your heart. From twenty yards away, they both heard Diana's cries. Without their noticing, she'd drifted off.

Jas kept looking at Greg. There was something in her manner, he thought. Something he recognized.

"Not bad," he said. "Even in a dress."

Jas winced. "Come on, you can do better than that."

"I was trying to be subtle."

"Oh yes, subtle indeed." Jas waved her hand above and behind her. "So subtle it went right over my head."

"I'll work on that."

She didn't respond. It took Greg a moment to realize that he'd lost Jasmine's attention. Following where her gaze had turned, he saw a big broad-shouldered man moving through the crowd. From his newspaper photos, Greg recognized Charles Whit. The managing director of ModoCorp was looking over the heads of those around him, surveying the crowd. Whit had never left El Nido after Brewster Tomaz's death, even though the murder appeared to have derailed his plans. He still talked occasionally about a world-class health mecca, but he no longer made any effort to get it built. *When the time is right,* he told folks now. Those who probed further heard complicated explanations about prohibitive economics in a limited market. To the merchants and bankers and anyone else in El Nido blessed with the least business sense, it sounded as if Whit no longer really intended to build a spa at Camp Mahrah. Given that, his continued residency in the valley represented something of a mystery.

Whit walked with a slight limp and carried a thick walnut cane, which he appeared to use mainly for clearing a path and pointing at folks. His face and neck and hands were the color of weathered copper, his light-gray eyes a striking contrast. The sun and wind had bleached his hair and wrinkled his skin, obscuring his age. He looked like a man who lived outdoors. He also looked like a man accustomed to giving orders. His eyes registered intelligence but not emotion; his cold steady smile had no root.

For all that, what most struck folks in El Nido about Whit was his eerily far-reaching knowledge of their community. He seemed to know something about almost everyone in town. How Ed Snell's grandpa drowned crossing the flooded El Nido Creek; how Constable Thomas Bell ended up locking himself in his own jail one night; how old George Garson robbed El Nido Bank in March 1916 while pretending to be showering at the adjacent Boxer Club. In the early going, Whit had entertained people by repeating such tales over beers at the Gaucho Tavern. Eventually, though, his mastery of their histories had started making some folks feel uneasy. So had the whiff of Christianity that in time began coloring Whit's conversation. *Christ is the center of my life*, he'd taken to declaring publicly in recent months. *If it's not right, I don't do it.* Such talk didn't sit very well with El Nido folks. Nor, for that matter, did Whit's insistent way of making you say hello back to him. The truth was, just about everything connected to Charles Whit had started to disturb a certain element in the valley.

"He irritates me, waving all friendly." It was the mayor's wife Tammy Rabe, who, with Diana Sanborn, had silently sidled up to where Greg now stood with Jas. "He did that at the public springs when I was swimming. 'Why don't you kiss my ass,' I said. He knows I don't want him waving at me."

Diana whooped and slapped Tammy's back. Just then, Whit spotted the three women. He grinned, and waggled his cane back and forth.

THE EL NIDO BAND began to tune up. They were an amateur group, pulled together from whichever local citizens had even the slightest bent for music. Teachers, carpenters, ranch hands, all sat side by side on the bandstand gripping their instruments. One played the trumpet, another the flute, a third kettledrums. There was a clarinet, an oboe, a bassoon, an alto sax, a French horn, a trombone, a tuba, a string bass. Families on the lawn started humming and clapping as the players launched tentatively into their first tune. A fourteen-year-old girl with straw-colored hair took the microphone. *Oh Nido, oh Nido, where the stars they shine so bright . . .*

"Charming little song, isn't it?" Charles Whit's voice was low and full of gravel. He was standing at Greg's elbow, watching the bandstand. "This your first visit to El Nido, Mr. Monarch?"

Greg studied the man before speaking. Whit's gray eyes seemed to have gone dead on him. He held his head at a truculent angle.

"I've visited before," Greg said finally. "But not for a while."

"What brings you here now?"

"I can't imagine you don't know. Everyone else seems to, even before I tell them."

"I wouldn't ask if I knew."

Greg turned back to the bandstand. "Okay, Mr. Whit. The sunshine brings me."

"Valley can get mighty hot."

"I'm partial to heat."

Whit smiled but didn't look amused. "Yes, so I hear. Understand you're an attorney. Criminal defense. Pretty big name over in Chumash County."

"It's a small county," Greg pointed out. "Easy to stand out."

The band kicked into its second tune, drums and tuba leading the way. Greg thought he recognized "You'll Never Walk Alone." Whit leaned over, spoke into his ear. "You planning to stick around El Nido long, Mr. Monarch?"

"I haven't decided. What about you?"

Whit moved his mouth even closer to Greg's ear now. "I haven't decided either."

"Yet you still consider Camp Mahrah worth protecting."

"It's an expensive investment."

"Armed guards to protect an abandoned camp?"

A trace of humor began to creep into Whit's expression. "Just a caretaker, Mr. Monarch."

"A caretaker with a rifle and an attitude."

"My caretaker's manners are misleading. They're not what they seem."

"What ever is?"

Whit looked genuinely delighted. He reached out, placed a muscular hand on Greg's shoulder. "We may get along yet," he said.

As THE BAND PLAYED on, Greg wandered through Sanborn Park, retreating ever farther from the music, losing himself finally in the thick stands of live oak that filled the park's lonely interior. He heard water running in the dark, then, with help from the moonlight, found the creek. He settled on its bank and leaned back.

What his father had most admired about the citizens of El Nido was their quiet, unforced sense of purpose. Growing oranges and running cattle involved certain verities and imperatives that left no room for much questioning. You rose, pulled on your boots, went to work, and saw the fruit of your labor. *It must keep the mind so steady,* his father would say with that fixed, inward look of his. Yet Dr. Paul A. Monarch never once thought of dwelling forever in what looked to be such an innocently bucolic province. El Nido to him was a place to visit and imagine, nothing more.

The crack of a twig drew Greg from his thoughts. He heard her voice before he could see her. "Thought I spotted you wander off this way," she said, sliding down the bank to where he sat. Jas Gest ran a hand through her hair. The moonlight glinted off her emerald-green eyes. "Figured maybe you could use some company."

"I came out here to think," Greg replied.

"About . . . ?"

He studied her. "What it must have been like," he said finally, "for you to watch Sarah Trant's trial."

Jas blinked with surprise. She settled on the bank next to Greg. "How do you know I watched the trial?"

"You pore through enough piles of old news clips, you start to notice the bylines."

"I'm delighted you noticed."

"What did you notice? I mean, back then five years ago, at the trial?"

Jas shrugged. "Big deal to have a murder trial of any kind here in the valley, but this one looked open-and-shut. Sarah Trant was the obvious suspect. They had a watertight case against her."

"Why did you choose to write so much about it?"

"Trials fascinate me. Especially murder trials. They tell a lot about people."

"You want to know about people?"

"Not particularly," Jas said. "I just like occasional confirmation of my worldview."

"Which is . . . ?"

Jas drew lines in the dirt at the creek's edge. "Let's save that for later."

"You expect there'll be a later?"

"Oh yes."

Greg found he couldn't look away from her. "Tell me," he asked. "How long have you been in El Nido?"

She shook her head. "Enough about me, okay?"

"Okay," Greg said. "Let's talk about Sarah Trant, then."

"Yes. Let's."

"You know Sarah? You spent time with Sarah?"

"I know her, yes. Not well, though. We weren't close."

"What does that mean?"

"We took a couple of hikes together. Drinks at the Gaucho Tavern sometimes. Single women need to buddy up over there to fend off the cowboys."

Greg chose his next words carefully. "Tell me, Jasmine. . . . What was Sarah like with you?"

Despite his caution, irritation showed in Jas's eyes. "What are you asking? Whether she ever acted like a murderer?"

Greg tried again. "Just wanted to know her state of mind. The Sarah I know cycles in and out. Sometimes she's there with you, sometimes she's lost."

Jas's expression softened. "Yes," she agreed. "Yes, that's Sarah."

Greg pushed himself up off the riverbank. "You could help me."

"How so?"

"Show me where they found Brewster Tomaz's body. Show me the murder site."

They rose silently and stepped carefully along the creek's moonlit bank, winding farther into the woodland. In the distance, the El Nido Band's music grew ever fainter. *This valley of ours . . . This valley so serene . . .* The forest closed overhead, obscuring the moon. They slipped on round worn boulders at the water's edge, they tripped over tree roots bulging from the ground. Greg struggled to keep his bearings. It all felt so overgrown here, so untended. Looking straight ahead, he found himself staring directly into a towering wall of dense foliage. He heard no sound now but for the wind in the oaks. "Have we lost our way?" he asked.

Jas looked amused. She was standing at the edge of the bank, one hand on her hip. "Not yet, Counselor," she said. "That moment may come, but not yet." She waved her other hand toward the water. "Here's where they found Brewster. Facedown, half in the creek, half out."

Greg turned to where she was pointing. The low bank, sheer elsewhere along the creek, here sloped gradually to the water, forming a flat crescent of bare earth. Like a small beach, Greg thought. From this spot a person could easily bend over and splash his face. Or dive in for a swim. That notion drew Greg's eyes to Jas. For a moment he recalled her rising from the creek on his first morning in El Nido. She looked at him as if she knew what he was thinking.

"Which way in the water?" he asked. "Head facing which way?"

"Head in the water, feet up on the bank."

Greg walked about, surveying the setting. He tried to imagine Sarah here, tried to imagine Sarah bent at the water's edge, slashing Brewster Tomaz's throat ear to ear. It wasn't that he couldn't conceive of someone committing such a brutal act; over the years his clients had exposed him to all manner of human possibility. It was the notion of Sarah doing it that gave him pause. From where could she have summoned not just the needed physical force but the savage volition?

Greg wished again that he had the autopsy report and photos. He hadn't expected to be denied for so long. Jim Mashburn still hadn't acquiesced. Such resistance, from a former colleague no less, aroused Greg's interest even more than the contents of the report itself.

"How could this have happened?" he asked Jas. "What was the state's theory at trial?"

"Theory at trial, Counselor? Or what happened? Which one?"

"Good point. I meant, what do they say Sarah did?"

Jas walked to his side, an arch look in her eyes. She suddenly pushed him hard, her open palms against his chest. Greg's feet slipped out from under him as he fell on the soft earth, landing on his back. In an instant Jas was on her knees above him, straddling his torso. Her curled right hand pounded into his hip once, twice, three times. Then the hand rose to his throat. Jas's fingernails dragged across his neck.

"That's how," she said. "You catch a man unawares, a woman Sarah's size could do just about anything."

Greg stared up at her. She still had him pinned. He could feel her thighs gripping his waist. "Brewster was a big man," he said.

"An old big man." Jas only now began to rise off of Greg. "An old man caught unawares."

Greg grabbed her right hand to hold her where she was. He pulled her hand back to his hip. "Why did you first whack me here?"

Jas shrugged. "Don't know. Just an impulse, I guess."

Greg shifted his hips, moving against her. She stayed with him. "Kind of curious," he said. "I don't know many women capable of slashing a grown man's throat."

Jas finally pulled away from his grip and rose to her feet. "You should get out more."

JAMES MASHBURN LONGED FOR a cigarette, but not even he, the elected district attorney of El Nido, could light up in the county building. They'd made the whole place smoke-free a year before. Reading the sentiment of the community, Mashburn hadn't opposed the move publicly, but among associates he railed against the lunacies of the politically correct crowd. Why couldn't he smoke a goddamn cigarette in the privacy of his own office? Did they fear he'd pollute Roy Rimmer's virgin lungs as the sheriff sat plotting tactics half a football field down a hallway? It just didn't make sense.

The peal of Mashburn's private phone line interrupted his thoughts. From the blinking lights on the panel before him, he could see it was Sheriff Rimmer, calling from down that hallway. He reached for the phone, then dropped his hand and instead looked about his office. There were times when this place made him feel weary, but he liked being a prosecutor. He felt suited for his job, even if he had more or less tumbled into it. He'd started out thinking he'd be a cop, of all things. Working as an Army Airborne MP had been fun. Jumping out of planes, driving fast cars, having patrol dogs as partners—what more could a nineteen-year-old want? Police science in college had felt different, though. He'd quickly switched to an English major, figuring he'd go to law school and become a criminal defense attorney. That's exactly how it worked out, at least for a while. It wasn't a bad role— he liked playing the maverick, he liked working for himself—but he gradually tired of saving so many loathsome characters from their just desserts. Once he tried prosecuting, he found he enjoyed it. Trials and cops were better than writing briefs. Helping victims felt good.

The ringing had stopped for a moment. Now it began again. Reluctantly, Mashburn punched the speaker button. "Yes, Roy," he said. "What is it you want?"

"What do I want?" Rimmer was sputtering. "For one thing, Jim, it would be nice if you answered when I buzzed."

"Done. What else?"

"Some strategy. We need to talk."

Mashburn felt a headache coming on. Rimmer loved mapping strategy more than anyone he knew. "What's this about, Roy?"

"A visitor who wants to come see you."

"A visitor?"

"Yes, a visitor. Our friend from Chumash County has called. Greg Monarch wants a meeting."

Mashburn tried to fight off the feeling of dread tugging at him. He'd been avoiding Monarch daily, yet expecting him. "I suppose he's still after the autopsy documents."

"No doubt," Rimmer said. "Maybe more, though. We spotted him at the band concert last night. Watched him for a while. Then he and Jas Gest headed toward the creek."

"Jas Gest? . . . Where on the creek?"

"Where do you think? The murder site, Jim. The spot on the creek where Sarah Trant murdered Brewster Tomaz."

Mashburn studied a crack in the ceiling above him. You could phrase that differently, he thought. You could say simply, the spot where Tomaz was murdered. Most probably, Sarah Trant had killed Tomaz. Most certainly, in fact. Yet Mashburn had been around courtrooms long enough not to place excessive faith in a jury's verdict. "Oh, that spot," he said. "Where you conducted such a fair and thorough investigation."

"How about focusing, Jim. Greg Monarch wants to come over this afternoon. We need to hold him off. Run him in circles while we get fortified. I'll tell him you're not available."

Mashburn flipped a pencil end to end, and watched it roll off his desk. He wondered how Greg had weathered the years. "But I am available," he said.

NOT UNTIL HE'D BEEN ushered into the district attorney's office did Greg entirely recall his days with James Mashburn. There'd been so many cases since then, so many lawyers, so many moments. He'd needed the sight of Mashburn standing before him to bring everything back. Then he remembered clearly. He remembered a pitcher of Graciosa Brew at JB's, a corner table by the woodstove, a bargain struck as the piano player's wife, Shirley, sang in the background.

How can I know you won't flip on me? That's what Mashburn had asked him that night.

Better to rely on me than the DA. That's how he'd answered.

They'd raised glasses then. They'd trusted each other. And because they did, they'd stopped the Chumash County DA, Dennis Taylor. Whether they should have was another matter. Both their clients, as Greg recalled, had gone on to ever-larger drug deals and ever-more-monstrous acts of brutality.

"Welcome to El Nido County," Mashburn said. "Been a long time, Greg."

"Yes," Greg said. "A long time."

At Mashburn's side, Sheriff Rimmer looked back and forth at the two lawyers. "You know each other?"

"Many years ago," Mashburn said. "For just a month or two. A case in Chumash County."

"You've come a long way," Greg said. "You're a prosecutor now."

Mashburn pointed him to a seat and settled behind his desk. "Yes, I'm a prosecutor."

Greg tried to adjust to that notion. Back when he knew him, Mashburn had not seemed the type. He'd lacked the necessary hubris. He wasn't nearly absolute enough to rise before a jury, point to the defendant, and declare without question or qualm that this— this—is the face of a murderer. Maybe such conduct didn't require hubris, though. Maybe Mashburn needed only a pure and unconflicted heart to do his job.

"So what can we do for you, Monarch?"

The question, coming as it did from Sheriff Rimmer, annoyed Greg. He looked at Mashburn. "Is there a reason why the sheriff has joined us today?"

"I wasn't in office during the Trant trial," Mashburn said, "and my predecessor is now a state judge. So I asked Roy to be here because he handled the investigation."

"I see," Greg said. "Well, then. Maybe the sheriff can explain why the DA's office told Dr. Montrose he shouldn't give me Brewster Tomaz's autopsy report and photos unless he was subpoenaed."

Mashburn responded quickly and sharply. "That's not true, Greg, and we have so informed Judge Solman. When Dr. Montrose contacted me, I advised him that he was a defense witness at Trant's trial, and the DA's office therefore had no voice in how he dealt with you."

"That's not what Montrose told me," Greg said.

Mashburn started to answer, but Rimmer spoke first. "So as not to disappoint you, Monarch, perhaps we should make this perfectly clear right now. We're not going to relitigate a state murder trial. That's not what a federal habeas proceeding is about. Autopsy reports, crime-scene reports, none of that is relevant to a habeas action. You don't start poring over the basic evidence in a habeas. You know that, Monarch. Or you ought to."

Greg dipped his head in apology. "Forgive me, Sheriff. I'm not as well versed in habeas actions as you seem to be. Just feeling my way."

Rimmer nodded vigorously, as if they were in utter agreement. "You're not even representing Sarah Trant, as I understand it. You say you're just poking around. Yet you're copying all your letters to a federal judge. Just what exactly are you doing, Monarch?"

"I thought he'd be interested."

"You shouldn't be sending him letters like that."

Greg rose, walked to Jim Mashburn's desk, and put his hand on the DA's phone. "You're right," he said. "Mail takes so much time. Let's call Judge Solman instead. Let's have a phone conference right now."

Rimmer stepped toward Greg, but Mashburn got to him first. "Okay, Greg," the DA said. "Okay."

From a file cabinet, Mashburn pulled out a large manila envelope and tossed it onto his desk. Greg picked it up. "Feels kind of thin, gentlemen."

Rimmer gripped the edge of the desk as if to keep himself steady. "That's everything. Autopsy report and photos, just as you asked. So let's not hail the judge once again, okay?"

Greg began to pull documents from the envelope. "What about crime-scene photos?"

"No." Rimmer was at Greg's side. "That's part of the investigative file. That's not part of what was handed over to the defense. And that's certainly not anything ripe for habeas review."

By now, Greg had the autopsy photos on the desk before him. He picked up one and looked more closely. "My God," he said.

Brewster Tomaz's neck wound went all the way to the bone of the spinal cord. It was almost six inches side to side, two inches in width, and at least an inch and a half deep. Everything inside Tomaz's throat appeared to have been severed.

"Nasty gash there," Greg said.

"Precisely," Rimmer replied. "That's what we call murder."

Greg scanned the six-page autopsy report. Then, more slowly, he reread the words on page two. _The slashing wound extends from the skin of the center of the throat down to the anterior surface of the vertebral column. This wound involves the skin, subcutaneous tissues, skeletal muscle, small vessels and nerves, and cuts the larynx in half in such a way that the epiglottis is separated from the rest of the larynx. The esophagus is also cut completely. . . . However, the wound does not involve the carotid arteries. . . ._

Greg turned back to the photo. His father hadn't been a surgeon, just a plain country doctor serving La Graciosa for thirty-five years. But growing up in his home, Greg had learned a good deal about anatomy. The practice of criminal law had also, from time to time, provided him an education about the insides of dead people's bodies. He'd seen slashed throats before. He knew the location of the carotid artery, he knew what it looked like. Brewster's was cut in half.

"Think your coroner missed something," Greg said.

Mashburn frowned. "What are you talking about?"

"Looks to me like you have a cut carotid artery here. But your autopsy report says no."

"Autopsy was done by the county pathologist," Rimmer said. "Assisted by a throat specialist. You know more than they do?"

Greg flipped back through the autopsy report.

There is moderate rigor mortis and no lividity. . . . The abdomen is scaphoid and on palpitation no organs are felt. . . . The upper portion of the left thigh shows a stab wound that ends in the bony tissues of the pelvis. . . .

There it was, on page four. _The cardiovascular system is devoid of any blood and the vessels appear to be empty, confirming the fact that the decedent must have bled profusely preceding death. . . ._

"Mr. Tomaz lost all his blood," Greg said. "That usually means you've opened up a main vessel." He looked back at the photo. The blood around Tomaz was a bright red. "And the color of the blood indicates it's freshly oxygenated. Which means it came from an artery. An artery close to the heart."

Mashburn rose, walked around his desk, glanced at the photo. The DA appeared to need a cigarette. "What's your point, Greg? Why does this matter to you so much?"

Greg put a finger on the photo and ran it along the victim's throat. "The vagus and laryngeal nerves run up the neck right there, right beside the left carotid artery. If the left artery is severed, so are those nerves."

Rimmer slapped the desk with the palm of his hand. "So the nerves were cut. Cause of death for Tomaz was a cut throat, isn't that the point? Wouldn't you agree?"

"Yes, of course," Greg said. "I was just wondering. . . ."

"What were you wondering?" Mashburn asked. He looked as if he truly wanted to know.

"It's just that these nerves are rather important," Greg said.

"How so?"

"You need them to talk. Cutting those nerves makes speech immediately impossible."

"So?" Rimmer demanded. "So . . . ?"

"So what I'm wondering," Greg said, "is how a dying Brewster Tomaz could have told Diana Sanborn that 'Sarah did it.' "

Rimmer's face had turned putty white, yet his eyes still seethed. "You're not a doctor, Monarch. You're not an expert pathologist. We had one on the stand. He said Tomaz could have talked."

"Dr. Montrose?" Greg asked. "That would have been Dr. Montrose?"

Mashburn glanced at his sheriff. "What does it matter who it was, Greg? None of this is ripe for habeas. We didn't just have experts say he could talk, we had jurors agree. You don't get to retry a murder case at a federal habeas hearing. You know that, Greg. You're wasting your time."

Greg began stuffing the documents back into the manila envelope. Mashburn, he knew, had a point. Both Congress and the Supreme Court had been narrowing the habeas window for years. It was hard enough even to get a hearing. To actually win relief was almost impossible. To get a federal judge to review old evidence was unheard of. *Barefoot v. Estelle*—that no doubt was the Supreme Court decision Mashburn would wave around if they ever really got going on this. *Barefoot,* invoking the "presumption of finality," declared that "the role of federal habeas proceedings is secondary and limited. . . . Federal courts are not forums in which to relitigate trials."

Yet Greg wondered: What if—just possibly—Sarah really was innocent? What if, for once, he had a case he really ought to win?

It shouldn't matter, he knew that. Sarah had a right to defend herself even if guilty. A writ of habeas corpus allowed state prisoners to seek release not because they were innocent, but because the government had unfairly convicted them. Greg, though, cared little about unfair convictions. He'd had his fill of milking procedural errors and technical violations. He knew it was wrongheaded for any self-respecting defense attorney, but he cared only about actual innocence.

Actual innocence. That opened the federal courtroom door like no other claim. That opened all sorts of doors.

Greg tossed the manila envelope across the table to Mashburn. "You're right, Jim, no doubt I am wasting my time," he said, heading for the hallway. "But at least now I understand why you've been so protective of this autopsy report."

F I V E

In the dark silence of her bed, Diana Sanborn twisted and turned restlessly, waiting for the night to end. As usual, it seemed to go on forever, trapping Diana in her memories.

They weren't all bad ones. All these years later, so much about growing up in El Nido still warmed her insides. Sharing a saddle with her grandfather when she was five, riding with his thick arms wrapped tightly around her. Owning her own mare at twelve. Going to May Day parties, sitting in the little brick schoolhouse. Listening to the stentorian if slightly off-key village blacksmith lead Sunday choir. Glimpsing a pair of booted feet sticking out from under the swinging door at Barney's Saloon, proof positive of an actual barroom shoot-out. Watching the first coming of the Southern Pacific train, rolling along the new sixteen-mile El Nido spur, heralded by trumpets and grand parties.

Diana often used to ride her mare Candy out to meet the train. One day when she didn't get to the stables fast enough, Candy took off on her own at the sound of the railroad's whistle. Diana found her down by the station, without rider or saddle, dutifully greeting passengers. Such a sight never fazed those who rode the El Nido spur. They were accustomed to all manner of irregularity. Sometimes the railroad engineers halted the train in the middle of fields to go duck hunting. Sometimes they made unscheduled stops to pick up passengers near their farms. Sometimes they let everyone pile out to pick apricots.

El Nido meant "the nest" in Spanish, and that's how Diana,

growing up, had felt about her valley. She couldn't remember pre-cisely when she lost that feeling of protection. It had vanished in increments—beginning no doubt with Thanksgiving Day, the year she was eight.

It was, as she recalled, the coldest day of a frigid winter. Icy rain had fallen in the valley the night before; at day's break, snow lay heavily on the mountaintops. As usual Diana's parents were some-where else, traveling in Europe, and her grandfather had business in San Francisco. So she spent the holiday with the Halder family. The Halders lived not far from the Sanborn ranch, their home set in an abundant orange orchard at the foot of the La Luna Mountain Range. Diana loved that home, where a half-dozen children were always scrambling about. Jenny Halder, just a month younger than Diana, was her best friend. For hours on end, they played together in worlds entirely of their own creation.

The Halders' ten-year-old boy, Kenny, was the one who first started talking about the snow that Thanksgiving morning. He wanted to roll in the bright white drifts covering the ridge above the Halder residence. After much begging, his older brother Charles agreed to take him up the slope. No more than a mile trek; they'd be back well before dinner. Jenny decided to join them, but Diana, helping Mrs. Halder roll out a blueberry pie, chose to stay in the warm kitchen. Jenny giggled and waved at her as she left the house. Three bustling hours passed, with the Thanksgiving feast almost ready to serve, before the Halders grasped that the children hadn't returned. Calls were made, alarms rung, a search team formed. Not until early next morning did they find the tracks in the snow where the trio had stopped and played. Not until midmorning did they find the three children's bodies at the bottom of Shady Canyon. They sat huddled together, frozen to death, the Halder home barely visible in the distance.

Kenny had slipped and broken an ankle, that's what the coroner eventually decided. He couldn't walk. Charles had carried him a ways, then stopped to rest. He'd taken off his own coat and wrapped it about his little brother. Jenny had curled up on Charles's lap. Then they'd grown drowsy as the chill air slowed their blood. Gradually, gently, they'd fallen asleep.

Diana roused herself and glanced over at the clock atop her

nightstand. With relief she saw it was, at last, five. A reasonable time to rise; her usual time to rise.

Diana climbed out of bed and moved to the window that looked out on the valley. She yanked open the thick, heavy drapes. Sunrise, her old friend. The brightening sky so cool and light and full of promise. El Nido followed an east-west configuration, uncommon in this reach of the California coast, where most ranges trended north-south. That, as Diana never tired of explaining to visitors, was why they enjoyed such exceptional sunshine for a deep valley. Gentle now in the early morning, lingering later in the pink-hued evening skies— Diana treasured the valley's light more than anything in her life.

She wrapped a soft terry-cloth robe about her and settled at a small oak desk in the corner of her bedroom. From a drawer she pulled out a thick leather-bound journal. Only here at dawn did she find it possible to put her thoughts on paper. She wrote almost every morning. At times she focused on recent events, at times distant ones, but always she sought understanding for how she now felt. Today she tried to record her memories of when El Nido began to change. She wrote slowly, laboring over her words, pausing often. After a while, she put down her pen and reached for a hairbrush. So much remained confusing. In her own mind, it was after Jenny died that the mood in El Nido shifted. Yet she understood this was her own particularly narrow way of viewing matters. For the grown-ups, other incidents certainly cast longer shadows.

Some happened well before her time, at the turn of the century or before. From her grandfather's stories, Diana knew there once came a big bearded man, digging holes. Then a rush of others, full of all sorts of plans for developing the valley. None of them lasted, of course. Eventually, Edward Sanborn and his esteemed Committee of Ten managed to quiet everything down; those they called "the demons of discord" all departed. Yet the demons left a lasting impact. Even as a ten-year-old, Diana was aware that certain folks turned their heads or looked down as they passed each other along the Main Street arcade. Conversations would begin with homey ebullience, then at mention of one thing or another, trail off. People who were once content, it seemed to Diana, had soured just a little.

They'd saved El Nido. That's what her grandfather always reminded her. El Nido hadn't been ruined.

Nor would it be ruined now, she told herself. Diana picked up her pen again. Before she could resume writing, a knock at her bedroom door interrupted the mistress of Sanborn Ranch. "Come on in, Alex, I'm decent," Diana called out.

Her foreman walked in balancing a tray in one hand. On it was Diana's customary breakfast—a pot of herbal tea, a glass of juice freshly squeezed from El Nido Valley oranges, and dry wheat toast. Alex put the tray at Diana's side. "Morning," he said. "I'm off to mend fence today up near the Signal Trail ravine, but thought you'd want to hear the news first."

Diana poured the tea, squeezed in a touch of honey, stirred. "By all means."

Alex placed a cloth napkin by her side. "It looks like Greg Monarch is going to stay," he said.

Diana kept stirring her tea. "Stay? Whatever do you mean?"

"Stay on the case, I mean. Represent Sarah Trant."

The cup in Diana's hand wobbled; tea spilled on the table. She grabbed the napkin and began rubbing the spot. Then her hand stilled, and she sat silently, staring out her window at a small herd of cattle. Greg Monarch's arrival in El Nido had alarmed her from that very first morning. Yet she had not wanted him to leave. Such conflict was no stranger to Diana, and also no comfort. Echoes from all quarters and all eras regularly competed for her attention. As usual, her grandfather spoke loudest. Diana pointed to the phone. "We certainly need to defuse Mr. Monarch, don't we now? Dial up Sheriff Rimmer, will you, Alex, please?"

Alex didn't move.

"Do it, Alex," Diana ordered. "Call the sheriff."

Still, the foreman stood where he was. He looked hard at her. "Why?" he asked.

Diana searched for an answer. For a moment, she considered wrapping her response in anger. *Such insolence, Alex.* But she and her foreman had been through too much together for posturing. "We've been over all this before," she finally said. "I'm counting on you, Alex."

He picked up the receiver. Not until the phone was ringing in his ear did Diana change her mind. She reached over then and pressed down the receiver buttons. The loudest voice, Diana had decided, couldn't drown out all the others. "Bless your heart, Alex," she said. "Let's not make that call just now."

Alex showed no expression as he put down the handset. "What about Greg Monarch?" he asked.

"Yes," Diana replied. "What about Greg Monarch?"

THIS TIME THEY BROUGHT Sarah to the attorney's conference room in handcuffs. The prison guard shrugged when Greg questioned their necessity. "She's a dangerous lady," he explained. "Dangerous to all of us."

Sarah didn't respond. She'd been dancing in her cell when they came to get her. Dancing and singing. *Summertime, and the living is easy . . .* She knew the guards had been watching, but didn't care. It made her feel powerful in a way. She swayed and tossed her hair, let her shift climb up her thigh. Through the two small windows, she could see the guards tugging at their trousers and shifting on their feet. Powerful, yes. That's how she felt. Even free.

"Sarah, I've decided to represent you," Greg said. "I've decided I'll help you with this habeas petition."

Sarah stared blankly at him. "Ah," she offered. "Well, now."

Greg leaned forward. "You hear me, Sarah?"

Sarah allowed a winsome smile to spread slowly across her face. She reached for Greg's hand. It had been so easy to draw him in those many years ago. He'd been so ready to let go. To choose danger and abandon over cautious endurance. To be foolish rather than dead. He'd made it to shore since then, she could see that easily enough. Now he hung back, at least from her. She felt so tempted to roil him once more, to knock him off balance. To let him feel again her disarray . . . hers, and his too. *Here's to the crazy ones, Greg. The misfits and troublemakers. What's the proper template, anyway? What's normal? Who's to say?*

And yet . . . she couldn't do that to Greg. She felt too protective of him. Disorder wasn't in his best interests these days. She admired his focused drive, his refusal to compromise or unravel. She respected his carefulness about human relations and other people's lives. She'd grown so tired of weak men whining in coffee shops to her. She loved

Greg for being different from all the others. Besides—she needed a first-rate lawyer just now, not a partner in chaos.

"Yes, of course I hear you," Sarah replied. "You're going to rescue me. Isn't that what you said? How nice, after all these years."

Greg stared at their entwined hands. "Can't promise a rescue, Sarah. My obligations will keep me in La Graciosa much of the time, and habeas pleas are remote long shots anyway. Just going to be your lawyer. We'll try our best."

Sarah began caressing his hand. Then she lifted his fingers to her lips. "Yes, our best," she murmured. "Our very best."

Through the window, the guard was staring intently at them. Greg pulled his hand from Sarah's grasp. "Listen carefully," he said. "I tried to visit your trial attorney, Reggie Dodge, but couldn't get to him. Bedridden and feverish, his wife says. Maybe pneumonia. So I really need you. Talk to me about Diana Sanborn. Why would she put Brewster Tomaz's murder on you? Why would she say she heard Tomaz making a dying declaration?"

Sarah ran a hand through her thick dark hair. "Why indeed?"

"Do you know Diana? What's your connection?"

Sarah started to answer, then stopped. An image of Diana on horseback filled her mind. That's how they'd met. Sarah on her knees, Diana atop a spirited roan. A cowgirl, that's what Sarah had fancied herself when she signed on at the Sanborn Ranch. Alex Ramirez had assured her she could handle the job. He'd assured her she would get the hang of waking before dawn to milk the cows, then laying the kitchen fire and starting breakfast for all the hands. She'd been at it for three weeks when Diana rode up one day.

"You're not cut out for this type of work," Diana barked. "Come on in the house."

They talked that first morning about El Nido. The boom and bust of a century before, Diana's grandfather, dry oil wells, Modo-Corp's plans, Charles Whit and Brewster Tomaz. Diana liked her spirit right off, her spirit and what Diana called her "passion to preserve." Diana wanted Sarah to be her special aide in the continuing struggle to protect El Nido. Diana's eyes blazed when she talked of this struggle. Some people felt overwhelmed in her presence, overwhelmed by her grand enthusiasms. Not Sarah, though. Diana's example reminded her how to stride down streets by herself, how to take everything in, how to imagine all sorts of stories and notions. Diana returned to her a sense of bravado. Diana saw her and heard her; Diana understood her. Maybe too well, it was true. Sometimes Sarah felt at Diana's mercy. Those moments always passed, though. Diana helped quiet the noise in her mind. Diana helped still the voices.

Keep up the fight . . . resist the temptation to turn inward. That was Diana's clarion call. Sometimes the "fight" seemed to imply something abstract and universal. Other times it sounded as if Diana were talking specifically about El Nido. She'd grown so tired of people being mistreated, Diana told Sarah over and over. Especially because of money. *Where there's a possibility of making millions, you can justify anything. But some things are right, some things are wrong. Always will be. When you victimize people for your own gain, that's wrong. Always will be.*

Sarah felt like standing and applauding sometimes when Diana talked. Sarah felt like doing anything for her.

"So you want to know my connection to Diana Sanborn?" Sarah shot Greg a look full of challenge. "That's hard to describe. I worked on her ranch for a while. We talked sometimes. She urged me not to seek insulation from the world. What do you think of such advice, Gregory?"

He shifted in his chair. It had been a recurrent theme in their time together: Sarah's insatiable appetite for exposure. *Let's go for it, Greg. We can have it all.* Truth was, he'd felt the same; her passions roused his own. Too much so, on occasion. Her turmoil matched something within himself, forming a combustible mix. Together they were volatile, turbulent. They could argue over anything—which friends to visit, how to spend the weekend—but the subtext was always the drive to define themselves. One night in the car she whacked him across the head so hard he almost drove off the road; another night, at a beach party, he straight-armed her into a trash can before an audience of dozens. They reconciled with equal fervor: Using her key to his cottage, she'd crawl into his bed just before dawn, her voice thick, her eyes half closed with desire. They were addicted to each other, caught in an endless, compulsive cycle of embrace and retreat, ardor and combat. He'd had to seal himself off from her finally. Either that, or lose his mind.

"Sounds like a smart idea to me," he said. "Sounds like Diana Sanborn understands you."

"Understands me." Sarah chewed on those words. "Understands me," she said again.

Greg tried to seize the opening. "Given your connection with her, why would she say she heard Brewster Tomaz's dying declaration?"

"Perhaps because it's true. Perhaps because she did hear him."

"I don't think that's possible."

"What you think doesn't matter, Greg. My own expert witness said differently. My own witness, right at my trial."

"Why is that, Sarah? Why did Dr. Montrose flip on you?"

"Who knows."

"I need your help here, Sarah, if you want mine. We have six months, just half a year."

Sarah studied the floor. "I guess the prosecutor got to Dr. Montrose. That's what's Reggie told me."

"How so? What happened?"

"I . . . I don't know. That's just what Reggie said."

"What else do you remember, Sarah?"

She pulled back from him. "Why . . . what for?"

"We have a chance here, Sarah."

"No. There's no chance."

"Yes, Sarah."

Tears rolled down Sarah's cheeks. Something wild showed in her eyes. "You're not going away this time?"

Greg hesitated, trying to craft an honest answer. "No," he said finally. "I'm not going away."

ALEX RAMIREZ ASKED PABLO to move by gently squeezing with his thighs. The whiskey-brown quarter horse had a lot of personality, but was in a cooperative mood today. He stepped toward the dozen heifers cringing before them. Alex lazily flicked the end of a coiled rope. He felt more at home in this moment than in any other his days offered.

Alex's father, and his father before him, had been among the proud California *vaqueros* who showed the others how to manage cattle in the New World. It was not an easy task. Lacking the proper grasses or hemp for rope, they made their own rawhide *reatas*; to rope cattle with these *reatas* required months of practice. Then you needed the right horse. *Quebrar el Caballo*—to break the horse—did not mean to break the spirit of the horse but to train it for the uses for which the rider might need it. The horse a rider chose for the day would depend on whether he planned to be roping, rodeoing, or cutting beef.

Patience, practice, observation—all were needed to earn the name *vaquero*. So was a particular way of looking at the world. Alex's grandfather, who was said to have roped three grizzlies in one day with nothing but his *reata*, often told him: A *vaquero* had a way of believing that if something went haywire he was lucky it wasn't worse, and if things went right, he was also lucky.

As he herded the cows into the Sanborn Ranch corral, Alex reminded himself of his grandfather's saying. Yes, that was the way to look at Brewster Tomaz's murder and Sarah Trant's prosecution. Things could have been worse. Brewster Tomaz could have lived, for instance. The notion roiled Alex. Never had a man so offended him. In middle age, Tomaz at least had managed to season his cranky bombast with lively stories about the valley, thereby winning considerable favor in El Nido. But in his later years, an intractable bile seeped into him that—to Alex's mind, at least—no narrative could redeem. Tomaz acquired pounds and wrinkles and flaps of skin, and in his expression, recurring traces of disdain. He showed up everywhere, at town meetings and park concerts and pancake breakfasts, as if he were an occupying army. He spoke little at these gatherings, mainly watching with blank pale-blue eyes. Many still respected him from a careful distance, yet even Diana Sanborn shrank from him in public. Particularly Diana.

"Hey there."

Alex started at the sight of Greg Monarch standing by the corral fence, then quickly regained his composure. He popped a toothpick between his teeth and rode toward Greg. "Hey there," he said back.

"I was looking for the mistress of the house. But no one answered at the front door."

Alex nodded, chewed on his toothpick, pushed back his straw hat. "Well, then," he said, "I guess she's not home."

Greg reached over and patted Alex's horse on his sweaty neck.

Minutes before, pounding on the thick oak double doors of the main ranch house, he'd sensed someone inside watching him. He'd stepped back after a while and looked up. A pair of second-story window shutters stood open; what appeared to be a shadow played on the edge of a pale blue curtain that fluttered slowly in the wind.

"Either that," Greg said, "or maybe she's just not available?"

Alex offered a shrug that suggested he was not inclined to bicker over words. "Or not available," he agreed.

"I was hoping to get some information."

Alex glanced over at the main house. For a moment, he tugged at his saddle's straps. Then he pulled the toothpick from his mouth and tossed it to the ground. "So you want to talk to me instead?"

THEY SAT ON GREAT blocks of hay in the barn. Outside, a hot breeze rustled through the bright sun-drenched valley; in here, all was cool and dim. "You looked quite at home," Greg began, pointing to the corral. "That is an art."

Alex accepted the praise with ease. "First you need to get your ideas across to your horse. I learned from my ancestors."

Greg searched his memory. "*Jineta*—isn't that what it's called?"

Alex smiled faintly at this reference to a centuries-old heritage of horse training. "Yes, that's right. My great-uncle Felipe often used that word." Then he added, "I hear you are staying. I hear you are Sarah Trant's lawyer."

"Looks that way."

"So now you're drawn to this case?"

"You could say that." Greg studied Alex. The foreman, so laconic and self-assured, held himself as if he owned the valley. "I'm trying to understand what happened here," Greg continued. "Five years ago. When Brewster Tomaz was killed, when Sarah was arrested."

"It's not complicated. People here don't like development much, but took a liking to the idea of a health spa at Camp Mahrah instead of something like an industrial plant. Sarah Trant didn't share that liking. Started acting really *loca*. Shouting, pushing, demonstrating. Brewster was her biggest target. Harassed him like crazy. When he turns up floating in the river with a slashed throat, it was obvious who did it. Jury stayed out, what, forty minutes?"

"I think it was forty-five."

"There you go."

Greg plucked at the bale of hay he sat on. "Tell me about Charles Whit and ModoCorp."

"Whit's a mighty sharp fellow. Mighty impressive . . . Can't say the same about his buddies, though."

"How so?"

"When Whit first came to town, he had a skinny young guy and a fat old guy with him. Public relations team, he called them. Hell. Maybe they do good with pencil and paper, but when they got out here in the country, they didn't know much. They tried to drive a Suburban across a creek that I row across. I know I can't cross water in a motor vehicle."

Alex paused, shook his head, continued. "This was middle of summer, pretty hot. The fat one is about 220 pounds, I'd say. Pretty round. Clearly he's sat at a desk a long time. No doubt has a four-year college degree. He walked a mile to ask me for help. I went to pull him out. That skinny fellow was waiting for us. I gave him a chain. He walks out in the water, hooks it to that nice chrome bumper. I tell him, someone will be mad when I yank that bumper off. Better hook it to the frame instead."

Alex pushed his straw hat to the back of his head, nodding at Greg. "That little skinny fella. He probably has a four-year degree too."

Greg stifled a smile. "Tell me about Diana and Sarah."

"What's to tell?"

"A good deal, I think."

Alex fell silent. The heel of his boots began to dig into the bale of hay. "That's not something I know about," he said finally.

"Why?"

Alex worked some more at the bale. "They spent time together alone."

"They were friends?"

"What can I say? One was the employer, the other a summer hire."

"Tell me about Diana's testimony. She heard Brewster Tomaz say that Sarah did it?"

Alex looked away. "Yes she did."

Greg spoke slowly now. "I think Sarah was framed. . . . I think you know that."

Alex removed his straw hat and started slapping it on his thigh. "Don't know any such thing."

"Then why did you tell me to get a look at the autopsy reports?"

"I just asked if you'd seen it. I was just talkin'. Diana Sanborn heard Brewster, that much is certain."

"How'd that happen?"

"Several of them, half a dozen I think, ran down from the concert when they heard the cries at the creek. The others stood back a few yards, but Diana, because she knew him, rushed to Brewster. Took him in her arms, cradled his head. That's when he talked. Low raspy whisper, hard to make out, but she heard him."

Alex stared hard at Greg and repeated: "She heard him."

Greg rose to leave. "Well, then," he said, "that's that."

IT REQUIRED ONLY A drive through the valley to realize there was more than one El Nido. Beyond the hamlet, the scattering of modern ranch-style houses that now sat amid the lush citrus groves offered an oddly suburban retreat for professionals wishing to flee the coastal fog. Closer in, on dusty side streets at the edges of the central arcade, small faded wood-frame homes provided housing for a mix of laborers, artists, lost souls, and wizened seniors. To the east, vast spreads reached toward Upper El Nido, some working ranches filled with livestock, others the estates of gentlemen farmers who, as a hobby, irrigated row after row of fruit trees. Such different stations and ways of life produced a certain tension, but not as much as an outsider might expect. Shared values, not obvious divisions, were what most colored the regular afternoon gatherings in Sanborn Park.

There, off to one side of the bandstand, Mayor Sam Rabe and his wife, Tammy, held court daily. El Nido had no smoke-filled backrooms. The mayor dispensed licenses and permits right on the sloping lawn, while citizens gave him a piece of their mind. Unneeded stop signs, speeding cars, blocked drainage ditches—whatever annoyed you received immediate attention, and often resolution.

An hour after his visit with Alex Ramirez, Greg sat on a bench by the Sanborn Park bandstand, listening to that day's litany of complaints. The town's beautification statute irritated one red-faced homeowner, who wondered whether he needed the city council's permission to paint his house. A vandal's theft of flowers and ornaments from the 150-year-old El Nido cemetery dismayed an elderly couple. The biggest ruckus came from a half-dozen citizens enraged over a rancher's newly built fence across a popular hiking trail. To Greg the six protesters, varying in age and manner, appeared to be a cross section of the El Nido community. Nothing, he reasoned, could unite these folks like a blocked hiking trail.

"May I join you?"

Greg looked up to see Jasmine Gest standing before him. She sat down before he could answer. "Word is, you're staying," she said, "You're going to handle Sarah's appeal."

"That's right."

"Well, then, maybe I can help."

Greg studied Jas. She acted so sure of herself, so comfortable in her world. He sensed something else, though. "Why do you want to help?"

"For one thing, I know Sarah."

"You weren't close. That's what you told me."

"I know her, though."

"You two don't seem to have much in common."

"You have X-ray eyes? You can see straight inside us?"

"I think so."

Jas appeared intrigued by the notion. She faced him straight on now. "Yes, I think so too. . . . Maybe I should wear lead underwear or something."

"Or maybe I should look away."

"No. . . . Don't do that."

Greg tried to regain his train of thought. "Okay, then . . . We were talking about Sarah. Could you explain a bit about Sarah here in the valley?"

Jas took her time, watching Tammy Rabe smother an El Nido citizen with a bear hug. Then she said, "Sarah didn't understand El Nido. She caught the love of nature here but didn't see that underneath it, just about everyone is a landowner. Everyone has an investment.

Shopping centers and car dealerships may be a sin to these people, but El Nido needs something to goose its economy. Just ask the poor merchants under the Arcade."

"A health spa brings in tourists with thick wallets."

"Precisely. Sarah missed that. Whit and ModoCorp were the devil to her. She didn't realize they were potential saviors to lots of people here."

"No one told her?"

"They tried. I tried. Jesus. You should have seen her this one night at the Gaucho Tavern. Really decked out, by the way. A drop-dead-sexy minidress. Dancing with the cowboys, singing, having a grand old time. She and the cowboys. Then Sarah sees Brewster Tomaz over in a corner booth with Charles Whit. Rushes over, starts in on them. Tomaz laughs and says something crude. So she picks up a glass of whiskey and tosses it in his face. If I hadn't hustled her out of there then, I don't know what would have happened."

Tammy Rabe was waving a finger in someone's face now. Sam Rabe looked as if he were taking a nap. "Tell me, Jas," Greg asked. "Were there other times you saw Sarah attack Tomaz like that?"

Jas glared. "What difference does that make? She has rights, Greg. No matter what, she still deserves a fair shake in court. She still deserves your help."

THE SUN HUNG LOW in the El Nido sky by the time Greg left Sanborn Park. He meant to return to La Graciosa this evening, and his cottage on Graciosa Creek. Both his law practice and his friends beckoned. There'd been three messages on his voice mail from Tim Ruthman, who was covering for him on a drug bust, and two from his buddy Jimmy O'Brien, urging his company on a fishing trip. *Come on, Monarch, the bass are practically jumping into the boat. . . .* Then there'd been the reminder from Cindy Seaman over at the county probation department. *We're supposed to have dinner together one night this week. . . . You didn't forget, now, did you, Gregory?* He hadn't. First, though, he had one more stop in El Nido. He drove east through the village, past the arcade and post office, plunging quickly into the citrus groves. Where the road curved right to Sanborn

Ranch, he instead turned left, onto a gravel path that climbed into the foothills on the north side of the valley.

If only Sarah were really innocent, Greg thought. He so much wanted her to be innocent. So much needed her to be innocent. Sarah was unstable, Sarah acted crazy, but that alone didn't make her a killer. El Nido regarded her as a killer, that's what made her one. . . . And yet, he had to admit . . . Sarah was capable of irrational acts. He'd seen enough in their time together. There'd been moments when she utterly alarmed him. There'd been moments when he couldn't begin to explain what she was doing.

Greg had reached the higher foothills now, in the rugged far end of the valley. Upper El Nido looked to him like the eroded course of an ancient stream. A ridge dotted with purple lupine and a scattered stand of live oaks separated it from the main valley. Facing west down the length of the basin, Greg gazed at foothills thick with cotton-wood and white alder and sycamore, ceanothus and sage and man-zanita. Closer, in the twilight, he saw a fast-moving creek tumbling from on high and bending sharply eastward, its banks decorated with strange black bands. Beyond, an emerald meadow shone through the open forest. Here was the El Nido of old, the El Nido that Greg had hiked with his father, the El Nido where Greg came to know his father.

Old Alder Road. Greg spotted the sign he'd been searching for. He turned down what seemed more a path than a road. After a quar-ter mile, he parked and began to hike into a narrow wooded canyon. Hearing the earth crunch under his feet, he looked down and saw he was again walking on black asphaltum. Oil oozing from cracks in the canyon walls had hardened into something that suggested a volcanic lava flow. Greg spotted the bones of several coyotes and deer. They'd been caught, he imagined, in the thick tarry flow.

The same crunching sound again claimed his attention. This time, though, it came not from under his feet but from somewhere behind him, off in the woods. Greg stood still and tried not to breathe. He could hear now only the chatter of birds in the forest. It wasn't pleasant to think you were being followed. Yet he felt certain there was someone behind him, back along the trail. The birds were convincing him. Another lesson from his father: Birds were brazen liars in certain matters, but they never lied to each other concerning the activities of man.

Greg heard the crunching again. One step, two, three. He turned around, peered through the trees, saw nothing. He moved off the path, into the edge of the forest. The silence bothered him almost as much as the noise. An annoyed landowner would come charging at a suspected trespasser. Who would hang back like this, trailing but hidden?

Greg walked back onto the path. He took a step, then another. A breeze drifted through the tree branches. Then came the crack of a twig. Greg swung around toward the sound. In a small clearing, some hundred feet away, two startled deer, mother and fawn, stood staring at him. Suddenly they bolted, bounding over a wild hedge of willows. Greg waited, but heard nothing more. There was nothing else to do. He turned and continued up the path.

At its end, Greg came to a small wood-frame cabin. *One Alder Road,* that was the address he'd found in the El Nido directory. Home of Buster Lloyd, El Nido's solitary paramedic. They called him an emergency medical technician, actually, an EMT. *EMT Buster Lloyd*— those were the words the coroner had scrawled near the bottom of the autopsy report on Brewster Tomaz. *EMT Buster Lloyd, first medical response on scene.* Nothing more. Greg had spotted the note just before leaving the DA's office. He'd never seen that name mentioned before or since.

Lloyd opened the door before Greg could knock. He was rail thin, over six feet tall, with a ponytail and a bushy beard. He squinted at the presence of a stranger.

"Buster Lloyd?" Greg asked.

"That's me. Who are you?"

"My name is Greg Monarch. I'm a lawyer, representing Sarah Trant."

"Who's that?"

"The woman convicted of killing Brewster Tomaz."

"Oh yeah, yeah. Tomaz. Boy, was his throat cut."

"That's just what I wanted to ask you about. What can you tell me about his injury? Do you remember what you saw?"

"Do I remember. Jesus, yes. That was the nastiest wound you

would ever want to see. Cut straight to the bone of the spinal cord. Everything sliced up. Just about everything you got in your neck."

"Carotid artery?"

"Sure. Carotid, epiglottis, everything."

Greg tried to sound casual. "Did you know that the autopsy report said the carotid wasn't involved?"

Lloyd took two steps back into his cabin. You didn't get much work as an EMT, Greg imagined, if you bucked the county coroner. "What?" Lloyd said. "No, hell, I didn't . . . I mean . . . Maybe I was wrong. . . ."

Greg tried another tack. "Was Brewster Tomaz able to talk when you got to him?"

Lloyd snorted. "Talk? You kidding? I cut your left carotid, that side of your brain starts dying instantly. We're talking maybe one second. And the left side of your brain controls speech. You can't talk without your left hemisphere. . . . Talking? Hell. I cut your left carotid, you're unconscious in seconds, dead in five minutes."

Greg suspected the answer to his next question before he asked it. "Buster, why didn't you tell the police any of this when they interviewed you after Tomaz's murder?"

Lloyd regarded him now as if he were a madman. "Tell the police?"

"There's a police report summarizing your interview, but there's nothing in it about talking or carotid arteries."

Lloyd clawed at his beard. "A police report on my interview? How could that be?"

"What do you mean, Buster?"

"The police never interviewed me. Nobody interviewed me. You're the first person to ask me about Brewster Tomaz's death."

—————— S I X ——————

Sheriff Roy Rimmer wiped his brow and tried to will himself to remain calm. If only Jim Mashburn could see things his way. Jim couldn't, though. Either that, or Jim didn't want to.

They were sitting in the DA's office. Out the window, Rimmer could hear children playing in the Sanborn Park fountain. The shrill noise annoyed him. How could Mashburn work in such a setting? It didn't seem possible. Nor did it seem possible for Mashburn to disregard him so often. Couldn't Mashburn see how fortunate he was to have a county sheriff with such a grasp of the law? Particularly the law as it functioned in El Nido County?

"Excuse me, Jim, but are you listening to me?"

Mashburn turned from the window. The sheriff's question appeared to summon the DA back to the matter at hand. There it sat on Mashburn's desk: Sarah Trant's amended habeas petition. This one, drafted by Greg Monarch, offered professionally printed blocks of type instead of graceful schoolgirl curls. Now it looked like a legal brief rather than an invitation to a birthday party. More important, it raised the stakes. No longer was Trant simply claiming the usual reasons—procedural errors, ineffectiveness of counsel—for why she merited a new trial. This revised petition, in no uncertain terms, accused the DA's office of enough "flagrant prosecutorial misconduct" to create a situation of "manifest injustice." What's more, it flatly declared Sarah Trant innocent.

Mashburn lifted the petition and began to read Monarch's words out loud: "The criminal justice system has utterly failed Sarah Trant.

Police and the prosecution, having decided she was guilty, set out to create a world of evidence in support of their theory. They altered reports, hid boot prints, tampered with witnesses. . . ."

Rimmer reached over and pulled the petition from Mashburn's hands. "You going to memorize that, Jim?" he asked. "Or do something about it?"

"Do something about it?" Mashburn yanked the petition back from Rimmer, rolled it into a cylinder, and began slapping it against his desk. "What do you suggest, Roy?"

Rimmer, staring at his empty hand, fought an impulse to lunge again for the document. His palm stung from what felt like a paper cut. Goddamn Mashburn. Who the hell did he think he was? Mashburn didn't even come from this valley. Mashburn was an outsider who'd moved from the coast and got himself elected DA because of a relative's political sway. What did Mashburn know about El Nido?

People with family money, people with privilege. Ever since he was a boy, Rimmer had watched them prance blissfully across the valley. So unlike Rimmer's own life. His family went back four generations in El Nido, but they'd lost their land decades ago. From his grandparents' time on, they'd worked for other people. Rimmer, in his youth, had tried to break that pattern. He'd scraped together every penny he had and bought a patch of land back up in the foothills. He meant to grow citrus, and raise cattle, and build a fine home. It had never worked out, though. He couldn't get financing, he couldn't get permits and variances, he couldn't get anything. The previous owners had never told him about the restrictive covenants that came attached to his land. They'd misled him about the quality of the soil as well, and the availability of water.

He'd ended up in law enforcement. The sheriff's department had an opening. Eventually he ran for sheriff and won. It hadn't been a half-bad move in the end. The pace of the sheriff's department suited him. He was out, moving around the county, meeting people. That was certainly better than sitting behind a desk or a plow all day long. Now people looked up to him, admired him, responded to him. Now people listened to him.

Rimmer came to Mashburn's side. "What do I suggest, Jim? I have all sorts of suggestions."

"Such as what, Roy? Going back and retrying Sarah Trant the right way?"

"Damnit, Jim, she was guilty. And she got convicted. That is the right way."

Mashburn turned on him so suddenly, Rimmer instinctively took a step back and raised a protective hand. "Did Reggie Dodge know all he should at the trial?" the DA demanded. "Did he get everything the defense was entitled to?"

Rimmer held his ground now. "Monarch is claiming actual innocence. *Actual innocence.* That is a crock."

"So why did my predecessor spin this one, Roy? He didn't need to. As you say, Sarah Trant is flat-out guilty. Karl Jackson had a solid case. Just what exactly in the goddamn hell happened here?"

Rimmer didn't answer at first. He squeezed his hands into fists and began pacing the room. "Karl Jackson needed more than a case," he offered.

"What are you talking about?"

"Doesn't matter at this point. We have to stop this Monarch fellow. Stop Monarch, and rein in that half-berserk federal judge."

"How do you propose to stop a federal judge, Roy?"

"Watch me," the sheriff said. He reached for the phone and punched in a number. "Rimmer here," he murmured. "Get me Whit. Pronto."

ALEX RAMIREZ SANK SLOWLY to his knees beside the broad brown carcass. She looked strangely hale, he thought, as if she were simply sleeping on the bank of El Nido Creek. Yet this heifer was quite dead. Just like the two others.

Alex fought a mounting sense of unease. He rose and surveyed this southwestern reach of Sanborn Ranch, as if searching in the landscape for an answer. When he'd found that first cow down by a bend of the creek, he hadn't known what to think. Hoof and mouth, an insecticide, a predator, nothing made sense. Old Dr. Pitts, their local veterinarian, didn't have a clue. Alex didn't like to lose even one head from his herds, so he'd called the state health boys right away. They'd shown up within hours, poking and prodding and taking all manner of samples. They'd been a garrulous friendly bunch at that first visit, full of promises and reassurances. Then they'd disappeared, and clammed up. Alex had never managed to get a written report from them, or even a clear word on the phone. No one would tell him what killed his cow.

Now there were three dead.

Alex raised a hand to his hat. The wind was up today, a real blow flowing down off the mountains. He turned toward Sanborn Lodge. Bury it, Diana had ordered after they'd found the first one. Bury it and fence off that stretch of the creek. He'd never known Diana to act in such a manner. With much protest, he'd followed her command, but had not stopped puzzling. No strangers with bags of poison could have visited Sanborn Ranch without his knowledge. Whatever killed his cows had to be in the soil or the water right here on the ranch. Just what, though?

In his frustration, Alex had twice hiked down to the river to study the area where the cows died. One time he plowed up the earth, only to find layers and layers of the rich fertile soil for which all of El Nido was renowned. Another time he took creek water to the county's one private lab, only to have the folks there tell him he had a crystal clear stream on his property. Yet there had to be something. There had to be.

On impulse, Alex lunged now at the dark brown earth. He began clawing at the stream bank, tunneling into the thick mud. Nothing but rich El Nido Valley soil, nothing poisonous, nothing evil . . . He dug deeper, rending the creek bank, throwing clumps of dirt into the air. It was senseless, he knew, but he didn't care. If only he could find an answer. If only—

A strange smell stopped him suddenly. Something offensive, like the odor of rotten eggs. He started to rise, but faltered. In an instant he was feeling dizzy and nauseated. His eyes hurt. So did his nose and throat and head. He crawled to the creek and retched until he had only dry heaves to offer. For a while he lay there, not moving. When he finally felt strong enough, he rose and lurched toward his pickup truck. By the time he made it to Sanborn Lodge, he was feeling fully recovered.

"Something made me sick out there," he informed Diana Sanborn.

He was pacing before her as she sat stiffly in a chair by her great-room fireplace.

"Whatever are you talking about?" Diana asked. There was steel in her voice. "You look just fine to me, Alex."

He stared hard at her. "We've got to deal with this," he insisted. "We have to understand why our cows died."

She stared back. "Perhaps you didn't hear me, Alex. I said you looked just fine."

He gave up then, suddenly realizing his misjudgment. He was being foolish, of course, to challenge her. He knew why she didn't want to face this matter. There was no swaying her. He would have to let her be.

DIANA SANBORN WALKED ALONG El Nido's Main Street arcade as if leading a procession. Past the ice-cream shop that offered nary a scoop of nonfat yogurt, past the bookstore that featured ponytailed folksingers in the back room, past the guitar shop whose proprietor plucked "This Land Is Your Land" from his front door. . . . Diana cherished all she saw. She waved furiously, she stomped her cowboy boots, she cried out greetings.

Only Tammy Rabe, the bounteous mayor's wife, was brave enough to block Diana's way. The two women found themselves facing each other in front of the El Nido Realty window. Photos there, of Spanish cottages and wood-frame cabins and six-thousand-square-foot ranch homes, offered newcomers to the valley the promise of an enchanted retreat. Neither Diana nor Tammy gave them a glance.

"What do you know about this Monarch lawyer?" Tammy asked over the jangle of her bracelets and earrings. "I hear he's filed some petition, and Sarah Trant is getting a new trial. We thought this was all settled."

Diana hung on to her hearty demeanor. "Now, don't go getting so riled, Tammy. A petition was filed, but that doesn't mean she gets a new trial. Doesn't even mean she gets a hearing. We will see. Nothing to worry about right now. Nothing to do."

Tammy gripped Diana's arm. "If this blows up—"

"Hush now." Diana put her hand on Tammy's mouth. "You're too loud. And too worried."

At the end of the arcade, Diana reached her pickup truck. In an instant she was barreling along Main Street. Then she was turning onto narrow, wooded Old Brook Road. She exhaled, happy to be off-stage finally. Out her window Diana could see El Nido Creek flowing by. Two miles to the east, Brewster Tomaz had breathed his last in these waters. A mile to the west, Sarah Trant counted her days.

The prison was Diana's destination. She stopped in a parking lot that overlooked the low whitewashed adobe complex, but remained in her truck. From the driver's seat, she studied the view before her. There'd been a health spa here once, she knew. Yet another of the many enterprises that failed during her grandfather's time. The wild catters had it even worse than the health nuts back then. Not a single well came in, despite all the auspicious reports about El Nido's fabulous oil springs. Flow those springs did, unceasing sluggish streams pouring out of the mountainsides, day after day, covering acres of land, crossing roads, literally paving them with asphaltum for hundreds of yards. Yet it was a heavy thick crude they yielded, with no apparent commercial value. What's more, their abundance was illusory; the prospectors eventually concluded that the oil seeped from shallow pockets near the surface, not great reserves deep in the earth. In the end, the springs mainly constituted a problem: All kinds of stock would get stuck in the tarry matter, leaving their bones as a warning to others. Farmers detested the stuff, speaking of "tar flat" as they would a trespassing horse thief. Each year they made a great show of burning the flow, making a wick out of a handful of hay. As a young child, Diana recalled gaping at a fierce blaze as high as a church.

That image vaguely troubled her. Why, she wondered angrily, must memories of the past always affect her so? She smacked at her dashboard as if to chase away her demons. *Don't give in to yourself*, she muttered. *Don't give in.* Snapping open her purse, she reached for a tissue and wiped her eyes. She turned to stare at the prison's windows. Through which one might she spot Sarah? Through which one might she learn how poor Sarah was faring?

"You okay, Ms. Sanborn?"

Diana jumped at the question, then turned to find Greg Monarch at her window. "What are you doing, Mr. Monarch? Following me?"

"Actually, my client resides inside."

"Yes, of course. That is true."

Greg bent down so his head was level with Diana's. "You visit the state prison often?"

"I go everywhere in El Nido, Mr. Monarch. I have friends everywhere."

Greg nodded as if that made sense. "The other day, I came to the ranch with a question for you. You weren't in."

"So ask it now, Mr. Monarch. Now that we've just happened to bump into each other like this."

"Okay, I will." Greg rested an arm on the pickup's windowsill. "Ms. Sanborn, are you certain you heard Brewster Tomaz's dying declaration?"

"Whatever do you mean?"

"Those few minutes when you held him in your arms, when you cradled his head. Did he really talk to you?"

Diana twisted in her seat to face him squarely. "Yes, he most certainly did."

"It's just that his throat was cut so badly, I don't think he could have said a word."

"Are you a doctor, Mr. Monarch?"

"No—"

"Well then, perhaps we should place our trust in the pathologists who conducted the autopsy, and thought Brewster capable of speech."

"Perhaps we should," Greg said. He studied this ebullient gray-haired lady rancher. Diana's cowboy hat sat on the seat by her side; her right boot rested lightly on the truck's accelerator pedal. "One other thing," he continued. "As I understand it from looking at the trial record, first time this dying declaration got mentioned in a police report is three weeks after the murder. Ms. Sanborn, why didn't you tell the sheriff's detectives about it right away?"

Diana turned to the prison. Her eyes scanned a row of windows set in the low adobe wall. "I was trying to protect Sarah," she said finally. "I cared about her. I didn't want her in such trouble."

"What changed your mind?"

Diana glanced at her watch, then reached for the key in her ignition. "My conscience, Mr. Monarch. My grandfather brought me up to be truthful. So I had to tell the truth. Now, please excuse me. I must go."

Greg leaned through her open window. "You looked troubled a moment ago. Also a product of your conscience?"

Diana started to turn her ignition but stopped. She settled back in the truck's seat, examining Greg's face. Then she reached into her purse, pulled out an envelope, and handed it to him. "A first for me," she said. "My first anonymous blackmail letter. Received it this morning."

Greg took the envelope from her outstretched hand. From it he pulled a single sheet of paper. *I demand restitution*, the unknown correspondent declared in hand-printed block letters. *I demand restitution for wrongs done my forebears in years gone by. Make amends, or I will kill you.*

"What's this about?" he asked. "What wrongs?"

Diana shrugged. "Who knows? The world is filled with wrongs."

AT DUSK, JASMINE GEST rode her charcoal Appaloosa, Dusty, along the equestrian trail that snaked through Sanborn Park. Just minutes from El Nido's main street, she was trotting through a densely treed forest that screened out all sights and sounds of the village. Normally this ride settled her mind, but not now. Memories of Sarah Trant's trial tugged at her. Such was one effect of Greg Monarch's arrival in the valley.

She'd thought it a distressing yet obvious affair. During the trial no one doubted Sarah's guilt, not even Jas. Especially not Jas, given what she knew about Sarah. She'd never told anyone the most damning things. Such as how Sarah zealously tracked Brewster Tomaz's movements through the valley, and how Sarah once took a steak knife to photos of the crusty old geologist. And how Sarah came unnaturally alive—eyes blazing, face flushed—in those moments when she talked of her campaign against ModoCorp. The fact was, sitting in the courtroom, not even Sarah herself had appeared to lay claim to actual innocence. Defiant, that's how she'd acted. Also peculiar. Each day she dressed up for her trial: special hats, colorful scarves, black stockings, rouge and lipstick. As if she were an actress playing a role. She kept glancing around at the spectators, while just about ignoring her lawyer. The more Jas thought about it, the more it seemed that Sarah had been expecting something—something or someone—throughout the proceeding. She'd appeared downright disappointed in the trial's final hours. As if events had not gone as planned.

Dr. Montrose's testimony definitely hadn't gone as planned. Reggie Dodge looked absolutely stricken when the pathologist started saying that Tomaz could have talked. Not even as lame a lawyer as Reggie Dodge would have called Montrose if he'd seen that coming. So what had happened there? Jas made a mental note to look into the matter. She also made a mental note to share her thoughts with Greg Monarch.

Jas had to admit that she found Monarch captivating. The way he watched her . . . He looked at her as if they were fellow travelers. He looked at her in a manner that compelled her to look back. He—

A commotion through the trees, over by the fountain, interrupted Jas's reflections. She could hear children crying. Jas reined Dusty in, then rode off the trail. Halfway across the park, she saw that a teenager, skateboarding, had collided with two toddlers. Parents were scrambling, but no one seemed seriously hurt. Jas started to turn back, then stopped. On a bench to the side of the fountain, she'd spotted a man hunched over in thought. A tall lean man with sandy hair. He seemed so coiled, even in repose. All skin and nerves and sense organs and brain. Greg Monarch. Just the fellow she wanted to see.

WATCHING PARENTS DEAL WITH salty tears and skinned knees, Greg didn't notice Jasmine until she was twenty yards away. She rode easily. Her jeans had a hole in one knee, her flannel shirt spilled out at the back. She dismounted with a quick springy jump. The green eyes opened wide, full of welcome.

"I was just thinking of you," she said.

"And I of you."

"Oh sure."

"Truth."

"Okay, then. . . . You go first."

"Okay," Greg agreed. "I was thinking about the night of the concert here in the park. Down by the creek, you said 'enough about me.' You said, 'later.' Now it's later."

"Aha. So you want my story. That it?"

"Sort of."

Looking amused, Jas settled on the bench beside him. "I've got no notches on my belt. That's my deep dark secret. No notches."

"Notches?"

"You know . . . marriages, divorces, baby announcements, marriage counseling bills, separation agreements, restraining orders . . . Nothing."

"Somehow, this doesn't surprise me."

"That obvious, huh?"

"Let's say you don't strike me as being part of the mainstream."

"You neither."

"No."

"There are times I'd like to be. . . . It's shameful what I sometimes long for."

"Do tell."

"In certain reckless moments, I find myself wanting to be like Barbara Stanwyck in *The Big Valley*. You know, with four strapping sons and all that. I want to pop cake into a groom's mouth and dodge rice. I want meddling in-laws."

"I won't tell anyone."

"I know it's unrealistic."

"You need to lower your expectations."

Jas laughed. Her hand reached out and came to rest on his forearm. "I lay low on the subject of notches usually. I realize how fragile men are. It's dangerous to confide mixed fantasies about *The Big Valley* and shared child custody. This makes you appear jumpy, and if there's one thing you shouldn't be these days, it's jumpy."

"I suppose you're right." Greg felt her fingers warm his skin. It was true—when she rode up, he'd been thinking of her. But also of Sarah. Meeting Sarah again after all these years had rekindled a welter of feelings he'd long kept at bay. Too many feelings, too many alarms, too many lessons. Now here was Jas, so stirring in her own way. He couldn't go there, not now. He needed to keep his senses about him. Yet he imagined Jas would be of genuine help in a place such as El Nido. Obliged to shuttle between La Graciosa and this valley, he'd not managed to gain full entry. He needed an escort.

"Shall we share our other thoughts?" he asked. "About the murder case?"

Jas patted his arm, then pulled her hand away. "Good idea. We were getting too serious here."

"Diana Sanborn," Greg began. "She's on my mind. A singular woman. Her testimony put Sarah away, yet she offered me her guest room."

Jas shook her head. "Not sure you should make too much of that. Diana Sanborn considers herself the grand hostess of El Nido. Her hospitality is automatic, and universal."

"She's a troubled hostess just now."

"What do you mean?"

"She was looking upset earlier today. I found her sitting in her truck, over by the prison."

"Upset about what?"

Greg, wondering whether to mention the blackmail letter, decided to hold back. "I think she has an enemy right now. Someone who worries her. Someone who has threatened her."

Jas gave him an odd look. "If Brewster Tomaz were still alive, I'd say him."

"Tomaz?"

"He was a real mean one underneath that crusty curmudgeon routine. It would especially come out in the Gaucho Tavern late at night, after he'd had a pitcher of beer. He'd get in just about anyone's face. Especially a woman if she didn't take kindly to him. He'd get downright scary sometimes. There were nights in there I thought he was going to smack someone good."

"But why would you think of him particularly as Diana's enemy?"

"Hard to explain. Something in the way they acted when they found themselves in the same room together. He'd glare at her, and she . . . well, she'd almost recoil. . . . Usually this happened at town meetings, when they were arguing over land-use issues. Diana loves the El Nido Valley. I don't think Tomaz really did, for all his knowledge of this place. So maybe that explains it."

"Maybe," Greg said. "At any rate, Tomaz is dead. Who else might threaten Diana?"

Jas fell silent. "ModoCorp . . . Charles Whit," she offered finally. Then she seemed to have second thoughts. "I mean, I don't really know. But that's a possibility."

Greg slid closer to her. "Tell me what you do know."

The bell started tolling atop the post office tower. After striking the hour, it continued, sounding the notes of a song that Greg couldn't quite recognize. Pedestrians and park visitors stopped to listen as they watched the sun settle below the tree line.

"What do you say we relocate?" Jas said.

Greg trailed in his car as Jas rode Dusty back to the stables. From there they drove west out Old Brook Road. They crossed over the highway leading to the ocean and La Graciosa, turning north into the mountains. The road narrowed and curved. Here the thick stands of oak gave way to open meadows and cultivated farmland. Greg watched a man working his field, guiding a battered red plow, a kerchief tied around his head. Two children ran up to him just then, hollering. Greg couldn't hear their words, but imagined they were calling him to supper.

"Over there." Jas was pointing down a dirt road that curved off to the left. Greg followed it around a sharp bend, then suddenly found himself staring at a long oval body of water that glowed under the darkening pink sky. Mountains thick with oak and sycamore cradled it on all sides; this was the only road in. "Welcome to El Nido Lake," Jas said.

Greg looked around at his past. There, to the west, in that shaded cove, was where he had often fished with his father. "I've been here before," he said.

They settled on a patch of pebbly shore just as the sun's last blush disappeared behind a ridge. "We were talking about ModoCorp," Greg reminded. "ModoCorp and Charles Whit."

Jas began tossing pebbles into the water. "Something funny between them and Diana. Something I'm not sure about."

"How so?"

"She never opposed them, not openly. Certainly not after Whit won over most of El Nido. Whatever's best for the valley, that's all you'd hear her say. But she got in their way, I think. She and her foreman."

"Alex?"

"You've met Alex?"

Greg nodded. He tried to hide his surprise at what he was hearing. "I didn't realize they opposed Whit's group. How do you mean, got in their way?"

"Tangled with them somehow. You could just tell. Whit and Diana at a meeting, their eyes would meet sometime, and it wasn't what you'd call friendly. Tense like. Alex made it worse. Sometimes I thought he and Whit would maybe throw a punch or two."

"What kind of meetings?"

Jas pulled her knees up under her chin and wrapped her arms around them. "Town hall meetings, mainly. They're held monthly, right in the mayor's living room. Quite a scene when Whit came. He with his PR team, everyone else so quiet and polite. Given Whit's size and manner and all, I guess only a drunk would dare to start an argument."

"What would Whit say?"

"Not much of anything. His PR boys usually did the talking, while he watched the crowd with those eyes of his."

"And the PR team's line. . . ?"

"The usual hooha. 'By telling the truth we hope everyone will be able to make a decision based on factual, accurate information and less on emotion.' Never got more precise. Always talked about a 'world-class health spa' but never showed us the plans. 'This will be good for everyone' was as specific as it got."

"How'd that play in the valley?"

"Tell you the truth, most just looked at Whit kind of blankly, especially in the early going. As I said, who's going to argue. He always had big loose-leaf notebooks full of tax-base growth projections with him, but no one ever touched them. A lot of the guys just leaned against Sam Rabe's walls with their arms folded, or walked the hallways with their hands shoved in their pockets. I don't think people really knew what to say. Except for Alex Ramirez."

Jas grinned at the memory. "I can still see him at the very first meeting with Whit . . . squatting against the wall, rolling a rubber ball to one of Sam Rabe's mangy mutts as Whit's guys talked on and on. Whit finally steps in and says, 'It's important that everyone who has a question about this project be given an opportunity to have all their questions answered.' Alex, still rolling the ball, his eyes on Sam Rabe's mutt, asks, 'What will you do if people oppose you?'

"For a minute, I don't think Whit knows what to say. Then he answers, 'Why . . . we'll pack up and leave.' So then Alex looks around the room and asks, 'Who here wants this man to stay in El

Nido?' No one speaks or moves. I mean it. Hands stay in pockets, arms remain folded. I think most folks just didn't know what to think. They weren't for or against, and surely didn't want to get in the middle of those two guys. That's how people are in El Nido. Alex runs with it, though. 'Well, now,' he says finally. 'Mr. Whit, I guess you got your answer.'

"That's when the bad blood started, right then. Whit kind of smiles at Alex in that empty way he has. 'We'll see,' Whit says as he gathers his books and walks out. 'We will see how everyone feels.' A week later, Whit hired Brewster Tomaz."

It was Greg's turn to toss pebbles into the water. The pink sky had deepened to magenta, then black; moonlight glinted off the lake. Somewhere a loon called. "What about Diana and Whit?" he asked. "You ever see them go at it?"

Jas thought, then nodded. "The Camp Mahrah acreage, like everything around here, derives from Spanish land grant days. Somewhere during all the land swaps and sales, the Sanborn family ended up with an easement across Camp Mahrah land. It had been granted many decades ago, so the Sanborns could get to their caliche mines over by the sandstone cliffs."

"Caliche?"

"Limestone gravel. They once used it in road building around El Nido, but no longer. It's been many years since caliche was worth anything. For that matter, the Sanborns' caliche probably was mined out long ago. Legally, though, the easement still exists. I can remember Diana just whooping at one meeting, that way she has. 'Way I see it,' she declared, 'the Sanborn family still needs access to its valuable caliche mines.' Then, late one night, to underscore that point, Alex trailered the ranch's backhoe right up the mountain and commenced to do a spot of caliche mining."

Jas laughed out loud. "He really mined that mountain. Swear to God."

Greg turned Jas's story around in his mind. He tried to fill in the dots, tried to weave a persuasive theory. But he'd somehow lost the thread. "What does all this amount to?" he asked. "Did Alex or Diana ever do anything that really stopped Whit?"

"Nope, can't say they did. Just gave him a little trouble at the meetings. Eventually, to no one's surprise, Diana lined up on Whit's side. Like I told you, a quality health spa would help the valley, add value to everyone's holdings. It was economics and market studies that stopped the spa, as far as I understand, not local opposition. El Nido is too isolated to draw a big enough crowd, it seems. To most folks' regret."

"So why do you think ModoCorp might be threatening Diana?"

"Don't know, really. I just tossed that out without really thinking. Sort of an instinct, based on what I saw at those early meetings. Now that you ask, I'm probably wrong. They almost act like allies now."

Greg kept throwing pebbles into the water. "What about Sarah? Where does she fit in?"

"Come on," Jas said. "She was stalking Brewster. She pushed the old man in the water."

Greg suddenly felt hollow. "You think Sarah is guilty, don't you?"

"Sure, but so what if she is?"

Greg could see both indignation and moonlight in Jas's eyes. "What do you mean?" he asked.

"I mean, maybe something terribly wrong still happened here even if she is guilty."

Greg waited, but Jas said nothing more. Instead, she looked at him steadily, in a way that made the heat rise in his face. He held her gaze for a moment, wondering whether she looked at all men like that. Then, sensing something moving, he turned toward the lake. A strange object, a black lump, bobbed in the water at the shore's edge. Greg rose and approached it. With a stick, he pulled it to the pebble beach.

Not just black, Greg saw now. It was black with a green metallic sheen, a not-uncommon coloring for the type of cormorant found in Central California waters. Greg studied the dead bird. The long hooked bill, the large fully webbed feet, the short strong legs—the cormorant was well equipped to dive for food, and to swim once it hit the water.

Not this one, though. Greg placed his hands on the bird's wet feathers, ran his fingers across its back. Then he rubbed his fingers together.

"Oil," he said, gazing at the water. "There must be a slick out there somewhere."

NEAR MIDNIGHT, AFTER A solitary dinner at the Rancho Café in El Nido Village, Greg drove the winding mountain pass that led to La Graciosa. A bright moonlit sky showed him the way. He had a promising plea-bargain conference scheduled with the Chumash County DA the next afternoon, then plans to meet Jimmy O'Brien at JB's Red Rooster Tavern. The eagerness he felt, heading home, surprised him.

Something terribly wrong still happened here.

Jas's words echoed in his mind. The El Nido DA's office most certainly had played this one fast and loose. Yet cops and prosecutors were always doing that. Most times, they knew they had the guilty party and simply wanted to make sure the jurors did also. That was wrong, of course—the state didn't get to put people away just because they were guilty, the state first had to prove their guilt. Still, there were certain moments when Greg wondered: What was worse, that or letting dangerous killers walk the streets of our cities?

He shuddered at a memory. Jason Pine suddenly disappearing one night . . . Jason Pine on a clandestine manic prowl through Chumash County. At dawn, he showed up at his terrified aunt's apartment, hollering and slamming things about. Only then did Greg turn him in, only then did he finally bring Pine down to the sheriff's office. It wasn't enough. When the DA learned Pine would talk only to doctors, not detectives, he responded with an ace card. *He won't talk, we've got nothing on him, so we're turning him loose.* Greg responded with his own ace card—a phone call to his reporter pal Jimmy O'Brien. *Want a good story about the DA letting a killer walk free?* A week later, Jason Pine ended up just where Greg wished him—in the Chumash County Mental Health Institute. Thanks to his clever attorney, there was no jail for Pine, just a bed and a window. That, and a prospect for release.

The scent of kelp disrupted Greg's reverie. He'd reached La Graciosa, wrapped as usual in a blanket of fog. His house, a half mile up-creek from the town square, rose like a promise before him. He parked and walked inside. On the way to the deck, he stopped to check for phone messages.

There was one. The voice on the machine sounded cheerful and familiar. It was, Greg recognized instantly, Julia Brass, Judge Daniel Solman's clerk. She wanted him to know that Judge Solman had reviewed his amended habeas petition on behalf of Sarah Trant. Reviewed it, and found it worth consideration.

Judge Solman has scheduled a status conference, Julia advised. He wants all lawyers in his chambers first thing tomorrow morning.

S E V E N

U.S. District Judge Daniel Solman rifled impatiently through the untidy pile of documents strewn on the credenza behind his desk. Such disarray annoyed him, yet he had little means to achieve order. These days he worked, literally, out of a suitcase. A colossal one-hundred-year storm, followed soon after by a moderate 4.4 earthquake, had left his customary federal quarters uninhabitable for eighteen months now. He'd been obliged to toil in temporary offices, and to travel, like a roving circuit magistrate, to hearings in outlying districts.

At least the Chumash County Courthouse, where he'd installed himself today for the purpose of considering Sarah Trant's habeas petition, offered the advantage of being located in his hometown. Solman had grown up in La Graciosa and attended Chumash State. He always welcomed the chance to revisit his roots. That the county courthouse occupied a former house of God made the return all the more pleasurable. Solman enjoyed sitting in the two-hundred-year-old *asistencia* and imagining its early use as assistant chapel for Mission San Luis Obispo de Tolosa to the north.

"Judge Solman?"

He examined the unfamiliar intercom box on his desk, looking for a button to press. Each office he sat in these days had a different tangle of machinery to decipher. "Yes, Julia?" he said finally, his hand loosely cupping the side of the box.

That seemed to work: Julia heard him. "The lawyers are present now," she said. "Jim Mashburn from El Nido County, Greg Monarch for the petitioner."

Solman stared at the papers spread on the desk before him. He wasn't sure why he'd urged Sarah Trant's habeas petition on Monarch that first night, and he certainly couldn't say why he'd taken matters a step further, to this status conference. He felt almost as if he were following an involuntary instinct, one that ran contrary to his normal bent. Yes, it was true, the initial impetus had come from Sarah Trant herself, from Trant's request that Monarch get a copy of her petition. Yet he would have sent her handwritten plea to Greg even if the prisoner hadn't asked. It was Greg's kind of case. From the mid-distance that their acquaintanceship provided, Solman had privately followed Monarch's course through the law with admiration. He wasn't the least like him; he didn't share Monarch's brand of brooding diligence, nor his affinity for abject souls and likely transgressors. Yet Greg moved him in some way. Greg, he had to admit, embodied something he lacked.

"Okay, Julia," the judge said. "I'm ready. Send them in."

WALKING SIDE BY SIDE with Mashburn into Judge Solman's quarters, Greg puzzled over the DA's manner. In the judge's waiting room, Jim had shifted about in his chair, struggling to make small talk, avoiding eye contact. For a moment Greg had imagined him feeling qualms about Trant's case. Yet now that didn't seem to be the case.

Settling into chairs before Judge Solman, Mashburn projected aggressive certitude, not ambivalence. "I'll be happy to," he said when Solman invited him to go first. He pulled a sheaf of papers from his briefcase and began. "Your Honor . . . What are we doing here? The petitioner is basically seeking a retrial. Boil all this down"—here Mashburn waved at the petition in Solman's hands—"and what she's doing is asking you, a federal judge, to retry her case. She's asking you to usurp a state judge's role."

Solman looked back and forth at the lawyers. "Isn't that what a federal habeas claim is all about?"

"No, sir." Mashburn rifled through the papers clutched in his hand. "I won't read everything we've cited in our response brief, just a bit from this most relevant Supreme Court decision."

Solman rolled his eyes. "Why do I think I'm going to hear a few lines from *Barefoot v. Estelle* at this moment?"

"'A presumption of finality,'" Mashburn said with emphasis. He looked over at Greg, then turned back to the judge. "That's what *Barefoot* talks about. 'The role of federal habeas proceedings is secondary and limited. . . . Federal courts are not forums in which to relitigate trials—'"

Solman held up a hand. "I know the language, you needn't go on. You can just brief me on all that."

Mashburn blinked back his frustration. "That's my case in a nutshell, Your Honor. If you know the language of *Barefoot*, you know my case."

"Well, then," Solman said, "I guess I know your case." He turned to Greg. "Let's move on. Mr. Monarch, you want to take a turn?"

Greg weighed his response. He saw he had Solman with him for some reason. Yet—knowing his college classmate to be a cautious and politically minded jurist—he still felt the need to supply the judge with a solid rationale for favoring Sarah's plea.

"Yes, Your Honor, I'll speak just for a moment," Greg said. "I think it's important for the Court to keep in mind that Sarah Trant is claiming actual innocence. That changes the equation a bit, Your Honor. *Barefoot* isn't the controlling case then. The key is *Schlup v. Delo*. No matter what procedural defaults you've got, no matter what you've waived or failed to raise earlier, Schlup lets you in the door if your case involves a fundamental miscarriage of justice. And *Schlup* says the federal district court isn't bound by the rules of admissibility that would govern at trial. The claim of actual innocence allows the habeas court also to consider relevant evidence that was either excluded or unavailable at trial."

Greg let a faint smile show as he looked back and forth between Mashburn and Solman. "We've got lots of that type of evidence, Your Honor. We're not entitled to retry everything in a federal court, but by claiming actual innocence we're allowed to show you evidence the trial judge and jury never saw. We get to pursue the truth for once, rather than just argue process. We get a chance to prove our claims."

"Excuse me, Greg." Mashburn was twisting in his chair, facing him. "You haven't raised these claims in the state system yet. You haven't exhausted your appeals in the California courts, which have jurisdiction over your client, and over all crimes of murder within the state's boundaries. You have no business in a federal court."

Greg shook his head. "Two years ago, the California legislature amended its statutes to exclude actual innocence as a basis for certain appeals. By doing so, I would argue that the state in effect relinquished its jurisdiction over claims such as Sarah's, and placed them squarely in the federal forum."

"How can you say—" Mashburn began.

"Besides," Greg interrupted, "even if the state were willing to hear Sarah's latest appeal, I don't believe her rights would be protected. It's El Nido County, after all, where this would eventually get remanded under a state proceeding. And I don't believe El Nido can be trusted to treat Sarah Trant fairly. I don't believe El Nido can guarantee Ms. Trant the basic protections of the U.S. Constitution."

Anger welled in Mashburn's face. "What do you mean by that, Greg? Just what do you mean?"

Greg remained still. In their brief time working together, he'd found Jim neither dim nor unprincipled. Back then, Mashburn had made sure they played by the proper rules. So why not now? How could Jim so earnestly dispatch Sarah Trant to the executioner? Didn't he see that neither of them really knew the truth?

"I mean something is going on in your valley," Greg said. "Somebody framed Sarah Trant but good, Jim. Somebody wanted Sarah in prison."

"For Christ's sake," Mashburn snapped. "She killed a man, Greg. That's why she's in prison. She killed Brewster Tomaz."

"No," Greg said. "That's not why."

Solman interrupted. "Gentlemen, let's stick to the legal issues for the moment, okay?"

Both lawyers turned to face him. Solman reached for the habeas petition on his desk. "Mr. Monarch has thrown in the usual language you find in these things," he said. " 'There are situations where the criminal justice system fails'—that's a nice hoary chestnut, don't you all think?"

Mashburn grabbed at that opening. "Fails for whom? For the accused, or for the victims? Or for all of us? I would argue that—"

Solman again held up a hand to stop the DA. "Point is granted. Hoary chestnut discarded." The judge leafed through the petition's pages. "But there's more than hoary chestnuts in here, isn't there? You've got a very funny-looking autopsy report in here, don't you?

And you've got a very funny-looking defense expert, don't you? That pathologist sounds more like a witness for the prosecution—"

"Your Honor." This time Mashburn was interrupting Solman. "No fewer than four California trial and appellate judges have reviewed all this and found no merit to Trant's claims. Do you propose setting yourself above them? Do you think you have a right to ignore all their findings?"

Solman chewed on that. Mashburn's words appeared to affect him. "Well, not ignore," he said. "Just review."

Mashburn had the look of a gambler now. "This is what riles the public, Your Honor. Murderers kill, murderers get convicted. Then come years of judicial delay. People are angry at federal intrusion into state affairs, people are genuinely distressed about violent crime. That's why you've got campaigns against federal judges these days. That's why you've got U.S. senators talking about ending lifetime tenure." Mashburn was almost out of his chair. "And that, Your Honor, is why you get citizens talking about impeaching federal judges."

Greg watched Solman as Mashburn spoke. The judge's expression had started to shift; his judicial air and sense of command were fading. Greg wasn't altogether surprised. He'd occasionally seen Solman dance near the edge of an adventurous act, but he'd always backed off eventually, settling for the assurance of established forms.

"You raise a valid issue, Mr. Mashburn," Solman said finally. "It is also true that our Congress and Supreme Court don't want the habeas process overused. They've narrowed the window, haven't they? They don't want state convicts to get bite after bite at the federal apple. Only one bite, they say. Convicts should get only one bite—"

"Your Honor, that's just the point." Greg was now sitting on the edge of his chair too. He'd been waiting for the conversation to reach this moment. "If you deny Sarah Trant's petition, she won't get another chance. She will have taken her one bite of the apple."

"You sure of that?" Solman asked, looking puzzled.

"It's in that new 1996 federal law. The Antiterrorism and Effective Death Penalty Act. One bite, that's what the AEDPA dictates. A single federal habeas petition, no more. If you deny her, Sarah Trant would need approval from the court of appeals to return to federal court. And if they say no, that's it. She can't take it to the Supreme Court."

"Judge—" Mashburn tried to interrupt.

Again Greg wouldn't let him: "Do you want to close the door like that, Your Honor? Would that not be constitutionally intolerable?"

"The law is the law—" Once more Mashburn couldn't finish a sentence. Greg was on his feet now.

"That's just it, Your Honor. The law is the law. The U.S. Constitution, the Fourteenth Amendment, due process—"

"Okay, that's enough." Solman waved them both off. Greg sat down, studying the judge. Solman was acting uneasy, as a man of caution and custom will when faced with making a genuine choice. Yet even as Greg watched him, Solman appeared to gather himself and will himself forward.

"Your office shouldn't have rigged it so much." The judge was frowning at Mashburn as he spoke. "Two or three crooked angles, fine, you're making sure the guilty don't walk. But it looks like your office crossed every damn line here."

"Your Honor—" Mashburn began.

"Gentlemen," Solman interrupted. "I've decided to schedule an evidentiary hearing on Sarah Trant's habeas petition."

EACH TIME GREG VISITED Sarah now at the La Luna Women's Correctional Center, he surveyed the other prisoners gathered in the communal visiting area. They came from all over the state, fed into this medium-security facility by faceless bureaucrats at a distant dispatching center. Some had the sickly pallor and hard worn faces of career cons, while some looked so fresh and vulnerable Greg wondered how they'd survive a week in this place. Drug convictions brought the majority here; often that meant they'd done a boyfriend's bidding. Either that, or they were here because they attempted to kill a boyfriend. Most people would be surprised to learn how many women tried to take contracts out on the men who beat them day and night.

Greg usually found the same guard standing by the door of the interview room where he met with Sarah. He was not a particularly menacing man, with his narrow shoulders and concave chest and big ears, but he had a habit of staring at Sarah with absolutely no expression. Once, when Greg tired of this routine, he taped a piece of paper over the interview room's small window. It worked for twenty minutes. Then the guard knocked and told him he had to take the paper down. Today, Greg thought of trying that maneuver again. As usual, their sentinel was watching them ceaselessly. With her back to the door, Sarah didn't seem to notice, but Greg sensed she felt his presence.

"Do you understand what I'm saying?" Greg asked. "Sarah, the judge has granted us a hearing. We're going to court. He's going to consider your petition."

Sarah nibbled at her lip. "May I talk a little?" she asked. "I so much want to talk to you."

Greg steeled himself, uncertain where she was heading. He slowly sank into a chair. "What, Sarah?"

"You're afraid of me, aren't you?"

Involuntarily, Greg leaned back. Sarah's hands rested on the table that separated them. They looked so scarred, like an old woman's. Or like those of someone who'd made too many frenzied attempts to escape from locked rooms. "You matter to me," he said. "That's how I feel."

She ignored his response. "I know one of the reasons you're afraid of me. It's because I haven't met the terms of my contract. You know, like in *Mr. Sammler's Planet*. Remember us reading Bellow together? The prayer over that nephew? I haven't done that. I haven't taken hold of my life—"

"Sarah . . ." Greg tried to interrupt.

She wouldn't let him. "I've never been very good at that business. I've preferred being naive, being an enthralled wide-eyed dupe. To some men, like yourself, it's a charming attitude in a woman. I understand. It can be funny. It can make the days seem more interesting. But somewhere along the line this mechanism can break down. It did with me. I know that I loved myself more when I was twenty-two than I have ever since."

Greg thought of Sarah at twenty-two. He loved her then too. He loved her that summer morning when she pointed her battered Mustang toward Canada and said *Come on, let's go*. Yet he had to admit he'd harbored other feelings as well. She was forever reciting her same string of stories, wanting him always to listen with wonder. . . .

She never could get them down on paper, though. She could never get anything down on paper. *I can't organize your interior*, he'd told her more than once. *We occupy our own rooms.*

"You did make the days more interesting," he said now. "Still do."

Sarah lowered her eyes, then raised them. "That last summer, Greg. You remember?"

"Of course."

"That last visit we had, when I came to you from the halfway house?"

"Yes, I recall."

"I drove away that day feeling like I'd tried to sell you a broken watch. I hadn't meant to sell anything. I wanted to voice a faint hope for our future. That's all. But then the tears came. So messy, so awful. Jesus. What a way to part. Sorry."

Greg reached for her weathered hand. "Nothing to be sorry about."

Sarah grasped his hands in her own but said nothing more. It looked to Greg as if she were listening to voices he couldn't hear.

"So," she said suddenly. "We get to have a hearing. The judge has given us a hearing."

Greg answered quickly, eager to keep her with him. "Yes, and not just a hearing. I asked for the right to depose state witnesses, and to conduct unlimited discovery. Judge Solman agreed. Because of 'un-usual circumstances,' he said."

"What does this mean?"

"It means we get to see everything the state has on your case, Sarah. They only had to disclose a part of their files back at the time of your trial. Now they have to hand over all they've got."

Sarah closed her eyes. She squeezed Greg's hands. Then, with one finger, she traced the lines in his palms. Realizing she was silently sobbing, Greg put an arm around her shoulders. "What more can you tell me about the night of the murder, Sarah? Down by the river, you say you confronted Tomaz, pushed him in the water, then ran off. Did you see anyone else?"

She looked as if she was going to answer, but didn't. Instead she began to hum, then sing softly. *Bewitched, bothered and bewildered . . .* Greg despaired. He grasped her by the shoulders, pulled her toward him, and held her close, as if that would keep her from slipping away.

"Sarah, Sarah. Listen to me. While you were running from the river, where was Diana Sanborn? Did you see Diana?"

Bewitched, bothered and bewildered . . . As Sarah sang, she ran her hand along Greg's neck. The feel of her fingers on his skin set him on edge. For a moment he was back with her, ricocheting up the coast on a hot summer night. "Sarah," he said. "Sarah."

A faint click and flash of light startled Greg out of his daze. He looked up, following the sound, and found himself staring, through a window, into the mirthless eyes of the thin gray guard. In the man's hands was a small automatic Nikon, which he held propped against the window, the open lens aimed at Greg and Sarah.

"Guess what?" Greg advised his client. "We've just had our picture taken."

——————— E I G H T ———————

Great flocks of blackbirds circled in the darkening sky. Wild-eyed deer, hares with astonishing ears, strangely crested quail, the sheer sullen walls of the La Lunas—taken together, they suggested an undiscovered world. Greg was riding a quarter horse named Harley up the Santa Theresa trail into Upper El Nido. Beside him Diana Sanborn sat her saddle squarely, as though it were a bench, with a silvered and tasseled strap tied across her lap. She'd blanched when he showed up unannounced at her front door. Then she'd said, "Come see my valley at dusk."

They stopped and dismounted above the steep drop that divided El Nido. Below them, the basin filled with an exceptional color of pink streaked with purple. Thin bands of light scaled the mountain faces, turning red-gold at the crest. Cottonwood and white alder and sycamore, ceanothus and sage and manzanita, prickly pear and yucca and abundant lupines—Greg's eyes roamed eagerly across the tableau.

"Here, we are *on* the El Nido," Diana said, her arm sweeping toward the horizon. "Not in, but on. Here's the El Nido known by its settlers. For others, for those in cars who follow the roads, El Nido puts on a disguise. You and I are seeing El Nido as it really is. If you stay here for long, Mr. Monarch, you will come to love El Nido as I do."

Greg said, "It makes you want to bow down to Mother Nature."

"There is more than Nature to thank for all this."

Greg looked at her but said nothing. He wondered if she'd intended such an edge in her voice.

"Places are shaped by how we behave, wouldn't you say, Mr. Monarch?" Diana was smiling now, dipping her head, looking recovered. The impish mischief in her eyes stripped twenty years away.

"I'd say everything's shaped by how we behave," he replied. "And why don't you call me Greg."

Diana clapped her hands. "Yes! Actions have consequences. A place's character and tradition, for instance. That's one consequence, wouldn't you say? One event connects to the next in a way that gives a place a particular . . . history."

"Yes, one event connects to the next," Greg agreed. "That I couldn't deny."

They sat in silence on a narrow ledge, studying the vista. It was almost dark now. Lights from the village twinkled in the distance. "You may call me Diana," she announced.

"Okay, Diana. So what's really going on in El Nido?"

"Whatever do you mean?"

"ModoCorp, Charles Whit, a health spa that gets talked about but never built. Even though everyone seems to want it. Everyone but you, that is."

Diana smiled. "Goodness, Greg. Your mind has been wandering far from Sarah Trant's cause."

"Has it?"

Diana clung to her smile. "I've never been opposed to Modo-Corp's plans. Just certain details. That is customary in these affairs. I'm quite eager for El Nido to grow, as long as it happens in a suitable manner. It has to grow, in fact, or it shall die."

"Sarah thought otherwise."

"Yes," Diana said, her smile now slipping away. "Sarah did."

"And Sarah worked for you?"

"For a summer. Hired on as a ranch hand, wasn't suited for that. Didn't last."

"Isn't there more to it, Diana?"

"What do you mean?"

"You two had a bond of sorts."

Diana looked steadily at him. She drew a breath. "Yes, you're right. . . . Sarah is full of passion. Sarah burns brightly. She has a soul that I recognize."

"It pained you to have to testify against her?"

"I almost didn't, it bothered me so much."

"Yet you did."

"Yes . . . I did."

Greg studied the basin below them. It had been another hot, dry day, the warm air pushed through the valley by a ceaseless breeze. Now though, without the sun, he felt chilled. He pulled his jacket collar tighter around his neck. "Why did you ask me to stay in El Nido, Diana? Why offer me your guest room that first weekend? What do you want?"

Diana rose, walked to her mare, began to pat her neck. Next she adjusted the horse's reins, tightened a buckle, checked a stirrup. Then she untwisted the silvered tasseled saddle strap. When she finally turned back to Greg, she seemed to be weighing something. "What I want you can't do," she said.

Greg came to her side. "Try me."

She looked at him without speaking. Twice she began to talk but didn't. She closed her eyes, then opened them. Finally, she said, "I want someone to fix the past."

Diana told her story as they rode back down the hill. She talked first about the winter she turned eight. She talked about a girl named Jenny, and a Thanksgiving hike in the snow, and three children huddled together against the arctic cold. Then she sighed and said, "I want to tell you more. I want to tell you about my sixteenth summer."

Greg, not knowing how to respond, simply nodded. They rode in silence, he waiting, she studying the sky. After half a mile, Diana began. She spoke slowly, measuring her words.

That summer, she said, a young man came to work on her grandfather's ranch. He was so unlike the others: not a boy at all, but a brooding, tightly wound twenty-four-year-old. She couldn't stop looking at him. He had pale blue eyes and jet-black hair. Sometimes he let her tag along as he toured the ranch, drilling holes and testing soil conditions for her grandfather. When he rested, he'd even talk to her a bit. She listened mostly, but in time found herself responding. It thrilled and scared her at once, how she opened herself to him.

Then he turned on her—so suddenly, she never saw it coming.

One night on the ridge, with too much whiskey in his stomach, and maybe too many of her words in his ear, all that moody intensity turned to anger. He slapped her once over something tart she said. Then he slapped her again, harder. When she cried, his eyes brightened and his hand curled into a fist. He yanked her shirt open, then went for her jeans. She couldn't tell which hurt more, the blows to her head or him ramming into her. At his climax he rose above her, propped up on his hands, hollering and swiping at her. For a moment Diana didn't know if she was being raped or murdered.

She never told anyone. Even as he was climbing off her, she knew she wouldn't. She had no choice really, since she well understood what would follow if she did. Her grandfather would kill her attacker on the spot, the instant he heard what had happened. Then he'd be charged with murder. Charged and maybe even convicted. Not even Edward Sanborn could kill his employees at will.

So the ranch hand stayed on, monitoring soil conditions for Edward Sanborn for almost eight years. When he left them, it was for another job just five miles farther into the valley. He never moved from El Nido. Year in and year out, first on her grandfather's ranch, then later on the streets of the village, Diana found herself obliged to pass silently by her attacker. Occasionally he'd nod a greeting, which she had to return.

"Thus both of us aged over the decades, silently sharing a secret," Diana concluded. "Now, isn't that a quaint love story?"

They'd reached the stables at Sanborn Ranch. Greg wondered why she'd chosen to tell him all this. "Is he still around?" he asked.

Diana offered an odd, faraway smile. "Alas, no. He passed on a while back. He's just a memory now. Although a persistent one."

Alex, approaching from the corral, greeted them and helped Diana dismount. She started toward the main house as Greg headed for his car. Then she turned and called to him. "You might as well know, Greg. My take on human nature is not all that favorable. Especially men's."

AS SHE STUDIED THE documents spread across the table, Jasmine Gest could feel his eyes on her. Sheriff Roy Rimmer was not being in the least lascivious, yet something in his manner made Jas tug at her black miniskirt. She wished she'd worn something else today. Rimmer turned away finally. Jas clutched at the buttons of her gray wool sweater.

Ah well, she thought. She had Greg Monarch beside her. She looked to him now for support.

"Sheriff," Greg was saying. "Should we repeat the question again? Are you having trouble concentrating today?"

The three, along with a staff lawyer from the DA's office named Donald Taub, were seated in a rented conference room at the El Nido Inn. The petitioner may conduct discovery and depose state witnesses, Judge Solman had ruled. So that's what they were doing. Greg had enlisted Jas as a temporary assistant to help sort through documents. They'd been at it three weeks now. Each day, they'd learned something new.

First came the intriguing revelation that Dr. Montrose's income from serving as a state expert witness had ballooned in the year after Sarah's trial—from $5,000 to $35,000. Then came a curious police report that made mention of a bloodstained blue-checked kerchief found just downstream from the murder site. Then an extraordinary report describing distinctive boot prints—a half-sole with diagonal nails—spotted on the creek bank right beside Tomaz's body. Finally—most astonishing of all—the account of one Judith Daniels, an El Nido spinster who'd reached the murder scene just behind Diana Sanborn.

A never-produced investigative file told the story. Half a year after the murder—one month before Sarah's trial—Judith Daniels had called the sheriff's department. *I saw someone that night,* she'd informed Sheriff Rimmer. *Someone running into the brush on the far side of the creek. Someone much taller and bulkier than Sarah. I saw him get as far as the yonder alder tree. Then he flat out disappeared.*

When he first found this report, Greg felt as if he'd stumbled on a hidden world, a parallel universe that operated by its own set of rules. Even in a system known for unconscionable deception, he didn't see how the prosecution could have kept this from Reggie Dodge.

"Sorry," Rimmer was saying. "Perhaps I am having trouble concentrating today. Please repeat the question."

Greg leaned over so as to get squarely into Rimmer's line of sight.

"The question is, how did these police reports not get turned over to the defense? Why was none of this revealed at Sarah's trial?"

Rimmer couldn't hide his irritation. "Those weren't official police reports. Those were just internal memos among our investigators. Sorting out what was legitimate evidence, that's what they were doing. Also, what was exculpatory. If it's not exculpatory, it doesn't have to be disclosed."

"The testimony of an eyewitness is not evidence, Sheriff Rimmer? And not exculpatory?"

Rimmer offered a condescending smile. "You're not from here, Mr. Monarch. Otherwise you'd know that Judith Daniels isn't right in the head. She's the village oddball. You lived here, you'd know that."

"The boot prints, the kerchief?"

"Prints were two days old, the kerchief months old. Not from the murder night."

Greg tapped the table with a pencil. "Sheriff, just what does constitute something worth mentioning in an official police report?"

Rimmer surveyed the room, as if looking for an example in a corner of the El Nido Inn. The strain of being required to answer this LA Graciosa lawyer's questions for three uninterrupted hours showed now in the set of his jaw and the clench of his fists. The sheriff's eyes finally lighted on Jas. "Well, now," he said. "Say if Jas here were attacked on the way to this deposition . . . Say she was raped . . . That would be a report. We'd write that up as a formal report."

Greg rose, and Rimmer started out of his chair too. The DA's lawyer, silent in a corner until now, jumped between them. "Okay, now, okay," Taub said. "Let's all settle down."

Greg remained on his feet. He reached for a pile of the documents they'd gained through discovery. "Sheriff, here is what you call a formal police report, I take it. It summarizes your department's interviews with Diana Sanborn on the night of the murder, and then again two weeks later. This, you agree, is a police report?"

Rimmer sat back down. So did Greg. "Yes, sir," the sheriff said. "That's a report."

"You know what's not in here, Sheriff? What's not in this formal police report?"

"No, sir."

"What's not in here is anything about Diana Sanborn saying she heard the victim's dying declaration."

Rimmer looked bored. "So it didn't get written down right away . . . That's not a secret, Monarch. Reggie Dodge worked that angle quite a bit during the murder trial, without getting anywhere."

Greg leaned forward. "Well, let's work it a little bit more, Sheriff. Are you saying you wouldn't have put it in a report that Diana heard a dying declaration?"

"For chrissake, Monarch, it eventually got written up. Take a look at those later reports."

"Three weeks later, to be exact."

"Okay, fine, three weeks. It's in there, isn't it?"

"Sheriff!" Greg snapped. "You think this kind of stuff is going to play once we get in a federal courtroom?"

Rimmer grinned. "That depends who the judge is," he said. "And who the lawyers are."

AT DUSK ON THE day of Sheriff Rimmer's deposition, Greg and Jas drove to an Italian farm family's café that stood among the avocado orchards a mile outside El Nido Village. "Best pizza and spaghetti in the West," she'd promised. With a bottle of Chianti, and a sky washed pale gold, and an outdoor table sheltered by a hundred-year-old live oak, Greg was willing to agree.

"They rigged the case, pure and simple," Jas said. "Isn't that right?"

Greg curled pasta onto his fork. "Pure and simple."

"Do you have what you need?"

"What I need is a new trial for Sarah. No way to know whether I have that. Judges don't issue habeas writs very often. No matter what's happened. Just like everyone else, they accept that cops and prosecutors cook their cases. As long as they haven't framed someone obviously innocent, judges usually let them have their way."

"Even Judge Solman?"

"Oh, I think particularly Judge Solman."

"But Solman granted you a hearing."

"That doesn't mean he'll issue a writ. Most who get to a habeas hearing still end up having their petitions denied."

"That's what you expect?"

"No. . . . Not at all."

Greg started tapping the table with his fingers. Jas studied his hands. "What, then?" she asked.

"Can't say yet. Too murky to expect anything . . . We just need to be aware of what's going on."

"I can't imagine you being unaware," she said. "Of anything."

He looked at her. "The folks who rolled Reggie Dodge aren't going to lie down now just because I came to town waving a habeas petition."

"No, I suppose not."

They sat in silence then, sipping their wine.

"What did you and Sarah talk about?" Greg asked.

"Sarah and I? . . . When?"

"Those times you were together. Those hikes you mentioned, those drinks at the Gaucho."

Jas's eyes danced. "You imagining some juicy girl talk, maybe? That what you had in mind?"

"Just asking . . ."

"The latest shoe styles   that's what we talked about. Hair news. Health tips were also big."

"Okay, okay." Greg held up his hands in surrender. "This is getting too serious again. Back to the case."

"I'm ready."

"One thing we need to do," he said. "That's ask Reggie Dodge about all these reports he supposedly never saw. We need to go over what he knew, what they didn't tell him. His testimony will be critical for us. He gives us the key to dozens of violations."

"You haven't talked to him yet?"

"I keep trying, but can't get past his wife. She insists he's still too weak to talk. Flat on his back. The pneumonia, or whatever it is, lingers. I stopped by his house yesterday but couldn't get a foot in the door. She won't even put him on the phone."

"I happen to know Mrs. Dodge fairly well," Jas said. "From the museum. Why don't I call her, see if that works? We could maybe visit them after dinner. They don't live far from here."

While Jas went to the pay phone, Greg watched a hawk float down the valley on a current of air, following the setting sun to the sea. Twice he twisted in his seat, sensing someone watching from the dense woodland beyond the café. Both times he saw nothing but trees.

"Oh God, Greg." Jas was at his side now, ashen. "I . . . Oh . . ."

"What, Jas?"

"It's Reggie Dodge."

"What?"

"He's dead. Died in his sleep last night. His wife found him in bed this morning."

"Dead of what?"

Jas exhaled slowly. "They don't know. The coroner has no idea."

Diana Sanborn labored to project the gusto that she knew was expected of her. Her surroundings didn't help, though. This weathered cabin, no doubt a charming retreat half a century ago, now stank of mildew and something fouler. Out a small window she could see only dust and rusting machinery and a barren landscape. She longed to be home at Sanborn Ranch, alone in her bedroom with her journal.

She wasn't alone, though. Nor home. Diana surveyed the room. Charles Whit stood in one corner, smiling without appearing the least amused. Sheriff Rimmer sat in a rocking chair by the fireplace, rapidly pitching back and forth. Near the front door, James Mashburn sifted through a briefcase, looking distracted.

"Sorry to call you all here in such conditions," Whit was saying. "But we seem to have a problem."

They were gathered at Camp Mahrah on a blustery Sunday afternoon. Diana wondered at the original use of this cabin. It wasn't big enough to be a dormitory for the children, not lavish enough for the supervisors. The head counselor's quarters? The cook's? Outside, she could hear the wind howling through the oaks. The campus sat on a plateau, ringed by a forest thick with vines and moss. No one could see in, no one could see out. Each time she visited here, Diana felt uneasy.

"A problem." Roy Rimmer contemplated those words. "No, not a problem. It's an absolute catastrophe. If Greg Monarch gets another week of discovery, the whole goddamn package is going to unravel.

Just what is going on? Monarch was supposed to be stopped long ago."

"Yes," Whit agreed. "That was the plan."

Both men turned to Mashburn. The DA glared back at them. "We wouldn't need a plan if you folks hadn't made such a goddamn mess of things to start with."

"Be that as it may—" Whit began.

"You're right," Mashburn interrupted. "Be that as it may, I now have a job to do. I tried to stop Monarch, just as we discussed. Went to two conferences with Judge Solman. Second one we even brought the attorney general with us, for chrissake. Solman wouldn't back down. We couldn't push him off this."

"We have to." Rimmer was up out of his chair now. "We've got to stop the bleeding."

"Excuse me, gentlemen." Diana offered a puzzled, ingenuous smile. "What more is there hidden away in your mysterious files?"

Mashburn leaned forward, hands on knees. "I ask the same question, Roy. Some of what's come out so far is news to me. Is there more to come? Pray share with us."

Rimmer waved him off. "It's not the documents I'm worried about now. It's Sarah Trant's mouth. And you, Ms. Sanborn, should worry as much about that as any of us."

Diana didn't look worried. "I don't believe Mr. Monarch has a clue about our situation in El Nido. He simply wants to rescue Sarah."

Whit poked at the fire with the tip of his cane. "Why do you say that, Ms. Sanborn? If I may inquire."

"We've spoken. He's never asked about El Nido. And Sarah's not talking, I'm sure of that."

Whit turned from the fire. "Why are you so sure?"

"Because Sarah doesn't really have anything to tell."

"She knows," Rimmer interjected. "She knows."

"But she doesn't know she knows," Diana said. "Bless her heart."

Whit sat down next to Diana. "Not good enough, Ms. Sanborn. I require considerably greater reassurance, as do my colleagues. We want Monarch out of El Nido, we want an end to this unexpected habeas proceeding. Otherwise, we quite reasonably fear, everything will blow wide open."

Everything. Diana turned that word over in her mind. So much it could encompass. *Everything.* By that did they mean the moment in El Nido history when Edward P. Sanborn so decisively dispatched the demons of discord? Or did they mean, more generally, that moment when life soured in El Nido? Moments, rather; there were more than one, of course.

"Mr. Whit," Diana said. "You talk as if you own this whole valley."

Whit stared at her. He waved an arm. "From yon mountain to yon mountain, I ought to."

"And from heaven to hell, Mr. Whit?"

Whit's smile did not register in his light gray eyes. "I'm sure you understand we need to quell this, Ms. Sanborn. Otherwise, it may be the end for all of us and, I'm afraid, for your cherished El Nido."

"Why make this point to me?" Diana asked, sounding irritated. "You and your colleagues are the ones with the power to quell this."

"And quell it we will, Ms. Sanborn. Don't you worry, given the stakes. I seek only your continued support in this effort. You've been with us for so long, it would be a shame to lose you."

Diana gazed steadily at Whit. "Yes," she said. "That would be a shame."

Whit moved his face closer to hers. "It's just that you've been so hospitable to Greg Monarch since his arrival. You offered him your guest room and your doctor. You visit with him. You seem to want him around."

"I was simply being a human being that first weekend, hard as that might be to understand. He'd been in an accident, he needed medical attention."

"And since then, Ms. Sanborn?"

"You and I are of different generations, Mr. Whit, and, forgive me, different backgrounds. Perhaps that's why you find my manners peculiar."

Whit rose and walked to the fireplace. He stood with his broad back to the flames, warming his hands. "I'm sure that must be it. I hope so, at least. My colleagues and I, we would feel just devastated if you abandoned us."

A man's holler out in the yard interrupted them. Through the window they could see Camp Mahrah's burly caretaker waving for his boss to come outside. "Please excuse me," Whit said as he headed for the door. "Always something to attend to around here."

"Mr. Whit," Diana called, just as he was about to step outside. "What are your plans these days for Camp Mahrah?"

Whit stopped, turned. "Maybe I'll develop all this as a religious center," he said. "Now that Christ has become the center of my life, that might just be its best purpose."

ALEX RAMIREZ STUDIED THE bull fuming at him from the far corner of the corral. He thought hard about tailing him, but questioned whether his horse possessed the necessary sensibility today. Pablo knew what to do, but he did not always wish to work in such close concert with the one who rode him—or anyone, for that matter. Alex respected and understood that impulse. He turned away from the bull. He'd leave him be for now. He'd leave them all be. Alex faced into the wind and turned up his collar. The animals were skittish today, anyway. This was a real blow. Up to fifty miles an hour, he judged.

A cloud of dust kicked up by the winds caught his attention. It was moving toward him, down the dirt road that led from Sanborn Ranch to Camp Mahrah. Then the dust lifted for an instant, and he saw under it Diana's white pickup, bouncing and lurching among the potholes. She was driving faster than the wind.

"Alex!" She called to him even before she climbed out of the truck. "Alex, over here. Get out of this blasted gale."

They sat in the pickup, watching a wall of live oaks bending with each gust. "Whit is agitated," she said. "And Whit is suspicious."

Alex looked unimpressed as Diana described her meeting at Camp Mahrah. When she finished, he popped a toothpick into his mouth. "What can Whit do?" he asked.

"Dear God," Diana sputtered. "You proud Latino men."

"Whit doesn't run the federal courts."

"But Whit has associates, Alex."

"We never see them."

"No, and I suspect we never will. But they're thinking of us."

Alex looked at her with raised eyebrows.

"They would be devastated if I abandoned them," Diana said. "That's what Whit told me. Devastated."

"Just like Sarah Trant was?"

"Alex! Dear God."

"We have become part of something that is not good."

She turned on him. "We're in the right here, Alex. We have a just cause. Sometimes that requires sacrifices."

"Human sacrifices?"

Diana glared at him. "It's more complicated than that. As you very well know, Alex."

"You can say so," he replied, "if you want."

Diana swung away from him and stared out the window. The bowed trees stood at nearly a forty-five-degree angle now. "I received another anonymous letter yesterday," she said. "Same message."

GREG WATCHED SARAH THROUGH the small window that gave onto the prisoner's meeting room. Usually they brought her to him; this time she was waiting. She appeared calm today.

"Watch out for her," said the guard at Greg's side. "She's dangerous."

Greg looked at him. It was the thin one with big ears again. "I've been so advised by your buddies more than once. I've got it now, I think."

The guard's face remained blank. "Reminders never hurt."

"Are you assigned full-time to Sarah Trant?" Greg asked. "You always seem to be around."

"Only when you're here, Mr. Monarch."

"I see," Greg said as the door to the meeting room swung open for him. "Much obliged for your guidance."

Sarah looked up at his entry. Her long dark hair, parted in the middle, framed a face full of hope. He was right about the calm he'd sensed at the window. He prayed that it might prove a good day for Sarah to talk.

"How are you doing?"

She offered a rueful smile. "Not throwing knives around today."

"Come on, now, you never did."

She raised her eyebrows. "Even I remember a certain motel room on a Canadian island."

"I meant here, in El Nido."

Sarah started to respond, then stopped. She looked down at her feet and clasped her hands together. "You sound so certain."

Greg searched for the right response. No, he wasn't certain. He just wanted to be certain. "You were framed, Sarah. . . ." That much was surely true. "Through discovery and depositions, we've been seeing all the evidence they held back at your trial."

"All the evidence?"

"Do you remember a blue-checked kerchief, Sarah?"

She looked wary now. "No . . . no."

"Who was wearing boots that night?"

"I . . . No one . . . I don't know. . . ."

"Why did Diana Sanborn want you convicted for Brewster Tomaz's murder?"

"She didn't, she didn't!" Sarah bit off the words, then looked dismayed at her outburst.

"Why do you say that, Sarah? What do you mean? What reason do you have to defend Diana?"

Sarah didn't answer. Slowly her eyes lost their focus. She rose from her chair, humming and swaying to a private rhythm. "Diana," she said. "I think something happened to Diana long ago."

"Has she told you?"

"No. . . . No. . . . I just sensed it."

Greg reached to still her. "I care more about what happened five years ago," he said. "At the river, between the two of you."

Sarah stopped humming. She looked at him. "I pushed Brewster Tomaz in the river, then ran away."

"Where was Diana?"

"I didn't see Diana."

"Why did Brewster Tomaz say it was you who cut him?"

Sarah stepped closer and wrapped her arms around him, as if she meant them to dance. "Maybe Brewster wanted to get me in trouble."

Greg held her off, gripping her arms at the elbows. "This won't do, Sarah. Your habeas hearing starts next week. You have less than six months to go. You need to stay with me."

Sarah studied his tightly curled fingers. "During Easter services that first year after we parted, I wrote a letter to you in my head and started to cry. The guy with me thought I was touched by all the banners and trumpets and the choir. I was saying goodbye to you. . . ."

"Sarah—what did Reggie Dodge tell you during the trial? What did he know about Tomaz's murder? What did he get from the prosecutors?"

"I have no idea. He barely spoke to me. Why don't you ask him?"

Greg slowed down now. He cupped her face with his hands. "Sarah, I can't ask him. Reggie Dodge is dead. He died last week, before I could talk to him. Some rare type of infection, they say."

That news appeared to undo her. She slumped into Greg's arms with a small cry, and stood close against him. "Oh my," she said. He held her now, trying to soothe. She responded, pressing against him, clinging to him.

Despite himself, Greg became aware that he could feel her thighs and breasts. A memory rose of the day he tackled her on the motel floor and lay atop her. Alarmed at his own feelings, he tried to move her away, but she wrapped herself tighter around him. "Sarah," he said. "Sarah."

Just then an arm reached between them. Following the arm came the prison guard's bony face. "Now, now," he said, "There'll be none of that in this prison."

AFTER ENTERING THE EL Nido basin on the main highway from La Graciosa, it was possible to swing south onto Old Brook Road and use it to approach the village. Greg, traveling back and forth between La Graciosa and El Nido, found he favored this more scenic if winding route. Old Brook Road ascended slowly to the east, winding gracefully as it followed El Nido Creek, whose clear sparkling waters it crossed and recrossed twelve times in four miles. At points the road passed under high banks fringed with giant sycamores, and at others it opened out into gentle dells dotted here and there with weathered farmhouses. Then, past the village, at Tiger Canyon, the outlet to upper El Nido, Old Brook hooked to the north and climbed sharply into the La Luna foothills.

Driving this route late on the day of his encounter with Sarah, Greg stopped and looked back over his shoulder when he reached the

Tiger juncture. All of the lower El Nido Valley spread before him, lu-
minous under a long blue sky. The setting didn't please him. He felt
too confined, hemmed in as he was by a sheer oak-covered cliff on
one side and the brooding mass called Gunpowder Mountain on the
other. He had no choice, though. By Greg's reading of the county
map, a gravel spur off this end of Old Brook provided a back way into
Camp Mahrah. He wanted to revisit the camp before the habeas
hearing began, preferably without being evicted so quickly this time.
He sensed that Charles Whit's machinations up there had a bearing
on Sarah's fate.

Greg mulled the tenuous links. Sarah Trant had openly fought
against Whit and ModoCorp. Diana Sanborn had fought them too,
but didn't want it to seem that way now. Diana and Sarah once had
some sort of bond. What had happened? If Brewster Tomaz didn't
make a dying declaration, then why did Diana belatedly step forward
with such a claim? There must be something in all this, Greg told
himself. Something that explained why El Nido County had found
Sarah Trant guilty of first-degree murder.

Or maybe not: Perhaps it was simpler. Perhaps he once again was
defending a murderer, and once again was trying to convince himself
otherwise. In truth, Sarah herself wasn't claiming innocence with
much vigor. Sarah was conveniently going away whenever Greg
pressed her. Games within games. That's what he'd been drawn into.
And what if he won those games? Might another unstable killer end
up walking the streets of a bucolic Central California town? Perfect,
Greg thought. Maybe he could bag another Lawyer of the Year
Award to boot.

Thus occupied, Greg didn't at first notice the car trailing him far
in the distance. Only as it began to close on him did he catch its image in his rearview mirror. Since there was no turnoff on this cliffside
road, and the gravelly curves made speeding up a reckless maneuver,
Greg slowed down instead. He wanted to see who was following him.

Whoever it was, he didn't appear to be in a hurry. Each time the
two cars rounded another bend they were closer together, but not
by much. Watching in his rearview mirror, Greg measured the slowly
narrowing gap. Not until they were fifty feet apart did he spot the
big red spotlights set in the other car's rear window. He had a black-

and-white on his tail. Property of the El Nido County Sheriff's Department.

Yet the man behind the wheel didn't look like a sheriff's deputy. At twenty feet, Greg could see him clearly. He had a fat face and a ragged reddish-brown beard. He was wearing what looked to be overalls. Greg had the sense he'd seen him before, but couldn't place where. He also had the sense that this wasn't the spot to get reacquainted.

Greg punched his accelerator, exploding in a cloud of dust and pebbles. Going into the first curve, he kept his foot on the gas. By the second bend he'd lost sight of the black-and-white. At the third he saw a dirt road off to the right that climbed into the mountains. A cattle guard blocked it. Greg braked hard, jumped out, threw open the gate. Once through it, he stopped and pulled the gate shut. Then he again hit the gas.

Ten minutes down the road, Greg decided he'd lost both the black-and-white and his way. He didn't know where he was. Yet the meadows and slopes looked familiar. He tried to envision the route he'd followed in the past half hour. It occurred to him he'd traveled in a wide arc, a sort of half-circle. He must now be in the foothills to the north of El Nido Village, heading southwest. He was, in other words, approaching the back end of Sanborn Ranch.

Ten minutes more and he was there. With an odd sense of appreciation, he drove down the trail that led toward the Sanborn stables, and then beyond to the main house. He parked near the barn and climbed out of his car, feeling as if he'd reached a sanctuary. Diana greeted him at the door to the kitchen.

"Glad you're home . . ." Greg began to say. Then he noticed Diana's expression. She appeared distraught.

"Sheriff Rimmer is looking for you," she said.

"Tell me about it. I've been in a chase—"

"Greg, you don't understand. One of the guards, out at the prison. He's saying he saw you have improper physical contact with Sarah Trant."

Greg's throat went dry. He tried to speak but couldn't.

"They've filed a report about you," Diana said. "Sheriff Rimmer has it in his mind to charge you with sexual misconduct."

Jasmine Gest, loping atop the Appaloosa she called Dusty, felt his eyes from one hundred yards away. Instantly, she sensed he was waiting for her. Fred Darvill, the wizened but still sharp-tongued eighty-year-old proprietor of El Nido Antiques, was not the sort to wander along the equestrian trail in Sanborn Park. He would more likely be found beside the spittoon in the Gaucho Tavern, or else beside his calculator and ledgers. Whiskey and profits, that's what interested the old coot. Except for now, on this warm autumn afternoon. Jas shifted in her saddle. What did he want with her?

"Hey there, Jasmine," Darvill called out. "Pretty sunset isn't it?"

Jas reluctantly reined in Dusty. Besides running his antique shop, Darvill served as curator at the local historical museum. She worked for him in a sense, although without getting paid, at least not in money. What he provided her was an acute ear on various rumblings in the community.

"Actually," she said, "I'd call it your average sunset."

Darvill spit a gob of tobacco-stained saliva onto the edge of the horse path, then suddenly launched into a volley of sneezing. Bent over, a red handkerchief to his nose, he heaved and snorted. With a bald sunburned head and a scratchy five-day-old white beard, he suggested to Jas a miner fresh from the Sierra foothills. "Damn allergies," Darvill muttered when he'd finished. "Happens whenever I even walk through the park."

Jas shook her head in sympathy. Darvill was an eccentric curmudgeon, but at least he could spin some droll tales, and he meant no harm. Born and raised in El Nido, he knew more about the valley's history than anyone, and cared about it in a way far different from his fellow merchants. Jas wasn't sure, but thought he'd even sided with Sarah Trant during some of her confrontations with ModoCorp.

"So why are you in the park, Mr. Darvill?"

The old man extracted a folded manila envelope from his jacket pocket and pressed it into Jas's hand. His eyes glinted. "The welfare of El Nido, that's why I'm here, Jasmine."

Jas glanced at the envelope but didn't open it. "I'm afraid you've lost me. What is this?"

Darvill moved closer and began to stroke her horse's neck. "Cattle . . . that's what it is. Dead cattle."

Jas searched her memory. "Is this museum business, Mr. Darvill?"

The old man started sneezing again. Bent over nearly double, he looked as if he were suffocating. Jas jumped off Dusty and came to his side. He reached for her arm to steady himself. His eyes had turned red and watery, yet still they showed a spark. "Not museum business, no, Jasmine. Newspaper business. Something for you to write about."

"Something for me—"

Darvill waved her off. "Got to get out of here, Jas. Damn pollen is going to kill me." He turned away, then looked back over his shoulder. "You didn't get this stuff from me, didn't even see me. But read what's in there. See what you think."

She watched him hobble down the path, then tore open the envelope he'd left her. From it she pulled out four typed pages and three photographs. Dead cattle, he'd said, and that's what the photos showed. Jas studied the pages. "CALIFORNIA DEPT. OF AGRICULTURE," read the uppercase words at the top of each sheet. Then, under it: "Confidential Document. Not For Public Release."

Jas looked up, searching the park for a sign of Darvill, but he'd disappeared. She turned back to the pages and began reading. Each page described in fine detail the death of a single cow. Three dead heifers, total. All in the El Nido Valley over the past six months. All at Sanborn Ranch.

Jas couldn't follow the technical jargon that filled most of the pages. She could tell only that they'd taken samples and performed tests, vainly searching for a cause of the deaths. One of the cows had lungs filled with fluid, but the two others had simply ceased breathing; it was as if their brains had stopped sending signals to inhale and exhale. *Precise explanation unavailable* is how the state bureaucrats put it. On each page, that same conclusion: *Precise explanation unavailable.*

That was all. Reaching the end of the report, Jas flipped back through the pages to the start and read them again. Obscure and qualify, that was the timeworn hallmark of state bureaucrats. Yet even for them, this report stood out. They didn't want to speculate, they weren't sure, they didn't really know. *Precise explanation unavailable.* That's all they could say.

Jas mounted Dusty and kicked her into a fast lope. Darvill was certainly right about one thing. This was something for her to write about.

AFTER REREADING JAS'S ARTICLE while sitting by the fountain in Sanborn Park, Greg walked across the street and along the Arcade. At the entrance to Gaucho's Tavern he stopped. From inside the bar he thought he heard the voice of Alex Ramirez. Greg stepped through Gaucho's swinging door. The room before him was dark and narrow, packed with six billiards tables, side by side. Off to the right, a chipped oak bar ran the length of the room. In the rear, a big-screen TV filled the back wall.

There was Alex, on the TV screen. He had to admit, Alex was effective. Greg ordered a Graciosa Brew and settled on a stool at the end of the bar nearest the screen. Alex stood before the camera without artifice: the cowboy hat pushed back on his head, the toothpick rolling slowly in his mouth, the eyes full of deadpan pride. "The state scientists came down and investigated. They found no explanation. We suspect some sort of virus. Just one of those things. It's not unknown. If you run cattle as long as my family, you see these things. . . ."

You did indeed, Greg thought. In Chumash County, he recalled from his history lessons, a brutal drought wiped out some three hundred thousand head between 1862 and 1864, leaving bleached bones strewn throughout the arroyos. It also left many cattle-baron families bereft. As the local historians told it, a young ranchero who lost everything hitched his wildest horse to a buckboard one windy moonlit night and rattled out of town, watched only by a solitary fevered old woman, propped up by her window. Out near the fog-enshrouded Clam Beach cliffs, it was said, he whipped his horse to a frenzy, then plunged with it over the rim to the wet rocks below, leaving only a broken wheel at the cliff's edge as a farewell note.

Greg found himself trying to sort out his thoughts about Diana Sanborn. She wasn't an ally; she was, in truth, an adversary, the person whose testimony put Sarah on death row. Yet he felt an inexplicable concern for her. A threatening blackmail letter, now three dead cows: What was going on? Why was this woman under siege?

Glancing up to the TV, Greg saw that Diana had joined Alex. "The state tells us a precise explanation is unavailable . . . ," she was saying. "Surely this will pass. . . . We live in a grand unspoilt valley . . ."

Greg sensed someone at his elbow. He turned to find Jasmine Gest on the stool beside him. They'd been regularly crossing paths like this, without apparent plan. Greg knew the contact wasn't as random as it seemed.

"What do you think?" Jas asked. "You believe them?"

"No, I don't. I wonder, though."

"About what?"

"Diana Sanborn seems to me a woman in need of help."

Jas regarded him with amused skepticism. "Not an appropriate feeling for Sarah Trant's lawyer, I'd say. Diana Sanborn is Sarah's worst enemy."

Greg put his bottle down. He'd grown accustomed to sparring with her. "Thanks for the input. But I think I'm still capable of deciding which of my feelings is appropriate."

"Ooooh," she said. "Such vehemence."

"I'm just trying to sort things out, Jas."

"You need to do your sorting all alone? God, Greg . . . Don't tell me you're one of those men who still needs his space."

"What I need," he said, "is more information."

She instantly turned serious. "Such as?"

"Diana and Sarah. Tell me more about the two of them together."

Jas mulled his question before speaking. "From what I can tell," she said finally, "Diana was Sarah's Svengali. Sarah adored her, worshiped her. Would do anything Diana asked."

"Why? What was Diana's hold on her?"

"You would need a shrink to answer that one. All I know is, Sarah changed around Diana. Got so sparkly, and focused, too. Especially when Diana did her grand-old-lady turn. The gracious-yet-commanding stuff. Sarah really came alive then."

"That displeased you?"

Jas lifted a beer to her lips. "It's just that sometimes I got the sense Diana was manipulating Sarah."

"Maybe she was helping Sarah. Galvanizing her. There are moments when Sarah needs that."

Jas tapped the bar counter. "You see all sides and possibilities, don't you, Greg? Nothing is ever black-and-white."

"What about you? Your world is lit by bright clarity?"

"Sometimes, yes, sometimes things are clear."

"So that's your worldview. At the park that first night, you said 'let's save it for later.' I've been waiting ever since."

"Sorry . . . You're still waiting."

"A bit more complicated than bright clarity?"

"Oh yes."

"Tell me about it."

"You have a few days?"

"I could find them."

"Warning . . . I'm a handful."

"I bet."

"Do you?"

Greg studied her. "You blame Diana for Sarah's situation?" he asked. "You think Diana egged her on? Set her against ModoCorp and Tomaz?"

She looked away. "Wouldn't say that exactly. Sarah had her own ax to grind, after all. She didn't need Diana to get her marching and shoving. . . . And yet, who knows? . . . I wonder . . ."

"Aha." Greg gave her a look full of mock surprise. "The matter is shaded, then."

Jas started to respond, but new voices distracted them. They glanced back at the TV. Alex and Diana had been replaced by a twenty-second "bright" concerning volunteer crafts programs in El Nido's elementary schools. Greg imagined himself up there on the screen, cornered by the camera as the anchor warned about "alarming charges" of sexual misconduct at the women's prison.

"You're right about one thing," he told Jas. "I do see all possibilities."

THE POST OFFICE TOWER bell chimed the seven o'clock hour as Greg walked through Sanborn Park. Dusk once again was falling. On the equestrian trail, a scattering of riders and bicyclists dodged the occasional walker. Greg realized that he'd grown accustomed to the rhythms of this town.

At the edge of the park's west boundary, he stopped. He was standing before the county administrative building. In the window of the district attorney's suite, he saw lights still burning. He studied them for a minute, then pushed open the building's front door. The staff had gone home for the night; he had the hallways to himself. He knocked at Jim Mashburn's door. The DA opened it himself, looking distracted. The sleeves of his brown cardigan were pushed up above his elbows. A pair of reading glasses sat on the bridge of his nose. In the gloom, Mashburn squinted. "Greg," he sputtered. "What are you doing here?"

"Saw your light on, thought we might chat for a minute."

Mashburn stood in silence. His displeasure was palpable. "Way to do that is to make an appointment. Call my office tomorrow."

Greg put a hand on the door to keep it open. "Come on, Jim. We need to talk."

Mashburn looked about, as if searching for a means of escape. He put a hand on his side of the door. For a moment they stood like that, gauging the pressure each could feel from the other. Then Mashburn shrugged, and waved Greg inside.

They sat across from each other, Mashburn barricaded behind a desk piled high with transcripts and briefs. Greg wondered what he'd find in those stacks if given the chance to explore. The federal discovery process had yielded multiple revelations, but surely Mashburn hadn't handed over everything.

"How are things in Chumash County?" Mashburn asked. "You still have that house on the creek?"

"Still there. But our buddy Dennis Taylor, as you know, has moved on. From Chumash County DA to state attorney general, just as he always planned."

"Yes. . . . Yes, I see Dennis from time to time."

"Ever remind Taylor of the summer you tussled with him over his grand jury probe?"

Mashburn held up a hand in protest. "*We* tussled with him. The summer *we* tussled with him."

"Yes, that's right. The two of us."

Mashburn rose and turned toward the window that gave onto a view of Sanborn Park. In the dark, illuminated only by a solitary streetlight's yellow flicker, the fountain looked like an apparition. "Hell of a lot has passed under the bridge since then."

Greg watched him. The moon lit one side of Mashburn's face; the other remained in shadows. "You were going to quit the law, I thought. Change your whole life. A new direction."

Mashburn turned toward him. "And you were going to stop defending killers. Told me you were sick of all that. That day we hiked in the dunes."

Greg reflected. He remembered an honest camaraderie with Mashburn, but he didn't recall saying such a thing. What did it matter, anyway? Whatever he'd said, they were just words, uttered years ago.

"I've had the chance to look at the responses you filed in federal court," Greg advised. "I'm wondering about them."

Mashburn stared at him. "Wondering what, Greg?"

"Whether you really want to make such representations to Judge Solman."

Mashburn walked back to his desk and sat down. "Stop, Greg. This is how it's done. You want to challenge the state's claims, do it in court. You're wasting our time."

Greg studied the DA. Yes, they had talked that day. After celebrating their victory over the local Chumash County prosecutor, they'd imagined other lives they might live. It had been just an afternoon's fantasy. Yet they had talked.

Greg said, "You claim in your response that Diana Sanborn right away told deputies about Tomaz's dying declaration. Right there at the river. On the very first night. Yet this isn't reflected in the initial police reports. It's also not what was represented five years ago at Sarah's trial. Or to me at any time since I started taking depositions."

Mashburn rubbed his temples, looking irritated. "That's all explained in my response, Greg. There was a lot of confusion back then about what was said when, to whom. One of the key deputy sheriffs went on medical leave because of a heart attack right after Tomaz's death, so files got mislaid and communications broke down. We've just now found that deputy's original handwritten notes. He spoke to Ms. Sanborn that first night. Looking at his notes, we found that he recorded mention by Diana of a dying declaration. It just didn't get into a formal report for a few days."

"Oh, come on, Jim . . ."

Mashburn held his hands palm up. "We have an affidavit from the deputy about this, Greg. We have a document expert affirming the handwritten notes are genuine, and five years old."

"And what do you think, Jim?"

"What do you mean?"

"You think this is how it happened?"

"Yes. . . . Damnit Greg, it can be proven."

"How do you know what happened?"

"How do I know? I have all this evidence. I have—"

"Jim, come on. You weren't there at the time, you weren't the DA. Where's it coming from?"

Mashburn hesitated. "Sheriff Kimmer," he said. "It's Roy's story."

Greg said nothing.

"But damnit, Greg, we also have Diana Sanborn. She agrees she spoke to this deputy."

Greg couldn't hide his surprise. "Diana? She goes along with this?"

Mashburn allowed himself a small, tight grin. "She most certainly does. We have an affidavit."

"You do? When did she sign it?"

"Just last week."

Greg labored to understand. To him, Diana had openly admitted making a belated report about the dying declaration. *I was trying to protect Sarah.* Why switch tales now? "How'd you get to her, Jim?"

Mashburn flushed. "I resent that, Greg."

Greg didn't care. An angry James Mashburn would be better

than this fellow. "Something lopsided here, Mr. DA. Something to investigate, maybe."

"You're way out of bounds, Greg—"

"One other thing," Greg said. "How do you sleep at night?"

Mashburn rose from his chair and started around his desk. Greg rose too. The DA stopped inches from him. "You sanctimonious hypocrite," Mashburn said. "A man of your morals shouldn't point fingers at anyone else."

"My morals?"

Mashburn's expression had turned stony. "Sheriff Rimmer tells me you were caught handling your client in the interview room. Just about to wet your willie, way Rimmer tells it."

"Yet another bit of fiction from the El Nido County sheriff."

"Everyone spins stories but you, Greg? Is that how it works?"

"How can you stand side by side with someone like Rimmer?"

Mashburn pointed Greg toward the door. "To be a prosecutor you have to make choices," he said. "You have to decide. And I've decided. I'm filing charges against you."

E L E V E N

Hot fierce winds roared through the El Nido Valley on the morning Sarah Trant's hearing was to start. The smell of sage and greasewood filled the air; the usual sound of birds had given way to the occasional buzz of a deerfly. Diana Sanborn, rising from a troubled sleep, immediately sensed something amiss. At her window, she pulled back the thick drapes. In the distance, at the far northwest side of the valley, she saw an ominous pall of reddish-brown smoke rising from the towering La Luna Mountain Range. It had been a dry year, and now, in October, the brush and timber were crackle dry. If prevailing winds shifted, Diana calculated, the fire might reach the valley by late afternoon.

She turned her ear to the window. On hot days you could hear the post office bell for miles. As she expected, it was tolling now. That bell always sounded at the report of a fire. The alarm brought out all the able-bodied men in El Nido, Alex among them. They'd soon be gathering at the edge of Sanborn Park, their arms full of backpacks and axes and water bottles.

Diana's thoughts drifted to other fires, long-ago fires in El Nido. She was seven when the most ferocious one nearly destroyed the entire valley. Her grandfather depended on her help even then. That first afternoon she filled buckets and rolled out garden hoses while Edward Sanborn consulted with his ranch crew and the local rangers. They all ate supper that evening under a big oak tree with the aid of a kerosene lantern. Then they hiked to the top of the highest hill on the ranch to inspect the distant blaze. The others all looked worried, so Diana matched their expression. Privately, though, she exulted at the thrilling wall of flames.

While they watched, the wind shifted suddenly toward the valley floor. By nine P.M. the fire, blown into unburned brush and timber along the hillside, had flared. By ten it had traveled eight miles, and was licking at the edge of El Nido's northernmost residential district. Diana's grandfather gathered tools and blankets, kissed her goodbye, and headed off to fight the flames.

The second day remained a blur to Diana. She remembered only a solid overcast of smoke over the entire valley, with no sun visible. She remembered almost everyone in El Nido madly fleeing from the valley by auto, buckboard, horse, and foot. Most of all, she remembered her grandfather returning to their ranch and staying put, refusing to believe that a fire would have the effrontery to burn him out.

By afternoon, their end of the valley was just about deserted but for Edward Sanborn's family and crew. By nine the trees and sky all around them glowed red. By ten the winds were howling at thirty miles an hour and the live oaks had begun to steam. Diana cried then, no longer so thrilled, but still her grandfather stood his ground. Not until nearly midnight, with the fire cresting the ridge just two miles from the ranch, did the winds shift, carrying flames back across already-blackened acreage. Without fuel, the hungry fire began to abate. "I knew we wouldn't be burnt out," Edward Sanborn told Diana, holding his granddaughter tightly in his arms. "I wasn't going to let that happen to us."

From her window Diana surveyed her perfect valley. Nothing stirred yet. No glowing red branches, no steaming oaks, no howling gale. Perhaps the winds would hold, perhaps the fire wouldn't reach them. To her surprise, Diana felt the slightest twinge of regret at that notion. Maybe El Nido needed a cleansing fire. A fire that consumed their history and legacy. A fire that allowed them all to start afresh.

Diana shook off such thoughts and turned her eyes to the mountain pass that led to Chumash County. Just sixty miles through that pass, Sarah Trant's hearing was about to begin in La Graciosa's auxiliary courtroom. Diana tried to imagine that vintage chamber, with Sarah sitting beside Greg Monarch at the petitioner's table. She tried also to imagine herself in that room. On which day, she wondered, would Greg Monarch call her to the witness stand?

"WELL NOW, GENTLEMEN," JUDGE Solman was saying, "it looks like we have some preliminary business to handle. Make yourselves at home. Sit down."

They were standing in Solman's chambers, Greg Monarch and James Mashburn. The two settled into chairs before the judge's desk. Greg had never felt personally warm toward Solman, nor connected to him by bonds of taste or outlook. At this moment, though, he keenly appreciated that Solman would be presiding over Sarah's hearing.

"I'd ask that this conference be under seal," Greg began.

Solman held up a hand. "Let's hear first what it's about, okay? Then I'll decide. Does the DA's office want to start?"

Mashburn reached for a file, opened it, studied the pages before him. "The problem we have here," he said, "is that there's an issue concerning Mr. Monarch. A prison guard reports he saw him, well, having intimate contact with Sarah Trant."

Solman flinched at those words ever so slightly, but enough for Greg to notice. His hand moved to his forehead. "What?" he asked.

Mashburn kept his eyes on the pages in his hand. "The guard described what he saw to his supervisor, who brought it to us. We feel we can't just sit on this."

"Is that so?" Solman asked.

"Yes. . . . We feel this needs to be revealed."

"Let me see the guard's report," Solman commanded.

From the file on his lap, the DA handed over a two-page document. Solman scanned it, then reread it more slowly.

"Why?" the judge asked. "Why do you feel this needs to be revealed?"

"At the very least because it speaks to the character of the petitioner's lawyer. More important, it may mean Greg can't continue in this proceeding. We may very well choose to file charges against him."

Solman turned to Greg with raised eyebrows.

"First, I dispute every word in this report," Greg said. "Second, the DA's office has never even questioned me about these charges. They've just been waving the report in my face. Mr. Mashburn says he 'may very well' file charges. I respectfully submit that's garbage. He's trying to force me off the case."

Solman took off his reading glasses and squeezed the bridge of his nose. "Is that what you're trying to do, Mr. Mashburn?"

"No, Your Honor. That's not what I'm trying to do. My intent is twofold. One is to enforce the laws of El Nido County. The other is to protect this case's integrity. We go forward with Greg on the case, Sarah Trant would have a great basis for an appeal. Incompetent defense counsel due to inappropriate emotional involvement . . . I can hear Ms. Trant's next attorney shouting such words even now."

Solman again studied the guard's report. He held the document as a shield between him and the lawyers. "Inapproriate emotional involvement?" he asked. "What exactly do you mean, Mr. Mashburn?"

The DA glanced at Greg. "It's not just what happened at the prison, Your Honor. We've learned that Greg and Sarah once had a relationship. They were lovers. They—"

"What the hell are you doing, Jim?" Greg was half out of his seat, his voice rising. "I don't know where you 'learned' that. . . . Actually, I can imagine. . . . But it's no secret, and nothing that needs hiding. It happened more than twenty years ago. It's irrelevant now. You know that, Jim. You know that perfectly well."

Solman was looking at Greg. "So that's why Sarah asked for you. . . ."

Greg ignored him. "Tell me, Jim. . . . Have your investigators interviewed Sarah Trant? Has Sarah confirmed the guard's report?"

Mashburn scowled. "She denied it. What else is she going to do? She loses her attorney otherwise. Perhaps her attorney even warned her that might happen if she talked. Perhaps—"

"Wait a minute," Judge Solman interrupted. "She's not making any accusation at all? She's disputing the accusation?"

Mashburn shifted in his seat. "Yes, sir, but—"

"So what's this about?" Solman interrupted again. "What are you doing?"

"As I said, we're enforcing our county's laws, and protecting our case."

The judge hesitated, tapping his desk with a pencil. His gaze swung from the DA to the defense attorney, then back again. The sight of Solman momentarily wavering reminded Greg that this man had that quality in him.

"Sorry, Mr. Mashburn," the judge said finally. "Your county's laws are of no concern at a federal habeas proceeding."

"But protecting our case does matter here, Your Honor. If this goes to appeal—"

"Okay, now." Solman waved Mashburn off. "I'll tell you what. I see what you have here, and I'm just not going to get into it. This is a federal habeas proceeding. You think you can pin a sex charge on Greg, give it a try. Go file over there in El Nido County Court. It's your prerogative. Give it a try."

Mashburn stuffed the guard's report back into his file as if it were contaminated. "Yes, Your Honor," he snapped. "We might just do that."

Greg stood up.

"Gentlemen," the judge declared, "we'll begin the hearing after lunch."

RISING FROM THEIR CREEKSIDE table at Stella's Café, Greg and Jas could smell smoke in the air. Their eyes instinctively traveled to the vast distant mountain range that separated La Graciosa from the hot inland valleys. The edge of an ugly brown cloud showed over the range's crest. A helicopter hovered silently off to one side. "Seems well to the north," Jas said. "Don't think that's near El Nido."

Greg didn't appear to hear her. "The one who puzzles me," he said, "is Mashburn. How could he be doing this? Defending the characters who prosecuted Sarah. Waving a phony charge at me. As if he doesn't have a conscience at all."

Slowly, Jas turned away from the mountains. "Of course, Mashburn might say the same about you. Defending an obvious killer. Playing games with the legal system. Obscuring the truth."

"Yes," Greg agreed. "He might."

She put a hand on his arm. "Jim Mashburn is no more sure of his role than you are. You both question what you're doing. You both have a conscience problem."

"Only in the law," Greg said, "would we call it a problem."

They'd spent the lunch hour analyzing the merits of Sarah's case. Despite everything damning he'd uncovered during discovery, Greg wanted more. A mind so inclined could still think Sarah looked mighty guilty. It would, Greg reasoned, finally come down to Brewster Tomaz's dying declaration, and that was the problem. Greg had managed to find a respected forensic pathologist who didn't think an expiring Tomaz could speak, but his was a qualified judgment. What with all the blood in the autopsy photos, Dr. Oscar Quagler, the medical examiner for San Luis, could only infer that Tomaz's carotid was cut. Which left the state a nice hole through which to run their own experts. The two doctors who did the autopsy would swear that the carotid hadn't been cut, and Dr. Montrose would agree with them that speech was possible. They'd end up with a stalemate, in other words. Nothing conclusive for either of them. Yet each lawyer would act as if he had God on his side.

Mashburn, of course, had someone of almost equal importance. *We also have Diana.* That's how Mashburn had put it. *We also have Diana.*

"Jas," Greg said as they walked the creekside pathway toward La Graciosa's courthouse, "that piece you wrote about the dead cattle at Sanborn Ranch. What's the inside story? What didn't you share with El Nido's citizens?"

Jas sniffed the air and glanced back at the mountain range. "Nothing more to know. I wrote what I had."

They were at La Graciosa's town square, in front of the courthouse. Greg looked at his watch. "We have time. Let's sit for a while."

They settled on a bench near the creek. The plaza was popular at midday. Shoppers and office workers strolled at the water's edge, lounged near the bear fountain, ate sandwiches under spreading sycamores. Here and there, someone called out to Greg, waving. The newspaperman Jimmy O'Brien, as usual full of exuberant bombast, came over to complain. *Small-minded editors don't want me to cover your hearing, damnit. Nothing to do with Chumash County, they say. What the hell. Got something else even bigger right now. Tell you about it tonight . . .* Then Tim Ruthman headed his way, openly seeking congratulations. Two days before, he'd won Greg's drug case for him.

"Just keep passing those potheads to me," Ruthman grinned. "Helps pay the kid's orthodontia bills."

Greg smiled back with genuine appreciation. Ruthman, with his broad shoulders and thick mustache gone half to gray, looked more like an aging linebacker than a lawyer. Yet he knew how to work a courtroom. Greg truly needed him, now that the habeas hearing was under way. "Might just have to do that, Tim. Going to be tied up before Judge Solman for a while. In fact, I'll call you later today. Two more files need moving off my desk."

Ruthman glanced at Jas with open curiosity. Greg made the introductions without explaining who she was. Ruthman shot Greg a sideways wink as he turned and left. Jas laughed. "That's okay, Greg," she said. "I like being a mystery."

They gazed out at the creek. Below them, at the water's edge, a mother was helping her young daughter feed bread crumbs to a trio of hungry ducks. Greg watched as the birds grabbed their morsels, then drifted downstream. *Birds in the water.* The image tugged at him. He'd sat with Jas once before, watching a bird in the water. But it was a dead bird. A dead cormorant mired in an oil slick in the middle of El Nido Lake. Dead birds, then dead cattle.

"Explain to me again about El Nido's oil, Jas."

"What exactly do you want to know?"

"You told me at the lake how it oozed everywhere but wasn't worth anything. Low-grade unusable oil, and only in surface pockets. Drove all the oil prospectors to ruin a century ago."

"Yes. That's true. But it took some of them a long time to realize they'd failed. Lots of stuff about that in our historical museum. Memoirs, records, deeds. Come by sometime, I'll show you. Because I volunteer there, they let me roam at will."

"I'll do that when there's time. Just give me an overview right now."

"Not sure I can. Trouble is, I haven't really read that stuff closely. Didn't appear terribly interesting, to tell you the truth. A bunch of failures, a bunch of false turns in El Nido's history. It wasn't the valley's destiny, it's not what El Nido is about."

"What do you mean?"

"I mean visions of oil fields quickly faded after one false boom."

Jas chewed on that, then continued. "You know, it's really something. Had El Nido's history been different, had the experts found the petroleum that they expected, the valley might be full of oil rigs instead of farms and orchards."

Greg was still staring at the creek. "It is something, isn't it?"

Jas watched him as if waiting for a signal, or another question. When none came, she moved closer to him on the bench.

"Why are you asking about this, Greg? What's it about?"

"Probably nothing."

Jas moved closer yet. She looked at him frankly, but he wouldn't meet her gaze. "What's with you?" she asked.

He kept his eyes on the moving water. "Sarah's execution date."

Jas raised a hand to his chin and turned his face toward her. "Who disappointed you so badly?" she asked. "Or did she scare you?"

"Let's go," Greg said, rising from the bench. "The hearing is about to start."

ON THE WAY TO the courtroom, Greg stopped to visit Sarah in her prison cell. With regret, he pointedly asked a guard to remain in full sight just outside the barred window. Sarah sat on her cot in a simple white cotton dress and sandals. She looked uncomfortable.

"They came and questioned me," she said. "About you. About you and me."

"Yes, I know. They're trying to knock me off the case."

Sarah raised her hand to her mouth. "How could they do that?"

"They're threatening to charge me with sexual contact with you, Sarah."

"They call that sexual contact? Jesus . . ."

"It's okay," Greg said. "Don't bother. It won't come to anything."

"The hearing . . . ?"

"It's about to start. They'll be bringing you into the courtroom in a few minutes."

"What am I supposed to say?"

Greg glanced at the guard watching them, then moved closer to Sarah, lowering his voice. "If I call you to the stand, you're to tell what happened. Don't hide anything, don't change anything. Just tell the truth. You pushed Tomaz, he fell in the river, you ran off, you saw no one else."

"I . . . but . . . I . . ."

"Don't worry. You won't be called right away," Greg said. "And maybe not at all."

"Oh . . ."

"Sarah, tell me something." Greg kneeled down to where she sat. "Did Diana Sanborn ever talk to you about oil in the El Nido Valley?"

That question transformed Sarah; her eyes grew focused and fierce. "No," she said. "We never talked about any such thing."

THERE'D BE NO JURY this time, just a solitary federal judge. Greg, entering the *asistencia's* courtroom, reflexively turned his eyes to the empty bench where Solman soon would be sitting. He didn't expect this judge, or any judge, to guarantee him justice—only a level playing field. He'd do the rest himself.

Greg glanced around. No more than a handful of spectators had claimed seats; the other lawyers and Sarah Trant had yet to arrive. Chumash County's auxiliary courtroom occupied what had been, a century before, the *asistencia's* modest church. It had a vaulted and beamed ceiling, but was compact and narrow, only twenty-five feet in width, with seats for just 150 in twelve rows. Not the usual venue for a federal proceeding; instead of dark walnut walls and thick carpets, this one offered whitewashed plaster and pink-hued, hand-laid cement. It would be odd, arguing a federal habeas here in La Graciosa.

"I hope you understand I had to do that, Greg."

James Mashburn was standing at his end of the attorney's table, unpacking his briefcase.

"Do what?" Greg asked, acting mystified.

"Protect my case."

"That's what you call what happened in Solman's chambers?"

Mashburn threw a stack of files on the table. "Yes, damnit, that's what I call it."

"Then why hope for my understanding? It's all perfectly clear, isn't it, Jim?"

Mashburn's frown showed more unease than anger. He took a step back. His tone softened. "What do you say, Greg. Shall we get on with this hearing?"

"Soon as Judge Solman gets here."

The DA, leafing through papers now, kept his head down. "I heard something over lunch. Heard there's a problem with Solman."

At first Greg didn't register Mashburn's words. Then he did. He turned to the DA. "A problem? What do you mean?" Greg started toward Mashburn, but stopped when he saw Sarah Trant being led his way. She kept glancing about, as if trying to understand her surroundings. Gone were the focused, fierce eyes.

"He had some out-of-town visitors with him in his chambers," Mashburn said. "Fainted or something, right in front of them. A van full of paramedics came, then a doctor. For a while they weren't sure whether he could preside at this hearing."

"All rise!" the court bailiff called out.

Through the door leading to the judges' chambers came a pale stiff figure wrapped in black robes. He reached the bench and stopped for a moment, surveying the courtroom. The judge's robes billowed and opened enough for Greg to see the hints of Solman's fine charcoal-gray suit. Standing before them with narrowed eyes and a stiffly set jaw, Solman suggested a man determined to stay his course. He wouldn't look at Greg.

"Good afternoon," Solman said. "Sorry for the delay. I was taken dizzy in my chambers. They say I'm just fine now."

"Your Honor . . ." Greg started to approach the bench, framing his motion as he walked. Something had happened in the judge's chambers, something had transformed Solman. "I would like—"

"Don't bother, Mr. Monarch." Solman was waving him away, his mouth pinched with annoyance. "There's no point filing a motion to delay. I've been given a clean bill of health. I most certainly will be presiding at this habeas hearing."

"Answer me, please. Did you not see that the left carotid artery had been totally severed?" In face of the witness's silence, Greg repeated his question. "Did you not see that the carotid had been cut?"

The petitioner went first at a habeas hearing, and Greg had started with Buster Lloyd, the emergency medical technician who'd examined Tomaz's bloodied body. Lloyd had cut his ponytail and bushy beard, so he looked nothing like the mountain man Greg had met weeks before at the end of Old Alder Road. He suggested now an eager junior executive at a bustling health maintenance organization. Which, in fact, he was. Health Shield, a giant Central California HMO, had hired him a month before, offering a lucrative post overseeing all operations in El Nido County.

"There was so much blood," Lloyd finally replied, frowning over Greg's question. "I couldn't really make it out clearly."

Greg nodded as if that were precisely the response he wanted. This was the third time Lloyd had ducked him. He'd expected something like this. They'd flipped Reggie Dodge's witnesses, so why not his? He just hadn't known which ones they'd get.

"But it was severed," Greg said. "To me, in your deposition, you said it was severed."

Another pause. "I'm not sure. . . . Yes . . . well . . ."

"Mr. Lloyd, you are under oath."

Without expression, Buster stared out into the courtroom. "I wasn't in a position right up close to his neck. I . . . I don't remember specifically seeing exactly the left carotid artery."

Greg approached, and stood within inches of the witness. "Would it refresh your recollection if you looked at what you told me in your deposition?"

This time the pause stretched on for twenty seconds. It didn't appear as if Buster would answer.

"Your deposition," Greg said finally. "Where you were also under oath?"

"Okay . . . yes."

Greg handed him his deposition and pointed at the relevant lines. Lloyd read, then looked up.

"Well, okay, yes," he said. "I recall saying that."

"But the question is, does it refresh your recollection of actually seeing the severed artery?"

Lloyd frowned and started to stroke the beard he'd shaved off. "We didn't explore the wound. We didn't open it up. There was so much blood."

"In your deposition you said—"

"But I never told the police that," Lloyd interrupted. "I never told them I saw a cut carotid."

Greg leaned against the witness stand railing as if he were this man's neighbor. "Mr. Lloyd, do you recall telling me that the police never even interviewed you after Brewster Tomaz's murder?"

Lloyd made a show of great puzzlement. "But there's a police report, Mr. Monarch. A police report of their interview with me."

Greg tried a flash of anger. "You're under oath, Mr. Lloyd. Yes or no. Didn't you say the police never interviewed—"

Mashburn interrupted: "Your Honor, I object. Asked and answered. He's badgering his own witness."

Greg headed for his chair before Solman could respond. "That's okay," he said. "No more questions."

BUSTER WAS ONLY THE start. Witness after witness took the stand sounding not the least like the people Greg had deposed. They qualified where they'd once been certain; they were vague where they'd once been precise. A deputy sheriff couldn't recall just where along the river he'd seen the strange boot prints with nailed half-soles. An audio technician couldn't explain the odd clicks heard on a taped interview with Sarah Trant. An evidence clerk wasn't sure she'd ever seen various now-missing photos of the murder scene. *It's possible but not likely. . . . It's hard to say. . . . The photos are blurry. I wasn't there. . . .* Greg hammered them hard, reading passages from their depositions, pointing out discrepancies between their words then and now. He'd deposed everyone he could find for just this reason: to pin them down before they were turned. Yet even with their previous testimony before them, the witnesses frowned and coughed and shifted about. *It's hard to say. . . . I wasn't there.*

"This reminds me of my murder trial," Sarah whispered during a brief lull. "Exactly the same. Poor Reggie. He hadn't a clue."

"We've got a clue," Greg replied, "but we've still got some terribly malleable witnesses."

"They're denying their own words. . . ."

"Yes. Plenty of baffled good ol' boy aplomb . . . Plays well in most courtrooms."

Greg was sitting as if coiled for attack, drumming his fingers on the attorney's table. Sarah looked at him with pleading eyes. "Thank God you're not confused, Greg. . . . Please don't get confused."

GREG WATCHED AS MASHBURN poured two spoons of sugar into his coffee, then reached for a peach Danish. They were in Judge Solman's chambers on the third morning of the hearing. Solman sipped a cup of tea behind his desk. Greg drank water.

"What's this about, Greg?" Solman asked. His voice now had a nervous edge to it almost constantly. "I'd like to keep these private sessions in chambers to a minimum. Public has a right to know what's going on."

What is this about. Greg wondered how to answer. The night before, he'd visited the spinster Judith Daniels to arrange her transportation to this hearing. Judith Daniels, the critical eyewitness who'd seen someone other than Sarah Trant fleeing upriver at the time of the murder. She'd not been called or even revealed during Sarah's initial murder trial, yet she'd been cooperative over the past few weeks with Greg and Jas. Coherent, too. Pot of fresh-brewed coffee always on the stove, like someone's grandmother. Sometimes a plate of just-baked chocolate-chip cookies. A round butterball of a woman with gray-black hair pulled into a bun. A little flighty maybe, a little jumpy, what with her odd quavering laugh and her eyes constantly darting about. But always certain of what she'd seen. *A figure in a slicker. Bigger than Sarah Trant. Ran like a man, hopped right across the river. Headed toward the yonder alder tree. Saw his body clearly in the moonlight. Not his face, though.*

Always eager to tell everyone, too. Until last evening, that is. *I can't, Mr. Monarch. No, I won't.* That's what she'd cried out, over and over. *I can't. I won't.* Greg tried to reason with her, tried to inquire, but to no end. The whole time, Judith Daniels stayed in her kitchen, slowly wiping her countertop with a wet dishcloth. No coffee, no cookies. Her countertop bare, bleached of all content.

"Your Honor," Greg said, "we have a new issue that just came up. It's about a critical eyewitness. For weeks she's been saying she would testify. Last night I visited her, to arrange for her to be here, and she just flatly refused. All of a sudden. I asked her why. She said that she'd been called on by Roy Rimmer."

"Roy Rimmer?" the judge asked.

Mashburn splashed coffee on the carpet as he leaned forward to explain. "He's the El Nido County sheriff, Your Honor."

"Rimmer came to see her and just got her very, very scared," Greg continued. "Asked her questions about what she saw at the creek, what she was going to say at the hearing, was she sure of her testimony, did she know what perjury was. She's not a stable woman to begin with, and Rimmer put her over the edge. Now she says she won't testify unless she can do it in chambers and there's an absolute guarantee her name won't be in the press."

"Your Honor," Mashburn said. "May I speak?"

The judge turned to him. "Yes, please do."

"First of all, Counsel here has given me no advance notice of this, so I have not checked into the facts of the matter. But I do know that Rimmer was planning to visit Judith Daniels. That is something we don't apologize about. She was obviously a potential witness at this hearing. She hasn't been deposed. We have a fair right to go out and talk to her regarding what her testimony was going to be. I don't believe the El Nido sheriff would threaten her or anyone like that. I resent that suggestion, in fact. I resent that greatly. This was fair exercise of our right. Nothing more."

Greg looked at the DA. "Jim, just how can you say what the sheriff did or didn't do?"

"He's under my direction. He functions as investigator for the DA's office. He does what I wish."

"What you wish. Well—"

"Enough." Judge Solman spoke sharply. "You two are supposed to address me, not each other."

"Your Honor—" Greg began.

"Enough," Judge Solman repeated. He frowned as he shifted in his chair. "Let me understand this, Greg. You're claiming that the prosecution has tampered with a defense witness?"

"That's exactly what I'm saying, Judge."

"This is outrageous, Your Honor." Mashburn's voice was rising. "He offers no proof. The sheriff has a right to visit this woman. An absolute right—"

Solman held up a hand to stop him. He glanced back and forth at the two lawyers. His frown had deepened into dismay.

"Greg," the judge said, "I think you've got an overactive imagination. Certainly Ms. Daniels has nothing to fear from El Nido authorities, or from testifying here in our courtroom. Tell her that, Greg. Tell her that it's not possible to believe otherwise about an entire county like El Nido."

"And if that doesn't work?"

The judge went stone-faced on him. "If that doesn't work, Greg, I can't help you. This is a public proceeding. I will not hold private testimony in chambers. And I certainly won't seal any testimony. And much as I wish, I can't control the press."

"You'd rather lose this witness's testimony?" Greg asked.

Judge Solman looked at him with vacant eyes. "You lose it, Greg. Not me."

ALEX RAMIREZ WIPED THE hot wet back of his neck and glanced at the darkening evening sky. Ashes had started to fall, resembling nothing so much as flakes of snow. If only they were, he thought. The wind had increased and swung about, taking the fire once more into burning ground. Trees and bushes glowed red in the distance. For three days now the blaze had been whirling like this in erratic patterns, driven by chaotic gusts. Turning back on itself, pushing toward the coast, lunging again into the valley . . . To Alex, it looked as if the flames were taunting El Nido.

How did this start? he wondered. A hunter's unextinguished campfire perhaps, or a carelessly discarded cigarette. Word was, a boy on Gunpowder Mountain first noticed the smoke at seven that first morning. Someone else saw a wisp at eight. But for both of them, the nearest telephone was miles away. Not until the Gunpowder Lookout spotted it did word of the fire reach the Forest Service. Since then, they'd matched every move of the fire with a well-timed counter-offensive. Shock troops charged its smoking flanks; special crews slashed firebreaks through thick chaparral; roaming units wiped up hot spots and set backfires; an airborne tanker dropped gallons of re-tardant. All this in one of the roughest portions of the La Luna Mountains, a country inaccessible except by trail, with only a few roads touching its valley borders.

They might just win, Alex thought. For all its disordered fury, the fire ran only 6,700 acres that first day, and 3,500 the second, far less than truly big conflagrations in this region. They had more than three hundred men now in the battle, and fifty miles of fortified fire line. The south side of the blaze was under control. Maybe it would never reach El Nido; maybe it would never reach Camp Mahrah. By reflex, Alex turned and looked through the pass toward Sanborn Ranch.

You can't let this fire reach the camp. That's what Diana had told him. Alex tried to imagine what might follow if he failed, but quickly shook off the thought. At least, he reminded himself, these flames were distracting everyone from Sarah Trant's hearing.

GREG APPROACHED THE WITNESS stand to continue his questioning of Dr. Oscar Quagler. The medical examiner from San Luis was highly esteemed throughout Central California, and frequently sought as an expert witness. Usually, though, he testified for the state. Getting him for Sarah's side had been a valuable coup. At least it had seemed that way until today.

"No, not exactly," the forensic pathologist was saying. "I couldn't possibly be that definite."

Greg held the man's own letter in his hands. A letter in which Quagler stated that he didn't believe Brewster Tomaz could have made a dying declaration. *I can't say with medical certainty he couldn't talk. But I'm willing to testify that I believe he didn't make that dying declaration about your client. I can honestly say I don't believe he was able to speak.*

"Doctor," Greg asked, "isn't it your opinion that Brewster Tomaz was unable to make a dying declaration?"

"No," the doctor repeated. "I couldn't be that definite. . . . You never know."

Greg rolled up the letter and began to tap it on the witness stand railing. "Let's go over this once more," he suggested. "Regarding the injuries to Brewster Tomaz's neck, and their effect on his ability to speak . . . As I understand your prior statements, you feel that the ability of Brewster Tomaz to speak was eliminated as a result of the injuries that he suffered. Is that not true, Dr. Quagler? Is that not the case?"

"Objection." Mashburn remained seated. "He's leading, Your Honor. Also, asked and answered."

Judge Solman addressed Greg without looking at him. "Mr. Monarch, what do you say we just allow the experts to tell us what they think, okay?"

Greg stared at the judge. Solman kept his head down, scribbling on a legal pad. Greg started pacing across the front of the courtroom, fighting for time.

He no longer wanted Dr. Quagler to say what he thought. Yet he had little recourse. This was his own witness, he'd called him to the stand. He studied the man now as if he'd never seen him before. The acclaimed pathologist had narrow sloped shoulders, a wispy mustache, and the look in his eye of a nervous feline. Had he always displayed that tic in his right cheek?

"Okay, Doctor," Greg proposed. "Let's make one more attempt here. Please tell the Court what effect you think the injuries had on the victim's ability to speak."

"It would have been compromised but not eliminated," Quagler said.

Greg moved closer to the doctor. "Not eliminated?"

Quagler's tic began jerking with added intensity. "That is correct. Not eliminated."

Greg suddenly felt empathy for the late Reggie Dodge. Dodge with Dr. Montrose, he with Dr. Quagler. They were kindred souls now. He pivoted from the witness stand. "No more questions," he said.

Solman tapped his gavel. "It's almost five, and a Friday at that. I think we've done enough for our first week. We'll reconvene Monday morning at nine."

As he rose from the bench, the judge finally glanced over at Greg. He appeared to be searching for something to say. "Counselor, you had some problems with that witness," he offered.

"Yes," Greg replied. "Not often that a habeas petitioner puts on a witness to bolster the state's case."

Solman looked away. "You are quite the maverick, Greg. Quite the maverick."

GREG AND JAS SILENTLY poked at salads as they sat on the creekside deck of Stella's Café in La Graciosa. What once had been wisps of smoke curling above the distant mountain range were now great mushroom-shaped clouds. The wind had picked up but had no fixed direction. It swirled about crazily, undecided where to go. The smell of burnt timber filled the air.

"I take it things aren't going so well," Jas said.

"So well?"

Jas slowly put her fork down. They'd spent time together this week in La Graciosa. Breakfast at the Apple Canyon Inn, where she was staying while covering the hearing. Lunch on the plaza. Dinner at Stella's. At the start, Greg had talked with animation about everything from El Nido history to trial strategy to his childhood in Chumash County. Listening and watching, Jas had seen such passion stored in his eyes. He'd gone away from her, though, as the week unfolded.

"I mean the witnesses," Jas said. "They're flipping on you, aren't they?"

Greg was watching the dark mushroom clouds. He didn't answer. An hour before, he'd tried to visit Judge Solman in his chambers. An *ex-parte* talk, without the DA present, was against the rules, but not uncommon with Daniel Solman. Greg had made it only to the judge's door. There a clerk had blocked his way. *The judge is occupied. That's what she'd told Greg. He can't see you alone, anyway.*

"Earth to Greg, Earth to Greg. Come in, please."

He turned to her. "Sorry, just drifting there."

"I was asking about the witnesses."

"Yes, they're flipping. Not surprising, though. It all makes sense. It's all to be expected."

"I see." Jas tried out her tone of sardonic challenge. "So you're the wise man here."

"No, not wise. Just aware."

He'd known for quite a long time, after all. That first weekend in El Nido, trying to get an autopsy report. *How big is this?* he'd asked Alex. Right from then, he'd sensed what might happen. Witnesses scared into perjury were the least of it. Prison guards trapping him in Sarah's arms, civilians in police cars chasing him through the mountains, armed men circling Camp Mahrah. Even that wasn't everything.

Greg shivered in the night air. He pulled his coat collar tighter around him. Jas's arch expression turned to concern. She put a hand on his arm. "Are you okay, Greg? Are you ill?"

Ill. The word jabbed at him. Reggie Dodge was dead, Daniel Solman fainting and furiously backpedaling. That was part of it too, of course. This wasn't just a legal battle. They were in a war.

"Don't worry, Jas. I'm fine."

"Greg . . ." Her hand came to rest on his neck. "You want my worldview now?"

He turned his attention to her. "You bet. . . . I've asked more than once."

"Despite how I act, not everything is so terribly clear to me."

"I know, Jas."

"At times I feel like someone who doesn't belong in the world where she's dwelling. Like someone separate from the life she's living. Like I'm acting all the time."

"You're not as alone as you feel."

"Greg . . . I've done this for so long, I'm not always sure who I am."

"I understand."

"Yes, I think you do."

Her gaze was direct, and full of feeling. No, Greg thought. She couldn't possibly look at all men like that. It would be so easy to let go with Jas. So easy once more to lose himself.

"I have a trip to make tonight," he said. "I'm going back to El Nido."

IT WAS STRANGE. THAT was the only way to put it. The fire now advancing directly toward El Nido didn't appear to require customary fuel. Flames exploded in burnt-out clearings and jumped well beyond the tree line; they looked as if they were feeding upon themselves. That, at least, was how it seemed to Greg as he drove on Old Brook Road, winding along the river's edge. You couldn't get all the way into the valley by the main route, which was blocked by rangers and fire trucks, but this ancient wagon trail remained open. In the dark, Greg listened to the winds slap the creek against its banks. At least there'd been no lives lost fighting this fire. Just one major injury, that's what Jas had reported over dinner.

A firefighter. He fell over a thirty-foot cliff in Pascual Canyon, breaking his leg. Possible internal damage. They carried him on an improvised stretcher to a nearby fire camp, but from there only a hiking trail led out of the mountains. They tried to airlift him, but the smoke and winds prevented landing a helicopter. Unwilling to wait, they instead carried the man to a tunnel at the nearby El Nido Lake dam. Through that tunnel there ran a pipeline that supplied water to El Nido Village, and beside the pipeline, a narrow-gauge railway, used by tram cars during the building of the dam. They put the injured firefighter on one of those cars and drove him through three miles of tunnel to the portal, where an ambulance was waiting. Hours of mountain hiking over sixty miles of rough terrain were cut to minutes. "There's lots of tunnels like that in the valley," Jas had said. "What a way of escape."

Greg had to admit, it was ingenious. So ingenious, in fact, that the thought of it wouldn't leave his mind. *Ways of escape*. As Jas said, El Nido was full of them.

Old Brook Road curved to the north now, toward the center of El Nido Village. Following it, Greg found himself at the rear edge of Sanborn Park. He parked and hiked through woodland, guided by smoke-filtered moonlight. He was looking for the spot on the river where they'd found Brewster Tomaz, the spot Jas had shown him weeks earlier. It wasn't hard to find. So many citizens of the valley had come to inspect it, they'd trampled a lush ravine into a bare clearing. Greg stood on the bank there and stared across the river. After a moment he moved fifty feet downstream to a narrow shallow bend, where he waded to the other side, jumping on boulders when he could, stepping in the icy water when he had to. Then he climbed a slope, heading toward the base of El Nido's foothills.

I saw him get as far as the yonder alder tree. Then he flat out disap-peared. That's what Judith Daniels had told Sheriff Rimmer about the strange figure who fled the murder scene. That's also what she'd told Greg more recently, before she'd grown too scared to talk at all. Greg surveyed his surroundings, squinting in the murky light. Live oaks and sycamore filled the forest. He stepped among them, branches scratching his face, twigs snapping under his feet. In the distance he could hear sirens. Then, off to the right, he saw it: A tree unlike the others in this stand. There were the coarsely toothed three-inch leaves, dark green above, paler green beneath; there the ascending branches with pendulous tips. White alders grew so fast along stream banks in the California foothills. This one, Greg estimated, was eighty feet tall, with a forty-foot spread. He turned back toward the river; up on this slope the tree most certainly was visible from the far bank. *Yonder alder tree.* Here it was, not fifty feet from the base of the foothills.

Greg hiked to it, then circled it. Again he circled it, widening his arc. Then a third time, and a fourth. The fifth turn carried him into thick brush at the start of the foothills. The sixth turn brought him to an opening in that brush. Greg knelt and pushed through it with his head and shoulders. Before him a dark cavern stretched into the bowels of the mountain. Greg pulled a small flashlight from his pocket and stepped inside.

The tunnel smelled of rotten eggs, recalling for Greg his first morning in El Nido. Asphaltum crackled under his feet, another re-minder. Greg stepped gingerly, wincing at the odor. The tunnel curved, hooking to the left. He must be circling the village now, arc-ing to the east end. Greg walked on until he estimated he'd covered a good two miles.

He slowed, then stopped. Time to rest. Greg rubbed his eyes. They felt so irritated. So did his nose and throat. He began to cough and gasp. He sank to the floor. There he sat, trying to focus.

Sarah was at the river that night, she didn't deny it. Maybe she'd even been there when Tomaz was murdered. But she didn't do it. No, couldn't have. Someone else did. Someone who escaped through this tunnel. Someone who . . .

Greg lost his train of thought. His head ached. He felt dizzy, and nauseated. He fought for each breath.

Someone who . . .

Greg closed his eyes. Then he forced them open. No, he didn't want to fall asleep in here. He tried to stand, but failed. He tried again, pushing himself off the tunnel's floor, grabbing at an outcropping. This time he made it to his feet. He still couldn't breathe without laboring. Less than a mile to go, he calculated. Maybe only half a mile. Greg put one foot in front of the other.

At first he staggered, then he didn't. Here in this last stretch the tunnel broadened and the ceiling lifted. Greg slowly stood upright, and found he could breathe more easily. With each step his head cleared. After five minutes, the dizziness and nausea passed. He looked around with eyes no longer burning. A rusted old pipeline, he now saw, ran along one side of the tunnel. He lifted his head to follow where it led. In the distance he spotted something bright. He stopped and shut off his flashlight. Then he laughed. Literally, here was a light at the end of the tunnel. Moonlight.

Reaching the portal, Greg stepped out of the tunnel and inhaled the night air. He was standing in a thicket of chaparral. Clearing a path with his hands, he slowly made his way down a wooded slope. Then he was in a clearing. A hundred yards off rose the Sanborn Ranch's tall red barn. Greg started walking toward the adjoining bunkhouse. He closed the distance silently. At the bunkhouse porch, he climbed three steps. He stopped, stood still. Before him was the usual inventory of saddles, shovels, gasoline jugs, and coils of rope. Greg had not a clue what he was looking for.

Then, under a bench on the far corner of the porch, he saw a pair of muddy boots. Greg reached for them, lifted them, turned them over. He'd expected the left boot to have rows of tacks pounded in diagonally across the half-sole. It didn't, though. The soles of both boots were smooth, unblemished. Greg ran his hand over them, feeling the glossy leather.

"What a surprise, Greg."

He turned slowly toward the voice. Diana Sanborn stood in the clearing before the bunkhouse, lit from behind by the moon and a high distant ridge glowing red with flames. Her long lavender skirt billowed in the wind. "Likewise," Greg said.

"Why would it be a surprise to you, Greg? This is my property, after all. I belong here."

"I meant the affidavit you gave Mashburn the other day. Swearing that you'd told the detectives about Brewster's dying declaration right then on the murder night."

Diana climbed the steps to the porch, came to Greg's side. She reached out and took the boots from his hands. "My goodness," she said. "These are so muddy. These certainly need cleaning."

"What happened the night of Tomaz's murder, Diana?"

Her eyes danced, her long gray hair whirled in the hot wind. "Bless your heart, Greg. What happened is not the point, is it? What we say happened, what we believe happened, that's the point."

"So goes the philosophy of the El Nido Valley?"

"So goes the philosophy everywhere, Greg. You know that. You are quite celebrated for knowing that, in fact. You win awards for knowing that."

Greg started to respond, then checked himself. She kept talking. "It's okay, don't you see, Greg! Everyone else here is playing that game. You won't get far unless you do too. So declare Sarah Trant innocent. Bless your heart. Believe Sarah Trant innocent."

Greg blinked as ashes from the sky filled his eyes. "Who wore these boots on the murder night, Diana?"

She looked at the objects in her hand. "These? These boots are two years old, as you no doubt can tell. They didn't exist on the night Brewster died."

"I reached your ranch through a tunnel. Ended over there in the chaparral. Started at an alder tree just beyond the murder site."

The ashes were falling on Diana too, on her shoulders and hands and eyelashes. She didn't notice, or chose not to bother with them.

"My grandfather used to pipe water from the river through that tunnel. Long ago, a century ago. It's been abandoned for at least fifty years."

"I got sick in there, almost passed out."

"No wonder. There must be precious little air in such a godforsaken place. You shouldn't have gone in that tunnel. No one with any sense would."

"It smells of rotten eggs in there."

Finally, a trace of anxiety showed in Diana's eyes. For a moment Greg thought he'd penetrated her armor. Then he followed her gaze. She was looking at the sloping hill behind the bunkhouse. A wall of flames had jumped a canyon and cleared the hill's crest. "I would think that a spectacular sight," Diana said, "if it weren't a scant two miles from my home."

——————— T H I R T E E N ———————

Sheriff Roy Rimmer paused to regain his breath. Sweat dampened the back of his uniform and dripped from his forehead down his gaunt cheeks. He didn't mind all the exertion. A fire in the valley demanded everything the sheriff's department had to give. In such a grave situation, the citizens of El Nido needed him even more than normally. They were seeking him out, calling to him, imploring him. There were roadways to keep clear, animals to rescue, families to evacuate. Rimmer hadn't stopped in hours.

Some forty-eight hours, to be exact. For two days now they'd been fighting the blaze as you did every chaparral fire in this reach of California. They flew airplanes for reconnaissance; they built camps at strategic points; they set up radio communication. For a good while, it all made little difference. While the citizens of El Nido watched and packed and loaded their cars, the firefighters found themselves struggling to stop a force of nature. The blaze, growing more focused as it marched into the valley, made spectacular runs into the higher, rougher backcountry. Several fire lines were lost, and two camps destroyed; once, a team of men were temporarily trapped by flames. Yet finally, man's wile and grit prevailed. They assumed command, they beat back nature. The fire still burned, but it was dying now. The gales had ceased, the humidity had risen. Each hour the fire burned more slowly, each hour they pinched it a little closer.

Rimmer loved the action. He didn't mind that his own role, in the end, had mainly involved traffic control. He'd been part of the battle. He'd fought the fire. So now he rested. Wiping his brow with a soiled handkerchief, he stood on a knoll near the far northeast edge of Sanborn Ranch, looking to the south.

Diana Sanborn's house rose in the distance, unscathed. Behind it, shrouded in a smoky haze, Rimmer could see the Sanborn barn and stables, also untouched. Down in the village, they told stories of how Diana and the La Graciosa lawyer stood their ground that first night, hanging wet sheets in front of windows, hosing down the barn, stomping out microfires. Rimmer didn't buy all that talk, though. The wind had shifted for Diana, that's what really happened. Just as it had for her grandfather decades before.

Rimmer wondered at the old lady's good fortune. The fire had crept to within yards of her buildings, right down to the clearing where she'd planted a small grove of orange trees. The round ripe fruit still filled green-leafed branches; from a distance they suggested to Rimmer a hallowed golden shield protecting the Sanborn legacy. Of course, he knew they were just oranges. He understood that much. He understood also that citrus trees were always the last vegetation to burn in the valley. Yet elsewhere, they'd gone up in flames. Elsewhere everything had burned.

Rimmer turned his back to the Sanborn house and surveyed the La Luna foothills to the north. Up there, for instance. Up at Camp Mahrah. Rimmer squinted, and shielded his eyes with one hand. Yes, you could see the camp's shadowy outline now. The fire had thinned the thick oak forest that surrounded Mahrah's flanks, the brooding cathedral-dark forest that protected and hid what existed within. For those who knew where to position themselves, and where to look, Charles Whit's property stood exposed.

Rimmer studied the scene with mounting worry. He could see the scorched brick common house, still standing. He could see the charred remains of two wooden lodge houses. He could see the kitchen and mess hall, apparently untouched. What else? Rimmer scanned slowly across the campus. Just as he had feared. There they were, barely visible through the forest, if only to the educated eye: Camp Mahrah's ancient oil wells and refinery.

Rimmer couldn't imagine how Charles Whit was going to respond. Whit usually maintained a mastery over himself, but this . . . It could very well throw the man into a frenzy. Whit had made it perfectly plain to him more than once that the rusty primitive oil wells of Camp Mahrah had to remain hidden. Rimmer didn't understand why, but sensed the reasons sprang from somewhere deep inside Whit. Whenever Whit talked about those oil wells, he grew so agitated. Pacing about, punching the floor with his cane, glowering at whoever stood before him . . .

What do you imagine happened up here, Roy? Why do you think the old pioneer wildcatters couldn't make a go of it when this land was theirs? They had these wells, they had a pipeline, they had a future . . . Something peculiar happened here, Roy. . . . Something terribly wrong.

Sometimes Rimmer would join in, to show his empathy, to let Whit know that the two of them shared similar sensibilities. *Yes, it was left for others to grow rich in the El Nido Valley. . . . Then proclaim that no one else could do the same . . .*

Whit always seemed to like that comment. In those moments, at least, Whit appeared to regard Rimmer with something approaching appreciation.

The sheriff, staring again at the tenebrous outline of Camp Mahrah, moved along the knoll now to gain other vistas. Suddenly he became aware that someone was standing behind him, off to the left. His hand darted to his revolver; he whirled to face his stalker. Then he saw who it was, and his hand dropped to his side.

"Morning, Sheriff," Greg Monarch said. "What a splendid view we have up here."

UNDER A THICK CLOUD of smoke that hung over the valley like a heavy gray lid, dozens of families huddled in the rolling green sanctuary of Sanborn Park. By noon residents from all over the valley had poured into the center of town, some on foot or horses, others driving soot-covered automobiles. They were returning, not fleeing. They came now to swap war stories, and reclaim their town, and give thanks that this hadn't been among their more cataclysmic fires. A six-year-old boy displayed his prized crayon set, a Christmas gift from a favorite uncle, all melted like water. A woman of the mountains named Harriet Parker—a packer and hunter who could throw a diamond hitch as well as any man—talked of being nearly trapped by flames while leading a loaded pack train up a narrow canyon trail. With aplomb, a teenage girl told of skinny-dipping in a meadow stream as ashes fell and a fire engine, siren blaring, roared along the canyon road across the river. A father of six with a red face and round belly recounted how he'd thought to escape the flames by riding his horse into an open barren field, only to have the fire explode about him anyway.

Greg Monarch listened to them all as he wound his way through the crowd. He settled finally on a bench near the Sanborn Park fountain. By necessity, Judge Solman had postponed the hearing. With the main mountain pass blocked, travel between El Nido and La Graciosa required a lengthy circuitous route. Sarah Trant, most of the witnesses, and all the lawyers "are sitting on the wrong side of the hill," Solman declared. Greg didn't argue in the least. He welcomed the delay.

Sweat darkened the front of his shirt. He'd been hiking as the day warmed up, but not aimlessly. He'd shadowed Roy Rimmer to that knoll after spotting him near the Sanborn property. There he'd followed Rimmer's gaze and seen the oil rigs. He'd seen also the look in Rimmer's eyes. When the sheriff left, he'd climbed the trail to Camp Mahrah.

Embers strewn across the ground still glowed faintly when he reached the campus. Burnt, toppled trees lay here and there amid blackened columns of oak and sycamore. Yet the fire had targeted its prey selectively; a good part of Camp Mahrah remained insulated by a thick green forest. Apart from the smell of burnt timber, the place to Greg felt much as it had during his first visit. Still no signs of life, no noises, no birds, no breeze. He toured the campus more slowly this time. There, as before, were a pair of knee-high rubbers, but now Greg saw they weren't a solitary pair. A row of these backcountry boots lined a wall inside a storage shed. On hooks above them hung an equal number of the white overalls Greg had once spotted through a window. They were thick, with zippered seals at the cuffs. Yards of steel chain lay coiled there also, and odd lengths of iron piping. In the brick central hall, Greg discovered a floor-to-ceiling cabinet stocked full of canned goods and bottled water. Outside, he found that Mahrah's playing fields had survived unsinged.

He turned and plunged farther into the untended camp wilderness, away from the cottages and open meadows. A trail took him ever deeper into the smoldering forest. He climbed, descended, forded a shallow stream. Suddenly he was in a small clearing. The oil wells and refinery rose before him, more rusted than charred. Six wells, of a sort Greg had never seen but in old photos. In their day, they'd been steam-driven affairs that could not have reached more than five hundred feet into the earth. The refinery looked even more primitive. It was essentially a still, cylindrical in shape, made of cast iron, with worms for condensing the vapors, and agitators to treat the oils. It could have held no more than a thousand gallons at a time, Greg estimated.

He took a step forward and suddenly faltered. Again, the smell of rotten eggs overwhelmed him. He found it difficult to draw a breath. Knowing where this experience was headed, he turned and lurched out of the field. Nearly blinded by tearing eyes, he found himself half sliding down a gentle slope. With the heels of his hands, he braked, and came to rest in a sitting position. He wiped his eyes, struggling to regain vision. He peered out at his surroundings.

Farther down the slope, where the ground leveled into a plain, he could see now a mammoth earthen pit, open but contained by a low levee. The pit appeared to be full of muddy water. Greg lifted his eyes. In the distance he could see four other pits, dotting a plain that was a good mile wide, maybe two miles long. The smell of rotten eggs was even stronger here than at the wells. Greg felt his head swimming. He fought to breathe. With concentrated effort he pushed himself to his feet and began his climb back up the slope. It took him fifteen minutes to make it to the cool still of Camp Mahrah's playing field.

"So, Greg Monarch, this is where you went."

Greg looked up from his park bench to find Jas Gest standing above him, hands on her hips. "With a few stops along the way," he said.

"I hope it isn't too forward if I say I was worried."

"I can handle that much brass from you, I think."

"Oh, there's plenty more where that came from."

"I'm well aware."

Jas smiled at that. "Okay, mister. Out of touch for two days in a valley full of fire . . . Sounds kind of interesting. Tell me about it."

Greg surveyed the park full of people, saying nothing.

"Come on," Jas urged.

Greg considered. He did need someone to confide in about the case. He couldn't deny that any longer. "I found a tunnel," he said.

"Yes?"

"A tunnel that leads from the river to the Sanborn Ranch."

It was Jas's turn to glance around the park. "There are dozens of old abandoned tunnels around here. That one was probably Edward Sanborn's water supply at one time."

"Precisely what Diana said."

"So?"

"It starts just up the bank from where Tomaz was killed."

Jas looked amused. "You have a theory? You think the murderer escaped through that tunnel?"

"It's possible."

Jas shook her head. "But not likely. That tunnel, all those old tunnels, were sealed up until about three years ago. The city engineers opened them up then because they were worried about accumulated gases. It was big news here at the time, fair amount of controversy. I wrote an article for the newspaper."

"I didn't know that," Greg said, unable to hide his disappointment.

"No, I guess you didn't. . . . What an adventurer you are. Where else have you been?"

"Camp Mahrah."

This time he had Jas's interest. "Mahrah? Why did you go up there?"

"I followed your Sheriff Rimmer up a trail this morning. Watched him studying the camp from a knoll. He seemed intrigued by what he was seeing. That intrigued me."

"Why? Nothing's going on up there. Whit doesn't even talk about development plans anymore. The camp's been abandoned for years."

"People meet there, though. People work there, stay there."

"How can you say that?"

"There was a conference of some sort up there just weeks ago."

"What are you talking about, Greg?"

"I'm talking about folding chairs, a long table, a dais, a freshly smudged white board."

"What an imagination."

"Also a fireplace, freshly laid with wood."

"You saw all this today?"

"Actually, I saw most of it the first morning I arrived in El Nido." He looked at her with appreciation. "The morning I saw you at the river."

"Oh, that morning."

A commotion off to the side interrupted them. Sam Rabe had climbed up on the bandstand with a megaphone in hand. The mayor was shouting announcements about road conditions, weather forecasts, temporary shelters, financial aid. Below him, Tammy Rabe appeared and began circulating through the crowd, her arms full of brochures and forms. Neighbors called to each other and reached for everything Tammy had to offer. A sliver of sunlight poked through the smoke. Somewhere in the park a boy tossed a Frisbee into the air.

"One thing I didn't see that first morning," Greg said. "Antique oil wells and a funny little refinery setup."

"Oil wells? . . . Where?"

"Up in Camp Mahrah's foothills. They've always been hidden by a forest of oaks. But the fire thinned the forest. You can catch a glimpse from Sanborn Ranch if you get in just the right place."

Jas started to say something, then stopped, realizing they weren't alone. She and Greg turned at the same instant to see Tammy Rabe standing directly behind them. She reminded Greg of a volcano about to erupt.

"What's always been hidden?" she demanded, stepping around to face them. "You can catch a glimpse of what, Mr. Monarch?"

He considered deflecting her, but decided not to. "Oil wells up in Camp Mahrah. Oil wells and a small refinery."

"How could you—" Tammy Rabe didn't finish her question.

Greg answered anyway. "The fire has deprived them of their cover, I'm afraid."

Tammy Rabe said nothing now. She looked back and forth at Greg and Jas, then up at the bandstand where her husband still was reading announcements. Her silver crescent earrings jangled as she whipped her head about. Her coral rings reminded Greg of iron knuckles. Finally she moved her thick red lips to within inches of their ears. "You two have stirred things up enough here in El Nido," she murmured. "You're making El Nido look bad. You're going to destroy El Nido."

"That's not my aim," Greg said.

Tammy Rabe appeared to be struggling to find the right expression. "Be careful, Mr. Monarch," she said finally. "While you are in El Nido, I advise you to be very careful."

ALEXANDER MOSS, PROPRIETOR OF El Nido's first livery stable, served also as the village's first constable. Reasoning that every town should have a jail, he built one in 1874 in his backyard, using stucco, timber, and tile. Moss was also the town's undertaker, though; he ended up using the jail more to store coffins than house criminals. Later, when a larger prison was erected behind Sanborn Park, the city fathers lifted Moss's jail off its foundation and transported the structure to a site beside El Nido's first church. Eventually Fred Darvill, in his role as historical society curator, claimed it for use as a modest local museum.

Greg had to duck his head as he passed now through the jail's doorway. Jas instinctively took his hand to lead him in the gloom. They stepped carefully through corridors filled with boxes, reaching finally the open room at the building's center. It had white walls lined by shelves, and, in its center, a long bare table. At one end sat Fred Darvill, waiting for them.

"Come on in," he grumbled, rising from his chair. "I'll bring you what you're after."

A piece of El Nido's history, that's what Greg had asked for. The history of El Nido's nineteenth-century oil boom and bust. Jas had urged him days before to visit the museum. He'd brushed aside her suggestion, meaning to follow that notion when he had time. For this he kicked himself now. He wasn't yet sure, but he suspected he should have started here.

Darvill shuffled back into the room bearing three thick brown expandable files. He placed them on the table, keeping his hand on them. The room's fluorescent light glinted off his bald sunburned head. He looked vaguely uncomfortable.

"This is everything," he said. "Like I told Jas, there's not a whole helluva lot." He pulled a paisley blue handkerchief from his pocket and wiped his nose. "At least not in the official record."

"You have allergies in here too, Fred?" Jas asked.

"Dust," he muttered. "Drives me nuts."

Still Darvill kept his hand on the files. Greg held out a hand. Darvill stared at him. "Why do you want to see this stuff, son?"

"I'm just curious about El Nido's history."

Darvill suddenly launched into a volley of sneezing. A fine mist from his nose evaded the handkerchief in his hand, landing instead on the files sitting before him. Darvill wiped them with the side of his arm, then, with a shrug, pushed them across the table.

Greg started pulling the pages from the files. Here were ancient news clippings, private correspondence, personal reminiscences, oral histories; here were dozens of voices speaking from the grave about a bygone time in El Nido. Greg rifled eagerly through the documents, scanning passages. He paused finally over a memoir titled simply "The Capitalist." He began to read.

There was a man they called the capitalist once in El Nido. A big bearded fellow by the name of Wallace Barley. He owned a fleet of whaling vessels which sailed out of San Francisco Bay. Late in the nineteenth century, Barley heard about the oil seepages to the south, in the mountains behind El Nido, and decided to investigate. What he saw—oil struggling to the surface at every crevice, running down the slopes like rivers—astounded him. Barley scraped together every penny he could and started drilling. The first well came up dry, then a second, a third, a fourth, a fifth. The sixth was make or break for him. He drilled down 550 feet, and in came a gusher. It was a thick tarry gusher, though: not the least usable. Undaunted, Barley built a refinery, thinking he could produce commercial-grade oil. But Barley knew little about building and operating a refinery. A fire soon destroyed his. Barley rebuilt, and refined, and proudly sent his first shipment of one hundred barrels to the East Coast. Only to have his good name marred when that shipment for reasons unknown disappeared en route. Barley tried instead to sell to the West Coast, but failed again when cheaper and better-quality eastern oil flooded the Pacific market. . . . To continue, Barley now needed new financing, which he pursued with unbounded vigor. Then certain East Coast refiners appeared in El Nido and sank their own wells. All came up dry or clogged with thick tarry goo. Word of the easterners' failure thoroughly debunked talk of a vast oil field in El Nido. Everyone's financing—Wallace Barley's included—quickly evaporated. Even in the face of ruin Barley tried to continue, but then his rebuilt refinery exploded for a second time. Broke and despairing, he finally gave up. They say he went mad and died of a morphine overdose, alone in an El Nido boardinghouse. . . .

Greg flipped through the documents. Here were reports on those that followed Barley. *Others bought his land and drilled where Barley first recovered oil. Very few wells had to be drilled, actually, as the oil was easily obtained from tunnels dug into the mountainside seepages. . . . In 1886 a pipeline was laid from a refinery in the El Nido foothills to the shores of Clam Beach in Chumash County. . . .*

Yet the results apparently weren't satisfactory. *This type of oil, the scientists decided, would never serve commercial uses. A large natural flow of surface oil cannot be regarded as a favorable indication of the existence of large oil deposits below, and heavy accumulations of asphaltum are a still less favorable indication. . . . After four years and $200,000, the prospectors lost their enthusiasm for oil. . . .*

Here, Greg saw, was where Edward Sanborn made his appearance. He'd been quietly buying up as much of the prospectors' land as he could get his hands on. Now he proposed his dream of an "agrarian paradise." *An agrarian paradise anchored by a choice, verdant oak-thick residential development on five hundred acres to the north of town. "Woodland," they called it. Instead of oil wells, graceful Spanish homes and acres of citrus spread throughout the valley. Thus did El Nido evolve as a truly isolated land. . . .*

A gnarled hand on his arm interrupted Greg. "Interesting reading?" Fred Darvill asked.

Greg looked up. He thought he saw mischief in the old man's ancient eyes. "Yes," he said. "I think so."

"Okay now, Sheriff, let's go back to the evening of the murder."

"Yes, sir."

For a moment Greg Monarch let Roy Rimmer ponder those critical hours on his own. He turned slowly, walked to the lawyers' table, picked up a file, flipped through pages. The sheriff's studied deference was getting on his nerves.

"Now, then," Greg continued. "At Sarah Trant's trial you testified that when you went down to the river that night, went to search the river—"

"Yes, sir   "

"—that you were specifically looking for footprints. Isn't that right?"

"Yes, sir."

"Good . . . Glad we agree on that much."

In truth, Greg wasn't glad about anything. He chafed at the need to be in this courtroom. With the fire thoroughly contained, Judge Solman had resumed the habeas hearing long before he could finish pursuing all that still intrigued him in El Nido. Clearly, Brewster Tomaz's murder and Sarah Trant's prosecution were mere props in some larger contest that stretched well beyond the Camp Mahrah conflict. To save Sarah, Greg needed to uncover everything that remained hidden to him in El Nido. Yet there was little chance to do so within the confines of this habeas hearing. He planned to feel his way, kick up some dust, keep his eyes open—and hope Judge Solman didn't hold too tight a rein.

"Now, then," Greg continued. "Sheriff Rimmer, isn't it true that at Sarah's trial you testified that you found only her footprints and Tomaz's at the river?"

"Yes, sir."

"And that was a flat-out lie, wasn't it, Sheriff Rimmer?"

Rimmer started to show some flash, then regained control of himself. He reached for a glass of water. "Not at the time, sir. When I testified at the trial, I totally forgot about the other set of boot prints we'd found."

"I see," Greg said. "So you went to the river that evening looking for footprints. You already answered yes to that. Do you want to change that answer?"

"No." Rimmer stared at Greg. "I went there looking for footprints."

"Okay. Besides the footprints of Sarah Trant and Brewster Tomaz, you found a third set, did you not? Boot prints?"

"Not the ones I was looking for. Those were old ones—"

"Hold on," Greg interrupted. "Please just answer my questions. That last required only a yes or no. Now. You saw a set of boot prints and you thought, Well, those aren't the ones I'm looking for. Is that your testimony?"

Rimmer went back to sipping his water. "Yes, it is."

"Tell me, Sheriff. Did you misunderstand the defense attorney's question at Sarah's murder trial? Is that your testimony?"

"No, I understood the question. I just had totally forgotten about the boot prints. If I'd remembered, I would have answered differently."

Greg frowned and paced. As he passed the lawyer's table, Sarah caught his eye. In her expression he saw growing hope. He touched her shoulder, then wheeled toward the witness stand. "Okay, I see. Okay. So you forgot about the prints. Let's just accept what you're saying, let's assume that it's true. But you surely would have put it in a report right then, right after you first saw the boot prints. Wouldn't you?"

Rimmer turned to James Mashburn with a silent command in his eyes. Greg stepped between them. Next Rimmer glanced up at the judge. Solman's hand rested on his gavel.

"Wouldn't you, Sheriff?" Greg demanded. "Wouldn't you put it in a report?"

"I supervise, Mr. Monarch. I wasn't the one actually on the line down there in charge of the operation. I wasn't the one writing the reports."

"So you didn't do a report on what you found at the river?"

"No."

"Did you take notes?"

"Yes. . . ."

Before Greg could frame his next question, Judge Solman intervened. "Excuse me, Counselor, may I contribute here?"

In a habeas proceeding, federal judges were allowed and often did interrogate witnesses directly. Solman had made little use of this power so far. Now, apparently, he meant to. Greg fumed. He'd been on a roll. Apparently, too much of one.

"Of course, Your Honor," he said.

Solman leaned forward, nodded at Rimmer. "Sheriff, didn't someone write up a report about these boot prints?"

Rimmer nodded vigorously. "Yes, Your Honor, the forensic technician did it. There was a forensic write-up on those prints."

"And was there a reason why you didn't consider that forensic write-up to be of any importance?"

"Yes, sir. The forensic team told us those prints were three days old. They could tell because there'd been a freeze earlier in the week. The prints were set in icy mud. I'm not sure of all the technical details, but it's in the report, which you have among our submissions. Bottom line is, we knew they weren't from the murder night."

"And did you make this report available to Ms. Traint's defense attorney?"

Rimmer appeared shocked at the question. "Of course, Your Honor. . . . I handed it to Reggie Dodge myself."

"Did Mr. Dodge ever bring it up again?"

"No, sir. He seemed to agree the boot prints weren't relevant. He said something like, 'Well, this isn't anything.' Never heard any more from him about it."

Judge Solman removed his reading glasses, wiped them, put them back on, and turned to Greg. "Counselor, you may continue. But I wouldn't use up much more time on this matter if I were you."

Greg stared at Solman. The judge looked away and began

scribbling on a pad. Greg turned next to James Mashburn. The district attorney was busily leafing through a sheaf of documents.

"Okay, then," Greg said slowly. "I'm finished with this witness."

DETECTIVE GARY GOOLAN, RIMMER'S chief deputy, moved to the witness stand with the measured, cautious look of a trusted second-in-command. He had thick black brows and a sparse mustache that barely covered the top of his thinly pressed lips. He kept glancing about, as if casing the courtroom. When he sat down, he remained, in the manner of his boss, on the edge of the chair.

"Detective Goolan," Greg began. "Can we agree that you interviewed Diana Sanborn on the night of the murder?"

"No, sir."

"You didn't interview her?"

"No, sir, I just talked to her."

Greg labored to maintain an even tone. "All right then . . . So you talked to her, you didn't conduct a formal interview."

"Yes, sir."

"In your conversation, did you hear Ms. Sanborn say that Brewster Tomaz had made a dying declaration, that Tomaz had said 'Sarah did it'?"

"In those exact words?"

Greg leaned closer to his witness. "You can answer that yes or no, Detective."

"The problem is, because I got sick, I didn't—"

"So what you're saying is, as far as you recall, Diana Sanborn didn't tell you Brewster Tomaz make a dying declaration about Sarah?"

"I didn't say that."

"You have no idea one way or the other?"

"I wouldn't put it that way."

It had been a long time since Greg felt the impulse to lunge at a witness. Over the years, he'd stifled that unfortunate tendency. Yet now, just for a passing moment, he imagined closing his fingers tightly around Goolan's neck. "Okay," he said. "Diana Sanborn's story. That would have been an important thing for you to put in your police report, would it not?"

"Yes, sir."

"So . . ." Greg walked to the lawyer's table, rifled through a file, pulled out a document. "So, let's look at your police report. Do you see what you wrote? Please read it for us, this part right here."

Goolan frowned, put on a pair of reading glasses. "Diana Sanborn was yelling, 'Oh my God, Brewster Tomaz is dead, someone cut Brewster's throat. . . .' "

Greg stopped him. "You wrote that?"

"Yes, sir."

"You didn't write that Diana Sanborn reported that Tomaz had spoken and identified the killer?"

"No."

"You didn't write it because it never happened?"

"No, that's not why. You can't—"

"Detective," Greg interrupted. "Let's look at your final report. The one you wrote two weeks after the murder. Still there's no mention of Diana Sanborn reporting Tomaz's dying declaration."

"That's right, I didn't make a reference to it."

"And you didn't make a reference because Diana Sanborn never told you anything about a dying declaration?"

"That's not so. . . . There's a reason. . . . I'd like to—"

"Yes or no, Detective, yes or no."

"I can't answer that yes or no. Do you want me to explain why—"

"Yes or no." Greg slapped the railing of the witness stand. "Yes or no."

"Hold on, now, Counselor." On the bench, Judge Solman was leaning forward, gavel in hand. "May I intervene here once again?"

Greg ignored him. "Is it your testimony, Detective, that if Diana Sanborn told you about a dying declaration, you would not have put it down in your report? Is that your testimony? Yes or no?"

Solman was banging his gavel now. "That's enough, Counselor, that's enough. If you don't mind, I'd like to get involved."

"Of course, Your Honor." Greg marched back to the lawyers' table. "Go right ahead, Your Honor. Get involved, Your Honor."

"You're risking contempt, Mr. Monarch. Let me warn you, if you continue in this way, you're going to put me into a position where this will have to get quite unpleasant. Do you understand that?"

Greg felt Sarah's hand on his arm. She squeezed his wrist, imploring him silently. "Yes, Your Honor," he said. "I understand."

Solman offered a thin smile. "Good, then. That's excellent, Mr. Monarch." He turned to the witness. "Detective Goolan, I have just a couple of questions."

"Yes, Your Honor. . . . Whatever you want to know."

"Detective Goolan, do I understand correctly that you suffered a heart attack shortly after Brewster Tomaz's murder?"

"Yes, Your Honor. Just hours after. The next morning. I went on medical leave."

"Did this situation affect how you handled reports about Tomaz's murder?"

"Yes, Your Honor. I lost track of things. I had notes that never got written up. There were things I was going to tell Sheriff Rimmer that never got told."

Judge Solman held up a document. "This is the El Nido County district attorney's prehearing response to the petitioner's discovery questions. This page here"—Solman pulled out a flagged sheet—"is a copy of your original handwritten notes from the evening of the murder?"

"Yes, sir."

Solman pointed to a paragraph. "Could you read this passage for us?"

Goolan took the page from him and again put on his reading glasses. " 'Diana Sanborn told me she heard Brewster Tomaz make a dying declaration. She told me Tomaz said "Sarah did it. . . ." ' "

"Your Honor, I object!" Greg was on his feet, and half shouting. "Who knows when these notes were written? Who knows whether this is an authentic document? I must register my formal protest about what's going on here. You're not even waiting for the state to make its case. You're doing Jim Mashburn's work for him. With all due respect, Your Honor, it seems clear that you've become a partisan for the respondent. Exception, Your Honor. I wish to—"

"Mr. Monarch!" Solman interrupted him with a bang of his gavel. Cold fury showed in his eyes. "Mr. Monarch, let's make something perfectly clear. I'm the custodian of the legal system here. We are seeking the truth in this courtroom. Nothing more or less. You want to get some points in the record for an appellate panel to read, you better make sure you're within bounds. Do you understand me? I won't have pyrotechnics in this courtroom."

Greg started to respond, but again felt Sarah's hand. This time she had his elbow, and was tugging. "You made your point," she whispered. Her eyes glinted with fear.

"Yes, Your Honor," Greg said. "I understand."

The judge was still clenching his gavel. "Mr. Mashburn, you want to be heard on this?"

The DA rose slowly. He glanced at Greg, then quickly away. "Your Honor, as you know from our response, we have a document expert affirming the handwritten notes as genuine and five years old. We also have a sworn affidavit from Detective Goolan. And—well, I hesitate to present the respondent's case out of turn here, but we will also have quite a critical witness who will corroborate Detective Goolan."

Solman raised an eyebrow. "That would be . . . ?"

Mashburn spoke so softly, Greg could barely hear him. "That would be Diana Sanborn."

DURING THE LUNCH HOUR on the resumed hearing's fifth day, Greg sat on a bench in La Graciosa's central plaza, savoring the lively scene before him. There was his old pal Alison Davana, strolling along the creek with a man Greg didn't recognize. There was Cindy Scamon from the probation department, chatting excitedly to a group of friends. There was Dave Murphy, the piano player at JB's Tavern, lounging in the sun with eyes half-closed. To them and others, Greg waved greetings. When he spotted two colleagues from the county defense bar, Ron Carson and Art Parrish, he called them over.

"Hey, stranger," Parrish began, with his usual deadpan delivery. "You in semiretirement? This your permanent park bench?"

"Retirement wouldn't be such a bad idea just now," Greg replied.

Parrish turned serious. "Hear Solman is giving you a rough time . . . Whatever we can do to help."

"Ditto," Carson offered. "If not with the habeas, with your other cases."

Parrish was tall and thin, and afflicted with a nervous blink. Except for an excessive fondness for Irish whiskey, Greg thought him a first-rate lawyer. Carson, shorter and calmer, and entirely sober, made up with dedication what he lacked in acuity. "Thanks, guys," Greg said. "Tim Ruthman has taken over what needs immediate attention. I'll holler if he starts sinking."

By now the plaza was teeming. A moment after Parrish and Carson left, Jimmy O'Brien stopped by. Then came a neighbor who lived two cottages down on the creek. Then a former client who'd managed to deflect a securities fraud charge. Not until half past one, with the plaza finally clearing, did Greg find himself alone. An untasted ham and cheese sandwich rested in his hands. His mind remained, as it had this entire afternoon, on Judge Solman.

No longer did Greg find his chief obstacle to be recalcitrant witnesses. Forensic technicians with bad memories were nothing compared to Solman's combative involvement. Solman wasn't just being cautious now. He was fighting Greg over every piece of evidence, he was leading witnesses with coercive questions, he was rolling his eyes at testimony he didn't like. Not even Reggie Dodge had to face someone like this federal judge. Greg longed to counter Solman in some fashion. Either that, or steer him into reversible error.

Greg rose and began stepping rapidly along the creek path. He had no destination, just the need to release energy. Maybe he'd follow the creek all the way to Pirate's Beach. Maybe he'd plunge into the dunes. Maybe he'd scale every last one of those majestic unspoiled mounds.

If only he could talk to Jas. It surprised him that he felt this need, but he did. When she told him she wouldn't be attending the hearing this week, he'd raised no objection. Now he wished he had.

Other business, she'd said. He wondered. Their last time together, after they'd locked up the historical museum, they'd had trouble talking. Over drinks at the Gaucho Tavern, she'd grown ever more quiet. They weren't arguing, not in their words at least. Just in their moods. He'd sensed her impatience. *There are times you hold back*, she'd pointed out. She'd tried to joke about it—*You sure do like heading for the train, mister*—but he'd heard no humor in her voice.

There was much he'd wanted to say in response. How not heading for the train had once cost him dearly. How he'd nearly come unhinged over another woman. How he'd learned the need to keep his balance. How, even so, he didn't always head for the train.

He'd not said any of that, though. Instead he'd told her, "Sarah's on death row. I have work to do in El Nido."

She'd smiled then, a mysterious, amused glint in her eyes. *So do I,* she'd said softly, as if reassuring him. With that she rose, ran a palm across his neck, and walked out. He hadn't heard from her since. He'd tried calling her twice in the past forty-eight hours, but hadn't reached her.

Greg, far down the creekside path, was nearly trotting now. On the outskirts of town, he followed Graciosa Creek as it curved into a narrow, densely treed glen. Dappled woodland sunlight filtered through the oaks, played off the rippling water here, giving this quiet hollow the feel of a hidden sanctuary. Greg settled on a rocky ledge beside the water.

If only he'd talked to her at the Gaucho. If only he'd explained. She would have understood. . . .

The sound of twigs cracking farther up the creek startled Greg out of his reverie. Through the thick shield of branches, he saw a man approaching. He was walking slowly, as if lost in thought. His head was down, his hands thrust in his pockets. Then he stopped, and lifted his eyes to the sky in the manner of a supplicant. Greg froze. Of all the places for Judge Solman to spend his lunch hour, how could he choose this glen?

Solman suddenly turned off the trail and scrambled through a ravine. Greg listened to the sound of his receding steps. Perhaps, Greg told himself, the judge simply hadn't seen him.

JAMES MASHBURN STARED AT Greg as they settled at either end of the lawyer's table. Judge Solman hadn't come out of his chambers yet for the afternoon session. Nor had the motley scattering of court-room spectators—the bored, the curious, the morbid—returned from lunch. Greg and the El Nido County DA had an empty chamber to themselves.

"Are you even going to put on a case?" Greg asked. "Wouldn't it be sort of redundant after everything the judge has done?"

Mashburn wouldn't take the bait. "Don't you worry, Greg. You better believe we'll put on a case."

"With Diana Sanborn as your star witness?"

Mashburn hesitated. "Well, you heard me say as much to the judge."

"Anyone else?"

"What do you mean?"

"How about Judith Daniels, for instance? Even if she is a batty spinster."

Mashburn frowned. "You heard the judge in chambers. You heard him say he wanted everything done in open court. Daniels won't testify in here, you know that."

Greg slid over to the chair directly adjacent to Mashburn. "Aren't you curious, though? Goddamn it, Jim, don't you wonder about what she saw?"

Mashburn's frown deepened to a scowl. Spectators had started drifting into the courtroom. The DA tried to keep his voice low. "This isn't an academic inquiry, for chrissake. I'm a prosecutor. You're a defense attorney."

"You're an officer of the court, Jim."

Mashburn rose and started to walk away. Then he turned back. Some of the spectators were studying them now. "You act as if only you have truth on your side, Greg. It's not that simple. You can argue the evidence more than one way. You say Tomaz couldn't talk, I have two doctors who insist his carotid artery wasn't cut. You jump up and down about those boot prints, I have a forensics tech who says they were days old. You think we cooked a detective's notes, I have a document expert who says they're golden. That's what courts are for, goddamn it. That's what trials are about."

"Settle down, Jim." Greg enjoyed seeing Mashburn agitated. "I was just asking whether you were curious."

Mashburn slapped the table. "This whole goddamn circus shouldn't even be in federal court. Solman made a mistake granting Trant a hearing. From his conduct, it appears he realizes that now. You think he's on my side, but maybe he's just trying to correct his course."

"They rigged Sarah's trial, Jim."

"Jesus Christ . . . We've gone over this before with Solman—"

"Tell me this," Greg interrupted. "Why do you think so many people want Sarah to be guilty? Why have so many people gone to such trouble to make sure Sarah is guilty?"

The noise of a door swinging open interrupted them. A guard was leading Sarah toward their table. Behind him, the court bailiff appeared. "All rise," he shouted. Out from his chambers strode the Honorable Daniel Solman.

"Mr. Monarch," the judge said as he settled at the bench. "Where are you in your case?"

"At the end of my rope." That failed to draw even a glimmer from Solman, so Greg continued. "I had hoped to include Judith Daniels in my case, but as you know, we can't get her to testify in open court."

"Then she won't be testifying at all," Solman said. "Isn't that what we decided?"

"Yes, Your Honor."

"Anything else for the petitioner?"

Greg hesitated. He'd hacked away at the case from all sorts of angles. He could keep hacking, but saw no point in fighting further on the present level. If they were going to prevail, it would be through means he didn't yet have at hand. Mashburn would certainly call Diana Sanborn and the ex-prosecutor Karl Jackson; if not, Greg could get them as hostile rebuttal witnesses. That left only Sarah Trant. He'd been putting off to the last minute a decision on whether to call her to the stand. Her effectiveness would hinge on which Sarah chose to appear. Greg couldn't be sure whether he'd be putting on a winsome plain-speaking woman or a muddled babbler. It really wouldn't matter, anyway. Both Sarahs—all the various Sarahs—were vague about the murder night. The notion of exposing any of them to Mashburn's cross made Greg shudder.

"Your Honor," he said. "We may wish to call Sarah Trant and certain other witnesses as rebuttal, after we hear the state's case. With the understanding that we may do so, the petitioner rests."

Solman nodded his assent without looking up. "Ready with your first witness?" he asked James Mashburn.

ON THEY CAME. Two executives from ModoCorp, a forensic technician, a document expert, two doctors, three sheriff's deputies, Roy Rimmer recalled for the state, a half-dozen El Nido residents who'd seen Sarah Trant's conduct about town. Each witness spoke with assurance and precision, each witness had a story to tell.

They talked of how Sarah Trant had stalked and taunted

Brewster Tomaz for months. They reported how Sarah Trant twice shoved Brewster Tomaz in full public view down by the river. One witness thought she'd overheard Sarah Trant actually plotting to way-lay Tomaz. The ModoCorp executives told how they'd been forced to seek an injunction against her physical intrusions. The two doctors declared themselves certain Tomaz's carotid artery had not been cut.

Sarah Trant admitted being down at the river, the detectives pointed out. She admitted arguing with Brewster Tomaz. She admitted pushing him into the creek.

"Actual innocence?" James Mashburn asked each investigator. "Detective, have you at any moment considered the possibility that Sarah Trant is actually innocent?"

"No, sir," each replied. "I never have seen any reason to consider that possibility."

Greg parried as best he could when it came his turn to cross-examine, but his mind was focused elsewhere. Diana Sanborn and Judge Karl Jackson would be the centerpiece of the DA's case, he reasoned; on them and no one else this hearing would turn. When would their turns come? What would they say? By the time Greg approached the stand to begin the cross of yet another El Nido State Park ranger, he was feeling almost as restless as the spectators sitting behind him.

It was late on Friday afternoon. Up on the bench, Judge Solman examined his watch. Greg intended only a quick, routine interrogation. Ranger Willie Wilton was a minor player, after all. He'd once encountered Sarah at a demonstration against ModoCorp. Mashburn had questioned him for just fifteen minutes, getting him to describe his observations of Sarah at the demonstration, and his efforts to calm her.

"Ranger Wilton," Greg began. "Did you ever write up a report documenting your encounter with Sarah Trant?"

"A report?"

Wilton appeared to be turning that notion over in his mind. He had thin graying hair pulled back in a ponytail, and pale brown eyes filled with concern. He'd been wavering over almost every question, as if he weren't accustomed to being interrogated.

"Yes, Ranger. A report."

"Well, no, sir."

"Okay. For the purposes of this hearing, were you ever asked to put in writing your memories of the demonstration?"

"No, sir."

"Did you talk to anybody involved in El Nido County law enforcement? In the sheriff's or the DA's office?"

Wilton turned wary now. "When?" he asked.

"At any time, sir. At any time."

"Well . . ." Wilton hesitated. "A couple days ago, yes."

Greg put down the file he'd been thumbing through. Wilton suddenly had all of his attention.

"To whom?" Greg asked.

"To . . . well, to Sheriff Roy Rimmer."

Greg squeezed Sarah's shoulder, then slowly approached the witness stand. He studied Wilton. "Where were you when you had this conversation?"

"In the sheriff's office."

Judge Solman interrupted before Greg could continue. "We're nearing five o'clock, Mr. Monarch. How much longer do you intend to go on?"

"I'm not sure, Your Honor. Not long." Greg struggled to sound obeisant. "Please let me continue."

Solman glanced again at his watch. "Okay, but let's not get bogged down here."

No sir, Greg thought. We won't get bogged down.

"Ranger Wilton, who called this meeting?"

Wilton shifted in his chair. "Sheriff Rimmer," he muttered.

"Speak up, please," Greg said. "The court reporter needs to hear you."

"Sheriff Rimmer."

"What did he say to you?"

"He asked me if I had been called to testify at this hearing."

"And what did you say?"

"Yes."

"Anything else?"

"No. We decided that we shouldn't talk about it to each other since we both were going to testify."

"I see. How admirable. You were both being so very scrupulous."

Greg nodded, paced. He felt Judge Solman's impatient eyes on him but refused to look up. Greg sensed something within his grasp, but didn't know what. He turned back to the witness. "Tell me this, Ranger. Did you and the sheriff talk about anything else while you were in his office?"

Wilton swallowed hard. "Anything else?"

"Yes, Deputy. Anything else?"

"No, sir." Wilton glanced up at the judge. "I swear to that, Your Honor. Swear to God."

Greg moved his mouth near the witness's ear. "Ranger Wilton, you've sworn to everything you say here. You took an oath before you sat down. "

"Okay, well. Okay. No is the answer."

It was like reeling in a big catch without knowing what you had on your line, Greg thought. He tried to reconstruct; he tried to grasp just what had caused Sheriff Rimmer to summon such a minor witness for obvious coaching. A thought occurred to him.

"Ranger Wilton, have you ever encountered Sarah Trant other than at that one demonstration back in October of—"

Wilton interrupted before Greg could finish his question. "I know what you're asking about," he cried.

Greg walked slowly to the witness's side. He tried not to show his confusion. "What is it I'm asking about, Ranger Wilton?"

"Object, Your Honor." Mashburn was on his feet now. "The witness isn't being responsive. There's been no question asked. This isn't—"

"There is a question," Greg interrupted. "I've asked him what it is that I'm asking him about. That's a question."

Judge Solman wavered. "It does seem to be a question. . . . Mr. DA, you want to be heard further?"

For a passing moment, Mashburn looked as if he were weighing options. Then he said, "I repeat my objection. . . . Monarch can't go fishing like this. He's got to ask a specific question."

Greg moved to the lawyers' table. He suddenly felt Sarah's finger on the back of his hand. He leaned down as if to study his notes, his head beside his client's. *Christmas Day six years ago,* she whispered.

Greg rose and turned to the witness before the judge could speak. "Isn't it true, Ranger Wilton, that you encountered Sarah Christmas Day six years ago?"

Wilton's eyes were fixed on Sarah now as if she were the only person in the room. "You're asking about the El Nido Lake campground, aren't you? That day when this woman came up to me to complain about her dog?"

Greg nodded vigorously. "Yes, that's it, Ranger Wilton. Tell me about that day, tell me about Sarah and her dog."

"It's just not true   " Wilton stopped himself as he looked over at Mashburn. "I mean, what's there to tell?"

Greg leaned down again to study his notes. Sarah's mouth barely moved. *Oil in the lake.*

Greg rose and approached the witness. "What's not true, Ranger?"

Desperation showed in Wilton's eyes now. "There's nothing to tell. . . . That's what I meant to say."

"Nothing to tell?" Greg repeated. He leaned closer to Wilton. "Ranger Wilton, don't you want to tell us about the oil in the lake?"

Wilton flinched at those words. "It's not true," he insisted. "Not true."

"Again I ask, Ranger. What's not true?"

Mashburn was rising to object again, but Wilton spoke first. "Okay, yes," he blurted. "She did say her dog had tramped around in some thick patches of crude oil at the edge of the lake. But I swear, she never told me that she'd seen oil spurting into the lake. She never told me about all the oil she saw gushing into the lake. I would have reported that, I would've told someone—"

"Your Honor!" Mashburn was charging the bench. "None of this is relevant, this is way far afield, I move all this be stricken, I—"

"—Sarah Trant never told me," Ranger Wilton continued. "I would have reported it, I never heard her—"

Solman banged his gavel. "Enough," he shouted. "Everyone stop."

At the lawyers' table, Greg clutched Sarah's hand as he waited for silence to fall. "Your Honor," he said when it came. "I ask for another delay of this hearing. There's obviously much I still don't know about the prosecution of Sarah Trant."

FIFTEEN

This time Greg kept a table between him and Sarah Trant. He'd wanted a chaperone, too, but still couldn't find Jas. It wasn't that she was missing. Neighbors had seen her on early-morning hikes, a store-keeper down the street had sold her fresh produce. Yet she was never home when he called.

His impulse was to go after her, knock on her door, make demands, declare something. He didn't have the time, though. Judge Solman—grumpily allowing that the state had withheld evidence about the ranger "even if its relevance is unclear"—had granted him a recess, but for only seventy-two hours. That, plus a weekend. Greg had five days.

Sarah held the key, or at least one of them. She sat now with one hand to her brow, watching him. The thin fluorescent bulb in the prison interview room was blinking off and on.

"I had a dream last night," she said.

"What about?"

"We were on the beach. . . . In the dunes . . ."

"You want to tell me more?"

Just then the light flickering overhead gave out entirely. Sarah sat in shadows, lit only by the glimmer from the window that opened onto the hallway. "No," she said. "There's no point."

"Okay, then . . ."

"Greg . . ."

"What?"

"I admire you so much. How you are. How you're handling yourself in the courtroom. How you're fighting for me. But don't let the rest of you go flat. Clear all the hurdles."

Greg leaned back in his chair. "Let's talk about the El Nido Lake campground."

Much to his relief, recognition showed in Sarah's face. "What we got the ranger to babble about yesterday?" she asked. "At the hearing?"

"Yes. Your dog, an oil patch, the ranger."

She ran a hand through her long dark hair. "I cued you on that, but didn't really understand what was going on. Why does it matter? What does it have to do with my habeas hearing?"

"I don't know," Greg said. "Let's walk through that day and see if we can figure this out."

Sarah fell silent. He waited. This had been their way so long ago. Sometimes moods moved through her like summer squalls. There was nothing to do then but stick around and bide your time. If you were of a mind to.

"What a day that was," Sarah was saying now. "So sunny and crisp. With a deep-blue sky and those thick cumulus clouds. Billowy white balls that looked like cotton candy . . ."

She stopped, distracted by the image. Greg reached out and lightly touched her hand. "Go on, Sarah."

She stared at his fingers where they brushed her palm. "My dog was playing at the edge of the lake," she continued. "Came back to me caked in a thick crude oil. Big ugly patches of the stuff were floating right at the edge of the lake. I complained to the ranger. Didn't do any good, not that I thought it would. Just wanted to tell someone. Just wanted to blow off a little."

"Was there more, Sarah?"

"More?"

"On the witness stand, the ranger. He talked about oil gushing into the lake. *She never told me about all the oil she saw gushing into the lake.* That's what he said. What was he talking about?"

"I . . . well . . ." She was pulling away again.

"Sarah, did you see oil gushing into the lake?"

"What are you after?" Her face twisted with anxiety. "All that happened long before the murder."

Greg gripped her hands firmly now. Hell with the guards, hell with the accusations. "I have a better question. Why don't you want to talk about this? Why haven't you ever told anyone about the oil at the lake that day?"

"But I did—" Sarah blurted the words out, then stopped herself.

"Who?" Greg demanded. "Who did you tell?"

"I . . . I . . ." Sarah hesitated.

"Talk to me, Sarah. Talk to me or I'm walking out of here for good."

"Diana Sanborn." Sarah, in her terror, almost shouted the words. "I told Diana. But she didn't want to hear about it, she didn't want anyone to hear. She told me to keep it quiet. She told me absolutely not to tell anyone else."

"Diana?" Greg chewed on that. "Did she say why?"

"No. . . . She was quite definite, though."

Greg had Sarah by the forearms now. He pulled her closer. "Sarah, I don't have answers, just ideas. But I know this is important. The ranger was alarmed, he thought he was being accused—"

"Well, he was." Sarah bit off the words. Her anger, Greg saw with appreciation, was stronger than her fear.

"Accused of what?"

"Accused of screwing up big time. Yes, I saw oil gushing, just pouring into the lake from somewhere off at the far bank. I told that ranger about it . . . oh, I hollered. He just ignored me, didn't seem to care. Or maybe didn't believe me. It was horrible, Greg. Hundreds of gallons, I imagine. Maybe more. All through the wetlands, up on the sand. A big slick about two hundred yards offshore . . ."

Tears filled Sarah's eyes. "The birds, that was the worst to me. Heron, egrets, sandpipers, ducks. All of them caked with that heavy sticky oil. They've got two endangered species out there, damnit. The California brown pelican and the snowy plover. Don't know what happened to them. Just terrible, so awful . . ."

"Sarah," Greg asked. "Tell me exactly. How did the ranger respond when you told him?"

"Like he didn't want to know, like he—" Sarah stopped. She turned to Greg with sudden surprise.

"What, Sarah?"

"It just occurred to me," she said. "I've been thinking all this time that he didn't care, didn't want to know. But that's not it, really. . . . It was more like he already knew."

Greg squeezed her hands so hard, she winced. "Could you see where the oil was gushing from?"

"That's the other thing that was odd. No, I couldn't see. The oil was coming from nowhere, just bubbling up from a marshy edge of the lake. So I went to investigate. Waded right in there. Dug around with my hands. So weird what I found—"

"How about an underground pipe?" Greg asked. "An ancient, rusty pipe, in the weeds or under the water?"

Sarah looked startled. "How did you know?"

"OVER THERE, RIGHT IN that spot."

Sheriff Roy Rimmer glanced at the small narrow glen where Charles Whit was pointing. They'd been walking through Camp Mahrah for an hour now, reliving the fire, assessing the remaining damage, contemplating what still needed fixing. The smell of wood smoke filled the air. Their boots crunched on charred oak branches.

"Eleven dead deer huddled together in that one spot," Whit said. "Quite a sight. Then you had all the doves. Looked like they were sleeping. Flames never touched them. All those beauties, suffocated by fire gases."

Rimmer turned away from the glen. He didn't care about the deer and the doves. To him the only part of the natural world up here that mattered were the mountain trout streams. He did like to fish. Damn fire probably ruined that, though. The trout would suffer severely this coming winter. Might die out completely when the rains carried the ashes and lye from the burned areas into the creeks.

"Your concern for the animals of the forest is touching," Rimmer said. "I thought you'd be more worried about those oil wells, now that you can see them from the Sanborn plateau."

Whit stopped at the mention of the oil wells. Yet to Rimmer's disappointment, he showed little in the way of real dismay. "Who'd ever be up there looking?" Whit asked.

Rimmer hitched up his trousers and tried to wipe tarry ashes off his shoes. "Greg Monarch, for one. Remember? He came up behind me. Must have followed me up there."

"You're not even sure he saw the wells, though. You don't know what he saw."

"He could have seen them. Can't get around that."

Whit still didn't react. "Nothing really to look at, anyway, Roy. Just part of El Nido's historical walking tour. A reminder of the past."

Whit resumed his trek through the camp. Rimmer trailed after, nursing a simmering resentment. He'd thought he might be able to affect Whit a bit today. But he could see now that it would take more than a little taunting to wipe the cold, empty look off this fellow's face.

"The past has links to the present," Rimmer said. "I think maybe Monarch is starting to figure that out."

Whit stopped again. "What do you mean? . . . Why do you say that?"

Rimmer took his time answering. First there was more ash to wipe off his boots. Then there was a horizon to study. "It's more than intuition," he said finally. "Mashburn briefed me about the hearing. Seems our prosecutor made the clever decision to put that El Nido Lake ranger on the witness stand. What's his name. Wilton."

Whit showed something now. Concern, Rimmer thought. Not alarm yet. But there was concern.

"Willie Wilton?" Whit asked.

"Yessir. Late yesterday, Mashburn puts Wilton on the stand to talk about a demonstration or something. But Wilton has other matters on his mind."

"Such as?"

"Christmas Day at El Nido Lake."

Whit flushed. Even in the forest gloom of Camp Mahrah, Rimmer could see his wrinkled coppery forehead darken with anger. "Mashburn asked him about Christmas Day?" Whit asked.

"No, no. Our friend Wilton just blurted it all out on his own."

"Jesus Christ."

Yes. Now Rimmer could detect alarm in Whit. Alarm was an unpleasant feeling, but surely it was preferable to what Whit usually showed. Over the months, the sheriff had grown unavoidably bothered by Whit's manner. The smile that seemed more like a sneer, the empty expression that hid such guile. There were times when Rimmer wanted to slam Whit's face against a tree trunk. He couldn't, though. His own fate, after all, was intricately tied to Whit's.

Not just Whit's, actually. Also to Whit's colleagues up north. Maybe someday Rimmer would be one of them. He'd like that. They saw the big picture, just as he did. They aimed high, just as he did. High, indeed. Those ModoCorp folks were reaching to the goddamn sky. Their computer server alone cost more than a million bucks. The Auspex, they called it. The Auspex something or other. First one of its kind went to NASA to guide space shuttles. Second went to ModoCorp.

Whit had briefed him on all this at the start, when they were wooing him. Rimmer had to admit, he'd been impressed.

All that stuff about exploring under the Gulf of Mexico, for instance. Miles into the earth's crust, searching for oil on a continental shelf that had already been intensively drilled. Searching for oil—and finding it. Yet not with drills. No. Instead, ModoCorp used computer technology. *We're taking the wildness out of wildcatting,* that's what Whit had said. *A petroleum company without rigs or roughnecks. A goddamn virtual energy company.*

At the least, it was an invisible one. Just an inconspicuous San Francisco office suite with a discreet nameplate on the door. Never a press release, never a public statement. Founded by Whit, first run as his one-man shop, then "grown" with the help of nameless investors. To be more precise, "absorbed" by a conglomerate, but with Whit still running his own show. That's how Whit put it. *People don't know we even exist,* he'd chortled. *People don't know how real we are.* Real—and, as Rimmer saw it, brilliant.

First they bought huge volumes of digitized seismic data. Then they hired the best geologists and gave them all the computer power they needed to analyze that data. Bingo. Without breaking a sweat they were finding new oil reservoirs in areas the major energy companies thought were uneconomical or all tapped out.

Whit had taken Rimmer up to ModoCorp's headquarters once. Obviously it was to soften him up, to get him on board, but even so, the visit was really something. A silent room full of earnest young college grads staring at computer screens. Some kind of green carpet covered the walls. An air-filtration system hummed softly up in the ceiling. Walking down an aisle, Whit stopped at one of the monitors, pointing at a display full of jagged lines and rich colors.

The fellow working that computer looked up with an eager, proud grin. *It's a topographic view of sandstone*, he explained. *See the lighter-colored areas? That's where the reflected sound shows a higher probability of finding petroleum. . . .Way down it is. Ten thousand feet under the sea floor . . .*

Then someone in an expensive gray suit stopped by. Thomas, just Thomas. Thomas, and a handshake. Thomas had dark slicked-back hair and pink cheeks. He also had his lines down cold. On and on he went, as if Rimmer were a venture capitalist with a pocket full of cash.

"It works so beautifully," Thomas explained. "Ships bounce sound signals off underground formations. We buy up the result. Enough 3-D seismic data to cover, say, the entire continental shelf of the Pacific Coast. Our computers translate the data. We scan for the best prospects. Then we buy leases. Either that or make deals with those who hold the mineral rights. It's all so low cost. A buyer's market right now."

Beaming over that notion, Thomas started to move on. Then he turned back, gripped by an afterthought, or maybe something he saw in Rimmer's eyes. "This isn't just about us making money, of course. You should understand that, Sheriff. This creates a new balance of economic power. Instead of cringing at OPEC threats, the rest of the world can now impose its own embargo on Iraqi oil. Instead of worrying about rising oil prices, we can expect prices to fall to their lowest level in years. This is a godsend for our country, Sheriff Rimmer. A godsend."

Rimmer spoke up then, to show them he was wise to their ways, and a not-unsophisticated player himself. "I assume that's why you have so much support in the right places?"

Standing at Thomas's side, Charles Whit intervened with a glacial smile. "You assume correctly," he said. "And that, my good Sheriff, is why we so much expect your support as well."

Eventually they'd gained it. Why not? When they first came to him, saying they wanted to buy his wretched piece of land adjacent to Camp Mahrah, he thought they were joking or something. As far as he knew, his rocky acreage on the backside of the camp wasn't worth a red cent. He'd long ago given up hope of growing anything up there. In fact, he'd given up hope of ever unloading the miserable property. Now these ModoCorp fellows were offering him a figure that was ten times the land's assessed value. He resisted initially, not trusting them. That's when Whit escorted him to San Francisco. We will make you a partner with us, they told him there at the Modo-Corp headquarters. You will prosper in the El Nido Valley.

Rimmer wasn't that gullible. "Why do you need me?" he asked.

We need your land as an approach and staging area. . . . And we need your support as the sheriff of El Nido County.

"My support as sheriff?"

Just in case we ever run into any trouble . . . It helps to have the law on your side.

Why not indeed? Why shouldn't he prosper as so many others had in the El Nido Valley? Besides, as the ModoCorp folks pointed out, this wasn't just about making money. This was a godsend for our country. The welfare of the nation mattered a great deal to Rimmer. He couldn't let everyone down.

"What did that damn ranger say exactly?" Whit was demanding now. They'd reached the edge of Camp Mahrah's playing fields. "What did Willie Wilton say?"

Rimmer held up two open palms. "I wasn't there . . . but some reporters were. Three of them, in fact. This is going to make the Sunday papers, I'm afraid. . . . You can read all about it tomorrow."

Finally, undisguised dismay spread across Whit's broad, weathered face. Rimmer exulted. "Should we sit down for a moment?" the sheriff proposed. "You look so under the weather."

WALKING THROUGH SANBORN PARK, Greg found himself no longer able to enjoy its charms. Conversations stopped or slowed down as he passed, and heads turned away. Here and there, someone glared openly at him. The latest news reports about Sarah's hearing had roiled people. More than a few citizens, in fact, had felt compelled to fire off agitated letters to the editor.

What in God's name does El Nido Lake have to do with Miss Sarah Trant killing Brewster Tomaz? . . . How could this murderess tarnish the reputation of our beautiful lake? . . . Ours is an unspoilt valley, no matter what that killer says. . . . Why doesn't this big-shot La Graciosa lawyer go pay attention to his own county . . . ?

Greg took this mainly as proud and protective folks blowing off steam, yet it was clear he'd crossed a certain line. He no longer was just battling the sheriff and DA. He now had adversaries scattered throughout the community. To be pitted against the valley's citizens in this manner gave him no satisfaction at all.

It didn't help that Jas still hadn't surfaced. It had been more than a week since they talked. Twice Greg had visited her home, a rented adobe bungalow just off Main Street. It didn't look as if she'd been there for several days. He couldn't deny it: He longed to know where she'd gone; he longed to know she was okay.

"Well, my goodness, look who we have here. Bless your heart, Greg, where have you been?"

Diana Sanborn had approached from behind. He hadn't seen her coming, but he'd expected her. He knew she walked the equestrian trail most afternoons at this hour. He'd counted on them crossing paths. They'd done so hardly at all since the night he helped her beat back the flames licking at her back door. Greg didn't know whether her circumvention was by accident or design.

"I've been at a federal hearing in La Graciosa most of the time, remember?" he said. "How about you?"

She laughed as gaily as she could manage. "Just counting my cows."

Greg hesitated. Talking in any manner to the state's star witness opened him to potential charges of tampering. Talking to such a witness about her coming testimony opened him to certain charges. Yet they'd merely bumped into each other in the middle of Sanborn Park. So random an encounter. So public.

"I imagined you'd also be spending a bit of time preparing for your testimony at the hearing," he said. "James Mashburn has promised us we'd be seeing you in the courtroom."

All hint of gaiety drained from Diana's expression. "What's there to prepare for? When I'm called to the stand, I shall simply tell what I saw and heard."

"Mashburn says he's got you on board."

"No one has me, Gregory."

"Mashburn must be mistaken, then."

Diana started to speak, then stopped. She peered at him with pensive eyes. "You must be sorry you ever came to El Nido," she said finally. "Everything is more complicated than you imagined. And now people are turning on you."

"Are they?"

"They're writing letters. They're talking."

"What are they saying?"

"They're just muttering. The one thing that unites everyone here is the valley itself. You cast the valley in a bad light, you have a big crowd against you."

"What does that mean?"

Diana glanced up the equestrian trail. "There's been talk, that's all I know."

"Is this a warning? Are you the appointed messenger, Diana?"

She looked genuinely bothered by that suggestion. "Far from it . . . I'm actually concerned for you, if you must know."

"That's reassuring to hear."

Diana said nothing in response. Greg wondered whether he'd managed to offend her. Then he saw she was merely distracted. Diana's eyes were locked on something across the street, under the Arcade. Greg followed her gaze. It took him a moment, then he saw what drew her attention: Jasmine Gest. Jas was striding with determination, as if on her way to an urgent appointment.

He reached her just as she was passing the open doorway of the Gaucho Tavern. His hand on her elbow stopped her. "You've been missing in action," he said.

She exhaled slowly. "It's called free rein, Greg."

"Just wondered what happened to you."

"Why? I'm not accountable to you. What's it to you where I go or what I do?"

Greg started to respond, but at that moment a laughing teenage couple collided with Greg. Then a mother with a double stroller forced him to the edge of the sidewalk. Greg regained his hold on Jas's elbow and guided her toward the entrance to the Gaucho Tavern. She tried to stop, bracing herself against his pressure. He ignored her resistance and pushed harder. In an instant they were standing inside the bar. A half-dozen East Valley ranch hands looked up from their pool tables.

"This is coercion, Greg. You're forcing me."

"Go ahead, slap me if you want."

"Not what I had in mind."

"Let's sit over there. In the corner booth."

He kept his hand on her elbow, but she walked with him now under her own power. As they settled in the booth, Greg waved to the bartender, who'd been watching them with a sullen stare. "Couple of Graciosa Brews," he called. "You know, that foreign beer from Chumash County."

Jas laughed softly. "Feisty today, I see. Good. Showing your anger is good for you."

"I'll show you anger," he said. "Damnit, what's been going on?"

"Talk to me, Greg. Don't bark commands."

She worked on her beer, watching him over the edge of her glass.

"Okay," he said. "I was worried. Thought something might have happened to you."

"Aha. We raised that flat line on your electrocardiogram, that it? Well, we can lower it, too. Raise it and lower it . . . Raise it and lower it . . ."

He looked at her with amusement now. "To have so much power must be intoxicating."

"I got tired of hanging around," Jas said next. "Waiting for you to welcome me in. Set out on my own. It was an interesting experience."

"What have you been doing?"

"Working on an article, Greg. Doing my job. Investigating."

"The topic being . . . ?"

Jas licked the beer's foam off the edge of her glass. "The topic being Sarah Trant at El Nido Lake on Christmas Day."

Greg struggled to understand. "You weren't at the hearing. . . ."

She looked now as if she wanted to slide closer to him in the booth. She didn't, though. "I talked to people who were. Couldn't believe the ranger blurting all that out. Sounded intriguing. I decided to chase after it a little. Kept me out of the county for a while. So being gone wasn't just a way to annoy you." Jas smiled. "Though I confess I didn't mind that effect."

Greg tried to think of what to say next. That she hadn't been in jeopardy, that she instead had simply struck out on her own, left him with a confusing mix of feelings. "So," he said finally. "What did your independent investigation turn up?"

"Why, Greg, I was wondering if you would ever ask."

He waved for two more beers. She pulled notes from a pocket.

It was clear, Jas began, that Sarah Trant had indeed spotted an oil spill on Christmas Day. There'd been some talk about oil at the lake, it hadn't been a total secret. Nor had it been a big deal. Maybe a couple hundred gallons, that's what Jas had heard. The routine, perennial seeping from the crevices of the valley's foothills. An independent contractor's cleanup crew worked it one night behind barricaded roads. Portable lights, bulldozers, skiffs pulling booms, skimmers sucking oil—they had it cleaned up by dawn.

"Lots of equipment and manpower for two hundred gallons of routine seepage," Greg said.

"They roll out the artillery here when the wetlands are threatened."

"All the same . . ."

Jas regarded Greg with appreciation. "Very good, Greg. There is more to this. I've been holding back."

"It wasn't just natural seepage, was it?"

"No, I don't think it was." Jas, despite herself, slid closer to Greg. "Get this now. Way I hear, it involves Charles Whit and ModoCorp. I'm told they'd been retooling those old oil wells up in Camp Mahrah. Don't know why, those holes are all dry. In fact, I always thought those holes never did come in. Still, that's what I'm told. They were fiddling with the wells, must have pumped up a bit of oil somewhere. Because they had oil running in a pipeline. And you know what that pipeline did? Burst on them. Whatever the cause . . . corrosion, stress from vibrations . . . the pipeline ruptured."

Greg's eyes flickered now in the dark of the tavern. His second beer sat untouched before him. "What kind of pipeline?"

"A gathering line of some sort, I hear. Gravity-fed, low-pressure. Meant mainly to carry crude from one storage area to another. Buried just eight inches underground. Except who knows? There's no regulation, no mapping, no permits. I tried to check. Get this, Greg. There's no record of the Camp Mahrah pipeline on file anywhere in our state government. It's not shown on the county's maps of oil and natural-gas pipelines."

"A ghost pipeline?"

"Something like that."

Greg knew the region of the spill. That's where he'd fished with his father. They might have cleaned up the mess right away, but it would take a long time for the lake and wetlands to recover. Years, maybe. Oil kills insects, which disrupts the food chain. Also, oil can seep into the soil, then resurface and create a new slick. Greg thought of the dead cormorant he'd found floating out at the lake. He imagined dozens more had died. Maybe hundreds. It was a migratory zone out there, after all. Who knew the full impact of Modo-Corp's decision to fiddle with ancient oil wells.

"Where's the state of California on this?" Greg asked.

"Good question. Initial response came from the Department of Fish and Game. They've got a special section just for oil spills. Their guys showed up immediately. Then they disappeared. Backed away. Hands off."

Greg was momentarily empty of questions. They sat in silence for a while.

Then Jas said, "It's kind of funny."

"What is?"

"While I was poking around in the archives on this, I came across clips about another oil spill. At nearly the same time. End of that year. At the ocean, northwest of El Nido. The Chumash Dunes region. In the dunes, on the beach, out to sea. That one was much bigger. . . . Thousands of gallons . . . I'm sure you recall."

Greg put down his beer. He most certainly did. Nearly seven miles of his beach had been damaged. His dunes. His wildlife habitat. His refuge. "People walking on the beach were coming back with feet just black with oil," he said. "Campers, bathers, the dune buggy crowd, they all abandoned the place. Even the surfers left."

"Yes, it was pretty bad."

"So what about it? Why bring that up?"

"Don't know, just thought it odd. Initial reports had state investigators speculating that the spill came from the oil wells they've got on floating stations two miles out to sea. But from what I can tell, they never confirmed that, never pinned that down. In later reports, their language always remained kind of vague. Maybe that's just how bureaucrats express themselves."

Greg knew the answer to his next question, yet still asked: "Remind me. This ocean spill, how close was it to the end of the year?"

"Two days after Christmas."

Greg spun his glass around on the table. "I wonder."

Jas stilled his hand with the tips of her fingers. "Greg, there's something I want to know."

He looked at her, waiting.

"How come you took this case?" she asked.

"Thought I explained. Judge Solman sent me the habeas petition."

"But why did he do that?"

Greg studied his glass. "Sarah asked him to."

"Sarah knew you?"

"Yes."

"You two go back a ways?"

Greg raised his eyes to hers. "Way back."

She covered his hand with her own. "It was Sarah who let you down?"

"I wouldn't put it that way."

"Do you worry I'll go crazy like she did? Is that it, Greg? You think all complicated, impetuous women end up off their rockers?"

He stared at her without answering. She held his gaze. "You did good work," Greg said finally. "But hey, Jas, come on. Don't go away like that again."

STEPPING SLOWLY AND AWKWARDLY, Greg walked backward toward the shore of El Nido Lake. That was the only way to move with all the gear he had on. A full-length quarter-inch wet suit and hood, a wraparound tempered-glass mask, a BCD inflatable bladder jacket, a twenty-two-pound weight belt, a Brut regulator, a snorkel, gloves, boots . . . What made walking particularly challenging were the giant adjustable ribbed scuba fins on his feet and the full seventy-two-cubic-foot air tank on his back. It wasn't possible to move or enter the water gracefully with full scuba gear on.

So Greg didn't try. He lurched without concern, looking over his shoulder as he moved deeper into the water. The lake reached to his shoulders, his neck, his forehead. He waved at Jas waiting on the shore, then began his feet-first descent by exhaling and slowly deflating the BCD jacket. Down he went into the heart of the lake.

This was the only way Greg knew to test his theory quickly. Were the El Nido Lake oil spill and the Chumash Dunes slick somehow connected? Had someone diverted the lake oil to the ocean, so it wouldn't be noticed in the valley? If so, that meant there must be some sort of bypass system at the lake, some sort of underwater pump tied to a pipeline that drained to the sea. Probably it was a pump normally used to divert runoff irrigation water, but Greg couldn't say for sure; nowhere did the public record indicate anything about such a setup.

Surveying the lake from the shore, Greg had spotted a small wooden shed on the water's edge, securely padlocked and nearly hidden by high weeds. That's where the motor would be, Greg reasoned, if there was one. Fifteen feet from it a utility pole rose from the ground with a small metal box attached to one side. A control panel, perhaps, with a simple on-off switch. Yes; Greg felt certain. Someone must have turned on the pump after the spill began. No one was going to confirm that theory for him, of course. Certainly not within the few hours he had left before Sarah's hearing resumed. He'd have to do his own verifying.

Greg could see the lake bottom now. He pumped air into his BCD to halt his descent. He hung suspended in the water above the floor, neither floating nor sinking. He looked around. Water is eight hundred times more dense than air, and that made for differences. Greg had gradually lost much of the world's light during his descent. Colors had been absorbed, one by one. First red, then orange, then yellow. The deeper Greg went, the darker and less colorful. Red and orange and yellow objects appeared brownish, gray, black. They also appeared larger and closer than they were: Light traveled at a different speed in water, magnifying objects by 25 percent.

A heavy clanking sound off to his left caused Greg to flinch. Was it really off to his left, though? Sound traveled four times faster in water, which made it hard to tell just where it was coming from. To Greg, the noise he heard seemed to come from everywhere around him. He weighed the matter for a moment, then let it drop. He flicked one fin in the water and began to swim.

He'd learned scuba diving from his father in the waters near the

Channel Islands, south of La Graciosa and the Chumash Dunes. When Greg had proved himself there, in the frigid, surging murk off Central California, his father took him to the clear still waters of Hawaii and the South Pacific. It wasn't the gear or culture of scuba that induced them to don wet suits and air tanks, but rather, the underwater world that diving made accessible. Majestic lava archways, brilliant coral formations, eels and sea urchins, sea turtles and white-tip sharks . . . All dwelling in a universe so still and insulated, so unlike the one they inhabited above the water's surface.

Diving didn't just allow relaxation, it required it. To swim about without fatigue in water's greater density, you had to let go. Rapid and jerky movements just wasted energy. Nice and easy, that was the way to move. Breathing worked the same way. If you took quick shallow breaths, you weren't getting much fresh air, or conserving what you had in your tank. To dwell underwater, you had to breathe slowly and deeply.

Calm it down, Greg reminded himself. Ease off . . . Inhale . . . Deep, slow . . . Exhale . . . Slower still . . . He was swaying effortlessly through the water now, following the circumference of the lake, orienting himself. If he had his bearings, the shed should be just over there, in that inlet. Did he have his bearings, though? It was hard to keep his focus in this world. Everything so muted and uncanny. Only largemouth bass and catfish for company. You don't swim fast or work hard down here, you—

Suddenly Greg saw it. Over to the right, by a sloping bank thick with willows. A pipe descending toward the lake bottom; a steel cylinder, maybe fourteen inches in diameter. Supported, it appeared, by a four-cornered structure made of wooden pilings. The pilings continued to the bottom of the lake; the pipe stopped some five feet off the bottom. Its end flared, and sat on a concrete base.

Greg flipped a fin and moved closer. This flared end, he saw now, was something attached to the pipe. It had a wide opening covered by a slotted grate. An intake head, Greg realized. If he was right, there would be a propeller shaft running down the inside of this pipe.

Greg swam closer yet. If he could stick his face inside the opening, he should be able to see the propeller and pump unit itself. The pump wasn't on, so there was no danger of being sucked in. Even if it were, the grate would protect him.

He had the pipe in his hand now. He moved down its length to the opening. He peered through the slots. Yes, just as he'd imagined. There it was, the shaft, the propeller—

Then he saw nothing. The blow came suddenly, something hard and unyielding cracking against the back of his head. At the same instant he heard a roar, and felt the pump's voracious suction pulling at his head, his regulator, his face mask. Greg dove and kicked away. Silt churned from the lake bottom clouded the water and his vision. Yet he'd be sightless anyway; his mask had been knocked off his face, and the human eye needs air before it to function. The roar grew louder, filling Greg's ears. Where it came from he didn't know.

Nor, Greg suddenly realized, did he know where his regulator was. His mouthpiece had been knocked away from his face. Greg had no way to breathe. A sense of suffocation gripped him. Stay calm, he told himself. He knew how to recover a regulator. The arm sweep, that's what you did. Greg lowered his right shoulder, then extended his arm out to his side and behind him until he could touch his tank. He swept his arm forward while extended, feeling for the regulator hose, waiting for it to hit his arm.

It never did. Greg's panic mounted. Was there no regulator hose there? He reached back directly now to where the hose was attached to the first stage. Nothing. The pump must have ripped it away.

He had no time to think anymore. In an instant, Greg unbuckled his weight belt and began inflating his BCD jacket. A buoyant emergency ascent, they called it. Last option in a disaster. As he began to rise, Greg looked forty feet up to the surface. He started to exhale, continuously, slowly. Make the sound, he told himself. A-a-a-a-h-h-h. Don't stop, keep exhaling. He'd have plenty of air to spare; the air compressed in his lungs would expand as he rose. Not only could he keep exhaling, he had to. Otherwise his lungs would explode.

A-a-a-a-h-h-h. He was halfway there now, twenty feet to go, then fifteen. Greg felt dizzy, his head ached. A-a-a-a-h. He thought of his father, who taught him this ascent, who taught him its greatest value: to know you could do it; to know you didn't need your air.

A-a-a-a-h-h-h. Five feet now. Through the water, he could see the blue sky. It must be a dream, but Greg thought he could see something else as well. Jasmine Gest's face. Oh Lord, what was that? Jas's hands, reaching for him?

I SHOULD HAVE GONE down with you, she kept saying. I should have watched over you. I shouldn't have gone away. Don't you worry, though. You're just fine. Take it easy, now. Keep still. Keep calm. Breathe easy. Nice and easy. Come on, now, Greg. . . .

Jas gently coaxed him back as they lay on the lakeshore. She'd peeled down his wet suit, pulled off his hood and gloves. Her drenched dress clung to her body. Her hair, loose and wild, brushed his face. He was supposed to feel confused in the aftermath of this, that's what the books said. He should have lowered alertness, unclear thinking, visual problems. Yet he didn't. He saw Jas plainly, saw her on her knees straddling him, saw her wet dress hitched up to her hips. When she leaned down, her breasts touched his cheek. He felt the press of her thighs, the stiffness of her nipples. He started to shiver. Jas, noticing, turned him on his left side and propped up his legs with the scuba equipment. Then she lay down beside him, wrapping herself around him.

"I don't have a blanket," she explained. "Trying to keep you warm."

"You're doing a fine job."

When the shivering stopped, he pulled her closer and kissed her. She tasted of the lake and the grass and something else, and she responded with an urgency that overwhelmed him. He felt her tongue on his neck, his ears, his chest. Then she rolled on top of him and pressed herself against him. She began pulling at his wet suit. Now he did feel light-headed. "Jas . . . ," he said.

Suddenly she stopped. She sat up, and looked around the lake with a worried air.

Greg watched her pull her knees to her chest and wrap her arms around her legs. The sun was drying out her dress, but it still clung to her. Buttons ran down the dress's front, holding the thin cloth together.

"What happened down there?" she asked. "Who's out there? We're not alone, are we?"

Greg moved closer to her. He hadn't wanted to dwell on that possibility just now. Perhaps the pump was on a timer and his assailant was an inanimate object; the blow to his head had been so unyielding. "Not sure," he said. "I may have cracked into a submerged boulder or log, for all I know."

She exhaled slowly. "I wish that were true," she said. Her voice was thick.

He felt her breath on his neck, he felt his blood pound. "Jas—"

She stayed him with a hand on his chest, then sat silently, gazing out at the lake. "Did you find what you were after?"

"Yes. . . ." He tried to gather himself. "An electric power pump, from what I could tell. The kind they use to lift large volumes of water at flood-control and irrigation stations. Thing like that lifts so much so fast, it creates a vortex. I can imagine what happened. Vortex pulled the water down, skimmed the oil off the top, just like scum in a bathtub. Then through a pipeline to the sea . . . Jas, all those thousands of gallons of crude out near the Chumash Dunes, I bet they came from here. I bet they came from El Nido, not from offshore wells."

Jas's brow wrinkled. "How could that be? El Nido is a dry hole once you get past all the tar and surface seepage."

Greg couldn't keep his eyes off the rising hem of her dress. He gently touched her bare, damp thigh. Her skin felt even smoother than he'd imagined. "I don't think so," he said. "The first day I came here, the proof was right before me. Up at Camp Mahrah. Not just asphaltum, but also a pool of oil. Then later, the fire burning away from the tree line, the fire burning in bare fields. El Nido's boom and bust. Wallace Barley's strange chain of disasters. Jas, there's oil under El Nido. Always has been. Real oil."

Jas watched Greg's hand as it now moved slowly along her leg. "I don't get it," she said. "I can understand covering up a spill. But if there's oil in the valley, why would ModoCorp hide it? Why not just pump it out and make a few hundred million?"

"I'm not sure. . . . But if I can find the answer, I think I'll know why so many people in El Nido wanted Sarah Trant convicted of murder."

"And how will you—"

Greg stopped her with a palm at her mouth. He pulled her to him by her shoulders. He reached for the top button of her dress. When he tugged at it, to his surprise all the buttons gave way. The dress fell open. Jas's mouth curved into a languid smile. "How'd you do that?" she asked.

─────── S I X T E E N ───────

Greg Monarch, by now familiar with the rhythms of a day in El Nido, approached Sanborn Ranch during that stretch of the afternoon when Diana customarily visited the village. Even then, he chose the backroad that led him most directly to the corrals and stables. He found Alex in his private quarters, hard by the ranch hands' bunkhouse.

"Time to talk," Greg said.

Alex was sitting on a frayed brown cotton sofa in a front room that faced toward the Sanborn barn. In the kitchen, a pile of dirty plates and pots tottered by the sink.

"About what?" Alex asked.

"Rotten eggs and dead cows."

"Rotten eggs?"

"The smell of rotten eggs."

Greg saw he had Alex now. The foreman glanced through a big picture window at the main house. "She's not here right now," he said. "But she'll be back soon."

Just north of the ranch they found the trailhead for a little-used route into the foothills. For half an hour they hiked in silence, through a land still untamed despite the nearby village. The prickly pear and yucca, the scarlet lupines and golden poppies, the oaks and sycamores and towering mountains—everything declared itself boldly. At dusk the two men stopped on a knoll above a sheer drop, watching the El Nido basin fill with color.

This land, Greg imagined, must so delight Alex Ramirez.

"In my family," Alex said, "there are many stories of strange acts."

"Tell me about them."

Alex lifted his eyes to the sky. "An uncle who thought his wife's heart resided on the wrong side of her chest, who took to pounding on her chest to put it right. A cousin who imagined himself able to cure all human diseases. A grandfather who sold two-hundred-dollar-an-acre land for one hundred."

"Why did he do that?"

"Because he felt it a shame that poor deserving men were compelled to do without simply because they lacked money."

"Is that such a strange notion?"

Alex smiled with appreciation. "You are right, I didn't think my grandfather so terribly strange. All the same, the telling of his story draws much clucking and eye rolling in my family."

Greg waited a moment, then said, "I myself have a strange story to tell."

Alex settled on the flat edge of a smooth gray boulder. "Okay. . . . Tell me your strange story."

Greg talked first of the asphaltum and pooled petroleum at Camp Mahrah, then of the oil spill at El Nido Lake. Lastly, he spoke about the tunnel that ran from the creek to the back of the Sanborn property. "I almost passed out in there. The smell of rotten eggs was overpowering. I found that same odor up at Camp Mahrah."

Alex said nothing at first. "A strange tale indeed," he finally offered. "But what of it?"

"That is my question for you, Alex."

In the gloom, Greg imagined his companion struggling, imagined a show of anxiety in his eyes. Perhaps not, though. "I have no answer" is all Alex would say.

"Let me talk more, then."

"Okay."

"There is oil under El Nido. Always has been, even though the boom went bust a century ago. And there's something else. Something that makes it not a good idea for this oil to be pumped right now. Something that few here want known."

"Okay."

"Something that you know about, Alex."

The foreman turned to him. "Why do you say that?"

"The dead cows on your ranch, Alex. You are too good a foreman to look the other way about them. You know why they died."

"No. . . ."

"Yes. And why they died is part of the mystery that no one wants known. Isn't that so?"

Alex rose and walked to the far corner of the knoll. He stood at the edge of the sheer drop. For an irrational instant Greg feared the foreman might jump. Then Alex turned toward him.

"There was a time when I thought myself capable of doing anything for this land," Alex said. "For this land, and for Diana Sanborn."

"It is always hard to know our limits and capabilities."

Silence then. On Alex's face, Greg could see the debate waging within.

"I will tell you another strange story," Alex said.

"Okay."

"It's true, I wouldn't just look the other way when my cattle die. I didn't. No one would ever give me answers, though. The state health guys came and went without ever telling me anything. Private labs were no help either. So one morning, I went out to examine the soil on my own. Down by the river, down where the cows died."

"What did you find?"

"Nothing, not a thing. I got sick, though. Really sick."

"Let me guess. You felt dizzy and nauseated. Your eyes hurt. So did your nose and throat and head. You had trouble breathing."

"Exactly."

"And . . . ?"

"You're right, there is more. I smelled something there at the river, just before I got sick. The odor of rotten eggs."

"What's your theory, Alex?"

"That's where you're wrong. I truly don't have one. I don't know why the cows died. They just stopped breathing. No one will tell me why."

"What does Diana Sanborn think?"

Alex stared out at the valley, saying nothing.

"Diana has enemies, Alex. She's in trouble. I can help her, but first I need to know what this is all about."

"You're not her friend."

"No, not exactly. But I am also not her enemy. Which is more than others can say."

"That's true," Alex agreed. He turned slowly from his view of the valley, and studied Greg as if taking his full measure. In that moment, something appeared to give way in him. He sighed and pushed back his hat. "Yes," he said, "she is in trouble."

"Tell me."

"I went to Diana straight from the river, that morning I got sick. Rushed to the house, found her in that sitting chair by her fireplace."

"Near where her grandfather's portrait hangs."

"Yes, with Edward Sanborn watching us from above. I was so full of myself. We've got to find out why these cows died, I told her. We've got to find out why the state health guys backed away."

"Diana's response?"

"Hardly any at all. It took me only a short while to realize why."

Greg waited for Alex to continue, but the silence stretched on. "I need to know, Alex."

"One more strange story."

"One more," Greg agreed.

Alex began to pace along the knoll. "In the early days of oil exploration in the El Nido Valley . . . Let's say you're right, that back then there really was oil here, not just dry wells."

"Okay," Greg agreed again. "Let's say."

"Let's say that oil was carried through a track of secret underground pipes from inland reservoirs all the way to the ocean. Let's say those pipes began to leak. Began to leak, and kept leaking. For thirty years, forty, maybe fifty."

"That's a long time."

"Let's say that as a result, a subsurface plume of oil formed in the center of El Nido Village. Right along Main Street and the Arcade, right through Sanborn Park. Then eastward toward Sanborn Ranch. Accumulated slowly, year after year."

"That would . . ." Greg stopped himself, waiting.

Alex continued. "Let's say a half-dozen years ago a newly arrived would-be developer in El Nido bought up a nice chunk of land in the foothills. Let's say this developer started bulldozing away. Let's say this developer stumbled upon evidence of that plume. Stumbled upon it, and realized it came from his property, from his oil wells, from his pipelines."

It was Greg's turn to stare out at the valley. "That's a problem for the developer, isn't it? He's responsible, as landowner and assignee?"

"Exactly. But it's a problem not just for him. It's a problem for the whole community. Who wants teams of overdressed strangers fanning across Main Street, waving probes and monitors at the Arcade and Sanborn Park? Who wants an environmental-impact report calling for the whole village to be torn apart? Who wants an enormous excavation? Minimize disruption, that's what everyone wants. Save the town. Maybe treat the plume with concrete and chemicals. Maybe try bioremediation."

"Or maybe do nothing," Greg said. He thought of Diana riding across her ranch one windblown evening, beating back the fireballs threatening to destroy her home. "No doubt many here would rather take their chances living quietly above an oil plume than dealing with the publicity and lawsuits and destruction of their town."

Alex was relaxed enough now to show a tentative smile. "You better believe it," he said. "Diana took me to one of their meetings. Pretty private gathering, up at Camp Mahrah. The sheriff, Charles Whit, the Rabes, the Arcade shop owners. Some talked about having to feed their families. Others kept insisting the hazard was overblown. Everyone agreed on one thing: They wanted the town to stay as it is. They didn't want El Nido torn up. They wanted to keep the plume secret. Fact is, they downright insisted."

"ModoCorp and the townsfolk were on the same bus? Each side, for their own reasons?"

"Exactly. Suddenly, if reluctantly, everyone had common interests."

"Is it possible just to sit on this? Is the town safe to live in?"

Alex stopped pacing and sat down next to Greg. "So many voices on that. You've got the ecology types wailing on about all sorts of hazards. Then you've got the shopowners pointing out that they've had this plume thing for decades with no problems. Fact is, Modo-Corp and Diana both paid for private studies, and neither came up with any direct evidence linking the plume to health hazards in El Nido. So yeah, maybe the town is safe despite the plume."

No direct evidence. Greg mulled that. "The plume doesn't explain the dead cows?"

"No, don't see how it could. But Diana assumed it did. That's why she resisted when I came barging in on her. That's why she wanted to ignore the whole business. She feared that if we started digging too far into the cows' deaths, the trail would lead to the plume. She preferred just to bury the cows."

"You couldn't explain to her . . . ?"

"Not that easy. Fact is, she's right. No matter the true cause of their deaths, the cows would probably lead to the plume, what with all the digging and testing. And Diana isn't at her most rational when facing that possibility."

Alex laughed with dark, rueful eyes. "Thing is," he continued, "even though she paid for a study, she doesn't really acknowledge the plume even exists. I once tried to talk it all out with her. She cut me off with a wave of her hand. 'Alex,' she said, 'it's just not true. If there were a plume, it could very well extend under Sanborn Ranch as well as El Nido Village.' She rose then and went to stand under the portrait of her grandfather. 'So,' she told me, 'there is no plume.' "

Alex fell silent. Greg asked, "You agreed with her finally?"

"How'd you know?" Alex looked at him as if beseeching his approval. "There was something in the way Diana stood there, insisting on the world being as she wished. I didn't want her to be wrong. I didn't want her to be vanquished."

"I understand."

"I know nothing else, Monarch. I don't know why the cows died."

"Can anyone else help us?"

Alex thought on that, then suddenly sat up straight. "One of the state health boys who came out to the ranch. An inspector for the environmental agency. He didn't act like the others. Looked like something was bothering him. He tried to talk to me one day, but his buddies kept interrupting, getting between us. Never saw him again, he wasn't with them their next visit. I forgot about him."

"His name, Alex?"

The foreman drew a breath. "He never told me."

JAMES MASHBURN, STANDING BY his office window, peering out at Sanborn Park's central fountain, tried to ignore the sound of Sheriff
Rimmer's impatient pacing. If I stay here long enough, he told himself, Roy might just disappear.

"Come on, Jim, we need to start throwing elbows now," Rimmer
was saying. "Monarch is tripping up our witnesses. He's roaming all
over the place, he's casting lines everywhere. This is maddening.
This is—"

"This is a lesson," Mashburn interrupted, turning from the window. "That's what it is, Roy. Just think how a lousy last-gasp handwritten habeas petition has brought everything to the brink of
utter exposure. Sort of gives you a new regard for habeas petitions,
doesn't it?"

Rimmer didn't look appreciative. "We should have shut Monarch
down a long time ago. That was the plan. It was a good plan. We covered all the bases. We got everyone from Diana Sanborn to Judge
Solman on board. But Monarch keeps twirling around like a windup
toy with a perpetual spring."

"He does," Mashburn agreed, "doesn't he."

Rimmer moved to his side. "This is my county. I'm expected to
keep things running properly. I'm expected to keep the lid on this."

"Who exactly expects that of you, Roy?"

Rimmer stared at the DA. "What do you understand about it
all?" he said in a low voice. "What does Greg Monarch understand?
You're just a pair of lawyers. Just two men enslaved by a bunch of
written rules. Rules that people never followed. Rules that people vio-
lated all the time. Rules that never, ever applied in El Nido."

Mashburn turned away and walked back to the window. Rimmer
had a point, he thought. He and Greg were bound by the rule of
law. Also by a sense of their roles in the system. *You could argue the
evidence more than one way.* That's what he'd told Greg when they
were debating in the courtroom. He'd meant it, he could defend that
stance any day. Yet what of Greg's questions? *Aren't you curious,
Jim? . . . Why do you think so many people want Sarah to be guilty?* If
only he could forge his own role. Not every day, not forever, but of a
moment. When that was needed.

"Don't worry, Roy," Mashburn said. "You're right. The legal system does bind me. As long as I'm the DA, I'll do my goddamn job. I'll defend the state's case. I'll be your advocate."

"Okay, then," Rimmer said, looking unsure how to take Mashburn's pledge. "What are you going to do?"

"Try to win . . . Try to stop Greg Monarch."

Rimmer thought on that, then asked, "What ever happened to the sexual-misconduct charges you were going to bring against him?"

The mention of that complaint made Mashburn cringe. "Chrissake, Roy. You know perfectly well we were just trying to harass him with that. Not even Judge Solman would go for it. If I filed in county court, it wouldn't come to anything until long after this habeas hearing ended. Probably wouldn't come to anything ever."

"Yes, no doubt," Rimmer said. "But Monarch hasn't stopped handling her in the meeting rooms. We've got a couple more moments on tape. They like to touch each other."

For a moment Mashburn entertained the notion of wrapping his fingers around the sheriff's bony neck. Instead he asked, "You're videotaping him now?"

"Whatever it takes, Jim."

"You put him on notice you're doing this?"

"Come on, now, Jim. What would be the point of that?"

Mashburn spoke slowly, stretching out each word: "To . . . make . . . it . . . legal."

"We don't need a legal tape. We just need something that convinces Monarch to back off."

Mashburn offered a faint smile. "Sorry, Roy. But I think that highly unlikely."

Rimmer studied the DA. "You sound so appreciative of Monarch. You part of his team, Jim? You know what else he's got planned?"

Mashburn lifted a document from his desk and waved it at the sheriff. "Don't have to be part of his team to see what's coming. Just need to look at the schedule when we resume the hearing next week."

"What?" Rimmer asked.

"If I don't call Karl Jackson to the stand, Monarch is going to, as a hostile rebuttal witness for the petitioner."

"Judge Jackson?"

"That's right, Roy. Your buddy. The fellow who prosecuted Sarah Trant for murder. The Honorable Karl Jackson."

AT DAWN IN HER bedroom, Diana Sanborn opened her journal and once again began to write. Her sleep had been filled with such vivid, precise dreams in recent weeks. Her mare Candy, the railroad, little Jenny Holder, her violent blue-eyed beau—the wondrous kaleidoscope, at once dark and exciting, hardly ever stopped now inside her mind. It was as if something was coming that required her to review her life, something apocalyptic. Diana felt it in her bones.

Not just her bones, though. She had more tangible evidence. Charles Whit and Sheriff Rimmer, for one thing. That gracious duo had dropped by to tell her of Greg Monarch's adventure in El Nido Lake. The postman had come too, with a third anonymous letter, this one even more threatening than the others. *You will die if you don't make amends. You will die if you don't provide restitution. . . .* Finally, there'd been Greg Monarch's visit.

Not to see her, though. Sitting her horse on a knoll off to the east, where she'd ridden to check on a dozen calves and their moms, she'd watched Greg roll quietly up to Alex Ramirez's quarters. Then she'd watched them hike off together into the foothills. They'd been gone three hours. She'd been waiting ever since for Alex to tell her about the visit, but he hadn't. Alex's silence terrified Diana. *I am alone now,* she wrote in her journal. *There is so much to hold together. It is all coming apart. Maybe that is best. . . .*

She stopped, put down her pen. *Maybe that is best.* She'd written those words once before in this journal. When Greg Monarch came, when Greg Monarch decided to stay and represent Sarah Trant. She'd imagined then a painless resolution, but of course that had been foolish on her part. There were prices to pay, consequences of actions, always and forever. To save El Nido, she'd forsaken a young woman whom she cared for. To save El Nido, she'd forged a bond with her enemies, she'd ignored the valley's poisonous plume, she'd let her cows die. And everything for naught, finally: To tear down the prison bars confining Sarah, it looked as if Greg Monarch was going to dismantle all of El Nido.

What would Edward Sanborn make of that? Edward Sanborn,

who in a public treatise once wrote that "it is the right and duty of a community to take such steps as may seem right against whatever is harmful to its welfare." *Whatever tends to retard the progress of a community should be looked upon as a public enemy, and the public have the right to rise up and abolish the enemy. . . .*

More and more frequently now, Diana found herself thinking of her grandfather, and those wondrous days when he was so vital and resolute. Neither storms nor anything else in nature could prevent him from going where he would. Whether in a saddle or a buckboard, he galloped across the plains, using his whip when need be. Which wasn't often, for his horses heeded him. They knew his voice, which seemed to inspire them to courage and trust. He had a similar effect on people. Once, after dinner, though the night was blustery and bitterly cold, he hitched up the horse and took Diana for a sleigh ride. The wind howled with fury, but the winter stars were very bright, and the sleigh bells made a haunting sound. Diana was bundled up to the nose, sitting beside her grandfather, where nothing, for that one evening, could get at her.

Diana closed her journal. Sheriff Rimmer advised that Mashburn was saving her until last. Yet Rimmer also warned that Greg Monarch might call her to the witness stand himself. Which process would be easier? Or did it really matter? Either way, there was no denying that the demons of discord had returned to El Nido Valley. Or rather, the descendant of those demons. She knew from where her anonymous letters came. She knew who was writing them. Diana picked up her pen again and opened the journal. *Here is my pledge: I shall take such steps as may seem right. . . . El Nido will prevail. . . .*

AS THEY WALKED ALONG the Arcade, Greg reached out to place a protective hand on the small of Jas's back. To his regret, he saw that she, by association, now also drew cold, hostile glances. At this moment, Sam and Tammy Rabe were staring at them from across the street, where they stood before the park fountain. Jas noticed but didn't appear to care.

"Where else can we explore El Nido's history?" he asked her.

"I'm not sure."

The oil wells of Camp Mahrah and Diana Sanborn's anonymous

letters were tugging at Greg's mind. There was a link between the two, he was certain of that. A link that he suspected went a long way toward explaining Diana's role in Sarah Trant's prosecution.

Greg suddenly stopped in midstep, struck by a notion. "Doesn't El Nido have a cemetery?"

They were there inside of ten minutes. The small overgrown plot of land sat in the heart of the oak-thick residential area called Woodland—Edward Sanborn's Woodland. Surrounded by a low stone wall and a wild lilac hedge, the El Nido cemetery suggested nothing so much as a quaint country garden. Large oaks spread their protective limbs over hundred-year-old graves. A rickety windmill and pump—donated by a young widow a century ago to "keep our city of the dead green"—irrigated the park's lush gardens.

In a way, Greg thought, here was a history of El Nido no one could dispute. With Jas at his side, he stepped slowly through the cemetery, reading tombstones in the still afternoon. The cemetery accepted its first four customers in 1870, and most tombstone dates were from the nineteenth century. Some markers were merely native stone with names of beloved ones scratched into them. Others were broken wooden crosses with fading, barely visible letters. Yet there were also some large granite headstones that bestowed recognition on entire families. You could, it occurred to Greg, piece together entire lineages from the words and dates in this cemetery. If not the story of an entire community.

"Look over there in the Alexander family plot," Jas said, pointing. "Julie Alexander. Not yet sixteen when she died in June 1897, one day before she was scheduled to speak at a state convention of the Women's Christian Temperance League in Chumash County. Largest funeral procession ever seen in El Nido up until that time." Jas swung her hand down another row. "There's Miriam Dayton. Twice widowed, eighty-four when she died, a tiny, nearly deaf gnome so stooped she was almost bent double. There's pictures of her in our files, and letters about her. Such sad anxious eyes. Spent her days knitting string washcloths, gathering eucalyptus bark for kindling, and waiting at the window for family members to return from horse-and-buggy rides. Yet she championed women's right to vote. Voted for the first time months before she died."

Greg turned to Jas. "You know everyone's history here?"

"Well, some . . ."

Greg pointed to a marker.

"That's James Boulin. Dead at age seventy-five of an accidental gunshot wound after overcoming a terrible case of tuberculosis. Took a ride in his pal Paul Wilson's new car. There was a shotgun lying on the seat. Wilson braked, the gun fell to the floor and went off."

Greg pointed to another marker.

"Wyman Williams, dead at twenty-eight because he got his dander up. Lost money in a card game at Hank Sidney's billiard parlor. Was still angry the next day, decided to take his losses out on the proprietor. Waited in an alley for Sidney to walk by on his way home for lunch, as he did every day. Except Sidney skipped lunch that day. So Williams finally came charging through the pool hall's front door, waving a gun. Sidney grabbed his own pistol and shot Williams to death on the spot."

Greg turned away from Jas and walked through the aisles, reading markers. There was the Wheelers' family plot, the Bullards', the Crowleys', the Danielsons', the Stillmans'. He stopped finally at a plot marked by a simple gray rectangle of granite. Here it was, what he was after. The Barley family plot. Wallace Barley's grave. Greg bent to study the nearly illegible names.

There was Lawrence P. Barley, who died in 1862. That must have been Wally's father, Greg reasoned.

There was Wallace Barley himself. Died in 1902.

Wally's wife Glenda, 1911.

Their son Thomas Barley . . . Another son, Jonathan Barley . . . Greg's eyes stopped at the name of their daughter. Gretchen Barley. Gretchen Barley Whitschenson. Born in 1890, married to one Joseph Whitschenson in 1915. Died in 1955.

Whitschenson. Could a later descendant have shortened that last name?

Greg's eyes moved farther down the granite rock, but there were no more names. That was it. The last addition to the Barley family plot had come more than four decades ago.

"Jas," Greg said. "You know anything about Wallace Barley's daughter Gretchen?"

Jas didn't answer. Greg looked up but couldn't spot her. He rose and started pacing through the cemetery. The foliage was so dense here, he couldn't see from row to row. Where had she gone? These disappearing acts were getting on his nerves. He glanced up at the empty road. He thought he heard something pushing through the brush. "Jas," he called, fighting a wisp of panic. "Jas."

She rose suddenly from behind a hedge at the end of the cemetery where she'd been on her knees, studying a splintery marker. She lifted a hand that was holding a bunch of withered leaves. "Here," she said. "Over here."

Greg tried to hide the alarm he'd felt. "I was asking whether you knew anything about Wallace Barley's daughter Gretchen."

"Got me on that one. Nothing about her in the archives. Far as I can tell, the Barleys didn't stay in El Nido long after Wallace died. I think I saw somewhere that the daughter moved to San Francisco."

Greg walked to her side. "Would you recall seeing anything about her own family? About her having a son?"

"Not likely we'd have reports like that from San Francisco. Why are you asking this? What's the point?"

"There probably is none," Greg said. "But let's take one more look at what Fred Darvill's got over at the museum."

THIS TIME THEY DIDN'T seek Darvill's guidance. Jas used her own set of keys to enter the closed museum. Greg took one wall of shelves, she another. For two hours they combed the stacks, flipping through mountains of files, not knowing what they were looking for. *General El Nido History*, read the label on one shelf. *Oil Exploration*, read another. Neither offered anything Greg hadn't seen before.

"I think Darvill showed you all there is," Jas said finally.

Greg didn't appear to hear her. He was striding down corridors now, his eyes surveying the building, his hands testing doorknobs. One led to a utility closet, another to a bathroom, a third to a small office. At a fourth, Greg stopped. The knob wouldn't turn. "This one is locked," he said.

"It's just a storage room, Greg."

"Can you open it?"

She fumbled with her set of keys, trying one, then another. The third key fit. She pulled open the door to a small room thick with dust and a musty smell. Stacks of boxes filled the chamber, reaching almost to the ceiling. "Over the years," she explained, "people from across the valley have dumped stuff with us when they moved away, or when their parents died off. We've never had much of a staff, so these boxes have just accumulated. Mostly household memorabilia. The idea has always been to index and organize everything one day. Don't know when that day will come, though."

Two at a time, Greg carried the boxes out to the museum's central chamber. Then he began pulling open the top flaps. He'd hoped to find some order to what he saw inside the boxes, but instead he found jumbles of dusty, yellowing documents that looked as if they'd been thrown in haphazardly during intermittent efforts at house-cleaning. His hands moved through chaos. News clips, receipts, and scribbled notes mingled with faded photos, birthday cards, land deeds, someone's employment contract. Greg picked up pieces of paper, straining to read pale illegible words. Nothing had meaning, nothing had import. Greg turned from one box to the other, moving faster now, fighting a growing unease. How many hours did he have left? It was late Friday. Just two days, forty-eight hours—

"Look at this." Jas was standing over the far box, holding a thick brown expandable file. With a large blue marker, someone had written three words on its side. "Committee of Ten," Jas read. She handed the file to Greg. "Sounds interesting, doesn't it?"

Greg opened the file. The pages were as crackly and yellowing as the others. The impatient handwriting slanted across the page at an angle, often spilling into the margins or curling sideways. Yet here was order. At last. Someone had felt compelled to keep a journal. Dates, a chronology, a narrative . . . A voice from the past, telling a story. It wasn't a story that Greg found surprising.

The early meetings among Edward Sanborn and his Committee of Ten. Their anxious concern at the encroaching oil wildcatters. Their passion to preserve and defend El Nido. Their love for their verdant oak-thick valley. And so their threats, their bribes. And their growing efforts at sabotage.

Setting the fire that destroyed Wallace Barley's first refinery. Arranging for Barley's oil shipment, bound for the East Coast, to be dumped in Panama. Flooding Barley's Pacific Coast market with cheaper eastern oil, shipped at deeply discounted rates by cooperative railroad men. Finally, the arrival in El Nido of East Coast refiners with ties to Edward Sanborn. East Coast refiners determined to keep hold of their monopoly, determined to squelch potential competition from Central California.

They bought land adjacent to Barley's. They sank phony wells that had to come up dry. They debunked talk of vast oil fields in El Nido. They discouraged financiers and other prospectors.

Still Barley struggled on, so the Committee of Ten blew up his refinery a second time. At last Barley gave up, broke and despairing.

Barley's wagon roads instead led the way for the next folks, wrote the anonymous memoirist. *Stouthearted adventurers in search of a home . . .*

Greg was turning through the pages so quickly now, he almost missed the quickly scribbled coda. It was just a single sheet, an afterthought at the bottom of a thick stack of pages.

Wallace Barley's descendants had to sell their land after his death. Yet for reasons unknown, they retained the mineral rights, despite all efforts of the Committee to purchase them. Edward Sanborn, in his final months, still talked of his failure in this matter. By then he'd watched the rights pass from one generation to the next. It was as if this family meant to keep a memory. . . .

Greg studied those words. *One generation to the next*

"Hey there," Jas called, waving her own stack of photos at the other side of the room. "More spoils . . . Look at these."

One by one he held them to the light. So faded, the black-and-white tones a blurred brownish tinge. Here were memories of a different sort—memories of Sanborn Ranch. Filtered, it seemed, through the lens of someone who worked there. He'd taken a few shots of his employers—there was a teenaged Diana with her grandfather—yet most captured the ranch hands relaxing in their bunkhouse, or toiling in a corral.

Greg moved slowly through the photos. A cattle drive, cowboys on horseback, someone sitting on a fence staring moodily at the camera, someone with a rope— Greg stopped, then flipped back to the photo of the moody young man on the fence. He had surly eyes and jet-black hair, and—yes—beside him, Edward Sanborn's granddaughter. Her fresh lively face was turned not to the camera but to him. *A brooding, tightly wound twenty-four-year-old.* Diana Sanborn's beau. It had to be. When had the assault come? Just after this photo was taken? Slowly, Greg turned the photo over. There, in light blue ink, in the right bottom corner, someone had scrawled something. Greg squinted at the pale letters and moved toward the window to get a better light over his shoulder.

The slam of a door stopped him. "What are you two doing in here?" a voice demanded. Greg turned to see Fred Darvill standing on the far side of the room. The old man's hands were shaking. His eyes looked as if they'd rolled halfway back in his head. Darvill took a step, then lunged toward Greg in a paroxysm of throat-rattling dismay. Greg stuffed the photo in his back pocket, grabbed the Committee of Ten file, and pushed Jasmine toward the exit.

"We've worn out our welcome," he whispered.

At first they couldn't open the front door. Greg vainly tried to yank back a jammed dead bolt. Darvill was closing on them with outstretched arms. Without effect, Greg slammed his shoulder against the thick oak panel. Jas pulled him away, flashing a key. In an instant she had the door open.

"After you," she said.

——— S E V E N T E E N ———

When Greg reached his room at the El Nido Inn just before ten P.M., he pulled off his dust-covered clothes and stood under a hot shower. He regretted that Jas hadn't stayed with him. *Somebody to see,* she'd explained as she drove off. He imagined her now beside him, and in that instant felt the warm water coursing down his body, kneading his muscles, releasing what held him.

"Are things complicated enough for you now?" she'd asked after they'd managed to escape from the museum.

They were standing then on the sidewalk outside Sanborn Park, catching their breath. Greg was rubbing his shoulder, where he'd slammed it against the door. "Getting there," he said.

Jas looked back at the museum. "I may have lost my volunteer job."

"What made Darvill so angry?"

"I don't think he was angry. More like scared, or upset."

"About what?"

"I'm not sure. Darvill doesn't scare usually. He also isn't one to keep things hidden. In fact, he shares things with me."

"But he also cares mightily about this valley, I presume."

"Yes," Jas said. "That's true."

Greg was toweling himself off, recollecting that exchange, when his telephone rang. Jas, on a cell phone, sounded like a distant, broken echo. Greg strained to hear. *In the canyon . . . I'm going to Judith Daniels's house . . . Just to try . . . Woman to woman might work . . . Will let you know . . .* Then they lost the connection. The canyons had swallowed her up. Greg fought to quell his sense of dread. He wished he hadn't talked to Jas about his critical need for the dotty spinster's testimony. He didn't want her going out alone like this. She wouldn't likely mind him, though, if he tried to call her off.

An hour later, the phone rang again as Greg was sitting on his balcony, staring at a moonless sky. He glanced at his watch as he lunged to answer it. Almost midnight. He would tell her—

"Is this Greg Monarch?" The man's voice on the other end sounded tentative. Greg struggled to adjust.

"Yes. . . . Yes. . . . Who is this?"

"Sorry, did I wake you?"

"No, but . . ."

"Didn't think I would."

"Who is this?"

"Name is Jeremy Rollins."

Greg searched his memory. "Do I know you?"

"No, no you don't. Not directly. But we have certain interests in common."

"Forgive me, Mr. Rollins, but is this going to become a guessing game? I'm too tired for that just now."

"It's you who must forgive me. I'm being too oblique. Sorry, I'm not accustomed to this sort of thing. I tried to talk to that ranch foreman weeks ago, but didn't do any better back then with him."

"Ranch foreman?"

"Yes . . . out at the Sanborn place."

"Alex Ramirez?"

"Yes . . . that was his name."

A notion occurred to Greg. "Mr. Rollins, are you by chance an agent with the state environmental agency? Are you the one who came out to inspect the dead cows?"

"Very good guess, Mr. Monarch. Except I'm no longer with the state. Quit a month ago."

"Reached retirement age?"

"The age of discontent, I'd call it."

"Alex talked of you but never knew your name."

"He managed to track me down, nonetheless. . . . Don't know how, but he reached me yesterday. Urged me to call you. Said you wanted to know more about the Sanborn cows."

Greg suddenly realized he'd never eaten dinner. "Mr. Rollins, I'm famished. Want to join me for a hamburger?"

THEY MET AT THE all-night diner on the canyon road leading from Chumash County into the valley. A ragged mix of bikers up late and fishermen up early had the place half filled. Greg guided Rollins to a corner booth and sat with his back to the wall. Two billiards tables stood off to their right, unused and unkempt, scarred by dozens of cigarette burns. One rough plank wall featured snakeskins and steer horns, another a twenty-pound stuffed bass. Biting into his hamburger, Greg kept his eyes on Rollins.

He had gray skin and a long narrow face, and resembled the career technocrat he was. Close-cropped white hair, a short-sleeved shirt, a tentative manner . . . Yet something in Rollins's eyes set him apart. An indignation, Greg thought. Beneath his composed demeanor, Rollins appeared to be deeply offended by something.

"So I understand you're here in El Nido defending Sarah Trant," Rollins was saying.

"Yes. . . . And I also find myself indulging in some historical research."

Rollins offered a skittish smile but didn't say anything. Greg tried to prod him. "I appreciate you calling me," he offered. "I've been wanting to meet you."

"Yeah," Rollins said, stirring a cup of coffee. "That's what Alex Ramirez told me."

"Okay, then. So can we talk?"

Rollins twisted around to survey the café. He drummed his fingers on the table. He rearranged a pile of sugar cubes. "I don't think so. This was a mistake, calling you."

Greg leaned forward, willing to gamble. "I know about the oil plume under El Nido. Shall we start there?"

Rollins looked surprised. "You know about the plume?"

Greg hesitated. He preferred collecting information to dispensing. "They've kept a pretty tight lid on it," he said. "A community secret."

"Yes, they have."

"So how do you know about the plume?"

Rollins knocked over his pile of sugar cubes. "A couple of scientists I know were hired privately to do some tests. Their contracts called for strict confidentiality, which for the most part they observed with due diligence."

"As I understand," Greg said, happy to be collecting again, "the plume developed from a leaking pipeline."

"Yes. . . . Slow leak from carrier lines."

"From how far back?"

"Maybe as much as half a century, when they were still prospecting for oil in El Nido. Leaked for decades." Rollins's eyes roamed around the café as he spoke. "But that plume is of no concern to me."

"Why not?"

"I've seen the private studies my colleagues did. No evidence of any danger, none at all. It isn't a refined by-product . . . just pooled oil that's been sitting there for decades, causing no pattern of harm. Believe me, if there were real dangers, I'd be the first to holler."

Maybe Alex's instincts were right, then, Greg thought. "So why all the hand-wringing?"

Rollins regarded him with exasperation. "Because even with these environmental red herrings, you always have certain terribly vocal folks wailing about toxic contamination. Some of them have heartfelt political agendas, but lots are just after a pot of gold. Commercial landlords, especially. They suddenly sound like tree huggers when they smell a chance to replace their weathered old shacks with four stories of brand-spanking-new stucco, courtesy of a bailout or settlement. There's no stopping them once they get their lawyers yelling about lawsuits and liability. I've seen this happen. One really fine funky old beach town not far from here just got ripped apart for no good reason other than the landlords' desire to go upscale."

Rollins began tapping the table with his knuckles. "Don't you get it, Mr. Monarch? El Nido has plenty good reason to hide the plume even if it's not harmful to anyone."

Greg studied Rollins, trying to assess what he saw in this man's cautious indignant eyes. "So why did Diana Sanborn's cows die?" he asked.

Rollins frowned, looked over his shoulder again. The café was nearly full now. Fishermen heading for the lake, farmers rising before the roosters, insomniacs seeking solace. Here and there, a face turned toward their booth.

"If the plume doesn't explain the dead cows," Greg continued, "it also doesn't explain why you're so angry."

"You're right . . . it doesn't."

A waitress suddenly appeared before them, offering a coffeepot. Rollins flinched; Greg waved her away. "What, then?" he asked.

Rollins began kneading his neck. "You'd think a place like this would be empty at such an hour."

"Not with so many folks trying to catch fish. You want bass, you've got to wake up before they do."

Rollins chewed on those words for a while. Then he shrugged and began to speak, keeping his voice low.

"Soon as I got out to the Sanborn Ranch, I had a notion what was up. Cows don't just stop breathing usually. They don't just lay down and die without any sign of disease, or anything toxic in the water or land. The wind was really up that day. A real blow, coming down from the foothills. Hard to ignore the odor of rotten eggs in the air. You put those two together, cows that stop breathing and a rotten-egg smell, well, it was pretty plain. At least to me."

"What?"

"Hydrogen sulfide, I figured. Hard to prove, though. They found nothing in the soil or water. They wouldn't. It would be in the air. That day for sure. Other days too, no doubt. But not all the time."

"Hydrogen sulfide? What's that? Where would it come from?"

"It's an air contaminant common in oil fields and refineries. Develops from petroleum refining, among other things. Highly toxic, quite colorless."

"And reeking of rotten eggs?"

"Even at low concentrations. Inhalation is the common route into the body. Passes easily from the lungs into the bloodstream."

"Symptoms include irritation of the eyes, nose, throat? Headache, dizziness, nausea, breathing difficulty?"

Rollins peered at him with curiosity. "Sounds like you've had your own encounter with the stuff. Probably in low dosages, though. In higher exposures, you get shock, convulsions, coma, and death. It can kill quickly, I tell you. It's a neurotoxin. Builds up in the blood, poisons the nerve and brain cells. Wrecks the centers of the brain that control breathing. Your lungs stop working. You die of asphyxiation. You can be overcome in seconds."

Greg slowly breathed in and out, involuntarily checking his lungs. "Twice I've smelled that rotten-egg odor. Up at Camp Mahrah. Then in a tunnel leading to the Sanborn ranch. Both times it went away as I kept moving."

Concern showed in Rollins's eyes now. "Stuff can deaden a person's sense of smell. Make him unaware he's being exposed. If the rotten-egg odor disappears, it may not necessarily mean exposure has stopped. It's said in oil refineries, if you think you've caught the smell of hydrogen sulfide and then it goes away, you're probably already on your way down."

Greg started to mull that, then decided not to. "The dead cows," he asked. "Couldn't they have been tested?"

"There's no specific, medically useful test for the presence of hydrogen sulfide in blood and urine. Tests will only show the resulting damage done to the brain and nerves and organs. We could have done that. I wanted to run those tests. But I got overruled by my supervisors at state health. I argued, even had some sympathetic ears. Then it went up the ladder, and we got stopped. Not just stopped, actually. Silenced. Total blackout ordered."

"Why?"

Rollins offered a faint smile. "I can only speculate."

Greg gazed out the café's front window. The sky had a hue to it that promised the coming sunrise. The more resolute fishermen, he imagined, already would be standing in their boats, casting. "So let's speculate," he said.

Rollins leaned across the table, his voice even lower now. "Like I told you, the wind was blowing down from the foothills that day. Down from the Camp Mahrah acreage, to be precise. Those cows on the creek were in a direct line from the camp. So that's where I think the hydrogen sulfide came from."

"What would the stuff be doing up there?"

"Remember, now, you get hydrogen sulfide as part of the byproduct waste of petroleum refining. Oil companies have to dump that waste somewhere." Rollins once more scanned the café, then turned back to Greg. "My guess is that ModoCorp has been using

Camp Mahrah as a dumping ground for toxic waste. From all their other oil fields along the Gulf and Pacific Coast. It would be easy. They've got isolated private routes in from the backside of their property. They could have moved hundreds of truckloads over the past five years. Maybe thousands."

"Why?"

"They have to put it somewhere, and have few choices. Oil waste, it's a multimillion-dollar business in its own right."

"I mean, why El Nido?"

"We've just discussed one possible reason. The plume. Hard to keep that covered up once they start openly pumping oil. Probably not enough oil in this valley to warrant the risk, at any rate. Maybe they never really meant to pump oil here. Could be they always planned Camp Mahrah as their central waste dump. It's the perfect spot for it, after all. Remote, heavily forested, small population, low density . . . It's a place where no one would notice what ModoCorp was doing."

An image suddenly rose in Greg's mind from the day he hiked alone into Camp Mahrah. He half sliding down a gentle slope, landing near a huge earthen pit full of muddy water. The overwhelming odor of rotten eggs, the protective white overalls, the tall rubber boots . . .

"I think I've seen part of that waste dump," Greg said.

Dimensions and colors mattered most to the former state health agent. Greg tried his best to describe for Rollins what he'd observed that day through dim, watering eyes. When he finished, Rollins slapped the table with an open palm.

"I'm willing to bet that El Nido citizens have a poisonous dump site hard by their lovely town." Rollins was still trying to talk quietly, but his voice was rising. "Besides the immediate dangers, you've got the potential long-term impact. Birth defects, cancer, kidney problems, respiratory troubles, eye ailments, chest pain, memory loss, headaches, trembling, depression . . . They've all been linked to this stuff. So much possibility here . . . And the folks don't have a blessed clue."

Greg labored to understand. "Doesn't ModoCorp have to tell someone? Doesn't this get regulated?"

Disgust showed in Rollins's eyes. "There's a huge gorgeous loophole in the hazardous-waste laws that exempts the oil industry from federal regulation. Some twenty years ago, Big Oil's lobbyists pushed a sweetheart deal through Congress. Lets them pump toxic waste out of a well, label it 'nonhazardous,' and dump it near towns without warning a soul. They don't even have to know what's in the waste. All they have to do is say this waste came out of ground where they sank oil wells. In any other industry, federal law would require the same waste to be trapped, labeled, and handled as hazardous material. But not the oil industry. That's how broad the loophole is. Nothing like it in federal law."

The crowd in the restaurant had thinned out now. The sun, low in the sky, reached through the café's window, warming the front tables. It would be a scorcher today, Greg imagined. "So this isn't just going on in El Nido?" he asked.

"Happens all over the place in oil country. You've got more than fifty-thousand oil fields producing waste that's got to go somewhere. The individual states could do their own regulating, but they're usually sitting deep in the oil companies' pockets. Result is, folks in thousands of communities end up having no idea what they've got in their backyards."

"Until an ill wind blows some of the stuff off site?"

Rollins looked at his watch, then suddenly rose to leave. "Precisely," he said.

Through bleary eyes, from fifty yards away, driving down Main Street, Greg spotted Jas Gest's car in the parking lot of the El Nido Inn. Relief mixed with a feeling of overwhelming exhaustion. He hadn't slept all night, and couldn't now. It was nearly nine on a bright, cloudless Sunday morning. Too bright, the sun harsh and relentless, already leaving no shadows. He had just twenty-four hours to go before the hearing resumed. One day to turn everything around.

There was no point, he understood now, to arguing either the law or the evidence. They weren't going to let him win that way. He could orate as much as he wished about the Fourteenth Amendment and due process. It would get them nowhere. Nor would trying to prove Sarah's innocence. Actual innocence . . . What a crock. He needed a hammer, that's what he needed.

Greg braked hard as he peered into the bright light. There she was, outside the motel, rushing toward him as he pulled into the parking lot. Something, he suddenly realized, was wrong. Jas nearly tripped in her haste to reach him. At his car, on the passenger's side, she grabbed the door handle, yanked, then collapsed on the seat beside him.

"Some guy followed me out to Judith Daniels's house," she gasped. "Got on my tail halfway through the canyon. I floored it, but he caught up. God, Greg, he nearly rammed me. . . . I could see him in the mirror. A fat red face, a big ragged beard. He was staring at me. His eyes were so awful. . . . I started looping onto backroads, but he kept coming. Damnit, Greg—"

"You got away finally?"

"Yes, but only after—"

"Did you get to Judith Daniels?"

"No, I couldn't. . . . I came back, I circled around on the old fire road, that's where I lost him. . . ."

He helped her out of the car and led her to his room at the inn. She paced about in agitation, then sank onto the bed. He came to her, sat beside her, put his hands on her shoulders. "Are you okay, Jas?" he asked.

"I'll be fine . . . now that you're here."

He began to rub her temples. His fingers moved gently along the side of her face, then down her neck and along her spine. She turned toward him, and the palms of his hands brushed her breasts. She arched her shoulder blades and moaned softly with parted lips. He stopped, and rose from the bed. "I'm sorry, Jas . . . I'll be back, I'm not heading for the train. . . . But I can't stay right now."

She grasped his hands. "Why . . . ?"

"There's someone I have to see."

E I G H T E E N

As if coming into a new country, Greg drove with slow watchful eyes through the lush orchards of El Nido's east end. The abundance startled him, for he hadn't been by this way for some time. He'd grown accustomed to approaching Diana Sanborn's property from the dusty, curving backroads. This Sunday morning he would be arriving through the main gate.

They had Sarah Trant in solitary confinement now. Assaulting a prison guard, they said. Sure, maybe so, that certainly was possible. He had no time to argue or sort it out, though. It wasn't Sarah he needed, anyway.

Diana would see him, Greg was sure of that. She had to see him. *We have Diana Sanborn*, Mashburn claimed. No. Not yet.

Greg parked in the gravel clearing to the side of the house, then climbed the steps to a wide planked front porch. As he was trying to decide between knocking or using the bell, Diana suddenly opened the door. She seemed startled to find him before her. At her side stood a young girl. Maybe ten years old, Greg gauged. Gentle blue eyes, a guileless face, long dark-blond hair pulled into a ponytail. They didn't look related.

"This is not a convenient time," Diana said quickly. "We're in a sort of a rush, I'm afraid. We're on our way out."

"You and I need to talk, Diana."

"It will have to wait."

"It can't wait."

Diana regarded him with a mix of irritation and unease. "This is

Ashley. The daughter of my ranch hand Edward. I'm afraid her pet pig is gravely ill. I know something about pigs, so she has come to enlist my aid. There's no time to waste."

Greg looked back and forth at the girl and the woman. He'd raised a pig once as a boy, he and his father in the home where he grew up, high in the wooded mountainside above La Graciosa. "I know something about those fellows myself," he said. "Let me help."

Ashley's pigpen sat at the bottom of an old orchard below a trio of ranch hands' cabins. It was a splintered wood-frame structure, painted a faded blue, fronted by a small fenced yard and shaded by a handful of orange trees. Through a small window Greg, with appreciation, could see sawdust on the floor. Sawdust was nice to root in, and made a warm bed.

"Winnie just didn't show up for supper," Ashley said. She had a tremor in her voice. "She's never missed a full trough."

Just then a small round pig emerged from the shed. She stood listlessly in the middle of the yard, regarding them with blank eyes.

"This is Winnie?" Greg asked.

"Actually," Ashley replied, "her full name is Winnifred P. Wombly."

"Almost certainly she's just plugged up," Diana said. "An injection of soapy water will fix that."

"I'd try two ounces of castor oil first," Greg said. "If that doesn't work, go to the soapy water."

Diana and Ashley both looked at him. "How enchanting," Diana said. "Our award-winning lawyer also knows pigs." To Ashley she suggested, "Why don't you run over to the bunkhouse and find us some castor oil."

Greg added, "And some clothesline. Just in case."

Ashley said, "Won't need to be tying up Winnie. Promise you that."

"Okay, then," Greg agreed. "No clothesline."

Greg watched the girl run off, then took Diana by the arm and guided her to a redwood bench by the low rail fence. "Let's sit here," he said.

THE VIEW FROM THEIR perch was of Diana's western range. Grazing cows meandered sluggishly, looking for shade. The sun had climbed higher. It was nearing noon. What did he have left? Greg wondered. Twenty hours?

"Sarah's hearing resumes tomorrow," he said. "It will be a critical week."

"I imagine so."

"At first I focused only on the law and the evidence. I knew little about El Nido. I didn't understand what had happened here. What was happening."

Diana showed nothing. "Happened here?"

"Come on, Diana. When I first came, you wanted me to stay in the valley. You had a reason."

"Happened here?" Diana repeated the words as if they would yield their own meaning.

The sound of Ashley's feet on the gravel road stopped them. She came running through the gate into the pigpen's yard, waving a small bottle of castor oil. In her other hand she held a length of clothesline. On her face was a small sheepish grin. "Just in case," she said.

Then Ashley reached down, grabbed Winnie by both her front legs, and upset her quickly. As Winnie opened her mouth to protest, Ashley turned the oil into her throat. The pig gave off a scream, high-pitched and hysterical, but it didn't last long. When Ashley released her legs, Winnie righted herself. The corners of her mouth turned up in a set smile. She stood her ground, studying them, as oil dripped from her lips. Ashley gently scratched her.

"Hope that works," Diana said. "Otherwise we're gonna have to try an enema."

Ashley came to her side. The girl raised her arms and offered Diana a shy, tentative hug. The mistress of Sanborn Ranch hugged back. "Bless your heart," Diana said. "Don't you worry, Winnie will be just fine."

From one of the cabins, they could hear someone calling Ashley now. The girl let go of Diana and turned to Winnie, who got from her a less tentative hug. Then she started out of the pigpen yard. "Thanks to you too, Mr. Monarch," Ashley called as she danced through the gate.

"The ways she moves," Greg said. "She reminds me of a ballerina."

Diana had a faraway look in her eyes. "She reminds me of myself."

Greg chose his words carefully. "You must want so much to preserve the valley for someone like her. As your grandfather did for you."

"Yes . . ." Diana began. Then she caught herself. "What precisely do you mean, Gregory?"

"The Committee of Ten. Wallace Barley. The refinery fires. The lost Panama shipment. The Eastern refiners and the phony dry wells . . . I know about it all."

"Oh, do you?" Diana didn't flinch. "How, may I ask?"

"There are amateur historians aplenty in the valley, it seems, who like to keep journals. Their families tend to dump boxes of memorabilia at the historical museum. There's much interesting reading to be found there, if you're willing to poke around in the storage room."

Dismay started to color Diana's expression. Then, through what seemed an act of will, she smiled grandly and swept her arm all about her, following the horizon. "Yes," she said. "My grandfather and his colleagues left us quite a legacy."

Greg spoke gently. "Maybe we can right wrongs, Diana, and still protect your valley."

Diana rose at those words and strode across the yard. She led Winnie back into the pigpen, then reached for a rake and fussed with the sawdust. Next she checked the food trough and refilled the water bucket. That done, she looked about, fixed on an orange tree, and began pulling ripe fruit off the branches. Finally, she turned to Greg.

"Is that possible?" she asked. "Is that really possible?"

"Yes, Diana. We can do this. We need to do this."

Diana studied Greg, then dropped the oranges at her feet. She slowly moved back to her seat beside him. "I've not managed to pull it off by myself," she said. "Doing right and protecting my valley appear to be mutually exclusive goals."

"Diana . . . Tell me what you've done. Tell me what's happened."

"You tell me something first."

"What's that?"

"How is Sarah doing?"

Greg spoke softly. "She's as you might expect someone in her situation."

"Does she . . . does she speak of me ever?"

"She defends you, Diana. She protects you."

Diana sat in silence for a moment, mulling Greg's words. Then she began. "I had to protect the valley. At first that meant resisting ModoCorp. At those early meetings, Alex and I, we did rather nicely. Had them stalled a bit, claiming easements over camp property. Then they hired Brewster."

"The game changed with Tomaz," Greg said. "Then some more when they rolled their bulldozers and discovered the plume."

This time Diana did flinch. "You know also about the plume?"

"Yes."

She waited for him to explain how he knew, but Greg sat still. Slowly, her shoulders sagged. Her body seemed to leak air. "So . . . ," she said. "It's out."

"No. Only I know. It's not out."

"Only you?"

"Yes."

As she weighed those words, Diana regained her vigor. He'd given her some room to maneuver. "Yes," she said. "The game changed. I couldn't let anyone know. Couldn't allow El Nido to be torn up."

"That gave ModoCorp leverage over you."

"Yes. Now we were partners of a sort. We had mutual interests suddenly. For different reasons, none of us could let the plume become public knowledge."

"Then came the oil spill at El Nido Lake."

Diana slapped the bench. "They were such fools. Fiddled with the old wells. Didn't understand about those pipes up there. Didn't realize they were rotted into nothing."

"A big oil spill would tell everyone there was oil in the valley. Which would cause certain folks to take a closer look, and no doubt discover the plume. Within months you'd have both a massive excavation and state-of-the-art oil wells. All across El Nido."

"Yes, precisely. Which was unthinkable, of course. So I didn't want the spill known any more than did Charles Whit."

"Thank goodness for the bypass pump. Only you would have known how to divert the oil from the lake."

Diana again looked startled at what Greg knew. "No," she said slowly. "Not only me."

Greg mulled that, then suddenly understood. "Brewster Tomaz. He would have known."

"Very good, Gregory. Yes, Brewster knew. He knew also that the bypass took it all the way to a submarine pipe that ran half a mile into the sea. They once used that pipe to transport oil directly to tankers sitting offshore. With a little cooperation from state investigators, you could make it look like the spill came from the ocean to the shore. Very nice solution."

"If only Sarah hadn't seen the leak," Greg said. "If only Sarah hadn't started yelling at state rangers."

"Just so," Diana agreed.

"At least you were able to keep her quiet. Good thing you had such sway over Sarah when she came to you with her news."

"She told you about that? . . . Well, yes, it was a good thing." Diana looked unsettled, as if something had been left unsaid.

Again Greg made the leap with her. "Sarah wasn't the only problem, was she? There was someone else perfectly willing to expose El Nido's oil secrets. Someone else who threatened everyone's interests."

Diana regarded Greg with open admiration now. "I am impressed, Gregory. Yes. Brewster Tomaz had an armlock on all of us. Brewster would never miss the chance to take advantage of people when he could. It was a lifetime habit of his, far as I can tell. Regarding El Nido's oil, he understood he was in an enviable position. He threatened to reveal the plume's existence. He blackmailed me."

"And he also played it against Whit and ModoCorp?"

"Yes."

"Anyone could have killed Tomaz. Everyone had a reason."

Diana offered a mirthless laugh. "You could say that."

"Diana," Greg pleaded. "What happened?"

She looked at him without artifice. "Whoever killed him had to. Sometimes that's the way it works. You do what's needed to make things as they should be."

"Who does? Who does what's needed?"

"We were all down at the river that night. I was there. Alex, Sarah, Whit, Rimmer. Half of El Nido. Choose whom you wish."

"El Nido chose Sarah."

"Yes."

"Why?"

Diana began fussing over the hem of her long skirt, pulling at a loose thread. "I tried to say I'd seen a strange hooded man rushing away. I tried to say that at the start."

"Tried?"

"Yes. Sheriff Rimmer wasn't interested."

"He wanted Sarah?"

"He and whomever he reports to."

"Why?"

"Oh goodness, Gregory." Diana couldn't hide her exasperation. "They had all sorts of reasons. She had to be defused. She'd seen the oil leak, she was yelling at rangers, who knew how long I could keep her quiet. They had to get her out of circulation. What's more, maybe even more important, she provided a clean, uncomplicated explanation for Brewster's murder. Sarah's guilt was the simplest to prove, the most obvious. You didn't have to bring in plumes and oil spills to explain her as the murderer. She was an eco-terrorist who'd been stalking Brewster. She was also an outsider. She was making El Nido look bad." Diana offered a rueful smile. "As you are, Gregory."

Greg tried not to sound like an accuser. "You went along with this, Diana?"

She hung on to her smile. "Sometimes, my dear Gregory, you must align yourself with folks who don't exactly warm your heart."

"Especially if they threaten to kill you."

"Whatever do you mean . . . ?"

"The blackmail letters."

Diana's smile evaporated. "You've figured that out too?"

"I've been prowling around your local cemetery. From what I saw there, I'm willing to bet that Charles Whit is Wallace Barley's grandson. Born to Barley's daughter, Gretchen. He wrote the letters, didn't he? He or someone who works for him."

Diana rose again from their bench and walked about the pigpen. She studied the horizon. "That's a fair surmise," she said. "Gretchen married a fellow in San Francisco named Joseph Whitschenson. Their son, if they had one, might logically have shortened his name."

"You've been fighting your grandfather's battles anew."

"Yes."

"Diana," Greg said. "I need to know. They wanted a dying declaration from Tomaz. . . . So you gave them one?"

She kept her eyes on the horizon. "Yes. . . . Yes I did."

Greg tried to hide his dismay.

"For all our needs," Diana was saying. "For the sake of El Nido. Sometimes we must cross lines. . . ."

"Where do you draw those lines, Diana? How do you decide?"

"You tell me, Greg. You're the expert. You win awards for crossing lines."

He forced himself to stay on track. "Who killed Brewster Tomaz? You? Whit? Rimmer?"

Diana's rich laugh filled the air much as it had his first day in El Nido. "Here's where it really gets amusing, Greg. The truth is, Sarah killed Brewster."

"How can you say . . . ?"

"I saw her do it. I went to the river with her."

"You were with her?"

"No, I hung back. I stayed at the edge of the woods. Brewster was making outrageous demands, insisting on his 'just desserts,' threatening to reveal everything. I'm afraid my response may have egged Sarah on. But I didn't realize what she was going to do. Honestly, I didn't."

Greg struggled to absorb Diana's words. He didn't believe her. And yet he knew she could be telling the truth. "What you're saying, then, is that Whit and Rimmer framed a guilty person?"

"Exactly. They didn't realize it, though. They didn't really know who killed Brewster. They just wanted the simplest story, and they also wanted Sarah put away. To achieve that, they thought they needed me to create a tale. They didn't. I neglected to disabuse them of that notion."

Greg's mind reeled. Sarah was guilty, Sarah did it. Sarah killed Tomaz. Okay, then. He could believe that. So what, though? They'd still framed her. You couldn't just ignore due process, the Fourteenth Amendment, the United States Constitution. A human being was sitting in jail facing execution based on what they'd done. A dangerously unstable human being, perhaps. Yet who finally was the greater threat? Sarah, or those who put her away?

"This is wrong," he said. "Diana, you know it's wrong. That's why you wanted me to stay in El Nido. You wanted me to fix the mess you made."

Something showed in Diana's eyes at that. A longing, Greg thought. A need. Yet she beat it back. "It's also wrong to destroy El Nido," she insisted. "My grandfather. He did what he had to. So did I. We can't let anyone destroy our valley."

Listening to Diana, the obvious suddenly occurred to Greg: The mistress of Sanborn Ranch didn't know about the waste dump. ModoCorp wouldn't have shared that part of their business with her; they'd have lost her if they had. He saw finally his path. Of course. It was the only way.

"That's right," he said quickly. "But that's precisely what Whit's gang is doing, Diana. Right now. Destroying El Nido. Why do you think your cows died?"

"The plume . . ."

"No, not the plume. The plume is only a theoretical hazard, with no proven effect. Hydrogen sulfide killed your cows, not old pooled oil. Hydrogen sulfide, blowing in the air from ModoCorp's waste dump."

"Waste dump . . . ?"

"Diana, they're dumping oil waste into Camp Mahrah from all their operations up and down the West Coast."

"What nonsense. That couldn't be. They'd need a dozen permits—"

"No, Diana. Whole thing is legal. They don't have to ask or tell anyone."

"A waste dump? . . . In El Nido?"

"It's true, Diana. . . . They need to be stopped."

Diana was trembling now. "Sarah's still guilty. Sarah killed Brewster."

"I need your help, Diana. We need to get this out."

"No!" Diana's eyes blazed with fear. "No one can know about the plume. . . . No one can tear up El Nido."

Greg exulted. Surely, he had her. "You have no choice, then," he said gently. "You give me what I need, or everyone will know about El Nido's plume."

"No choice?" Diana cried. "You're wrong there, Gregory. We always have a choice."

—————— N I N E T E E N ——————

They saw each other in the same instant. James Mashburn glanced up from the bench where he sat just as Greg Monarch turned his way. They nodded. Then Greg moved toward the El Nido County DA.

It was Sunday evening on La Graciosa's central plaza, a dormant time in the life of Greg's hometown. He relished the sense of repose the plaza offered at the end of a weekend. By then the weekly Thursday night farmer's market—with its blockaded roadway and makeshift produce stands and outdoor barbecue grills—had receded in memory. The plaza and surrounding avenues were swept clean, posters removed, benches replaced. Not a store clerk or shopper stirred. In the window of Stella's Café, Greg could see waitresses stacking chairs and wiping tables.

He'd be home soon, Greg told himself. Sarah Trant's hearing was to resume in the morning, in the *asistencia* that stood as it had for two hundred years on the far side of the plaza. Whatever was to happen would come this week.

"The game's almost over," Greg said to Mashburn. "Almost time to count our chips."

The DA slid over on the bench, offering Greg a seat. "Not a game, Greg. Not any kind of game."

"No. . . . Of course not."

They sat in silence for a moment, watching the creek. Greg wondered if Mashburn had the same absurd impulse he had just then, which was to talk strategy together, to plot jointly how they would conduct matters when the hearing resumed in the morning. Of course, if he shared all he knew with Mashburn, at the end of the tale Sarah would still be the one who murdered Brewster Tomaz. A framed murderer, but a murderer nonetheless. Without actual innocence, Greg felt he had nothing, despite what the laws of the land promised.

Something else now occurred to Greg. To tell more, to tell Mashburn why they'd framed Sarah, to tell about ModoCorp and oil plumes and waste dumps, he would need to betray Diana Sanborn. Greg, to his surprise, found himself incapable of doing so. He wouldn't be the cause of El Nido's ruin.

"You've shown me nothing new, Greg." Mashburn sounded more sorrowful than combative. "I've been willing to listen, okay? But all I've seen is the same old stuff. Yes, they were sloppy. Yes, they cut some corners and polished a few rough spots. But that's not extraordinary. You know that."

Greg looked about the plaza. "You aren't offended by what you've seen, Jim?"

Mashburn started to respond, then stopped. In Jim's expression, Greg thought he saw feelings not unlike his own. The DA looked as if he wanted to share concerns and impulses. The DA looked as if he longed to feel at least a shred of valor.

"Well, Greg," he said. "Of course I've seen things that offend me. What the hell, though. I often do. It's certainly not unusual. You don't want to be offended, don't look too closely at how we seek justice in this world."

"There are other ways to avoid being offended."

"Sure there are. But they all involve lying down on the job."

"Maybe that's what's needed sometimes."

"Can the crap, Greg. You want *me* to lie down. You'd never do the same. Never."

"What if you flat out knew you were nailing an innocent person?"

"That's not the case here, Greg."

"You don't know."

"Chrissake, Greg, you're all tangled up with this woman. You can't see—"

"Tell me this," Greg proposed. "If Reggie Dodge had known

about the boot prints, do you think he could have put on a better case? Or if Reggie Dodge had known about Judith Daniels's eyewitness account? Or if Reggie Dodge hadn't faced belated recollections about a dying declaration—"

Mashburn leapt up from the bench. "Enough, Greg. For the love of God. Sarah Trant's appeals have been filled with these arguments for years. They don't make her innocent. She killed that old man, damnit. Face facts, Greg. Face that your ex-lover is a killer."

"Now, wait—"

"No, you wait. I'm not lying down for you. We're adversaries, Greg. That's how it works. You don't like the rules, don't play in the game. There's no right or wrong. Just winners and losers . . ."

Greg stopped fighting. It was dark now on the plaza, and empty. He sat still on the bench, looking up at Mashburn, taking the measure of this man. What he saw gave him reassurance. "Come on, Jim," he said. "I know you don't believe that."

FROM THE WINDOW OF his chambers in the *asistencia*, Judge Solman watched Greg Monarch and James Mashburn talking in the plaza. When the two lawyers rose and parted, Solman returned to his desk and the files before him. He'd come here on this Sunday evening seeking a moment alone before the habeas hearing resumed in the morning. He wanted to consider how he'd ended up in such a regretful position.

If he had it to do over, he never would have stopped by Greg Monarch's office with that handwritten habeas petition. What compelled him to do so? Solman couldn't fix on a satisfactory answer. Of course, he was facing the question with hindsight now. At the start he hadn't the slightest notion of the quagmire attached to this petition. If he had, he might very well have shredded Sarah Trant's sorry little plea the instant he received it.

He hadn't shredded it, though. Instead, he'd walked it over to Greg. He couldn't turn back the clock now; he had to continue forward, as they all did. That, unavoidably, had been among the several matters he'd been pondering these past five days. He hadn't granted Greg a delay just because the state withheld evidence. He'd needed his own respite. He'd bought time for himself as well as the defense attorney.

He'd seen such outrage in Greg's eyes these past weeks. Sitting in the courtroom, it had been hard to look down at that man after a while. Solman had found himself turning away, scribbling on his legal pad, staring at the ceiling . . . anything but gaze upon the consequences of his own chosen conduct.

He wished he could reverse course now. He wished he could stop what he was doing. He couldn't, though. There were too many forces at play. Too many forces to defy. He saw no means of escape.

JASMINE GEST CAME TO Greg later that night as he sat on his deck at home, watching Graciosa Creek flow by. There'd been no plan or phone call. She just showed up and settled beside him on his redwood swing.

"You mind?" she said. "I need a place to stay during the hearing."

"And if I did . . . ?"

"I would leave."

He pulled her to him. "Don't leave."

Jas's hand moved to his neck. Her lips brushed his ear. "Then don't go away anymore. Especially when I'm gasping for breath in a motel room. Moaning, too. Gasping and moaning."

"A deal."

They sat in silence. Greg knew he hadn't managed to hide his apprehension from her. These days, he rarely could hide anything from her.

"What will happen tomorrow?" she asked.

"Hard to say."

"You have a plan, though."

"Is that a question?"

"No," Jas said. "It's not a question."

Greg ran a hand through her hair. "You think you're so smart."

"I know you."

"Funny . . . I don't."

"I know that too."

Greg's hand roamed down her back, coming to rest on her hip.

He could feel her thigh through the thin cotton dress. "Yeah, sure, I have a plan. I always have a plan."

She studied him. "Want to talk about it? Tell me what bothers you so?"

"What bothers me," Greg said, "is what always bothers me."

Jas hesitated, then spoke. "Tell me about Jason Pine. Tell me the end of that story."

It was so like her to do that, Greg thought. To make such a leap. To know where he was.

"Okay," he said. "Jason Pine." As he began, it occurred to him that he'd never told anyone the end of the story.

IT REALLY WAS A nice bit of courtroom handiwork, Greg had to admit. At Pine's murder trial, he couldn't even get Jason's mother or minister to testify on his behalf. Nor could he call a medical expert to the stand, for the court provided no funds to hire one. All he had going for him—to counter three state doctors' testimony that the defendant was drunk on the murder night, not mentally ill—were the records from Pine's twenty-two-month stay at a private psychiatric hospital in Delaware. Only by chance did Greg, poring through those handwritten sheets, notice certain tenuous references to "pseudopsychopathic schizophrenia." The term meant nothing, really. It could be applied broadly and subjectively to anyone a doctor thought might have some characteristics of a schizophrenic. Or rather, it once could be applied. No longer; the American Psychiatric Association dropped it as a recognized diagnosis the very year Pine was being treated in Delaware.

Normally, Greg wouldn't have been able to get these Delaware records admitted without testimony from the doctor who wrote them up. It was here Greg undeniably hornswaggled the district attorney. "Come on, Taylor," he'd urged. "Defense has no money to fly in experts. Let me use the records. Stipulate their entry into evidence." Maybe Taylor was overconfident, maybe Taylor foolishly succumbed to a sense of fair play. For whatever reason, he agreed. Which decision—Greg couldn't help observe—had its own consequence. Putting the records into evidence meant Greg could talk about them in his closing argument. Any good lawyer can testify better than an expert—that was a maxim learned in law school, then over and over in the courtroom. Greg certainly proved its verity at Pine's trial.

"Ladies and gentlemen," he told the jury, "we don't have a psychiatrist who is going to testify today. The defendant is indigent. He can't afford to fly in experts. You noticed that, unlike the state, we didn't have a psychiatrist testifying for the defense. What we do have are all the psychiatric records, which we furnished you, entered into evidence. In those records you can see mention of many things. An alcoholic abusive father, a depressive mother, early-childhood trauma, an overindulgent grandmother, antisocial behavior. But most important, there are diagnoses. Doctors diagnosed him. Doctors called him mentally ill."

Pseudopsychopathic schizophrenia—over and over in his closing, Greg repeated that term, until it sounded like an ominous threat. Dates and times, explanations, narratives. *Pseudopsychopathic schizophrenia.* Then, with perfect timing, he backed away from that meaningless phrase. It's up to you to decide whether Jason is sane, Greg told the jurors. Just because a psychologist or psychiatrist or other expert says he's competent or not, that doesn't change things. It's up to you. Here's what you need to think about: Would a normal person do what Jason Pine did? Would you or your friends or relatives? *This murder was so horrible, nobody in their right mind could have done that. Nobody in their right mind.*

After deliberating for just two hours, the jurors unanimously agreed. Pine, declared insane, went back to the mental hospital instead of prison. To the mental hospital, where a doctor soon declared that he wasn't insane after all. Where a doctor eventually insisted they therefore had to let Pine go.

"THAT'S JUST WHAT A judge felt obliged to do in the end," Greg told Jas. "Jason Pine walked free because I convinced a jury he was insane, when he wasn't. Six months later, he strolled into another convenience store. Again he thought he saw his ex-girlfriend, and again he pulled the trigger. A bullet to the heart. This one had no children, at least."

Jas put her arms around his neck and curled against him on the redwood swing. "It's not your fault Greg. You did nothing wrong. You did precisely what you were supposed to do."

Greg felt the warm pressure of her body. He clung to her with a sort of desperation.

"I know that," he said. "And I'm going to do it again."

─── T W E N T Y ───

On a dark fogbound morning such as this one, there was nothing to be seen of La Graciosa's central plaza. Now all the familiar objects that normally provided Greg his bearings were hidden. The park benches, the bear statue, the winding creek, even the *asistencia* itself, had vanished behind a thick gray wall. Greg moved slowly toward the courthouse, stepping with care.

It was nearly half past eight on Monday. Sarah Trant's habeas hearing was to resume in forty minutes. Greg wanted to talk once more with his client; they'd brought her from the El Nido state prison late the evening before. Feeling gravel underfoot, he turned up the unpaved path that circled to the sheriff's private jailhouse entrance at the rear of the building. A guard led him down a hallway toward her cell. It had been days since he'd seen her. Days that had emphatically challenged his own understanding of her role in Brewster Tomaz's death. He no longer was certain how to approach his client. *A defense attorney shouldn't hear what he doesn't need to know.* Greg, though, longed to know everything.

"How nice," Sarah said. "My savior has returned."

She was sitting on the edge of a cot. The effect of her tenure in solitary confinement showed. She blinked with uncertainty.

"Not sure you should call me that, Sarah."

"Oh." His tone stopped her. "What's changed?"

He held back, reluctant to take her where they had to go. He cast about for other topics. "Did you really assault a guard?"

She looked away. "That skinny guard with big ears tried to get handsy when I was alone on mop brigade outside the mess hall. Told me I should be nice to him. Nice to him like . . ."

"Like what?

"Like I was nice to my attorney."

"What happened next?"

"I pushed him away and got out of there. That was all. An obvious case of assault on my part. So yes, I confess. I'm guilty."

Greg drew a breath. "Sarah," he asked. "You want to confess to anything else?"

Confusion showed in her expression now. "Confess . . . What do you mean?"

A ray of sunlight reached through the cell's small window, warming the side of Greg's face. He could see a patch of blue sky. The fog was lifting. "Sarah, the thing is, Diana Sanborn says she went down to the river with you that night. She says she stayed back at the edge of the woods. She says she saw you kill Brewster Tomaz."

Sarah sat still for a moment. Then she rose from her cot and walked to the window. She wrapped her hands around the iron bars that kept her from the plaza. "I pushed him into the river, I know I did that," she said. "I also know I ran off afterwards."

"You're not certain what happened between those two moments, are you, Sarah? You've never been certain. Whenever we've gone over that night, you've acted confused."

"I imagine slashing his throat . . . there's a vision in my mind." She began to weep. "I couldn't have, though. How could I?"

He came to her and held her in his arms. "In your mind, Sarah. You sometimes can't separate your dreams from reality, can you?"

"I think I can, but sometimes . . . Oh, Greg, it gets confusing. It gets so scary."

"Why would you have charged Tomaz with a knife that night, Sarah? Can you remember how this started?"

"He was going to ruin El Nido. He was helping ModoCorp. I had to stop him. . . ."

"That night, though. What happened that night?"

"Diana . . . she was so tormented by Tomaz. He was threatening her, scaring her. He was hurting her so much . . . I just—" Sarah stopped and turned away. "That's all I remember."

He pulled her back to him, cupping her face in his hands. He stroked her cheeks, searching for understanding in the feel of her skin. Sarah changed around Diana, that's what Jas had told him. Diana had a hold on her. Enthralled her with the history of the valley, her grandfather, unspoiled Eden. Sarah, wide-eyed, lapped it up. Greg could see why, given Diana's subtext. Good and evil sharply defined in an otherwise bewildering universe. A world of unblemished clarity, high purpose, intricate meaning. That's what Diana offered Sarah. Just what Sarah always wanted. Diana fed Sarah's eternal hunger.

"She's not your friend," Greg said. "Diana betrayed you. She gave you up for the murder."

Sarah twisted out of his arms, turned back to the window. "That's not true," she said. "Diana is my friend."

EMERGING FROM HIS CHAMBERS, Judge Solman walked slowly to the bench, keeping his head down and his eyes averted from all who'd gathered for Sarah Trant's habeas hearing. When he did finally speak, he offered only a brusque greeting, then began leafing through documents.

"Your Honor—" James Mashburn began.

"I trust we're all up to speed now?" Solman interrupted. "Are we ready to get to the end of this proceeding?"

"Yes, Your Honor," Mashburn replied. "The state has been ready for some time now."

Solman glanced vaguely at the petitioner's side of the table. "Your Honor," Greg said. "I'm ready to proceed."

Solman nodded at Mashburn. "Call your next witness."

"I call Judge Karl Jackson."

The former prosecutor of El Nido County was a tall, thin man with an oddly serene manner. Watching him stride through the courtroom toward the witness stand, Greg Monarch searched vainly for any sign of menace. Karl Jackson had the look of one who would make a good drinking companion any evening at the Gaucho Tavern. He'd grown up in El Nido County, Greg knew that much. After law school at Berkeley, he'd opened a private practice, but after four years had joined the DA's office. He'd worked his way up, year by year. Eventually he ran for the office of district attorney and won. He was reelected six times. Then the governor appointed him to the state bench.

"Judge Jackson," Mashburn began. "Good morning."

"Good morning," Jackson replied, with the tone of one who thought it indeed was.

The two of them, the former and present district attorneys, proceeded to engage in a gracious dance. Mashburn had decided to call Jackson to the stand himself, rather than wait for Greg. Now he lobbed softball questions, guiding Jackson carefully through the prosecution of Sarah Trant. Why he'd chosen to charge her, why he'd disregarded certain pieces of evidence, why he thought it unnecessary to share various matters with the defense attorney. Most central to all his reasoning, Jackson explained, was Brewster Tomaz's dying declaration.

Here the witness pointedly looked up at Judge Solman, sharing a collegial moment. He had the victim naming his killer, Jackson pointed out, and a highly respected member of the community hearing him do so. What more could you want? The jury had listened, the jury had delivered a verdict. That's how the system worked. It wasn't the district attorney who convicted Sarah Trant. It wasn't El Nido County, or the state of California. It was a jury of twelve El Nido citizens. God bless the jury system. What could be preferable? What could be a more wonderful defense against abuse?

When it finally came time for his cross, Greg approached this witness with deliberation. He didn't expect to make his case on Jackson's back; that would come later today. Nor did he expect Solman to let him get too far. For the moment, his aim was simpler. He wanted this good honorable man to explain himself.

"Judge Jackson," Greg began. "You were the prosecuting attorney in the murder trial of Sarah Trant?"

"That's correct."

"And you were involved from the start, right?"

"From the night Brewster Tomaz was murdered."

"You asked for a murder in the first degree verdict, correct?"

"Correct."

"And you asked for the death penalty, right?"

"We had a death-penalty hearing, that is correct."

"Well," Greg said, moving closer to his witness. "You asked for the death penalty. You didn't have the hearing by accident, did you?"

For the first time, some of the contented geniality slid off of Jackson. "No, we didn't. Right. We filed a notice."

"Okay, then." Greg circled around to the lawyers' table, picked up a file, then turned back to the witness stand. "To start out with, I'd like to review what you didn't do as part of your job of prosecuting Sarah Trant and asking for the death penalty. You didn't, Judge Jackson, think that the extra set of boot prints found at the murder site were significant in any way? Is that what you indicated on direct? Is that still your testimony, Judge?"

Jackson frowned now. "That doesn't capture the context," he said. "But yes, at the start of the trial the boot prints were not considered a significant issue."

"Do you recall looking at those prints yourself?"

"It's hard to say. I had the sheriff's office—"

"Yes or no, Judge. You never looked at the boot prints that you decided weren't significant in a death-penalty murder trial?"

"I can't imagine that I didn't. . . . But I have no specific recollection of looking at them."

"Isn't it a fact that you depended on Sheriff Rimmer to determine what you were shown concerning the crime-scene evidence?"

Jackson reached for a glass of water. "That's how it always worked. He had control of the evidence. I visited him, or he came to me and showed me what he had."

"You looked only at what Sheriff Rimmer showed you, is that your testimony?"

"I asked to see everything, and I assumed that Sheriff Rimmer showed me everything. I know of no reason for him not to show me everything."

"I ask you again, Judge. Did you or did you not see those boot prints?"

"To the best of my recollection . . . I have no specific recollection."

"Do you recall conferring with the forensics tech who decided they were three days old?"

"There again, I'm not sure. The sheriff's office handled that."

"Yes or no, Judge."

Now Jackson looked as if he wanted to slam a gavel down somewhere. Up on the bench, Judge Solman reached for his. "I can't imagine I didn't," the witness said again. "But I have no specific recollection."

"Do you recall sharing the matter of the extra boot prints with Sarah Trant's trial attorney, Reginald Dodge?"

"As I understood it, Sheriff Rimmer provided Dodge with those prints."

"Do you have any independent knowledge that Dodge was provided those prints?"

"I can't imagine he wasn't."

"Yes or no, Judge."

"Okay, no, I have no independent recollection."

So it went for much of the morning. *I can't imagine . . . I have no independent recollection . . . The sheriff handled that . . .* By midday, Greg had heard his fill of slippery responses. This good, honorable man was not explaining himself in the least. Out of the corner of his eye, Greg watched Mashburn absorb his predecessor's performance. What did Jim think? What could Jim possibly think?

Just past noon, Greg approached Jackson with his final set of questions. "And you didn't believe it was worthwhile to look at photos from the murder site yourself?" he asked. "To see if what the police told you was the truth?"

"I didn't think they reflected a contested issue."

Greg moved his mouth near Jackson's ear. "You've been a lawyer long enough to know that when I ask a question you're supposed to answer it. Isn't that right, Judge Jackson?"

The witness glanced up at the bench. "Yes," he said evenly. "Of course."

Solman shifted about, and Greg tensed, preparing for his intervention. It didn't come, though. Solman was busily scribbling something on a pad before him. Greg tried to read the judge's expression. He realized now that Solman hadn't intervened all morning. Was he going to give him room to roam today?

"Is there a chance," Greg asked Jackson, "that you just preferred not to know what the sheriff's detectives were up to?"

"No, sir." A tinge of pink showed around Jackson's jowls.

"Okay, then," Greg suggested. "Let's talk for a moment about the so-called dying declaration. Detective Gary Goolan has told us he heard from Ms. Sanborn about this right away, on the night of the murder, but just didn't manage to get it into his reports until weeks later. Does that sound believable to you?"

"As I understand it, he did tell his colleagues. Then he—"

"No, no. I don't think that comes close to being a responsive answer. Please answer my question."

"Detective Goolan did report what he'd heard—"

"We seem to be having some problems with the acoustics in here," Greg interrupted. "Let me try again. Yes or no, does that sound believable to you?"

Jackson summoned a faint smile. "Yes, it does."

"Do you still have confidence in his account of Diana Sanborn's statement to him?"

"Yes, I do."

"You are telling us you don't find anything unusual about anything in that statement?"

Jackson looked up at Judge Solman again. Greg followed his glance. To his surprise, Solman was frowning at the witness.

"Yes or no," Greg said. "Yes or no, Judge Jackson."

"No. . . . I don't find anything unusual."

Greg slapped the railing before him. "Tell me, Judge Jackson, do you think this is some kind of sport?"

"No, I don't, sir. . . . Absolutely not, sir."

"Do you realize that Sarah Trant sits here facing execution based on the evidence you put on? Do you realize that?"

"Yes, of course I do."

"You sit here and defend this type of evidence?"

"Yes, I am defending it."

"Are you telling us the truth, Judge Jackson? Are you telling us the whole truth? Are you telling us nothing but the truth?"

"Yes, sir." Jackson's eyes blazed. "Yes, sir, I most certainly am."

"Is Sarah Trant really the greatest menace in this courtroom? Is there possibly someone else here who represents an even greater peril?"

Mashburn jumped up. "Objection, objection!"

Solman was finally reaching for his gavel. "That's enough, Mr. Monarch. . . . You're pushing too far now. . . . You must stay on track."

"I am on track," Greg insisted. "Judge Jackson, isn't it true you withheld the boot prints from Reggie Dodge? Isn't it true you withheld Judith Daniels's eyewitness account? Isn't—"

"You only need turn over material to the defense that's exculpatory," Jackson interrupted. "We followed the law."

"The law? . . . The law?"

"Yes, the law," Jackson said. "The California Rules of Criminal Procedure—"

"No!" Greg thundered. "Excuse me. We're talking here about something called the United States Constitution. We're talking about the Fourteenth Amendment. We're talking about due process of law. That's what we're talking about. Are we not, Judge Jackson? Are we not—"

"Objection!" Mashburn called. "Objection."

"That's quite enough," the judge declared. "Stop, everyone, stop. I've been giving you latitude today, Mr. Monarch, but you're way out of bounds now—"

"It's not me who's out of bounds," Greg snapped. "Tell that to this witness. Tell that   "

"Counselor!" Solman was banging his gavel. "That's quite enough. If you can't settle down, I'll throw you in jail. Don't think I won't, Mr. Monarch. Don't make that mistake."

Behind him, Greg could hear Sarah sobbing. "Greg," she gasped. "Please . . . I need you. . . ." He turned and walked back to the lawyers' table, his eyes on Jim Mashburn. At least he'd had an impact, that much he could see. To the judge he said, "You're right, Your Honor. That is quite enough. No more questions."

AT THE LUNCH BREAK, Greg picked up a tri-tip sandwich at Stella's Café, then hiked along Graciosa Creek, following it to where it curved into the narrow wooded glen that had become his sanctuary during the hearing. He'd retreated more than once to this quiet hollow, where the sunlight filtered through the oaks and played off the rippling water. He sat in his customary spot, on a rocky ledge beside the water, and waited.

The sound he was hoping for, of someone stepping through the surrounding thicket, came just moments later. Then the form of a man appeared out of the dense brush. He was walking quickly, as if in a hurry to reach a destination. When he saw Greg, he froze. This time, though, he didn't turn and flee.

"Well now, Greg," Judge Solman said, trying to hide his fluster. "I didn't know we had a common interest in shady glens."

"I did," Greg said. "I've seen you here before, more than once. Several times, in fact, during the lunch hour. Not a bad way to escape from the hearing."

"I've not seen you."

"I think you did, once at least. At the start of the hearing. I was sitting on this very ledge. You turned off the trail and slipped down that ravine over there. Since then, I've made sure to keep out of your way."

Solman's fluster deepened into embarrassment. "Well, okay, Greg. Yes. It would have been improper for us to meet."

"Yet we need to, don't we?"

"What do you mean?"

Greg weighed his words, not sure how to pursue the opening he sensed. "You sure have sandbagged me, Judge. What was it you said? *Just thought you might be interested in what's crossed my desk. . . . The way she puts things . . . This is her last chance.* Jesus. Thought you'd meet me halfway, at least. You granted the hearing, after all. Now you're thinking of throwing me in jail."

Solman stood where he was, unwilling to close the distance between them. "We can't be talking like this. Alone, without the other lawyers. It's against all the rules."

"I'm delighted to hear that you are so concerned with rules," Greg said.

Solman took two steps toward him. "Listen to me, Greg. Getting a habeas hearing doesn't mean you automatically win. You put on evidence, so does the state. I thought your gal had some interesting business in her petition. The state has answers, though. And you, Greg, have a temper. Any judge would be reining you in as I do. Some judges would already have you behind bars."

Greg studied the creek. "How'd they get to you?" he asked after a while. "Tell me, Judge. What did it take?"

Solman advanced now, stood above him. A vein had started

throbbing in his neck. "Elemental principles of law and government in this country," he said. "That's what got to me, Greg. Those principles restrain federal intrusion into a state's affairs. Look at what the Ninth Circuit just said the other month in rejecting that *Delaney* habeas: 'We are sensitive to the independence of the California courts and of that state's sovereignty.' "

"Oh, come on, Judge—"

"No," Solman interrupted. "You can't just blow up the fundamental balance of power between state and federal courts. You can't dismantle the entire underpinning of the legal system."

Greg stared at Solman. "You've got to act, because the state won't, Judge. The state won't because it's they who created this gross injustice."

Solman looked away. "Fine. Then keep arguing your case. Do the best you can. We'll see where it leads."

"There's no jury, Daniel. It's going to be up to you."

Solman tugged at his collar. "I'm trying to keep things on track. That's all. On track. There will be a reviewable record out of this. I need to pass appellate review."

"Hey, Daniel." Greg spoke quietly, straining to keep a tone of argument out of his voice. "Don't you dream sometimes of just doing the right thing?"

Solman began absentmindedly touching the pulsing vein on his neck. "The right thing," he said. "As if that were a fixed object that we all could recognize. It's not, though. Unsettling as it may be to you, trials rarely yield incontestable truth. We traffic in the world of reasonable doubt."

"Come on, Daniel. You gave me my seventy-two-hour delay, which I needed. And today, on the bench, you gave me some leeway. You also looked quite unhappy with Karl Jackson. Acts of a man with a conscience, I'd say."

"You read too much into my gestures."

"No, I don't buy that. Something has happened. What turned you back to me? The sheriff's testimony? Karl Jackson's? Or was it all those long hours of thinking over the past five days?"

Solman held up a warning hand. "I haven't turned back to you, Greg."

"Then you're lined up with a bad sort on this one."

"Bad sort, perhaps," the judge said. "But they include just about every big hitter in the state."

"Well beyond California, actually. Big hitters all across the country, from what I can tell. I still didn't expect this of you. Back in law school, you were ever the politician on the podium. But you stood for something, Daniel. You were a leader."

Solman looked as if he'd received a body blow. He turned and walked toward the water. There he stood, examining the creek. "No, I didn't expect this of me either," he offered finally. "Maybe that's what I've been thinking about during the recess. . . . On top of that, it didn't help today to see a respected judge disgrace himself on the witness stand."

"Tell me, Daniel, during your thinking, you reach any conclusions?"

Solman held his hands cupped together as if in prayer. "Nothing so certain, I'm afraid. Only questions occur to me, not answers. It occurs to me, for instance, that maybe I shouldn't have ever accepted appointment to the bench. I wonder now if I made a mistake. Be honest, Greg. Back in law school, did I strike you as having a particularly wise and noble judicial bent?"

"Well, I . . ." Greg, face-to-face with this man, found he couldn't lie. "Not really, Daniel. Sorry. I must confess."

Solman nodded his absolution. "It is a hard thing to admit . . . but I'm not a particularly brave person."

"I'm going to help you be one," Greg said. "In court this afternoon, I'll give you what you need."

Solman was pacing now, and didn't look as if he'd heard Greg. "I thought Sarah Trant's was a curious plea, maybe even a worthwhile plea. I concede that. I thought it might intrigue you, and, well, to be honest, I guess the notion of arousing your concern attracted me. But there was so much I didn't know. If only I'd understood back then what a tangled box we were opening."

"It is tangled," Greg agreed. "But we're going to untangle it. You'll have good reason to rule for Sarah. You won't even have a choice."

Solman stepped to where Greg sat on the ledge, and settled beside him. "I realize some people are willing to lose everything in the defense of what they deem to be right and just. Not me, though. Can you understand, Greg? I don't wish to lose everything."

"Of course I understand. But you won't lose at all."

"Besides," Solman continued. "Who knows what's right and just?"

Greg kept his eyes on the creek. "Yes, precisely. Who knows?"

DIANA SANBORN LINGERED IN La Graciosa's plaza, just as they'd planned. She strolled about, stopping to look at the sculpture of a bear, then the ducks in the creek, then the face of the two-hundred-year-old *asistencia*. She'd not been here very often, for she only rarely ventured from the valley. She found La Graciosa's central core pleasing. Like El Nido, it had weathered the forces of time. This plaza reminded her of El Nido's arcade. Without the oil plume, she surmised.

Instead they had fog. She'd nearly caught her death this morning, accustomed as she was to rising in a warm dry valley. The sun finally had burned off the heavy mist, yet still Diana felt a chill. She pulled her scarf more securely around her neck and let her mind drift. It wasn't, she had to admit, entirely accurate to describe the El Nido Valley as dry. They didn't have fog, but they did, in rare moments, have legendary cloudbursts. In her twelfth year, Diana had seen one. She could recall it now with as much clarity as ever.

The clouds that day had been gathering in a great black bank in the west for some hours. Thick masses piled up on the already accumulated clouds, until they seemed miles thick, dark and threatening. On the opposite side, from the northeast, loomed a similar bank of clouds. As the hours passed, the dense masses advanced on each other. The winds seemed to cease, but higher up among the clouds, Diana could hear a low brooding roar. The roar deepened then, and the leaves rustled. At first a few drops fell, as large as rocks. Soon they came faster and so thickly that Diana couldn't see fifty feet away. Small ravines were waist deep in water, the flat ground a good inch. Still a greater roar could be heard. Down the channel of El Nido Creek came a wall of water five feet high and a hundred feet wide, sweeping everything in its course.

A cloudburst, it was later explained to Diana, was simply a point of condensation between two opposing currents of air, both saturated with moisture and suspended for some time over a small territory. Yet to Diana that day it had looked like the end of the world. In a certain reach of the El Nido Valley, she still could see the cloudburst's history written in the pile of rocks that covered nearly a four-square-mile canyon. At the mouth of the canyon, the debris remained over one hundred feet deep. They estimated that some one hundred million cubic yards of earth and rocks were swept away that day. It was hard to imagine the force of a torrent that could, in an hour or two, cast forth such a mass. Yet Diana had seen it with her own eyes.

The sound of steps pulled Diana from her reverie. Looking up, she saw James Mashburn exiting the *asistencia* by the side door he always used. Diana turned quickly and cut across the plaza at an angle that would intersect with the DA's path toward Stella's Café. They met in the center, near the bear sculpture, just as Diana had calculated.

"Mr. Mashburn," she sang out. "How nice to encounter you. How convenient, in fact. There is something we need to talk about."

Mashburn regarded his star witness with puzzlement. They'd gone over Diana's testimony ten days before. He thought they had everything nailed down. She'd told her story without a hitch during the practices. "Need to talk about?" he asked. "What do you mean?"

"It's about my testimony this afternoon. I must talk to you before that happens."

Puzzlement gave way to concern. Mashburn took Diana by the elbow, guided her toward Stella's. "Come," he said. "We'll get a quiet table on the deck."

They sat near the railing, with the creek drifting by at their feet. Each poked at a salad. Diana threw bread crumbs to the ducks on the stream's bank while Mashburn watched and fidgeted. Theirs had always been more a respectful relationship than a close one. That Mashburn wasn't a native of El Nido didn't help. In truth, Sheriff Rimmer had handled most of the contacts with Diana. He'd prepped her for this hearing, just as he had for the original trial. Mashburn had monitored them from afar, as if disdaining that type of involvement. Diana couldn't recall when they'd been alone together like this.

"I've been thinking about the evening of the murder," she began.

Mashburn froze, a forkful of lettuce halfway to his mouth.

"So much I blocked off, so much I couldn't bear thinking about. So much going on, everyone in a frenzy. A person gets confused. It's hard. . . ."

Mashburn leaned forward. "Diana, what are you saying?"

She reached for a handkerchief in her purse. She dabbed at her eyes, then began.

It didn't happen as she told them at the trial, Diana explained. She didn't just come upon Brewster after he'd been attacked. She was standing in the woods beyond the creek. She saw Sarah down at the river. Sarah with Brewster. She saw Sarah push Brewster in the water. But then Sarah ran off, just as she has always claimed. Someone else came running up. A man; at least she assumed it was a man. Taller and bulkier than Sarah. Broad shoulders, thick forearms. She couldn't see his face. He had a hooded jacket tied tightly over his head. He also had a knife. She saw it glint in the moonlight when he lifted it to the sky. She couldn't see what he did with the knife. Only that he lifted it. Then he ran off too. Not in the direction Sarah went. Across the river, into the brush on the far side. Got as far as the big alder tree over there. Then he flat out disappeared.

Mashburn by now had put his fork down. "Why didn't you tell us this before?" he demanded. "Back then, at the time of the murder?"

Diana found a dry spot of her handkerchief and applied it to her eyes again. "I did. . . . I'm afraid I most certainly did."

Mashburn looked both furious and in great pain.

"I told all this to Sheriff Rimmer back then," Diana continued. "He came to me saying that the spinster Judith Daniels had seen a third person, a man, running from the river. I started to tell him that I had too. Sheriff Rimmer stopped me. He told me not to dwell on that. They had so much evidence pointing toward Sarah Trant, so much evidence putting Sarah at the murder site. Since we all knew Sarah did it, we shouldn't muddy things up. Besides, that Judith Daniels, everyone knew she was a dotty old lady, terribly disturbed. Wouldn't be a reliable witness in any case. We were better to forget the third man. Better to stick with Sarah."

Tears were rolling down Diana's cheeks now. Mashburn, seeing that her handkerchief was a sodden ball, handed her his napkin.

"I let Sheriff Rimmer convince me," Diana said. "I don't know why. Then I forgot about it. No, that's not so. I put it aside. I put it away. Until now . . ."

Mashburn reached for his glass of water. "Tomaz's dying declaration . . . Are you saying you didn't hear that?"

Diana put down the napkin and rearranged herself in her chair. "I heard Brewster. Yet the memory haunts me now. He was whispering, gasping. Something awfully guttural . . ."

Diana hesitated, as if lost in a memory. Mashburn leaned forward. "Go on," he urged.

Diana nodded her thanks for the encouragement. "The truth of the matter is that I now think Brewster was just making noises, to which I applied meaning."

Mashburn sat back in his chair. He felt about for his napkin, then realized Diana had it. She, noticing, handed him her clean one. He dipped it in his water glass, wiped it on the back of his neck.

"Your story," he said. "It fits exactly with Judith Daniels's."

"Yes," Diana agreed. "Also with Sarah Trant's testimony at her trial."

"You're . . . You . . ." Mashburn was having trouble speaking. Diana waited for him. "If this is true," he continued after a moment, "your account knocks out the entire underlying theory of the trial. It's an entirely new story. It . . . it changes the theory of the case."

"I'm afraid so. But I felt I needed to tell you. This has weighed so awfully on me."

Mashburn's expression hardened suddenly. "Maybe you're lying. How can I believe you? You're telling me you committed perjury back at the trial. Why not assume you're lying now? It certainly is possible. Likely, even. No, I'm sorry, Diana. You just can't be trusted anymore. What you're telling me is worthless."

Diana sighed. "I realized you would feel that way, Mr. Mashburn, even though it was your own sheriff who coerced me. Yet I have corroboration for my account."

"Corroboration?"

"Yes. My foreman, Alex Ramirez. He was with me that evening. He was standing beside me in the woods."

"Your foreman . . . ?" Mashburn fell silent, lost in thought. Slowly, his look of wary concern faded. To her surprise, Diana thought she saw a glint in his eyes now. "Are you sure of all this?" he asked finally. "Let's hear it again."

By the time Diana finished walking a second time through her story, Mashburn was drumming his fingers on the table. He rose suddenly. "It's going to come out anyway," he told Diana. "So let's get it over with."

THE CONFERENCE IN JUDGE Daniel Solman's chambers began at 1:30 P.M. Mashburn sat off to one side, Greg between Diana and Sarah. The two women traded tentative, fragile glances, while from across his vast desk, Solman gazed at everyone with uncertainty. "I don't know what this is about," he said slowly. "How do you want to proceed, Mr. Mashburn? You asked for this conference."

The DA nodded at the court reporter seated in a corner of the room. "This should all be on the record," he suggested.

"It is," Solman assured him. "Don't you worry."

"Fine," Mashburn said. "We're prepared to start, then. I'm just going to ask Ms. Sanborn to speak to the Court."

"So we should swear her in?" the judge asked.

Mashburn glanced at Greg, but Monarch was studiously riffling through a file. "I guess that's a matter for the Court to decide," the DA said. "Perhaps I should explain. Walking to lunch today, I encountered Diana Sanborn out on the plaza. She needed to speak with me, she said. We went over to Stella's, sat on the deck. She seemed terribly upset. Terribly. So maybe we should just hear from Ms. Sanborn."

"Will she be making representations of fact?" Solman asked.

"I would have to say that is correct, Your Honor."

"Fine," Solman said. "Ms. Sanborn, would you kindly raise your right hand? . . . Do you swear to tell the truth, the whole truth, and nothing but the truth, so help you God?"

In her grandest voice Diana declared, "Yes, I do."

"Okay, Ms. Sanborn," Solman said. "What would you like to say to the Court?"

For the third time on this Monday, Diana Sanborn walked through her story, this time before a judge and court reporter.

Someone else came running up. A man, taller and bulkier than

257

Sarah . . . I told all this to Sheriff Rimmer back then. . . . He told me not to dwell on that. . . . I let Sheriff Rimmer convince me. . . . Then I put it aside. . . .

As she spoke, Judge Solman sat ever straighter in his chair. He reached for a pen and a legal pad. His eyes, at first fixed on Diana, slowly moved to Greg. He kept them there until Greg looked up at him. Solman finally interrupted Diana. "The dying declaration, Ms. Sanborn? Did you hear that or not?"

Diana softly exhaled. "I heard something, Your Honor. But as I reflect back now, I'm sure it was only a meaningless noise, a dying gasp. I'm afraid I applied the meaning. Either that, or maybe Brewster just meant Sarah was there, Sarah pushed him. . . . It was all so unclear. . . . I'm sorry."

Judge Solman frowned. "You testified at the murder trial with such certainty, Ms. Sanborn."

Diana pulled the handkerchief from her purse, dabbed at her eyes. "I am so sorry. I'm afraid I let Sheriff Rimmer influence me. It was he who took all my statements. It was he who prepared me for my testimony. I'm not accustomed to murders and courtrooms. . . ."

To Greg's left, Sarah was sobbing now, stretching her arms out toward Diana. To Greg's right, Diana was blinking back tears and turning to Sarah. Solman looked back and forth at them. Then his eyes returned to Greg. "Very interesting, Mr. Monarch," the judge said. "Fascinating."

Greg tried not to show anything. Jim had bought Diana's new tale, that much was certain. It looked as if Judge Solman was heading that way also. Mashburn no more had the instincts of a prosecutor than Solman had a feel for the bench. Their sense of conflict was all Greg needed. That, plus Diana. Diana, the mistress of Sanborn Ranch, the virtuoso of high theater.

Who could say whether Diana was committing perjury in Judge Solman's chambers? Is there not always doubt? Is not evaluating such a matter up to a jury or judge? It didn't matter anyway, Greg told himself. Lawyers regularly strive to fool jurors and judges, so how absurd to worry about a witness's possible perjury. The ethical distinction between lying to jurors and pulling the wool over their eyes was surely a fine one. All Greg knew was his own role. He was Sarah Trant's champion against a hostile world.

Greg leaned forward. "Your Honor," he said, "I think the record should reflect that Diana Sanborn's testimony here is totally consistent with what Judith Daniels told police soon after the murder. It is also totally consistent with what Sarah Trant has always said."

Judge Solman allowed just the barest glimmer of appreciation. "Yes," he agreed. "I suppose the record should reflect that much, shouldn't it?" Then he asked, "Anything further, Mr. Mashburn?"

"No, Your Honor. I felt I had the obligation to offer this—"

"Well, then," Greg interrupted. "Does that mean we now come to the question of relief, Your Honor?"

"Relief . . . ?" Solman blinked in confusion.

Greg turned to the DA. "Jim, tell me this. Does the State intend to continue defending this case?"

Mashburn appeared as perplexed as the judge, and also wary. "Now, wait just a minute," he said. "I didn't come here to surrender. No, sir. I'm still representing the State. I believe I have two obligations. One is total candor with the Court—"

"Which you have consistently offered," Solman offered. "Unlike the sheriff of El Nido County."

"I've tried . . ." Mashburn spoke now as if stepping through a minefield. "But it was Ms. Sanborn. . . . I would have come forward anyway, but it was Ms. Sanborn—"

"Excuse me," Greg interrupted. "I guess I'm having a little trouble hearing in here. What was it we said about relief for my client?"

Solman finally took Greg's cue. "It does seem clear now that the petitioner is entitled to relief, Mr. Mashburn. The only question is, how much?"

"It seems clear?" Mashburn sputtered. "The only question is how much?"

"I believe that's what I said," Judge Solman murmured.

The DA stared hard at Greg, realizing finally where this was heading. "We're going to make our own rules of the game?" he asked. "Is that it, Greg? Rules we can believe in?"

"It's an idea."

Mashburn sat in silence for a long moment. Then he drew a breath and swung toward the judge. "Okay," he said. "I'll give a little here. . . . Yes. . . . Obviously there is some relief justified in this particular case. Yes. . . . I agree relief is warranted, and I think we're talking now—"

"About what relief," Solman said.

"Yes," Mashburn agreed. "What relief."

"May I propose something?" Greg asked.

The DA and judge turned to him. "Given what we've heard here," Greg said, "I ask that the Court consider releasing Sarah Trant outright at this point. I ask that the Court find Sarah Trant, by clear and convincing evidence, actually innocent of Brewster Tomaz's murder."

A silence fell in Judge Solman's chambers. No one appeared to know what to say. Sarah Trant and Diana Sanborn fussed with their handkerchiefs. Daniel Solman and James Mashburn gaped at Greg.

So Greg continued: "Given what we know about Sheriff Rimmer's conduct, there's clearly no basis for holding her. You've got witness tampering, suborning perjury, hiding critical evidence. . . . Just about everything but a dying declaration by Brewster Tomaz. If I may say so, Sheriff Rimmer merits a trial here, not Sarah Trant."

"But . . ." Judge Solman rubbed his temples, trying to keep up with Greg. "Customarily, if I were to issue this writ, if I were to grant the habeas petition, you'd get not freedom but a new murder trial in state court. Mr. Monarch, convicted murderers just don't walk out the door at a federal habeas hearing."

"Yes, Your Honor," Greg agreed. "Not normally. But this is an exceptional case. We're not only looking at outrageous prosecutorial misconduct. We're looking at a petitioner's actual innocence. We're asking that Sarah Trant walk free not because she was unfairly convicted, but because she didn't kill Brewster Tomaz."

Solman examined Greg now as if finally seeing him revealed. He said nothing for a moment. Then he turned his attention to the DA. "Mr. Mashburn, what do you say? Mr. Monarch raises an interesting question, doesn't he? You have a response?"

Mashburn's mouth opened but no words came. He was still a prosecutor, despite everything. "You mean we just let her go?" he asked finally. "She walks? How can—"

Solman interrupted. "It needn't be put just like that. What I'm thinking is, I issue the writ. Then the district attorney's office simply decides against retrying the case. Nice and easy. No need, then, for judicial dramatics."

"Hold on, now," Mashburn said. "How in heaven could I not retry—"

Solman interrupted again. "The question is, how are you going to defend this? How could you retry her if I grant this habeas appeal? All your evidence is tainted, everything Roy Rimmer touched. You don't have a dying declaration. Instead you have a mystery man fleeing across the creek."

Still Mashburn held back. "Your Honor, I said relief was warranted, but I never said—"

This time Greg interrupted. "Jim, after what you've heard, you really want to win here? That's what you want?"

Those words stopped the DA. Mashburn turned slowly to Greg. Amused recognition crept across his face. "I thought there weren't winners and losers in this game, Greg. Just right and wrong."

"Only if you say so, Jim."

Mashburn rose and paced about. He stopped at the window that gave onto a view of La Graciosa's plaza. There he stood, his back to the room, his hand on a pane of glass. When he finally turned around, he was beaming. "Well, hell," he said. "Yes . . . I say so."

Solman regarded the two lawyers with wonder and open relief. "I don't believe we're any longer in an adversarial relationship here," he said. "For the record, we'll still hold oral argument tomorrow as to what precisely the relief should involve. But I can tell you right now, I'm planning to issue the writ. I'm also planning to declare Sarah Trant actually innocent. Counselors, are we in agreement on that plan?"

"Yes, Your Honor," Greg said.

All faces swung to the El Nido County DA. "So are we agreed, Mr. Mashburn?" Judge Solman asked.

Mashburn's eyes were fixed on Greg. Without turning his head, he spoke to Solman. "I don't see how I can object, Your Honor."

—— T W E N T Y - O N E ——

From his stool at the bar of JB's Red Rooster Tavern, Greg nursed a whiskey as he listened to the saloon's piano player, Dave Murphy, pound out his brand of country blues. Anytime now, Greg knew, Dave's wife, Shirley, would appear, ready to sing by his side. No doubt Jimmy O'Brien would come barreling in. Some of the local lawyers would be there, certainly Tim Ruthman. Maybe Alison and Cindy. Even Kim Rosen might show up. He'd not been to JB's in months. With satisfaction, Greg saw it hadn't changed a bit. The ancient mahogany and maple bar, the billiards tables, the potbellied stove, the kerosene lamp, the branding irons, the steer horns . . . JB's was permanently frozen in time. So, too, were Greg's memories of the place. He'd celebrated more than one courtroom victory here, and fought with more than one woman.

Tonight was an occasion for celebration. They were almost at the finish line. Mashburn had caved, Solman was on board. Very likely, Sarah would walk tomorrow. Sarah's actual innocence demanded as much; actual innocence opened so many doors. Yet Greg didn't feel like celebrating just yet.

"You lost me somewhere."

Greg looked up to find Jas Gest on the next stool. "I told you to meet me here," he said.

"I don't mean that, Greg. I mean, you lost me in that courtroom. What happened today? You're behind closed doors in the judge's chambers for half the afternoon, then the hearing is postponed again."

Greg signaled the bartender to pour Jas a glass of white wine. He tried to look casual and pleased at the same time. "We had a break-through today. Diana Sanborn came forward with a revised story. Seems not Sarah but a strange hooded fellow is the killer. Fits exactly with Judith Daniels's account. Diana saw him running from the river waving a knife, but was persuaded by Sheriff Rimmer to forget that bit of information."

Jas's eyes widened. "My God . . . She just came forward. . . . How did that happen?"

Greg nursed his drink. "Actually, she approached Mashburn with it during the lunch hour. He felt obliged to take it to the judge. That's why we were in his chambers."

Jas was studying him now. "I see. . . . So you just learned of this in his chambers?"

"That's right."

"Must have been quite a surprise."

"It was that."

"Wonder what moved Diana to flip."

"Her conscience, maybe?"

Jas nodded, lost in thought. "So where are things now?"

"I've asked the judge to issue the writ. Also to release Sarah out-right. Solman will grant these requests tomorrow."

"How can you be sure?"

"Mashburn didn't object. Mashburn agreed relief was due."

Jas let out a low whistle. "Now I see why you win awards." She looked as if she wanted to say more, but didn't. Instead she waved for a second round of drinks. At the piano, Dave was launching into a tune Greg recognized. "Angel from Montgomery." With apprecia-tion, he turned to watch Shirley at the microphone.

"Well, then, Greg, we should celebrate tonight, shouldn't we?" Jas was tugging at his arm. "Let's dance."

He held her closely, feeling her against him as they moved with the music. His eyes roamed the room, though. They weren't finished, he was sure of that. This wasn't over.

Jas's right hand was sliding down to his hip now; she was slapping playfully at his haunch. In an instant, the gesture reminded Greg of another day. They by the creek in the park, she pushing him down and straddling him, simulating the murder . . . Slapping at his hip before slashing his throat. Why had she done that?

"Jas, did you ever read the autopsy report on Tomaz?"

"Yeah, sure."

"Besides the slashed neck, wasn't there something else?"

Jas looked oddly at him. "Yes. . . . Remember? . . . The left hip, a knife wound into the pelvis bone . . ."

"The bone?"

"I'm sure of it. At the trial, I remember hearing that the tip of the blade broke off into the bone."

He'd missed that, or forgotten it, so intent was he on the carotid artery.

Jas patted the side of his head. "Poor boy. Just can't stop taking it apart, can you? Come on, relax. You've won, Greg."

No, he hadn't. Not yet.

He stopped dancing. "Where's Diana?"

"Why should I know?"

"She's staying where you are, at the El Nido Inn. I told her to come over here with you. Didn't you see her?"

Now Jas stopped dancing also. "I did see her," she said. "But she wasn't heading this way."

"Where was she?"

"She was at the front desk, checking out."

A FULL MOON GUIDED Diana Sanborn through the wooded, curving mountain pass. She required no light, though. She could find El Nido blindfolded.

She rolled her window down as she drove, wanting to feel the breeze on her face. The air gained a growing clarity as she plunged ever deeper into the canyon. She'd go back to the coast tomorrow, she'd finish the job she'd started for Greg Monarch. But tonight she needed to sleep in El Nido.

What a job it had been. Diana wondered how her grandfather's obligations compared. Would he have gone as far as she had? Most certainly, if obliged. He recognized no limits. Once, he and another rancher, crossing a vast plain in a small buckboard, came to a deep and wide wash barring their way home. It was late in the day; driving around the wash would involve a matter of miles and several hours' travel, taking them far into the night. *I'm not going around it*—that's what Edward Sanborn declared. The other rancher, frightened out of his wits, leapt from the buckboard just as Diana's grandfather put the whip to his team. An instant later, in unity, horses, carriage, and driver bounded over the wash. Edward Sanborn made it home in time for dinner.

He never chose his battles unwisely, though. No doubt her grandfather would have managed to avoid the situation she faced. Diana hadn't realized it would come to this. A step at a time, that's how they'd been drawn in, until she couldn't retreat. Would she ever be forgiven?

Diana was descending now into the El Nido Valley. She drove through the village, empty and unlit at this hour, then plunged into the citrus groves of the East End. Sanborn Ranch's gates rose before her in a welcoming embrace. She parked behind the main house, smelling the air as she climbed out of her pickup. She glanced over at Alex's bungalow. The lights were off, which by it-self was not odd. But where was Alex's truck? With regret, Diana turned to the house. What a shame he was out. She had an urge to talk to him.

Diana flipped on lights as she moved through her kitchen and pantry. In the great room, she stopped before the portrait of Edward Sanborn. Those potent ice-blue eyes so often had focused on her. She'd basked in the attention, yet in truth she'd also squirmed at times. She could never hide from her grandfather. He saw every-thing. Everything, that is, but what happened to her one moonlit evening in the summer of her sixteenth year. It would have appalled Diana's grandfather to learn of his ignorance regarding this matter. Yet knowledge would have been worse. All these decades later, Diana remained sure of that.

She wrapped her arms about her. A chill had settled in the valley this evening. Diana glanced at the great stone fireplace. Someone had laid it with oak logs and kindling. How nice of Alex, or whichever ranch hand thought to do this. Diana struck a long stick match against the mantel and touched it to the kindling. The fire grew quickly in the crackle-dry wood. Diana sat on the hearth, draw-ing warmth as she stared into the flames.

Then she heard a sound. Not exactly of footsteps, she thought. More of a thump, as if something had fallen to the ground. Upstairs, she judged. Almost directly above her. She started to rise and look up. So it was only out of the corner of an eye, turned sideways, that she saw the flames suddenly erupt. They leapt toward her with a rau-cous roar. Scorching heat washed over her, then pain of a sort she'd never felt before. All she could see was a bright white light. She was on the ground now, rolling away from the fireplace. She thought she heard a pounding on a door. Something red and wet was falling down her forehead, down her nose. The flames had stopped barking at her, at least. She lay still, waiting for the pain to cease.

JUST PAST DAWN, IN the first pink light of day, Greg descended into the El Nido Valley. La Graciosa had been fogbound when he left; here all was crystal clear. On impulse he pulled over to the side of the road. Not until he climbed out of his car did he realize this was where he'd collided with a tree trunk on that first morning he came into the val-ley. Over there was where he stood, watching Jasmine Gest rise slowly from a blue-green lagoon. Greg walked over to look once again at that bend in the river. He was in no particular rush.

They had Diana in a private room at the El Nido Community Hospital. She'd survive, they'd reassured him. In a good deal of pain right now, though, and not yet ready for visitors. It could have been much worse. A nasty scalp wound, a moderate concussion, but only first-degree burns, mainly along the side of her body. Luckily, the blast had blown her away from the flames. It was James Mashburn who'd first given Greg the news, calling him at JB's Tavern. Mash-burn in turn had heard about it from Sheriff Rimmer.

The firewood had exploded on her, that's what they figured. The logs had been packed with black mining powder. It was an old ranch trick to booby-trap logs like that when you suspect someone is steal-ing your firewood. Soon enough, a stove or fireplace explodes in the thief's home, and you've got your culprit. One of Diana's hands, knowing that full cords had been disappearing from ranches all around the valley, must have packed some of their wood. Then somehow those logs had ended up in the main-house fireplace, instead of stacked outside as bait. Hell of an accident.

Greg would have to wait to see Diana. Maybe by the end of the day, they'd told him. Or maybe tomorrow. That would be soon enough. He had other business to transact first anyway. From the ledge where he stood, Greg scanned the creek coursing a hundred feet below him. A fly fisherman caught his attention, just as one had on his first day. There were no naked willowy bathers about this morning, though. Greg lifted his eyes to the horizon. So little had changed. The ravines and orchards and vines, the pale morning sunlight. Greg turned back to his car.

They'd be waiting for him at the entrance to Camp Mahrah. That's what Charles Whit and Roy Rimmer had told him when he'd reached them late last night. One hour past dawn, they'd said. He was early. No doubt they would be also.

Where the road turned to dirt and narrowed into a path, Greg parked his car and began walking. At the splintered wooden gate with the hand-lettered Do Not Trespass sign, he waited only for a moment. Then he stepped around the barrier. New growth, he saw, had already started to obscure the fire that had scorched this part of the valley. Burgeoning willows overwhelmed blackened columns of oak and sycamore, promising a needed food source for the wildlife that fed on them. Someone had made sure to rebuild the watershed structure. They'd replaced culverts and set stone to buffer runoff areas. Greg eyed with appreciation the bales of straw, the boulders, the check dams, the armored stream banks. Whoever ran this camp knew how to manage the land.

"Welcome to Camp Mahrah, Mr. Monarch."

Charles Whit had suddenly appeared fifty feet in front of him without notice. He somehow filled more space than even his considerable size dictated. Greg stepped toward him, then stopped as he noticed Sheriff Rimmer well off to his right, standing in the shade of a spreading oak. "Why don't we all gather together," Greg suggested.

Whit offered his cold, steady smile. "An excellent idea," he said. "Both of you, please join me. We'll walk to the lodge."

They fell in line together, Whit commanding the center. Even with his limp and cane, he moved along at a pace that required the others to step quickly. As they walked, Rimmer aimed fierce looks at

Greg, but Whit kept his eye on where he was headed. They were in the heart of the campus now, passing along the side of the playing field. There was no evidence of a fire here at all; they'd reseeded with abundance. All the charred buildings had been stripped and rebuilt with fresh timber. As before, a strange silence filled Camp Mahrah. Greg looked up at an empty sky and sniffed, but couldn't detect even the hint of rotten eggs. There was no wind today, so perhaps that made a difference.

Whit pointed the way to one of the lodge houses. Greg recognized it as the one where, through a window, he'd seen the evidence of a meeting long ago. Whit stood at its door, holding open a front screen. Greg had Sheriff Rimmer at his back. Reluctantly, he stepped into the room. The two other men followed him, then closed the door.

Whit pointed to a rocking chair by the fireplace. "You ought to find that comfortable, Mr. Monarch."

Greg waited for the others to sit down before settling into the rocker. They were in straight-backed chairs, placed just far enough apart that he needed to swing his head to look at one, then the other. He pulled his rocker back to gain a wider perspective.

"On the phone last night you spoke of an urgent matter we needed to discuss," Whit said. "So let's discuss."

Greg looked back and forth at the two men. "Yes," he agreed. "Let's discuss."

Rimmer erupted. "Are we to guess what this is about, Monarch? What is this, Twenty Questions?"

"More like Jeopardy," Greg replied. "Wouldn't you say?"

Whit's smile grew wider, even as he fixed Greg with empty gray eyes. "Just what do you mean?"

"For a remote insulated valley, there's been so much danger. Sudden deaths such as Reggie Dodge's. Little accidents such as mine while diving out at El Nido Lake. Now Diana Sanborn's fireplace explodes on her. The mayor should put up a sign at the city limits. Something like, 'Hazardous Zone, Proceed at Your Own Risk.' "

Rimmer was shifting restlessly in his chair. Whit moved not at all, but looked even more impatient. "I don't mean to sound rude," Whit said. "But get to the point, Mr. Monarch."

Greg rose and walked to the fireplace, where he put a foot on the hearth, a hand on the mantel. "The point," he said, "is that it's time to call your dogs off."

Rimmer started to respond, but Whit waved him into silence, then turned to Greg. "Mr. Monarch, when I first met you at the park during that band concert, I told you we may get along yet. I still feel that way. You do your job well. I like that. I admire talent and discipline almost as much as I appreciate the willingness to do what's needed. I see now why you are so celebrated in Chumash County."

Greg ran his hand along the fireplace mantel as he looked past the seated men to the window behind them. A stand of oaks shaded and obscured his view. He could see only the corner of another lodge house, and the edge of the distant playing field. That and, for a passing moment, what had appeared to be the outline of someone moving slowly among the trees. It occurred to Greg that he needed to speak his piece as quickly as possible.

"I know everything now," he said. "The plume, the oil spill, Brewster Tomaz's blackmail efforts, the alliance with Diana, the need to defuse Sarah." Greg looked hard at Whit. "I also know about the waste dump."

Until those last words, Whit had appeared entirely at ease. Mention of the waste dump drew a response, though. The wrinkled skin reddened around his receding forehead. "You're making a mistake here," Whit cautioned. "Be aware, Mr. Monarch. You are involving yourself with forces you should avoid."

"I'd be more than happy to take a wide detour," Greg said. "That's why I've asked to speak to you."

As Whit digested those words, he relaxed once again. "A deal . . . That's what you're here to offer, isn't it, Mr. Monarch?"

"Precisely." Greg left the fireplace, returned to his rocker. "As I say, you call off your dogs. That means Diana Sanborn is safe to walk the streets of El Nido, and so is Sarah Trant when Judge Solman releases her."

"Which," Whit interrupted, "I understand he plans to do this very day."

"If I can get back to La Graciosa in time. We may need another day or two."

Whit appeared lost in thought. "Yes. . . . Well, Ms. Trant's release does alter matters, doesn't it? . . . But I interrupted you, I'm afraid. Please continue."

"Calling off the dogs also means you withdraw your considerable pressure from the DA's office." Greg thought of Judge Solman. "And from the entire legal system, for that matter. On their own, the judge decides whether to issue a writ, and the DA decides whether to retry."

"I'm flattered, but you overestimate our powers."

"I don't think so."

"You also ask for a lot."

"I'm not finished. You also seal off the old wells up here in Camp Mahrah, and dismantle the pumps."

Whit studied Greg with fascination. "You are amazing, Mr. Monarch."

"Something else," Greg continued. "You shut down the waste dump, rehabilitate the land, and do something worthwhile with Camp Mahrah. Develop a regional park, or make that world-class health spa a reality, not just a decoy."

Sheriff Rimmer was on his feet now, advancing toward Greg. "Are you mad, Monarch?" he demanded. "There's oil under here. This is my chance. . . . You can't—"

From where he sat, Whit stopped Rimmer with the end of his cane. "Take it easy, Roy," he advised, pointing the sheriff back to his chair. "You had best sit down."

Rimmer glowered but slowly complied. Whit turned back to Greg.

"Anything else, Mr. Monarch? Have we reached the end of your list?"

"Just one more thing. Sheriff Rimmer here. He's served his county nobly all these years. He deserves a restful retirement. That would surely please him more than facing the conspiracy and obstruction of justice charges that Judge Solman no doubt is presently contemplating."

Whit brandished his cane before Rimmer could respond. The sheriff gripped the arms of his chair, staring wide-eyed at the two men before him, but said nothing.

Whit asked, "And in exchange for all this, Mr. Monarch?"

"Silence."

"Can you elaborate a little?"

"Silence about the plume, to begin with. That will save your people about four hundred million dollars in cleanup costs and criminal fines. And silence about the waste dump. That will save your people many times more dollars . . . lots more."

Whit's eyes traveled to the window now. Greg followed his glance. He saw nothing but the trees rustling in a slight breeze. "The waste dump is a perfectly legal operation," Whit observed. "Nothing to hide."

"Then why is it run as a clandestine operation through the back-roads? Why doesn't anyone in El Nido know about it? Why go to such lengths to conceal everything?"

"ModoCorp is a privately held company. It needn't make public all that it does."

Greg slowly rocked back and forth. "My turn for appreciation. You are being so ingenious, Mr. Whit . . . but also a little incomplete."

"Am I?"

"The dumping is legal," Greg said, "but only because there's a gaping loophole in the hazardous-waste laws. No one really knows about this loophole. Got passed without anyone paying attention. It starts getting into the news, people start getting aware, there'll be hell to pay. At the least, enormous pressure to reverse things, change the law, kill the loophole. It would ruin the game for everyone. That's why you need the waste dump kept secret. That's why you and your colleagues at ModoCorp will value my silence. You people surely don't want to ruin your sweetheart deal."

"You presume much about our wants."

"Not just your wants, actually. It's a far bigger game, isn't it?"

Whit couldn't stop himself from gloating. It showed in his tone, and in his eyes. "You're right, Mr. Monarch. It is far bigger. There are national interests involved, reaching to the highest levels. That's precisely why I advised you against getting involved. So many interests, so much power, so much money. You're trying to take on all sorts of forces. You're—"

"Actually," Greg interrupted, "it's you and your ModoCorp colleagues who will be taking on these forces if we can't come to terms here."

Whit stared at Greg. "What do you mean?"

"I mean you'll have a nasty problem if you blow everyone's sweetheart deal just because of your little situation in El Nido. Not only ModoCorp has a compelling interest in keeping this thing covered up. Mr. Whit, to put it plainly, you let this blow, you'll make lots of powerful folks very unhappy. I imagine you won't fare well."

"And . . ." Whit's eyes looked as if they'd momentarily gone out of focus. "And . . . how exactly would you make it blow? Who would pay attention outside of the valley if you start hollering? No one cares about El Nido's waste dump. This isn't big news anywhere else."

Greg continued his rocking. He made a note in his mind to buy a chair just like this one for his house. He found the rhythm soothing. "What if, say, someone threatens to leap off a La Luna mountain cliff in protest of your waste dump? A few people, actually. A devout core from El Nido who would do anything to preserve their valley. That would make for quite a public relations mess, wouldn't you say?"

"Preposterous."

Greg smiled. "I'm afraid that Sarah Trant and her friends are precisely that. . . . Sarah loves how that native Colombian tribe hogtied Occidental with just such threats of mass suicide. . . . And remember, Sarah will soon be out of jail."

"The U'wa tribe," Whit muttered, recognizing the reference. He was unable to hide his dismay. He glanced again at the window. Greg, trying to follow his gaze, saw only trees.

"As you might imagine," Whit disclosed, "we're not alone up here at Camp Mahrah. This lodge house is surrounded."

"Yes," Greg said. "As I might imagine."

Whit turned to him. "They swindled my family, you know. The community of El Nido, a century ago. They stole our legacy, and utterly destroyed my grandfather. We've been brutalized by these lovely folks."

"That was long ago. Those who hurt your family aren't alive."

"Their descendants are."

"Yes," Greg agreed. "And they appear as determined as their forebears to preserve this valley."

Whit flared at that, but didn't argue the point. "My family kept the mineral rights, God knows why. By the time they passed down to me, I was already doing quite well in the oil business. I'd taken on 'investors.' I'd been 'absorbed,' as they say. I had partners just loaded with supercomputers and high-tech geeks. We were in the Gulf, and laying plans for the Pacific Coast. I didn't need El Nido Valley for the money. Coming here, buying Camp Mahrah, settling in, it mainly meant a chance to vindicate my grandfather, to reclaim finally what was his due."

"Forgive me," Greg said. "But wasn't it also a chance for retribution?"

Whit shifted in his chair. "Yes, Mr. Monarch, yes it was."

"No matter what it took?"

Whit looked at him steadily. "Yes."

"Sending threatening blackmail letters through the U.S. mail is a federal crime that carries grave consequences."

"For those who do it."

"Or those who cause it to be done."

"If such a link can be proven."

"Yes," Greg said. "But given what we now know, that shouldn't be too difficult."

The tips of Whit's fingers, gripping his cane, had turned white. "You are good, Monarch. But this isn't enough. You're not holding a full hand."

"How about motive. Does that round things out?"

"Motive?"

"Brewster Tomaz knew about the plume and the waste dump. No doubt he knew much more. He was threatening you. He was black-mailing you."

Whit started tapping his cane on the floor. "Such speculation . . ."

"You had the motive. You had reason to kill him."

"Sarah Trant's on trial, no one else—"

"Unless new evidence is introduced."

Whit raised his cane and pointed it at Greg. "This is all a bluff."

"You will prosper no matter what happens here, Mr. Whit. . . . Maybe the two grandchildren can work something out."

"The two grandchildren?"

"You and Diana."

Whit was adrift now. His cane hung loosely in his hand. "A waste dump instead of oil wells . . . Necessary in my business, and even ap-propriate for this blasted place . . . But not what I'd counted on. That hadn't been the original plan."

"It couldn't have been what your grandfather wanted here."

Whit sat in silence, staring out the window. Then he turned to Greg. "I wasn't sure what we'd be doing with you."

"I understand."

"Now I know."

"Yes?"

Still the smile didn't show in Whit's pale gray eyes. White teeth flashed, though. "We're going to make a deal with you," he said.

—— T W E N T Y - T W O ——

Higher and higher she flew, first her feet reaching toward the sky, then her head. Long dark hair billowed in the wind. Intense hazel eyes danced with glee. "Oh my," Sarah Trant called out. "Yeeha . . ."

From a bench by the fountain in Sanborn Park, Greg and Jas watched as Sarah pitched back and forth on one of the park's playground swings. She'd tried the jungle gym already, and the merry-go-round, and the hanging bars. Jas wanted to join her, but Greg, for the moment, was keeping a hand on her arm.

"My savior," Sarah had sighed when Greg met her at the prison gate this morning. Following the briefest of final oral arguments, it had taken Solman only twenty-four hours to issue his writ and declare Sarah's actual innocence. Late that same afternoon, Mashburn had announced he wouldn't retry Sarah Trant. They'd led Sarah down a corridor to freedom at dawn the next day.

"My savior," she repeated to Greg as he drove away from the prison.

"For once," he said. "Finally."

"Just in time," she said, laughing.

He glanced at her sideways then, and saw the familiar flicker of exuberance play across her face. He raised a hand to her cheek and gently brushed the hair from her eyes. For an eager moment he imagined her restored. Her manner vaguely unsettled him, though. When he tried to talk to her about the future, she simply nodded and sighed and clung to him.

"ModoCorp is packing up and going away from El Nido," he told her just before they reached Sanborn Park. "No more oil spills, no more anything. There's going to be a regional park up at Camp Mahrah."

"Who do we fight, then?" she asked. "Who do we go after?"

The courts no longer had jurisdiction over her. Greg had placed a call, so far unanswered, to El Nido's one group-care home. He'd try again later in the day. He'd do whatever was needed. "Sarah," he said. "The battle has ended. No more speeches, no more demonstrations, no more talking. We settle down. We keep a low profile. We fight no one."

She looked as if she was sulking, but said nothing more. In an instant she was out the door and at the playground.

"A complicated, impetuous woman," Jas observed as Sarah headed now toward the fountain.

Greg turned from Sarah to Jas. "They're everywhere," he said.

"You have a problem with that?"

Greg spoke softly. "Not at all."

She put a hand on his wrist. "Something terribly wrong happened here, Greg. You fixed it."

"Yes . . . I suppose I did."

"You did good, Greg."

He wrapped her in his arms. "Okay, Jas . . . thank you. . . . Everything's fine."

An angry cry interrupted them. They looked up to find Sarah dancing in the fountain, bare legs flashing, her skirt hitched up to her hips. An outraged matron with two young children in tow was shouting alarms at this display. Jas started giggling as she and Greg jumped up to intervene. "You know what?" she said. "I think Sarah and I have some things in common."

FROM SANBORN PARK, GREG once more drove through El Nido's abundant East End. He soaked up everything with hungry eyes, for he didn't think he'd be passing by this way again anytime soon. The sun hung low in the sky. Another dusk was painting the valley brilliant shades of pink and purple. It wasn't hard for Greg to imagine why people came to El Nido and decided to stay. He wished them all well, them and their protected valley.

The gateway to Sanborn Ranch now rose before Greg. He drove through and parked as usual in the back. This time, though, he knocked at the front entrance, as he had on the day he first met Diana Sanborn.

Alex Ramirez opened the door. He gazed at Greg with dark, solemn eyes. "They brought her from the hospital late this morning," he said. "She's waiting for you."

Greg followed a nurse who led him up a curving flight of stairs and down a corridor. He entered Diana's bedroom by himself. For a moment he hung back at the door, watching her. She lay slightly propped up in her bed, breathing heavily. Her face was swollen, her forehead and arms wrapped in thick white bandages. She peered up at him, first with groggy eyes, then with recognition.

"What you must think of me," Diana whispered.

"And you of me."

She tried to smile, but it looked more like a grimace. "We are a pair."

"A victorious pair."

"Yes, so I've been told," Diana agreed. "I must say I'm very impressed at your achievements."

"Our achievements. You were magnificent with Mashburn and Solman."

She stared deep into Greg's eyes now. "Okay, our achievements. Yet I was simply righting my wrongs. I want you to know how anguished I've been about Sarah. What I did was required, it was mandated by people with power over me. But I never imagined she'd end up on death row."

"She was guilty," Greg said. "You weren't framing an innocent person."

A faint tremor played across Diana's face. "Yes. . . . Still . . . that's no rationale. . . . I never could sleep at night after her trial. I stayed awake for long hours, writing in my journal. Then, finally, you arrived." Diana reached for his hand. "I was so happy when you came to the valley. Scared, but happy also. I saw a way out of this."

Greg pulled up a chair and sat down beside Diana's bed. He spoke as gently as he could. "There's more to it," he said. "Isn't there, Diana?"

She closed her eyes. Minutes passed. Greg waited. He glanced at the nurse hovering in the hallway. When he turned back to Diana, she was watching him with eyes now wide open and crystal clear. "Of course there's more," she said. "Isn't there always?"

"It wasn't just your valley you were protecting by handing over Sarah, was it?"

"What do you mean?"

"You were protecting the one person who mattered to you more than anyone in the valley. The person who cared most about you, the person who would do anything for you."

"My goodness . . . ," she murmured.

"Alex killed Brewster, didn't he, Diana?"

"That's preposterous. . . ."

"It had to be a man. The hip wound, the broken blade tip in Brewster's hip. Only a man was strong enough to do that."

"Oh dear, Gregory . . . There are many men in El Nido Valley. There is, for example, our mysterious hooded fellow with the broad shoulders."

"The boots in the bunkhouse . . . The tunnel."

"All explained, all discounted. Besides, why would Alex kill Brewster?"

"For you, Diana. Because he thought that's what you wanted."

"I wanted a cranky old geologist killed over a land dispute?"

"He wasn't just a cranky old geologist, Diana. Was he?"

She maneuvered to sit up. He helped her with an arm around her back, and a pillow. Then he pulled a photo from his jacket pocket. As he held it before her, she gasped.

"Recognize that young man sitting on the fence? Recognize your brooding, high-strung beau with the jet-black hair?"

"Where did you . . . ?"

"In the boxes at the historical museum. Fred Darvill came charging at me just as I was studying this one, so I stuck it in my pocket and didn't get around to looking at the back until this past weekend."

"The back . . . ?"

He turned the photo over, held it before Diana. "As you can see, somebody scribbled the names of those in the photo."

She peered, then sank onto her pillow, once again closing her eyes.

"Brewster Tomaz," Greg said. "That's the young man's name, as I read it. I should have realized. You said your young man drilled holes and tested soil conditions for your father. A budding geologist. Of course. Funny how time plays tricks. I looked at our murder victim always as a grizzled old goat. I never thought of him as being a young man once. Yet he was. As were you a young woman. By my calculation, he would have been twenty-four when you were sixteen."

Diana opened her eyes. "Yes, that's right. That's how old we were."

"After all these years . . ."

"He was going to ravage me again. Twice. At both the start and end of my life."

"Alex knew what he'd done to you back then?"

"Yes, Alex knew. . . . But, Greg, you must understand. . . . So did Sarah."

"All three of you were down there at the river that night with Tomaz. Sarah argued with him, then pushed him in the river and ran off. What followed wasn't planned. Brewster threatened you, no doubt. On impulse, full of passion, Alex advanced toward him. You stayed back, watching your foreman until he fled across the river. Then you ran to Brewster yourself. Maybe to sneer at his dying face, maybe to make sure he was dead. That would have been understandable. But others were approaching now. So you scooped him up, held him in your arms. In an instant, you had to choose. You were frantic, you were torn. But above all, you feared for Alex. You had to protect Alex. So you pointed the police toward Sarah."

Diana's laugh sounded utterly genuine. "My goodness, Gregory. You surely do love stories, don't you? But don't you see, however you figure this, it's still just a story. That's how you lawyers build cases. You weave narratives to ensure someone's conviction or acquittal. Or—" Diana gazed at Greg with tender eyes. "Or sometimes, to make things be the way you wish them to be. Bless your heart, Greg. You so much want Sarah to be innocent. So this is your story."

"And you so much wish Alex to be innocent."

"Indeed," Diana agreed. "The fact is, we could devise all sorts of narratives regarding Brewster Tomaz's death. Any of them could be right or wrong. Who knows? You'll never reach truth in this, Greg. Only a verdict."

"That's not enough for me."

Diana's face filled with sympathy. "Oh, Gregory, I do understand. We need to make clear who the victims and villains are, don't we? The world being so confusing, it needs that much clarity at least. So let's say this, shall we: Justice was served, whoever killed Brewster Tomaz."

Greg lifted his eyes to her bedroom's picture window. In the distance he could see the mountain pass leading to La Graciosa. He'd be home by dusk. "Okay," Greg agreed. "Let's say that."

Then he turned to her. "Tell me this at least, Diana. . . . What have I done here?"

Her grand smile filled the room now. She whooped with pleasure as she waved at the wondrous vista. "You have restored my faith in mankind, that's what you've done, Gregory. You have shown us the way. You have shown us how to protect ourselves. You have saved El Nido."

With effort, she reached up from her pillows and threw her bandaged arms around Greg. "Bless our hearts," she said. "We were such innocents until you came to our valley."